SPOTLIGHT

USA TODAY BESTSELLING AUTHOR
REBECCA JENSHAK

Rebecca Jenshak
www.rebeccajenshak.com
Cover design by Lori Jackson Designs
Cover illustration by Sarah Jane
Editing and proofreading by Rebecca at Fairest Reviews Editing Services and Sarah at All Encompassing Books

This is a work of fiction, created without use of AI technology. Any names, characters, places or incidents are products of the author's imagination and used in a fictitious manner. Any resemblance to actual people, places, or events is purely coincidental or fictional.

This one is for all the girlies who have ever felt unlovable. I wrote Flynn for you.

AUTHOR'S NOTE

Thank you for purchasing *Spotlight*. I hope you will enjoy Flynn & Olivia's story.

Spotlight utilizes American Sign Language throughout the story. ASL has its own syntax, grammar rules, and structure that is different from written and spoken English. There are varying thoughts on how to properly write sign language in fiction.

Most of the time my characters are signing and speaking at the same time. For those instances, I chose quote marks and italics. If the characters are not speaking as they sign, it is italicized only.

Additionally, I want to thank everyone who helped me in this process. Any errors are mine and based on my experiences or those who I consulted with.

SPOTLIGHT

CHAPTER ONE

Olivia

"I'M NOT READY TO GO HOME TOMORROW," RUBY SAYS as the hotel door clicks behind us.

"I am." I toss my purse on the entry table. "I miss Greer, and Gigi still isn't responding to my texts."

My sister opens the mini fridge and pulls out the small bottle of white wine that we opened last night. "Everything is fine. Gigi is just dying for you to meet a nice young man and give her another great-grandbaby."

"I gave her one. It's your turn."

"Oh no. I am far too busy doing… things." She waves a hand in the air as she trails off without a good excuse. "One last drink?"

"Yeah. Why not?" I walk over to the window and stare out at the New York City lights.

I flew across the country with Ruby so that she could meet with her publisher and sign copies of her newest book that releases next week. It's been a blast to see my sister in her element as a bestselling author, but I'm ready to go home. Back to my daughter. Back to work even.

"Did you get that guy from the bar's number?" she asks as she pours the wine into two glasses.

"No," I say, like the idea is impossible. "Why would I do that?"

"Maybe because he was cute and really into you."

"He was not." In my experience, guys are only into the version of me out at the bar, not the reality of my life as a single mom.

"He was. And why shouldn't he be? You're pretty and smart and—"

"Not interested in dating right now."

She rolls her eyes at me as she walks over to where I still stand at the window. "You can't swear off dating at twenty-four. The right guy is out there."

"Now you sound like Gigi."

Grandma Gloria, who we've called Gigi for as long as I can remember, is amazing, but she has it in her head that I am missing out on experiences. She hasn't outright said that, but when I asked if she could babysit Greer this weekend so I could go with Ruby on this trip, she agreed immediately and even suggested we stay an extra day or two. She's always inviting Greer to sleep over at her house or offering to help so I can "go out, have fun, meet some new people." And by people, she absolutely means men.

I am not just any other twenty-four-year-old, though. The people I meet when I step out of my normal routine are living their best lives, going out and sleeping in. We have one fun night together and then they either ghost me because they absolutely know they don't want the responsibility of dating a single mom or they give up quickly when they realize my schedule isn't as free as theirs. And don't even get me started on trying to date a single dad. Nothing shines a mirror on your exhaustion like sitting across from someone who fought their kid over putting their shoes on an hour earlier.

"I'll take that as a compliment."

"Thanks," I say, taking one of the wine glasses. "To my insanely talented sister. I'm so proud of you."

Ruby's expression turns bashful. She clinks her glass to mine despite her obvious displeasure at being the center of attention. "I couldn't have done it without you."

"You absolutely could have and did."

"No. You read it first and gave me a ton of great feedback. You're a born editor. You see problems and offer great suggestions that make my books so much better."

She's overselling my part, by a lot. "I offered a few minor suggestions."

"No." She shakes her head and her eyes light up with amusement. "That assessment is so wrong; I don't even know where to start."

"If I'm good at it, it's only because I'm your biggest fan."

She smiles at that, and we face the window, looking out together as we drink in silence.

Eventually, Ruby rests her head against mine. "I should pack. What time is our flight in the morning?"

"Ten. The car will be here to pick us up at seven forty-five."

She groans. "Okay. I'm off to bed. Are you staying up?"

"Yeah. I'm not tired yet."

"Maybe you should go down to the hotel bar and see if your cute guy is still there."

"Good night," I say with a laugh.

Ruby flashes a grin as she heads into her room and closes the door.

I drain the rest of my wine and then glance around the suite. The publisher put us up in a really nice hotel. We each have our own bedroom, and the living area alone is nearly bigger than my entire apartment back in Arizona. It has a dining table that can seat twelve and a balcony that overlooks the busy streets.

Unlike Ruby, I've already packed, so I grab my phone. Dozens of texts wait for me from friends, but what catches my eyes is a new text from Gigi. Finally. I open the text to a picture of a smiling Greer. I'm happy to see my daughter's face, but it only makes me miss her more.

While I'm still holding my phone, it vibrates with an incoming call from Jake.

My gaze narrows as I stare at my ex's name flashing on the screen. Actually, calling Jake an ex gives him far too much credit for the one decent night we spent together, but it's easier than explaining to people he's my baby's daddy.

"Hello?" I answer, keeping my voice low.

"Hey, finally." His tone is part irritation and part relief. "Did you not get my texts?"

"One second," I say as I unlock the sliding door that leads to the balcony and step outside.

I don't love New York City the same way some people do, but I love the way it lights up at night.

I use the view to push away the frustration that always seems to surface while talking to Jake. Co-parenting is hard. Putting the phone back to my ear, I say, "I'm in New York with Ruby. I told you before I left, I would be hard to reach."

He's silent on the other end.

"What's up?" I ask. We aren't friends, but we are friendly. Still, he isn't calling without reason.

The cold wind whips around me as Jake says, "I'm not going to make Greer's birthday party next weekend."

"What?" That frustration that I was trying so hard to let go of comes roaring back. "You promised."

A chill moves down my bare arms and legs. I'm cursing my short dress and the winter breeze, but I want to soak up the last night here, even if I am eager to get back.

"And I meant it at the time, but something came up at work and I can't miss it," Jake says, a hint of annoyance creeping in more with each word, like explaining it to me is the real frustration and not missing his daughter's birthday.

"That isn't how promises work." My teeth grind down as I walk out toward the edge of the balcony, resting my elbows on the ledge and peering down. The street is still busy with bumper-to-bumper traffic. People out enjoying their night, hurrying to parties or bars or back home. That's where I wish I were. Home in sweats and not having this conversation.

Jake sighs, further driving home the point that he thinks I'm the unreasonable one. "I have some vacation time in early June. She can come to San Diego then, and I'll take her to the beach or Sea World."

"June?! That's six months away."

That's a long time even by my standards, but to the five-year-old in question, it will feel like a lifetime. Greer can barely comprehend waiting a week for something she's really excited about, let alone several months.

"It's her birthday, Jake. She'll be devastated if you aren't there. Can't you rearrange your schedule or have someone else cover you?"

"I can't. I'm sorry. This is the best I can do," he says, with a note of finality. I can't force him to be here. I know because this isn't the first time he's bailed or the first time I've tried to talk him out of it. He's never missed her birthday though.

Dread washes over me as I picture Greer's face when he breaks the news to her. She mentions her dad every single time we talk about her birthday next weekend—and it's basically all we talk about. She's been counting down for weeks and saying how happy she is that everyone will be there.

"I'll call her the day of, and my assistant already mailed her gifts. She picked out a new princess costume that I'm sure Greer will love and a pink iPad."

"That is more than we agreed to spend." We have always had a strict fifty-dollar limit on birthdays. Co-parenting can be tricky when it comes to gifts. It's like each birthday, holiday, or celebration we're both trying to make up for the fact we're raising our daughter separately. Both of us going above and beyond in our own ways. Jake's way is with money, and I don't want our daughter to grow up having more stuff than memories.

"Fuck, Liv, there's no winning with you."

Maybe I am the irrational one. My current frustration makes it hard for me to think straight. The budget rule was my idea. And yes, it was set with good intentions, but I can't deny I've been extra grateful for it so that Jake doesn't spend a lot more than I can. I want Greer to have everything her heart wants, but I also want to leave room for her to use her imagination and creativity.

The sigh I let out takes all the remaining energy I have left and blows it right over the ledge of the building. This is why I can't escape for a night or weekend like a typical single twenty-something. The responsibilities are always there, and I'm holding it together with duct tape and safety pins.

"Whatever. You can tell her when you talk on Sunday, but do not mention June unless you are certain you can make it work."

There's a pause that makes my hackles rise.

"I was hoping you could tell her. I don't want to ruin our weekly call. If you give her the news tomorrow, then she'll have a day to adjust to the idea."

He's making me the bad guy, but if I'm honest, I want to be the one to tell her. That way, I can hold her while she cries and remind her how much we love her. And I don't want to ruin their Sunday afternoon video chat any more than he does. It's the one day of the week she has his attention, and I know how much she looks forward to it. Every kid deserves time with their parents. Even if I want to punch said parent in the nose. I can resent his decision and still want to protect Greer from it as much as possible.

"Fine." I exhale and close my eyes, turning away from the city and facing the room.

As Jake says his goodbyes, making more promises that I'm uncertain he'll keep, I focus on the city noises that filter up to the rooftop. The glide of tires over the road below and the squeal of brakes rolling to a stop. A horn honks in the distance. A slight thump of the bass from another hotel room and the occasional laughter or loud voices.

After I end the call, I cradle my phone in both hands and linger a moment longer, pushing away the irritation of my call with Jake. He doesn't get to ruin my last night in New York and Greer's birthday.

Sure, my plans for the rest of the night are getting ready for bed and sleeping, but now I'm likely going to be thinking of him while I do both activities. The number of hate dreams I've had about Jake is truly impressive.

"Ten more seconds," I speak the words out loud as I soak in just a few more moments of the city sounds.

"Ten. Nine. Eight. Seven. Six. Five. Four. Three. Two." I pause. "Two and a half—"

A deep chuckle rumbles from the shadows, and I suck in a startled breath.

"Hello?" I ask cautiously as I sidestep closer to the door leading back inside. I swear to God if I get murdered up here, I'll be so pissed.

"Sorry. I didn't mean to scare you." I finally see him, or part of him. He stands on the balcony of the room next door, cast in shadows. He doesn't move, but I still feel a prick of unease at being out here with a stranger.

"Have you been out here the entire time?" I ask, glancing at the door again, just in case I need to make a run for it. I'm fairly certain I could outrun him in the time it would take for him to leap over the balcony wall.

"If you're asking if I heard your conversation, then yes, but only because interrupting seemed rude."

"And eavesdropping isn't?" I ask, quirking a brow. I probably shouldn't provoke this strange guy, but I can't seem to help it. I'm still prickly from talking to Jake.

9

"I was here first, so technically you were eavesdropping on me."

"You weren't talking," I point out.

"Actually, I was having a pretty nice conversation with myself until you showed up."

I huff a small laugh. There's a playfulness in his words and a tone that loosens some of the anxious energy I've been holding.

His voice softens as he adds, "Sorry. I should have gone inside or said something, but I like it out here and you seem to be having as shitty of a night as I am. Plus, I'm a gentleman. I couldn't just leave you out here all alone."

It's an oddly sweet confession from a complete stranger.

"Who's Jake?" he asks. "Boyfriend? Husband? Dad?"

"That's none of your business."

"Doesn't matter, anyway. He sounded like a jerk."

I open my mouth to defend Jake, because that's what I usually do, but this mystery man doesn't give me a chance.

"If he's not going to make it this weekend, I am happy to take his place."

"What?"

"I love a birthday party, and I just happen to be free."

The audacity is almost charming. Almost. With my luck in men, he's some sort of psycho serial killer.

"I don't even know you." I study his profile in the dark. He leans against the stone wall of the balcony. Long jean-clad legs crossed at the ankle. He slouches forward slightly, but I can still tell by the width of his shoulders and the bulge of his biceps that he's tall and muscular. I wish I could see his face better. His profile boasts a straight nose and wide mouth. His hair curls around the bottom of the baseball hat on his head, but I can't make out the color. Not black, but not blond either, somewhere in between.

"Sure you do. I'm your next boyfriend."

I smile and laugh softly to myself. The moonlight flashes against his teeth enough for me to tell he's smiling, too.

"Thanks for the laugh. I needed that." Cocky isn't my type, but at least I'm not standing out here sulking anymore. I start for the door to head back inside.

"Wait," he calls out. "You can't just leave me out here. Who will I talk to?"

Pausing, I glance back at him. "The same person you were talking to before I came out and interrupted you. You can finish that nice conversation with yourself."

"I like talking with you better. What's your name?"

"I'm not telling you that." I should leave it at that and keep walking, but something keeps me rooted in place.

"Fine. Tell me something else about you then."

"Why?"

"Because I don't want to go back inside yet, and I get the feeling you don't either."

There's something about his honesty that has me considering it. What's another minute or two?

"I hate the cold," I say finally.

His deep laughter skates over my skin, leaving goosebumps.

"It isn't *that* cold." His hands are shoved in his pants pockets and his shoulders are slightly hunched to block the wind.

"It's cold to me."

"You must not be from here."

"No. I'm not."

He chuckles again, as if realizing I'm not going to tell him where I'm from.

"Me either. I like it though. I didn't grow up with real winters either, but I love snow and ice, and all that."

I shiver just thinking about it. "Not me. My winter accessories are only for show." Cute boots and scarves that I pull out of the back of my closet for a week or two each year. Most winter days in Arizona can be braved with a sweatshirt or a light jacket, but there's usually a small window where the mornings dip below freezing.

"Tell me something else," he says.

"Umm…" I'm a little embarrassed that nothing immediately comes to mind. For one, this is a bizarre scenario, so making idle chitchat with a guy that could still turn out to be a serial killer is not at the forefront of my mind. But also, I'm not used to guys wanting to know things about me beyond the usual: What do you do? How old are you? Followed up by, do you want to come back to my place? And in the rare instance they ask me to tell them something interesting about myself, I freeze up. It's too much pressure. For the past nearly six years, my world has revolved around Greer.

But standing out here in the dark with a complete stranger, I don't feel any pressure to be charming. It isn't like I'm ever going to see this guy again. So, I think for a second and then rattle off the first things that come to mind.

"I want to start a garden, but I have no space in my current apartment for any more plants. I like action movies but only if they have a romantic subplot. I read several books a week. I don't understand the appeal of pumpkin spice beverages. When I was in high school, I went to the state championship for cross country. And I cannot go on one more bad date."

I don't hear his laughter this time, but I can sense it as well as see the slight lift and fall of his shoulders as his body shakes with the movement. His reaction breaks the dam that usually has me freezing up.

"A runner?" he asks, sounding impressed.

"Not anymore. I had a couple scholarships to colleges, but I didn't go."

"Why not?"

"Life." It's my usual canned reply, but then I remember I'm never going to see this guy again. "I got pregnant."

"You have a kid?" His lips curve with a bigger smile than I'd expect. It isn't like most guys recoil in horror, but they rarely look this… happy about it.

"A daughter. She turns six next week."

He's quiet, as if considering my answer or maybe

waiting for me to say more. I clamp my mouth shut. I've already overshared, but for some reason I still don't want to leave. If anyone asks, I'll blame it on the cold numbing my brain, but really, I think it's him.

"What's your name?"

I could tell him. Even if he were a serial killer, which I've pretty much ruled out at this point, I don't know how a name is going to change anything, but I feel like I've already said too much.

"Fine. Doesn't matter."

Now I laugh. "At least you're honest. You'll forget it in an hour anyway, right?"

"I know I've only known you for a few minutes, but you aren't the kind of woman a guy forgets so easily."

My cheeks heat even though I'm certain that was a total line.

He shifts slightly and the lights reveal a sharp jawline and full lips that are quirked up in a smile. "A person's name is usually the least interesting thing about them, so if you're only offering a few pieces of information, I want the ones that tell me more about who you really are."

It's a more insightful answer than I was expecting. It's probably still a line.

"I'm not sleeping with you."

He barks out a laugh in the night air and it loosens some of the tension. He has a nice laugh, deep and throaty.

"I'd say the thought hadn't crossed my mind, but I'd be lying." Another quiet chuckle leaves his lips after the admission. "Won't tell me your name, not sleeping with me, but you will stand out here and talk with me?"

I should go inside and get some sleep before our early flight.

"You know, there's a bar downstairs filled with women who would probably be willing to do a lot more than talk." An image of some other woman entertaining this guy flashes through my mind, along with an unexpected hit of jealousy.

He probably would have talked to anyone that walked out here. I'm not special. I was in the right place at the right time. But the thing about moments like this is that they feel special regardless of your better instincts. Fate. Destiny. Luck. Whatever you want to call it. I'm a hopeless romantic at heart and this stranger in the dark asking me questions is the most romantic thing that's happened to me in a long time. How sad is that?

"Is that a no?" he asks.

"I haven't decided," I say, but don't make any move to go inside.

"Was the guy on the phone your boyfriend?"

"No. I am very single." And in case he thinks that's an invitation, I add, "I'm not interested in dating right now."

"That bad, huh?" he asks with a tinge of disbelief in his voice, like dating is awesome. Maybe for him it is. Actually, even without fully seeing him, I get the sense that he dates a lot and is great at it.

"I'd like to blame the men I've been out with, but honestly, it's me. I'm a terrible date."

"What? No way. I don't believe that." His gaze rakes over me and it's the first time I realize he might be able to see me better than I can see him.

"It's true. I promise you." I cross my arms over my chest. "Now tell me something about you."

"I'm an open book. What do you want to know?"

"Why are you in the city?"

He takes a beat, as if considering his words carefully. Maybe not such an open book after all.

When he finally answers, he says, "I had a job interview today."

"And it didn't go well?" I ask because he did say he was having a crappy day.

"It was a long shot. I knew that before I came, but I had to try."

"I'm sorry."

"Thanks. What about you? What brings you to the city?"

"I'm here with my sister. She had a job thing, and I tagged along."

"That's cool. Older or younger?"

"She's three years older."

"Other siblings?"

"No, just the one."

"You're the baby of the family, like me. I have older brothers."

I don't often feel like the baby. Ruby has always looked out for me like an older sister, but I had to grow up fast when I got pregnant, and somewhere in the past six years, I've taken on more of that eldest vibe. Though she would still cut a bitch who crossed me.

"Speaking of siblings," he says, reaching into his pocket and pulling out his phone. He stares at it, a grin pulling up one side of his mouth. "They've been blowing me up all day to hear about the try—, I mean, the interview."

His smile falls, and he slides his phone back. The air shifts around him. He has a cocky playfulness about him, but this is a first glimpse of just how shitty he's really feeling.

"Was it that bad?" I ask.

He blows out a breath that is visible in the dark night, and I can feel the weight of his emotions, disappointment, most likely. Maybe shame.

"No. In fact, it went well. Or so I thought. They want to go in a different direction."

"I'm sorry." And I am. I don't know this guy's name or anything about him, really, but I know what it's like to reach for something and not get it, no matter how badly you want it.

"Anyway, enough about me." He pushes off the balcony, standing to his full height.

My heart pounds a little faster as he comes toward me. He's even taller than I assumed. Broader too. With each step he takes, the light brings him into better view. The black T-shirt he's wearing stretches across his chest in a way that hints at the muscle underneath.

Confidence oozes from him. It's in his fluid, athletic

movements and the easy way he talks to me. His face is the last thing the light hits. His dark brown hair is covered by a white Minnesota Twins baseball hat. I guess that's where he's from, but I don't ask since I'm not prepared to answer the same question.

His mouth is pulled into another half smile that gives him a certain charm. He's one of those guys that is more handsome the longer you stare at him. Which I now realize I've been doing for several moments.

If we weren't standing out in the cold, I'm certain that I'd be blushing.

"I knew you were beautiful, but the closer I get, the more out of my league I feel." His voice has a direct line to the butterflies in my stomach.

"You're full of shit." The traitorous butterflies flutter anyway.

"I've never been more serious in my life." His brows pinch together. "I feel like I've seen you before."

I'm positive that's a line, but dammit, it's working. I'm flushed and smiling. I think that half glass of wine went to my head.

"Maybe in another life."

"Either way, I'm glad we both ended up on this balcony together."

"I should go in," I say, but don't move.

"Come have a drink with me." He tips his head toward his room.

"I don't think so."

"Why not?"

"Maybe I don't want to."

"Nah." He grins and shakes his head. "That can't be it."

A small huff of surprise leaves my lips. The balls on this guy.

"Invite your sister too, if you want. I promise to be a perfect gentleman."

Biting the corner of my lip, I glance inside. Ruby is probably sleeping by now, but I don't want him to know that. I also don't really want her to come. Which is how I realize *I* want to go. I want to spend more time talking to this guy and I don't want to dissect it too much. And really, what could it hurt? I'm never going to see him again and it's my last night in New York. Gigi would be proud. I can tell her I had a flirty conversation with a stranger, and she'll stop harassing me to go out more, at least for a week or two.

"Fine. One drink."

His grin widens and makes my stomach flip nervously. I hope I don't regret this.

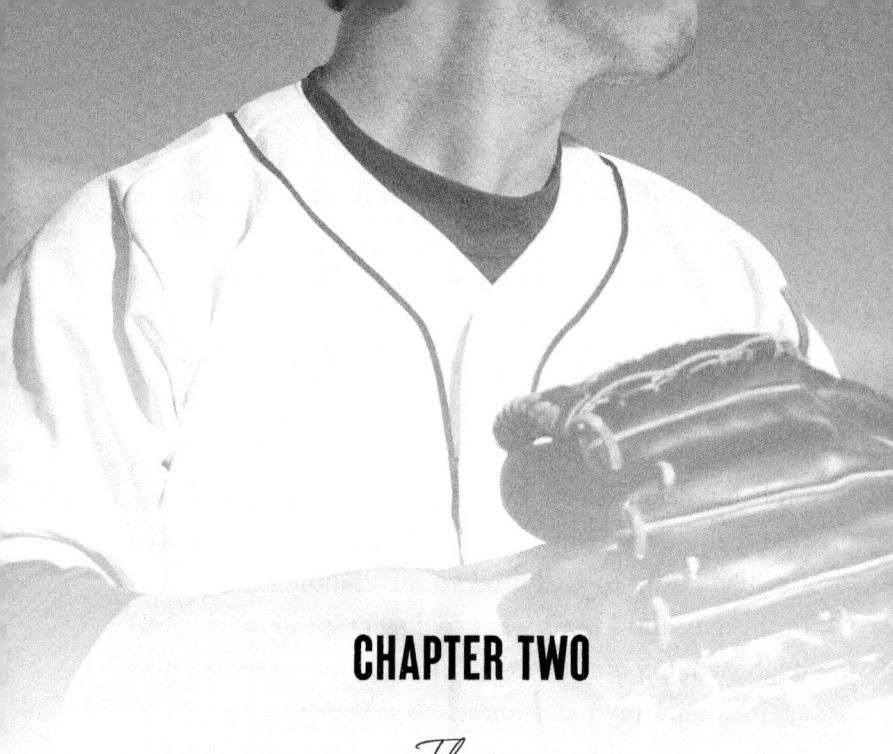

CHAPTER TWO

Flynn

I WAKE UP TO MY PHONE VIBRATING IN MY POCKET and a warm, soft body pressed against me. My eyes flutter open and a smile curves my lips at the sight of the woman in front of me. Her hair smells like coconut. The memory from last night plays like a movie in my head.

"You smell good," I tell her. "And I can't get over how beautiful you are."

She blushes. "Well, you're hideous."

I bark out a laugh and her lip curves into a shy smile. She's fucking with me. That's fine. I don't need her to say she's attracted to me. I feel it.

We talked all night. *Just* talked. I can't remember the last time I did that. It was… nice. More than nice. It was one of the best nights of my life. I still don't know her name, or anything about her really, but I might know her better than any other woman I've met.

I shift ever so carefully. My entire body hurts. Between the tryout yesterday and falling asleep on the small hotel couch with one arm underneath her, I feel at least ten years older. Worth it.

My phone vibrates again. I move slowly, careful not to wake the mystery woman. My throat hurts from talking and my eyes burn from lack of sleep. Worth it. So fucking worth it.

I pull my phone from my pocket and grimace when I see my agent's name on the screen. Everly is calling to give me some rousing pep talk about not giving up and saying something like, "we'll find the right team for you." I'm not ready for that kind of optimism just yet.

As I slip my phone back into my pocket, there's a knock at the door. I still, wondering if I imagined it. The knock comes again, louder this time.

I manage to get up without waking the woman in front of me and pad to the door. Everly stands on the other side.

"I need you to get downstairs immediately." The urgency in her tone has my body going alert.

"Good morning to you too."

"Here." She shoves mouthwash at me. She has a brush

21

in her other hand. "Do you have a shirt that's less wrinkled? Never mind. You'll do."

I glance down at my shirt. It is wrinkled. Almost like I slept in it. "What's going on?"

"I'll explain in the elevator. We have to go *now*."

"One sec. I—" I glance back to the couch. She's curled up to make herself more comfortable. Blonde hair falls over part of her face, but a hint of a smile peeks out.

"Fine, I'm attracted to you," she admits with a coy smile.

"I knew it." I did, but hearing it lights me up.

"Don't let it go to your head, Hotshot."

"Too late. The most beautiful woman I've ever met just told me she was into me."

She laughs. "That is not what I said."

"No? I must have misunderstood."

"Come on," Everly breaks through my thoughts. "It shouldn't take long."

Everly wouldn't tell me I needed to be downstairs immediately if it wasn't urgent but every step away from my room makes me panic a little more.

I don't even know my gorgeous mystery woman's name. She was adamant about not sharing personal information even after we confessed intimate details I doubt either of us has told anyone else.

"This wine is better than sex."

My brows rise. "It's not that good."

She makes a low sound deep in her throat and her blonde hair falls over one shoulder.

"You must not be having sex with the right people."

"That's probably true. I can't remember the last time one managed to get me off."

"You're serious?" I ask when she doesn't laugh it off.

She nods and takes another drink of her wine. Her blue eyes are like nothing I've ever seen before. Bright and sparkly like sapphire in the sunlight. My brothers would give me so much shit if I ever said that out loud, but I don't care.

"Let's go, Holland." Everly power walks down the hallway. She jabs the elevator down button, and it opens immediately. "You look like hell. Did you spend all night drinking away your sorrows?"

"I—"

Everly shoos me into the elevator. "Less talking, more walking."

I stumble inside. On a good day my agent is hard to keep up with, but right now it's impossible. She thinks I'm hungover, or still drunk. But it isn't alcohol clouding my mind.

My body is having a very visceral reaction to the thought of her not knowing good sex. As in, it would like to show her how good it can be.

"You've definitely been having sex with the wrong people."

"I'm starting to think there isn't a right person out there. At least for me."

"I don't know if I'm the right person or not, but I can guarantee you this, gorgeous. If you were mine, I'd make it my life's mission to get you off well and often."

As soon as the elevator doors close, Everly moves in front of me. She spritzes some sort of floral spray in my face with no warning.

Whatever the hell it is tastes awful and I grimace. "What the hell, Ev?"

"Colt Backer is here."

My stomach dips. "What?"

"He called me this morning and asked to meet. That's all I know." Everly continues fussing over me, smoothing out wrinkles in my shirt and running her fingers through my hair.

After my tryout yesterday, the GM of the Renegades called personally to tell me they were going in a different direction. Would it have stung as much if it weren't the fourth time in a month I'd heard the same thing from every team I'd met with? I don't know, but I know that my heart trips over itself as I walk toward him, wondering why he's here and what it could possibly mean.

Colt stands from a small table in the hotel restaurant when he sees us approaching.

"Nice to see you again," he says. He's a foot shorter than me, but still has an air about him that demands respect and admiration. He's immaculately put together from the crisp, custom suit to his freshly polished shoes. He makes me feel like a slob, even after Everly's pampering, but what do I care since he's not signing me to his club anyway.

"You too, sir." I glance at Everly for any hint on what to say or do here, but her face doesn't give anything away. "What can I do for you?"

Colt waves for us to sit down. His dark skin crinkles slightly around his eyes as he smiles at me. "Sorry for the impromptu meeting. It's early and I know you have a flight back home in a few hours, so I'll make this quick."

I tip my head in a nod for him to go on. My flight isn't until this afternoon, but I am eager to get back to the woman in my hotel room. Colt takes a few moments, like he's collecting his thoughts. His expression goes contemplative, and he takes a sip from a to-go coffee cup.

Internally I'm tapping my foot and motioning with my hand for him to get on with it already, but I stay still and silent while he considers his words. I don't want him to know I'm sweating it. Maybe acting chill makes me seem too detached, but yesterday I was eager and excited, and that didn't bode well for me either.

"I'm sorry we don't have a spot for you this season. It wasn't an easy call to make. In fact, even now I'm sitting here wondering if I made the right decision." He narrows his gaze at me like maybe he's about to change it now. Hope fills my veins, and my pulse quickens.

I can't put into words what it would mean to me to pitch for the Renegades. They're my dad's favorite team. His dad, my grandpa that I never met, loved them and passed it down to him, and I guess he passed it down to me. I can remember him watching them on the TV and listening to the games on the radio while he worked in the garage. Putting on that uniform would be a dream come true. It would mean I made it.

"You're going to be a hell of a pitcher, Flynn," Colt says in a very matter-of-fact tone.

And just like that, any hope I had is squashed. You're *going to be* a hell of a pitcher. Not, *you are* a hell of a pitcher.

"Thank you." I'm shocked the words come out as polite and friendly as they do. I'm tired of people telling me I'm not ready, not good enough, not there yet. I've been working my whole life for this, and it always feels just out of grasp.

"You're young with a long career ahead of you. What I need and what you need are at odds right now. I admire you and I'm looking forward to watching you progress, but right now the team needs someone with more consistency and experience. You get a few more seasons under your belt, stay healthy, and work on taming that fastball, and I'll be one of *many* general managers fighting to sign you."

"With all due respect, sir, what we *need* might be different, but what we *want* is the same. You want a pitcher that will lead you to a pennant and I can promise you that no one wants to stand on that mound again more than me. I know I'm young and that there is still work to do, but I'm ready for it. I will outhustle every other player on your roster. I come from a family of professional athletes so that isn't a claim I make lightly. You're right I don't have a lot of experience, and some might say that makes me a risk, but that's not how I see it."

"How do you see it?" His lips part with a grin. He has a gap between his front teeth wide enough that most people would have fixed it with braces. God knows he could afford it. Somehow it fits him though.

With a shrug I say, "I'm going to be the best pitcher in the league. I just need someone to put the ball in my hands so I can prove it."

His smile widens as he continues to stare at me. I'm not sure how long goes by before he stands. I guess that means we're done here.

Everly gets up to shake his hand. They exchange a few words that I don't hear. I'm slower to get to my feet. I meant every word I said. I'm not blowing smoke or saying what I think he wants to hear, but I'd be lying if I didn't hope that it'd also sway his decision.

Colt shifts his attention back to me and extends a hand. I take it and he grips my palm tightly as he says, "It's my hope that our paths will cross again."

Not sure what to say, I tip my head in a nod and manage a small smile for him.

As soon as he's gone, Everly blows out a breath.

"I'm sorry I dragged you out of bed for that. Nice job, though. You handled it well."

"Not well enough," I say dryly.

"We will find you the right team, and Colt and every other team that passed on you is going to regret it. Mark my words." She's fiery and gets this look of lethal retribution every time a team goes in another direction, like she's personally affronted as much as I am. That look and her ability to tell people off in a way that somehow comes across as polite and professional is why I hired her.

I have four older brothers looking out for me, and the truth is I'm not always great at advocating for myself since I didn't need to that often while growing up. And I'm learning that there is so much formality and hoop jumping in professional sports that I'm happy to let her manage all that and let me do my thing on the field. I just need to find a way back onto the field.

"I'm heading to the airport. Go home, relax, and I'll be in touch early next week. I have a call with Kansas City and Baltimore this afternoon and a dozen messages from other teams. New York passing means someone else gets the opportunity to sign the best pitcher in the league."

I don't know if she truly believes that, but Everly smiles at me, hazel eyes dancing with amusement and determination, and I know at the very least she's going to operate like she does. That's good enough for me.

"Thank you," I say.

With a nod, she turns on her heel and walks across the marble lobby floor toward the front doors. People scurry to get out of her way. God she's terrifying.

I give myself two more seconds to feel sorry for myself but then I remember there's a gorgeous woman upstairs in my room.

I take off in a jog toward the elevator and smash the

up button with my palm. Last night, she made me forget about everything going on with baseball. I want to go back to that bubble with her.

The doors finally slide open, and I step inside and hit the floor number. I tap my thumb against the side of my leg as the elevator moves at a snail's pace. It stops at the third floor and a woman with a housekeeping cart smiles politely. I move to the side to make enough space. We stop again at the fourth, but no one is there, then at the fifth for the housekeeper. By the time I get to the eleventh floor, I am vibrating with impatience.

I'm out the door the second I can squeeze through, and I jog down the hall until I come to my room. I pat my pocket for the key, only to realize I didn't bring it. Instead, I pull out my phone and navigate to the app.

"Come on. Come on," I mutter quietly while I wait for the light to flash green. When it does, I push into the room, gaze going right for the couch where I left her.

The room has that stillness that already tells me she's not here, but I check every room and even out on the balcony just to be sure. Then I retrace my steps and look for a note or any sign that she left me some way to contact her.

Nothing.

Fuck.

Wait. She's staying in the room next door. I run back out to the hall and pound on the door next to mine. It flies open and a housekeeper gives me a soft smile.

"Can I help you?" she asks.

I look past her to the empty suite.

"Sir?"

"No. I'm… Thanks." I run a hand through my hair and walk back to my room. I call down to the front desk, but all they can tell me is she already checked out.

Defeated, I drop onto the couch. I pick up the wine glass with her pink lipstick smudged on the rim.

She's gone and I didn't even get her name.

CHAPTER THREE

Olivia

"**A**NOTHER NEW DISPLAY?" RUBY'S VOICE STARTLES me from the top of the ladder where I'm adjusting the twinkle lights that frame the front window.

I steady myself before glancing down at my sister. "You scared me. I could have broken my neck."

"Please. You're only a few feet off the ground. At worst you would have broken an arm." With a small grin she extends a coffee cup in my direction.

"I couldn't keep it Valentine's Day themed forever," I say. Nor did I want to. Love shmove. "What do you think?"

She barely glances at it before nodding. "Looks good."

I climb down and take the cup from her. She has her

backpack hooked over one shoulder and a pencil holds up her red hair in a messy bun.

"How did writing go today?" I ask. She spends most mornings at a small coffee shop down the street writing her next book.

"It didn't." She won't quite meet my eye as she adds, "I beat three levels in Royal Match though, so quite a successful morning if you ask me."

I know better than to pick at her when she's having a rough writing day. No amount of talking it out or inspirational speeches pull her out of it. She needs a couple of hours to mull it over and then inevitably she'll start picking my brain and we'll brainstorm wherever she's stuck until she's excited again. "Do you want to get lunch?"

"Yes." Her eyes light up. "I have a call with my agent later and I'll never survive without carbs and cheese."

"Pizza it is," I say. "Let me put the ladder away."

Gigi comes out from the back room holding a stack of books.

"Oh good," she says when she spots Ruby. "I have a stack of new orders for you to sign."

"I'll do it after lunch," Ruby says. She's been saying she'd get to them for two days now and Gigi gives her a loving but no-nonsense stare that says Ruby has run out of excuses.

"You sign books. I'll grab pizza and bring it back," I say. Now that I've thought about food, my stomach is growling and impatient.

"Okay. Thank you."

I nod my acknowledgment. "Gigi, do you want anything?"

"No thanks. I have leftover soup and homemade bread today." The level of excitement in her expression seems to contradict the idea of leftover anything, but Grandpa has been packing her lunches for as long as I can remember, and they are the gold standard. He packages things up like a pro, always adds something from every food group—including dessert. When Gigi pulls out her lunch, anyone nearby always stares in fascination at the spread. But my favorite part is the notes he writes her. Every single day her lunch comes with a handwritten note, usually on a Post-it, occasionally a receipt or lined paper. Sometimes the notes are sweet, sometimes funny. Poems, jokes, drawings, or just a simple I love you.

After I put away the ladder, I grab my purse and leave Ruby with Gigi to sign books. Outside, the weather is sunny and warm. We had a rainy, cold Valentine's Day last week, but since then, it's felt like spring has arrived.

The pizza shop is only two blocks away and I'm early enough that I beat the lunch rush.

"Hey, Olivia." Tim, the owner, smiles from behind the cash register. He's wearing a Mustangs hat and reading the newspaper. "Dining in or carrying out today?"

"To go, please. The usual."

He puts down his newspaper to ring me up. It's open to the sports page and the top headline mentions the Mustangs. There's a grainy black and white picture underneath of what I assume is one of the players. Tim notices me looking and smiles.

"I bet your grandfather is excited about the season. Hope this new guy is as good as they're saying he is. I'd like to see them win just once in my lifetime."

"He's always excited during baseball season," I say, handing him my card and stealing another glimpse at the paper. The photo is upside down and not all that clear, but the guy looks familiar. Something tickles in my brain, a memory or connection I can't quite make, but before I have time to decipher it further, Tim hands me my card back and the receipt.

"Give us about fifteen minutes."

"Thanks," I say and head back out the front door. There are tables and chairs underneath a blue awning, but instead of sitting, I walk down the sidewalk enjoying the sun and fresh air.

I love downtown Lake City. Small businesses line the streets. Most have been here since the 1950s. Other areas around downtown have grown, putting in chain restaurants, department stores, and housing subdivisions, but everything in this five-block radius is filled with the old city charm and character. It's a mecca for art galleries, cozy restaurants, and bookstores. In fact, this area is home to three of the city's best bookstores: a used bookstore, my family's, which is The Book Nook, and Plot Twist. They are the newest of the three to the area but have won best city bookstore two years running. Not that I'm counting or anything.

I stop in front of Plot Twist. They have a great location at the end of the block where people park and walk up to the other stores. The front window always has original artwork and changes weekly. It's part of their schtick. People stop just to stare at the window display and this week's is an ode to the start of baseball season. The linework is incredible, depicting a man's profile as he winds up to throw a pitch. And underneath are a variety of books about baseball—from fiction to memoirs. It's good, not just the artwork but the concept. So good I'm mad that I didn't think of it.

By the time I get back to our bookstore with lunch, my brain is buzzing with new ideas for the front display. I'm obviously not going to copy their idea, but at the very least we should move some of our most popular baseball books to the front tables. Spring training starts next week, and people around here love the Mustangs—even if they have been on a fifty-year losing streak.

I set the food down on the back table with a thunk.

Ruby and Gigi look up at me from where they sit on the opposite side. Gigi's lunch is already laid out in front of her, and just like always, it's a masterpiece. Soup, bread, cut carrots and celery with hummus, mixed fruit, a thermos of tea, and an oatmeal raisin cookie.

"What's wrong with you?" Ruby asks, lifting one eyebrow as she reaches for the pizza box.

"Did you see Plot Twist's new window display?"

"Yes," she says slowly, like she can't understand why that's caused my mood to shift.

"I feel like such an idiot. It didn't even cross my mind to do something for the start of baseball season. Grandpa must be so disappointed in me."

"Your grandfather doesn't care one bit about window displays and you know it." Gigi lifts the spoon to her mouth and takes a small bite, still watching me.

She's right. I know she's right, but no one loves baseball more than him. I should have at least considered it.

"I want everyone to love this store as much as I do. We just need to get them in the front door." I believe that with my whole heart. After all, that's what happened to me. My earliest memories are sitting on a bean bag chair in the children's section with a stack of picture books while Gigi helped customers and worked around the store. It's a magical place, filled with love and books—and really aren't those the same thing?

"Is that why you've changed the front display three times this month?" Ruby asks.

I slump down in my seat and take a slice of veggie pizza from the box. "I'm figuring out what appeals to sidewalk traffic."

"She's trying to beat Plot Twist for best bookstore this year," Gigi says so matter-of-fact that my jaw drops.

I have never spoken that dream out loud.

Picking up on my shock, she says, "You stomped around here for a week when last year's awards came out."

I hadn't realized I was so obvious about my disappointment. I know it's a silly dream, but this bookstore means everything to me, and Gigi created something really wonderful that has been a part of the community for thirty years. I want the entire city to love it as much as I do.

"Do you still have that old pink bike with the basket on the front?" I ask Gigi.

She nods thoughtfully. "Yes. I think it's in the shed at home. Why?"

"Can I borrow it for the display? I have an idea that I think will blow theirs out of the water."

Gigi offers me a soft smile. She might think I'm taking it too seriously, but she'd do anything for me. "Of course."

"I can go with you to grab it after my call. Maybe we can talk out plot issues on the way?" Ruby asks hopefully.

"Deal."

By five o'clock, we have finished the new window display and fixed Ruby's plot issue. She pulled out her laptop as soon as we were done and cozied up in one of the comfy white chairs in front of the magazine section. It makes me so happy to see her fingers flying over the keys.

Greer busts through the front door with the same kind of energy. My daughter only has one speed lately and it's a full-out run.

"Momma!" she yells and flings herself at my legs. Her

blonde curls are wild from the day, framing her heart-shaped face.

Grandpa enters the store a few feet behind her. I smile at him briefly before hugging Greer.

"Hey, sweet girl. How was your day?"

"Good," she chirps, peering up at me with her arms still wrapped around my waist. "Grandpa took me for ice cream, and he said we could bake cookies tonight."

One side of her mouth is covered in chocolate—evidence of the ice cream—and yep, now so are my pants. "Sounds like Grandpa is going to be chasing you around the house to get rid of the sugar zoomies!"

She giggles and unlatches herself from me, heading to Gigi next.

"Thanks for picking her up," I say to Grandpa. He gets her from school every Friday to give me extra time at the store. He's in his usual outfit of navy dress pants and a short-sleeved button-down shirt. Much to Gigi's dismay, he hasn't updated his wardrobe in thirty years, not even the Mustangs hat perched on his head is from the last decade.

"Any time." He nods his head toward the window behind me. "Looks nice. Is that your grandmother's old bike?"

"You like it?" My smile widens. "I was going for whimsical springtime vibes."

"I don't know what *vibes* are, but it looks real nice, sweetheart." He stops in front of me to place a kiss on top of my head.

I follow him to the counter. Gigi is closing out the register for the day, and Greer sits on a stool kicking her feet and talking a mile a minute about everything she did at school.

"And then we played freeze tag until Axel threw up on the gym floor. Then we went outside and…" she continues, detailing all the most memorable parts of her day.

When she's done and finally takes a breath, Gigi says, "That sounds like quite a day."

Grandpa leans in and kisses Gigi's cheek.

"And how was your day?" she asks him.

"Real good." He nods, mouth curving up. "New scoreboard is up and working, and the benches got a fresh coat of paint."

Grandpa is the facilities manager at Fletcher Stadium where the Mustangs play. He's worked for the team in some capacity all my life. I've never been a big fan myself. We all go as a family to spring training where Grandpa points out all the updates they've made in the past year.

"Can we make chocolate chip cookies tonight?" Greer asks. She has a habit of changing the topic as fast as she talks.

"What about double chocolate chip cookies?" Ruby appears with the cheeriest expression I've seen from her all day. I'm not sure if it's because she finally figured out her book or if Greer's infectious smile and happiness has rubbed off on her—probably both.

"Are you coming over too?" Greer asks her aunt.

Ruby nods and leans on the counter in front of her.

"Of course. I wouldn't miss Grandpa's cookies. Plus, I need to go grocery shopping, and I heard you're having spaghetti."

"Spaghetti?" Greer's green eyes widen comically as she looks between Gigi and Grandpa for confirmation.

"With meatballs and garlic bread." Grandpa rubs his stomach.

"Well now I feel left out," I whine playfully, although there is a small part of me that wishes I were going to be hanging out with my family tonight. The much larger part is excited for a night out with my friends. It's my best friend Sabrina's engagement party so it'll be a fun time, but there's always a point in the evening where I miss Greer so much I feel like I can't breathe. It's more about me than her. I know that when she's there, she's well-loved and taken care of, and Greer looks forward to staying over at her great-grandparents' house. But tomorrow morning I'll be anxious to pick her up and see her sweet face.

"I'll save a cookie for you," Gigi says to me.

"I won't." Ruby smirks.

"Jerk," I mouth and stick my tongue out at her.

She makes a face back and just like that we're kids, poking and taunting each other until Greer is in a fit of giggles that almost sends her falling off the stool.

"I think that's our cue to get home." Grandpa lifts her into his arms.

I step forward and kiss my daughter on the cheek. She wraps her arms around my neck.

"Tell Aunt Brina hi for me, and Uncle Archer that I've learned how to sign all the letters of the alphabet, and Uncle Brogan that I've been practicing my touchdown dance."

"Okay. I will try to remember all that." I squeeze her hand. "Be good. Have fun. I'll see you in the morning."

"Bye, Mommy!" She waves as Grandpa carries her away.

"Wait. Can I catch a ride with you?" Ruby grabs her backpack and runs after them, leaving me and Gigi in the store.

"You should get out of here too," Gigi says.

"We don't close for another hour."

She raises both brows as she looks around the quiet store. So far, my new window display is not doing the trick of bringing new people inside. Maybe Grandpa is right. What even are whimsical springtime vibes?

"I'll stick around for a bit. You go have fun. Enjoy your night with friends." She shoos me with one hand.

"It's early. No one is there yet."

"Then go home and change." She looks me up and down. "Maybe go to the bar first, chat up some nice young men."

I snort a laugh. "There are no nice young men at the bar on a Friday evening."

She gives me a disapproving head shake and mutters something about wanting more great-grandbabies while she can still pick them up.

"Okay. Okay. I'm going." I get my purse from the back

room and scan the store for anything that needs doing before I go, but everything is exactly as it should be.

Gigi motions with her head when she sees me lingering.

Laughing to myself, I lift a hand to wave goodbye and then head out of the bookstore. It's a short drive to my apartment. I change into a dress for tonight and redo my makeup and hair while blasting all my favorite pop songs that I usually skip because they aren't appropriate for Greer's little ears.

Even taking my time, I'm ready to go before it's time to leave. Sabrina and Archer rented out the back room of a popular restaurant and bar for tonight. Nerves bounce around in my stomach. The guest list is insane. Archer plays professional football for the Mavericks and so does his best friend, Sabrina's brother, Brogan. All their teammates are sure to be there. I've only been around the whole lot of them once before, but they're a big, rowdy, intimidating, but loveable group.

I think Gigi is secretly hoping I'm going to meet one of Archer's teammates, fall madly in love, and give her a dozen more babies. She's still offering to take Greer so I can go out and meet people any chance she gets.

My mind flitters back to the last time she watched Greer while I went to New York with Ruby. Brown eyes, a playful smirk, rough hands. My stomach flips at the memory of him.

I met someone. And was promptly reminded why I stopped dating. He snuck out while I was sleeping. I've done the walk of shame before, but it never felt as awful as waking up that morning and realizing he'd left without a goodbye. I mean, how embarrassing that he had to leave his own room to get away from me?

I shake off the memory and negative thoughts and check my reflection in the mirror one last time before I head out the door.

I turn up the music in my car and try to reclaim the happy, excited mood from earlier, but my thoughts keep drifting back to that hotel room. I have replayed that entire night from start to finish so many times. Each time I do, I look for the clues. I mean, sure, he was ridiculously hot and charming, but he didn't seem like a phony. I guess good phonies never do seem that way.

A billboard near the exit catches my attention. Brown eyes. Playful Smirk. My heart lurches and I blink a couple of times. I swear that looked just like him. I turn my head to get another look, but I'm already past it.

"Okay, you've officially lost your mind," I say to myself with a small chuckle as I get off the freeway. Now I'm seeing him on giant signs? I've reached a depressing low. For the first week after I got back to Arizona, I thought I saw him everywhere—on TV, on the street, and every time my phone pinged, my heart jumped. It was irrational since I didn't give him my phone number or my name.

At the restaurant, I spot our group immediately. Archer and his teammates stand out—taller and broader than everyone else. My nerves are back, but as soon as I spot Sabrina and the blissed-out smile on her face, I relax.

43

"Congratulations!" I say, embracing her tightly.

Her laughter tinkles next to my ear. "I'm so glad you're here."

We pull back and she gives me a once-over with an appreciative nod. "You look hot."

"So do you." Then again, she always does. Her long, red hair is curled and falls over one shoulder. She's in a pale purple dress that looks gorgeous against her pale skin and makes her brown eyes pop wider.

Her fiancé, Archer, steps up next to her, sliding one arm around her waist as he tips his head at me. "Hey, Olivia. Glad you could make it tonight."

"Me too. Greer wanted me to pass on her congrats and let you know she's mastered signing the alphabet."

"Is that right?" His smile lifts higher and hazel eyes twinkle with admiration. Archer is deaf. He wears hearing aids, but he also signs—something Greer has thrown herself into learning ever since she met him. I don't know how he did it, but Archer won over my daughter in record time. It usually takes her a while to warm up to men. I could probably read a whole lot of things into that, but the simple fact is she's predominantly around women. With the exception of Grandpa, of course.

"She's very excited to show you the next time she sees you."

"I can't wait to see it. Tell her I'll drop by the studio after her class on Wednesday."

"She'll love that."

Someone nearby laughs loudly and the three of us

look over at the commotion. I must have reverted back to being nervous because Sabrina laughs softly and says, "Let me introduce you to some of the guys. They're not as intimidating once you get to know them."

I'm not so sure of that, but I follow as she and Archer work their way into the circle of men.

"Sabrina!" The guys all yell and lift their drinks to cheers the bride-to-be.

"What about me?" Archer asks, looking around at his friends.

The guys laugh, but a few tip their beers in his direction.

My gaze travels around the circle. Almost as if on cue, each of the guys looks from the happy couple to me.

"What did I say? Best behavior tonight," she scolds them playfully. Grabbing my hand, she tugs me farther into the center and begins to introduce the guys.

Some of the more well-known Mavericks players I recognize, like Cody St. James, Merrick Thomas, and of course Sabrina's brother Brogan Six. He lifts a hand above the crowd to wave at me. I mirror the action, but then Sabrina is pulling me away to another group of guys. Someone, Archer, I think, hands me a glass of champagne.

I take a small sip as Sabrina begins to introduce me to Archer's brothers. Knox, the motocross rider, Hendrick, the former NFL player. I can see the resemblance in them and Archer. I smile and then glance over at the last Holland brother.

"And this is Archer's youngest brother, Flynn."

I glance over at the last man in the circle with one of those friendly, too-bright smiles reserved for first introductions. I've heard a lot about Flynn. He's a professional baseball player that has been crashing with Archer and Brogan after he was cut from the Twins. Sabrina has mentioned him a few times, and I even saw him once, briefly, when I stopped by the apartment. He was passed out on the couch so we didn't speak, but the point is I know of him, and Archer is the kind of good guy that makes me believe his brothers are all equally as nice.

Which is probably why my stomach lurches so violently when I'm met with familiar brown eyes. I stare at him the way you might an optical illusion—waiting for the man in front of me to morph into someone else.

Because this guy? I know him.

The playful smirk I remember twists with recognition and shock.

"This is my best friend, Olivia," Sabrina says. Her voice sounds far away like she's in a tunnel. Or maybe I am.

I hear Hendrick and Knox's greetings, but I can't seem to look away from the guy I have thought about every day since New York. Who am I kidding? Every minute. Granted, a lot of those thoughts were anger that he snuck out while I was sleeping and couldn't be bothered with saying goodbye, but I haven't been able to shake him.

I open my mouth to say… something… anything, but nothing comes out. Did he know this whole time? That night was he laughing and waiting for me to recognize him? Was it all some joke to him?

An embarrassed flush spreads through me.

"Olivia," Flynn says my name slowly like it's part of a puzzle he's just figured out. He extends a hand.

"You have to be kidding me," I say under my breath but loud enough that Sabrina hears.

A wrinkle forms between her brows as she looks from me to Flynn and back. "You two have already met?"

"Flynn was crashing at our place that night we watched Greer," Archer reminds her.

"Oh, right."

"That's not it," I say, then shake my head and look directly at Flynn as I say, "I mean, no, we haven't met."

Flynn pulls his hand back, that playful smirk returning, like he's amused at me pretending not to remember him. Oh, I remember him, but we haven't met. At least not officially.

Flynn Holland is the guy from New York. Correction, he's the *asshole* from New York.

CHAPTER FOUR

Flynn

I CAN'T TAKE MY EYES OFF HER. *OLIVIA*. HOLY SHIT. IT'S really her.

I take a step forward and her body stiffens. So many things rattle around in my brain. I don't know where to start. Questions I want to ask her, things I want to say.

"I can't believe you're really here."

Long, blonde hair. Big, blue eyes. I've pictured her face a million times since New York, but staring at her now, my memory didn't do her justice.

Those bright blue eyes glint like cut sapphires as her gaze goes from confused to shocked—possibly pissed. At me? I'm not sure.

"Am I missing something?" Archer asks, dark brows raised. Without speaking, he signs, *What the hell?*

"We have met," I say to her. "Maybe you don't recognize me in the dim lighting."

If she doesn't want to tell everyone about the night we spent together, that's fine by me. All I care about is seeing her here. *Now.*

Instead of dignifying my comment with a reply, she attempts a weak smile at Sabrina. Unfortunately for her, no one is letting the awkward moment drop.

"In any case, nice to meet you." I extend my hand toward her.

Her stunning blue eyes flick to my palm and up. "Flynn, is it? You look more like a Richard or a *Dick.*"

Claws out. *Meow.*

I'm grinning at her and she's looking back at me like I am the spawn of Satan.

Silence stretches out around us. Hendrick is the first to break it, laughing nervously and then covering it with a cough.

"Who wants champagne?" Sabrina asks.

"Love some," I say without looking away from Olivia.

Her gaze narrows, but she doesn't break my stare. Everyone else politely moves toward the bar, leaving us as close to alone as we're going to get in this crowded place.

"I can't believe it's you. Didn't I say I'd seen you before?" I ask, shaking my head with disbelief. "And you said—"

"Maybe in another life," she finishes the statement for me and for a second, her angry demeanor softens.

"I need another drink," she says, staring off into the distance like she's in a haze.

I walk with her to an open section of the bar. Filled champagne flutes sit on the bartop and she takes one, brings it to her lips, and takes a long gulp, then side-eyes me like she can't quite believe I'm really here either.

That feeling is mutual. I'm basically gawking at her, but I can't seem to stop. I'm still so stunned. God. I must have thought about her a million times. And she's been here the whole damn time.

When she's drained the entire glass, she finally angles her body toward me. The earlier fire is back in her gaze. "Was New York some kind of joke? Did you know who I was the whole time?"

"What? No." Is she for real right now?

Her piercing stare narrows as if she's not sure she believes me. I consider telling her that if I had known who she was, I would have already tracked her down. That night has lived rent-free in my head ever since. It isn't often that you meet someone and connect with them like we did. I wouldn't call it love at first sight, but I would say it was a hell of a lot more than lust at first sight.

"I had no idea who you were," I say, my tone low and serious. "But I'm really happy to see you again."

She snorts a laugh, stare moving back so that she's looking behind the bar toward the shelves of liquor bottles. "I'll bet."

"I'm so for real right now. I must have thought about you a thousand times since that night." That number is low, but I can already tell that she's hesitant to believe anything I say. Less seems better.

Squaring her shoulders, Olivia glares at me. I've never seen eyes so blue or a mouth so kissable. Her brows lift, indicating that she might have said something.

"Sorry, what?" I ask. She's so damn pretty it's distracting.

An exasperated scoff leaves her mouth, and she mutters, "Unbelievable."

She starts to walk off and I put a hand on her forearm to stop her. Tingles race up my arm at the feel of her warm, soft skin.

"Wait," I say, voice closer to pleading than I'd like. "Can I get your number or take you out sometime?"

"Seriously?"

"Uhh…"

"I don't think so." She takes a step and so do I.

"Why not?" I ask.

"I don't date."

"Ever?"

"Not since the last dozen attempts."

"Because none of them could get you off?" I ask quietly.

Her face flushes. "Oh my god. I can't believe I told you that."

"Nothing to be embarrassed about."

Her face scrunches up adorably and she gives her head a little shake. "Look. I like your brother and Sabrina is my best friend, so let's just forget about New York and everything we said and did there, and try to enjoy tonight for them. Okay?"

"Not likely."

Exasperation flashes across her features. "I'll see you around."

This time I let her leave. I stare after her and feel a smile tug at the corners of my mouth. "You can count on it."

The bar is filled with Archer's friends and teammates. I've met most of the guys already, but as I walk up to Brogan, he motions with his head for me to join them and says, "Baby Holland, let me introduce you to the guys."

"Guys, this is Flynn. Aka Flynn the Flame. Aka Baby Holland. Aka—"

"They get it," I say, then smile at the group crowded around. I nod my hello to each of them as Brogan points and calls out their names. Tripp, Cody, and Merrick.

"Good to see you again," Tripp says to me. "How's the arm?"

Instinctively, I make a fist with my right hand and squeeze until I feel the muscles contract all the way up to my shoulder.

"Rested and ready to get back out there." So ready. The sooner I do, the quicker I can prove myself.

"I'll bet." Tripp's grin widens. "The Mustangs are lucky to have you."

Merrick lifts his beer toward me. "Here's hoping you can pull them out of their slump."

"Slump?" Tripp's brows rise. "They haven't had a winning season since the eighties."

"Nineteen seventy-six," I say.

An awkward silence hangs around the circle. The Mustangs are the worst team in the league, but they were the only one willing to take a chance on me, so I feel something like loyalty to them. Don't get me wrong, I wish I were playing anywhere else next season, but I plan to seize the opportunity.

"Well, I, for one, am stoked you're sticking around. I missed you, little bro." Brogan places a hand on my shoulder and squeezes, then shakes me like a ragdoll. I'm taller than him, but he's a big, muscular dude, and I think he likes to remind me of it any time he can.

"I'm excited to have a reason to use my season tickets," Cody says. He's the Maverick's quarterback and has a more serious vibe about him than the others. "And I'm sorry about how things went down with the Twins. That was some impressive pitching for being pulled up at the last minute. Not a lot of guys could handle that kind of pressure."

"Including me," I say, feeling like I'm out there on the mound in front of thousands of fans and walking batters left and right all over again.

"Don't even sweat it. You'll get another shot," Brogan says, ever the optimist.

"Yeah, for sure," I add, trying to mimic his optimism—except I don't feel it. "I'm going to grab a drink."

Instead of heading to the bar, I go out a side door to the outdoor patio to have a few minutes of peace.

My steps slow when I spot Olivia.

She doesn't see me and her voice filters out softly. "Five. Four. Three. Two."

She pauses.

"Two and a half," I say.

She swivels around to face me.

"Sorry. I came out here to get away. Seems great minds think alike." I shove my hands in my pockets. "Mind if I join you?"

"It's all yours. I was just leaving," she says.

"Stay. I have so many questions I've wanted to ask you since New York."

"Is that why you ran off while I was sleeping?"

Ah. Well that makes more sense why she's pissed. She thinks I left her. I mean, I did leave her, but not because I wanted to. "Something came up. I went downstairs for a few minutes and when I came back, you were gone."

"Which is where I'm going now. Bye, Flynn. It was…" She falters like she's struggling for the right word, "interesting seeing you again."

She's gone before I can reply. I would have taken great, good even, but I guess interesting will do. It was *interesting* to see her too. And by interesting, I mean fucking fantastic.

CHAPTER FIVE

Flynn

OH, *HOW THE MIGHTY HAVE FALLEN.*

That's my only thought as I get a tour of the Mustangs training headquarters.

I have been inside a lot of baseball facilities in my day. None as small or run-down as this one. Which isn't really a fair statement. It's clean and appears well taken care of, but it doesn't have any of the sparkle and extravagance that other teams flaunt.

I can tell the walls were recently painted and the floors shine with new polish, but it's obvious that no real money has been put into the club since... maybe ever.

I try to keep my face from showing all this as the Mustangs general manager, Charles Harper, leads me through a series of hallways, grunting out names as we pass rooms. Weights. Therapy. Media. Kitchen. He walks too fast for me to get a good look at any of them, and maybe that's the point. Best not to look too closely.

I grip my duffel tighter in my left hand as I follow him. I knew signing with the worst team in the league was going to be an adjustment, but any optimism I was holding on to flew out the window the second I stepped inside the door.

My stomach swirls with dread and the feeling that I have managed to go from the height of my career to the bottom in six months' time. It's just one year. One season to show everyone what I'm capable of and get back on track.

Last fall I pitched in the playoffs for an incredible team. I thought I was on my way to the top. This place is going to be a daily reminder that staying at the top takes a hell of a lot of work.

"We're all excited you're here," Charles says. His mustache pulls at the corners, indicating he might be attempting a smile.

Before I can reply, a man I recognize approaches.

"This is your catcher, JT Ryan." Charles opens his stance as JT steps up to join us.

"Flynn Holland. Welcome to the team." JT Ryan stands in front of me, sizing me up but in a non-confrontational way. He's baseball royalty. His dad is a Hall of Famer who played with four different teams over his career and won the pennant with three of them. JT has been with the Mustangs since he was drafted six years ago. Before that, he played in college and helped his team win a national championship. I don't know how he ended up here. Or why he hasn't left. But the Mustangs are damn lucky to have him.

"Thanks. I'm…" I search for the right word. Happy isn't accurate. Excited? Not exactly. "Looking forward to it."

The *it* being the baseball season. I'm itching to show everyone what I'm capable of.

"I'll let JT give you a more in-depth tour," Charles says, pulling his phone from his pocket in that way people do when they're anxious to get back to work. "Really great to have you here, Flynn. Let me know if you have any questions."

"Thank you, sir." I nod to Charles as he steps away.

JT places both hands on his hips and his smile pulls up. "I'm so stoked you're here. I'm a fan, actually. I saw you pitch in game six against Kansas City."

He whistles, grin lifting higher at the same time he chews fast on a piece of gum, and starts walking, leaving me little option but to follow him.

"How's the arm? Did you take some time off after the end of the season?" JT fires questions faster than I can answer them. He stops in front of an older man coming out of a small office.

"This is Earl," JT introduces him. "You need something around here, he's your guy."

I give Earl a polite once-over as I try to guess his role here. There are a lot of people behind the scenes that make an organization run, but I've rarely had them called out as the go-to guy.

"Hello," I say.

Earl looks like every TV sitcom grandpa. Gray hair, a light tan, creases around his eyes and mouth, clean-shaven. He's wearing an off-white, short-sleeve dress shirt with a pocket on the left side. His pen and glasses are tucked inside, and he smells faintly of spearmint.

"I'm the facilities manager," he says as he extends a hand. He has a warm smile and a firm grip. "Nice to have you. Some arm you've got, kid."

Kid. Everywhere I go it seems people are hung up on my age, like a few years makes a difference in my abilities. I've spent my life proving people wrong and I guess that's going to continue here. When will it be enough? But Earl oozes a friendliness that keeps the word from annoying me too much.

"Thanks, I appreciate it," I say, squeezing his hand before I pull my arm back.

"If you need anything, anything at all, holler." He flashes another smile that I feel myself mirroring.

"Yeah, I will."

He tips his head to me in acknowledgment before walking off.

JT continues the tour. He walks slow but talks fast, pointing out every nook and cranny of the small facilities, much like Charles had, but in much more detail. I'm struck again by the difference in size and extravagance from the other teams I visited. It's staggering, really. I never thought a lot about the disparity between the top teams and the worst. It's no wonder, really that they've had a hard time signing talented players.

JT shows me the indoor batting cages and a weight room with one of those garage doors that opens to a side parking lot. Music is pumping and a couple of guys are using the squat rack.

They both lift a chin to JT and then their gazes move to me. I raise a hand in a wave, but neither return the gesture.

"That's Gunnar and Bo," JT says. "You can always find them in the weight room. And don't even think about changing their music. Nice guys, though, once you get to know them. I'll introduce you later."

Judging by the icy stares, I'm not sure they're all that eager to meet me. It's been a whirlwind since I signed last week. Interviews and photoshoots, mostly highlighting the excitement of three brothers playing professional sports in the State of Arizona. Four if you count Brogan, but since he's not blood, most of the headlines have only featured me, Archer, and Knox. A baseball player, a football player, and a motocross rider. It's been fun to commemorate the moment with them, but I can see my teammates might not be so excited about the attention I'm getting. It's either that or they're worried about my performance last season. Though, I'm not sure I could make the team any worse.

Next, I see a lounge area with a large TV and big,

leather couches. It's next to a kitchen that smells like coffee and burnt popcorn.

"Microwave, refrigerator, water cooler." JT points to each and then taps a finger on a clipboard hanging on the wall. "Sign-up is here. Whenever you get a chance, you can put yourself down for a few days."

"Sign-ups for what?"

"Throughout the season, we all pitch in to make sure there is always food around for the team and staff," he says. "My wife makes the best coffee cake muffins. You want to get in early on my days because they go fast."

What in the potluck hell? I've fallen a long way from the catered food and delicious cafeteria options I had access to with the Twins.

"You don't want to eat anything I make," I say.

"A lot of the single guys bring in donuts or order pizza or something." He waves it off, so I do too. One year. That's it. One amazing season and I'll be out of here.

Then finally, we're stepping out of the building and onto the field. My eyes drift closed, and I inhale deeply. One thing that's always the same with baseball stadiums, that smell. Grass. Dirt. Sunshine. Is there any better scent?

A few guys are out here, running in the outfield; others are playing catch. Spring training doesn't start until tomorrow, but there's an eager energy in the air that gives me my first hint of excitement since I signed with the team.

"Want to throw me a few?" JT asks.

I'm in jeans and a T-shirt, but the enthusiastic look on his face has me nodding.

His grin widens. He leans down and plucks a baseball off the ground, then tosses it to me.

My fingers smooth around the ball and that familiar sensation of comfort spreads through me. While I grab my glove out of my duffel and head up to the pitcher's mound, JT gets in his gear.

We play catch for a few minutes, while I get warmed up. It feels fantastic to be out here. Amidst all the chaos of the off-season and busting my ass in tryouts and meetings to find a team, I almost forgot how much I love this sport. There's nothing better than standing out here in the sunshine with the ball in my hand.

"Warm yet?" JT asks as he throws the ball back to me.

"Getting there."

"All right, then. Let's see that fastball." JT punches his glove and squats down behind home plate.

I pull my shoulders back, stretching my muscles, then tip my head side to side. I throw the first pitch, a fastball just like JT wanted, but at only eighty percent.

He catches it and tosses it back. We do it three or four more times until my arm is loose, and this feels like any other field, with every other team. There's a familiarity in baseball, probably in most sports. Everything changes as you move from team to team, but everything is somehow exactly the same.

The sun pricks the back of my neck as I get into a zone. JT nods that he's ready, and I wind up and give him everything I've got. It feels good. No. It feels fucking fantastic. It's the first pitch I've thrown in months that wasn't in front of coaches and general managers—people picking apart my every move so they could decide whether or not I was right for their team.

I realize some of the weight of that is gone now that I have a spot. Maybe it isn't the place I wanted to end up, but now that I'm here, I'm ready to get to work.

After a few pitches at full speed, JT stands and lifts his mask with one hand. His grin stretches across his face as he yells, "You're putting on a clinic."

I don't immediately understand his meaning but then follow his gaze to right field where guys have stopped what they were doing to watch.

I get it. I'm the new guy and they all just want assurances that I'm not going to come in, throw like shit, and cost them a bunch of games. Although honestly on this team, winning any games would be an improvement over their previous seasons.

When they realize we've noticed them, they go back to playing catch. I've got the bug now. I don't want to stop.

"Got time for a few more?" I ask, hopefully.

His nod is immediate. "Definitely."

So we keep at it. I throw to him, trying out all my pitches and seeing which feel rustier than others. I have work to do, no doubt about it, but my arm feels great and anticipation hums through me. Out here I can forget that I'm playing for my last-pick team and that I blew an amazing opportunity just months ago—one I dreamed about my whole life.

All this buzzes through my brain as I pitch to JT.

The familiar *whoosh* as the ball sails through the air followed by a *thwack* of the ball hitting the catcher's mitt time and again has every muscle in my body relaxing. I dream of that sound.

I'm not sure how long we're going, but at some point, I stop trying to throw hard and instead focus on getting back to my rhythm. Speed is great, but precision and accuracy make or break a pitcher.

Sweat drips down my temples when JT finally stands and jogs up to the mound. He doesn't remove his face mask and a pit forms in my stomach. I'm teleported back to the last inning I pitched in game six of the World Series. I'd been unhittable up to that point and then I just lost it. I don't know what happened. I couldn't put the ball where I wanted no matter how hard I tried. I was all over the place. Inside. Outside. High. Low. When I tried to pull back on the speed to regain some precision, it was like I was lobbing softballs.

I knew it was coming. I knew I was going to be pulled from the game if I didn't get it together. Still, I fought as long and as hard as I could.

No pitcher wants to get pulled, especially not like that. And not when you know your career depends on it. Walking off that mound I knew it was going to be a fight to get back. At least I thought I did. The last four months have shown me just how fast an entire league can turn on you.

JT holds the ball in his glove. He stops two feet away

and finally lifts the mask. His brown eyes twinkle with excitement, and that uneasy feeling turns to confusion.

"Was that the best you've got?" he asks.

Shit. Maybe I'm still lobbing softballs.

I reach up with my right hand and rub the back of my neck as I flounder for an answer.

He laughs, then pulls his glove off his right hand and holds his palm out in front of him. He opens and closes it a few times, staring at it with an expression I can't make out.

"Even when you were holding back, I've never felt anything like that," he says, voice filled with wonder.

For a second longer, I'm still confused. But as his boyish grin, one I'm already becoming accustomed to, lights up his face, understanding hits me. Along with relief.

He forms a fist with his hand and then hits me with it lightly. "You throw like that all season and we're going to be unstoppable."

Archer's gaze roams around the space, still all blank, empty walls and sparse furniture, as he enters my apartment.

"Is this everything you have?" he asks.

"Yep." I've been in paid housing since I left college or, most recently, crashing on Archer and Brogan's couch, so I don't have a lot: couch, coffee table, TV, bed.

"*It's temporary,*" I tell my brother, signing the words as I speak. My brothers and I all learned sign language. It helps in situations where it's loud or there are lots of people or when he's too busy looking around at my drab apartment to watch my face.

"It's depressing as hell," he says.

A laugh shakes my chest. "The location is good and it's not like I'm going to be spending a lot of time here. I'm close to the Mustangs' facilities and there are restaurants and bars within walking distance."

With an expression that seems to say, *if you say so,* Archer plops down on my only piece of furniture.

I grab two Gatorades from the fridge and bring them to the couch, taking a seat on the other end. "It's a six-month lease. Why get a lot of stuff if I'm just going to move it all again?"

He accepts the drink and studies my face for a second, brows pinched and mouth in a straight line, then nods slowly.

"Have you met the team?" he asks.

"Some of them. I went by the stadium earlier today and threw a few pitches with JT Ryan."

"Oh yeah?" One side of his mouth pulls up into a smile.

None of my brothers have really mentioned my performance in the World Series that caused me to be let go from my team and forced me to spend the next few months clawing for another opportunity. Sure, they've offered their support and told me to keep my head up, but they've tiptoed around my shitty pitching.

Now, though, I can see he's thrilled at the thought of me being back out there and of things going well. Having four older brothers is like having a whole bunch of parents, except they're more overbearing and less comforting. Oh, and there's a lot more ribbing. Or I assume that's what it's like since I didn't grow up with parental figures that weren't my brothers. Our mom died when I was young, and our dad wasn't around much.

"What have you been up to since the season ended?" I ask, kicking one foot up onto the coffee table.

"Not much. Sleeping in, working out, helping Sabrina at the dance studio." At the mention of his fiancée, Archer's expression goes soft. Helping at a dance studio for kids doesn't sound like the most exciting way to spend his months away from the rigorous schedule of professional football, but if it makes him happy, I guess that's all that matters.

"Speaking of Sabrina." He gives me a sideways glance that makes me want to squirm in my seat. It's the classic big brother look, the one that says *I'm about to get up in your personal business whether you like it or not.* "You didn't tell me that you saw Olivia in New York."

There's no question in his statement, but I know at least a dozen are swimming in his head.

"I didn't know it was her," I say.

He gives me the same disbelieving look she had. Am I absolutely kicking myself that I didn't take one look at her and instantly place her? One thousand percent. But two months and thousands of miles separated the first time I saw her to the second. I wasn't expecting her.

"I'm serious."

"All right." His voice lifts an octave.

"How does Sabrina know her?"

"They worked together at Lilac Lounge when Sabrina danced there," Archer says.

I'm still filing away that information when my brother bumps my knee with his.

"So, what happened?" he asks.

"Eh…" I run one hand over my jaw.

Archer groans. "Please tell me you didn't hook up with her."

"What if I had?"

"She's Sabrina's best friend."

"O-kay." I don't see how that changes anything.

"I love you like a brother, but—"

"I *am* your brother," I interject.

Grinning, he continues, "You're young and having fun and I totally get it, no judgment here, but she isn't the kind of girl you hook up with and then ghost."

"First of all, ouch." I level him with a glare. "I don't do that."

That disbelieving stare is back again.

"And second, I would never ghost Olivia. She's…" My words trail off as I try to come up with an adjective to describe her. Stunning. Feisty. She doesn't hold back her emotions or thoughts, and I find that incredibly sexy.

My brother is still looking at me like he thinks I'm full of shit.

"Fine, yes, I've hooked up with women and never texted them back for a repeat, but I never make promises that it's anything more than a one-night thing. I don't know where I'm going to be in six months or a year, so it's nicer than stringing them along for months and then hopping town."

"Yeah? Is that how you're selling it?" He arches a brow. "How *nice* of you."

"Fuck off." I laugh, relaxing into the couch and feeling lighter than I have in weeks. "It doesn't matter. That isn't what happened with Olivia. I met her by chance at the hotel and we stayed up all night talking."

"*Just* talking?"

"Mostly talking."

He groans again. I could put him out of his misery and tell him I didn't hook up with her, but this is more fun.

"Lighten up." I elbow him.

"Just promise me you won't do anything that I'm going to have to apologize for later. Sabrina likes you, but she will still plot your death if you hurt her best friend."

"I will be a perfect gentleman. Just like my big brothers taught me."

This time when he lets out a low groan, I laugh. Making your older siblings sweat is one of the few perks of being the youngest.

CHAPTER SIX

Olivia

EVERY FIRST SATURDAY OF THE MONTH, THERE'S A farmers' market at the end of the block. It brings in a big crowd and all the nearby businesses open early, some set up outside, and people wander up and down the streets. We always get a lot of foot traffic, and it's a good opportunity to remind the community that we're here and welcome them inside.

I'm lingering near the front of the store adjusting displays that are already perfect. I can't help it. I have this nervous energy, wishing I could just drag people inside and gush to them about books and make them love this place as much as I do.

Ruby is here signing new stock of her books we got

in yesterday. My favorite display in the entire store is the one that's dedicated to her books. I'm so proud of everything she's accomplished.

Greer is with Gigi at the market and the store is still empty.

Ruby yawns next to me and then declares, "I'm done."

"Oh, uh, there's actually another box in the back room."

Her hair is pulled up in a messy bun and she gives me a wry expression.

"If I get coffee, will that help?"

"Only if it comes with a scone," she replies dryly.

"You got it." Laughing lightly, I take off out the open front door. The air has a nip to it, but the sun is shining, and seeing so many people milling around makes warmth spread through me. It's an even bigger crowd than normal.

Maybe news of the market is starting to reach a wider audience?

I'm smiling as I walk along the sidewalk, exchanging hellos and good mornings. It isn't until I get closer to Plot Twist that my stomach clenches. While our store is empty, this one is bustling with people already.

"How?" I whine quietly.

My steps slow as I approach. There is a line to get inside. Again, hooooooow?!?!

Two women stand at the back of the line, grinning and careening their necks to see to the front.

"What's going on?" I ask them.

"That hot new baseball player for the Mustangs is here." Her face is flush with excitement.

"Hot new baseball player?" I ask, mostly to myself. I walk around the line to the front and then push my way through the door to get inside.

"Excuse me. Sorry. I'm not butting in line. I promise," I say when I get more than a few dirty looks.

I've never been inside Plot Twist, and it feels a little like crossing into enemy territory, if I'm honest.

The bookstore is smaller than ours and has a more dated feel, like a library or your grandfather's den. The lighting is dim, and the color scheme is all wood and dark colors. I glance around for Walter, the store owner. He's a grumpy old guy who has perfected his resting asshole face.

When I don't see him, I go back to scrutinizing the space. The shelves are packed too tightly with books, and the table displays are basically just piles of books with no clear indication as to why they were bunched together. The signage denoting each section, *historical*, *non-fiction*, *sports*, *fiction*, *children*, look like they were handwritten. To be fair, the penmanship is artsy and beautiful, but it still strikes me as something a bargain store would do instead of a place that won best bookstore the last two years.

It takes me a few seconds to catalog all this and then turn off the critical eye I usually reserve for my own work. I've worked so hard, and it's difficult not to look around and see the ways I believe our store is better.

Still, it has that same sense of home and joy that all

bookstores have. I love the smell of books—old and new. When I was a kid, I'd go to the library, open a book, and stick my nose right in the center to take a deep inhale. Ruby said it was gross, but I just love everything about books. They're family and friends, connection to a big world out there.

Music plays from the speakers, something classical but lively. The line of people snakes through the right side of the store past recipe books and through the minuscule romance section. Without thinking, I search for my sister's books. I'm not all that surprised when I don't find any. We have pretty much covered that market. Our Ruby Madison books come signed and with anecdotes about the author. Things like, "she wrote chapter twenty-two right over there in that chair" or "I was with her when she got the call that this one hit the New York Times Bestseller List!" People love those little insights, and Gigi and I are so proud of Ruby that they slip from our lips easily.

Finally, I spot the front of the line. Under the handwritten SPORTS sign a man stands in front of the bookshelves. He has a Sharpie in his right hand and his left is draped around the shoulders of a little boy wearing a Mustangs jersey.

No, not a man. *Flynn Holland*. He's dressed in a long-sleeved gray shirt and jeans. He has this effortlessly handsome way about him. Sporty, casual, but undeniably attractive. I gawk at him for several seconds while he takes a photo with the boy who can't stop glancing over at Flynn with wide-eyed admiration.

After a woman, who I presume is the boy's mother, stops taking photos, Flynn squats down to the kid's level and says something to him I can't make out. Whatever it is, the kid beams bigger. Then Flynn holds out a fist and the kid bumps his against it.

It's heartwarming, but right now I don't want my heart to be warmed. Especially by him. *In someone else's bookstore.*

As the little kid jogs off, Flynn stands. His gaze roams from the line over to me. My feet move toward him of their own accord.

There's a flicker of surprise on his face but is quickly replaced by a wide smile. "What are you doing here?"

"What are *you* doing here?"

"Wait, is this your bookstore?" He glances around as if he's seeing it for the first time.

"No."

When I don't offer any other explanation (frankly, I'm still too shocked to come up with one), Flynn says, "My agent thought it would be good to do some community events. I wasn't sure a bookstore was the best endorsement, but the owner is a fan. And I mean, look at that line."

"I saw it," I mumble under my breath, then scoff. "Unbelievable."

"We need to move the line along," a young woman says quietly. She's a bookstore employee, judging by the official way she speaks. She at least has an apologetic look as she does so.

"Do you want me to sign something?" Flynn asks me.

"No." The word comes out with a little too much force.

The line patrol shifts uncomfortably as neither Flynn nor I move.

"Give us just one more minute." Flynn holds up the same hand that has the Sharpie to the woman. He angles his body, so his back is to the rest of the line.

"It's so good to see you again. I was hoping I'd run into you." He picks up a shirt off the table. "Turn around."

"What?"

He makes a circle motion with his finger.

I turn, still too stunned to object. He places the shirt against my back, and I feel the marker as he scribbles on the material.

"Is this going to be a regular occurrence or a one-off event?" I ask. I can't believe they brought in an athlete. Why not an author at least?

"I told him I'd stop by as often as I could to sign jerseys. I'm not sure about future events. With the season starting, I won't have a lot of time. Where is your store? Do you have my jersey? I'd love to come see it sometime." He finishes and I turn back to face him.

"No."

"No, you don't have my jersey at your store or no, I can't see it?"

"Both."

"Why not?" he asks, laughing softly.

"We don't sell sports memorabilia, and you can't help another store sell books and then come by mine."

"Because....?"

"I'm really sorry," the woman managing the impatient line interrupts again.

"It's fine. I'm going," I say.

I start to walk off, but Flynn calls after me.

"Olivia."

I stop and glance back. He holds up the shirt in his hand and then tosses it to me. I don't get my hands up in time and it hits me in the face. I inhale a waft of starched cotton and permanent marker. My hands grip around the fabric and I pull it down. Turning on my heel, I weave back through the line until I'm out on the sidewalk again. The line has only grown. I finally stare down at the shirt he gave me.

The front has the Mustangs logo and on the back, his last name and number eighteen. It's the same number all his brothers wear for their mother. It was her birthday. I know this because I looked him up after our run-in at Sabrina's engagement party. I know a lot about Flynn Holland now. Things I could have known months ago if I hadn't demanded we not share any personal information that night we spent together.

Right next to the eight, Flynn signed it, *Dick*. And what I presume is his number is scribbled underneath.

"What is going on with you today?" Ruby asks as I remove every book from our front table, setting them on a cart to place back on the shelves. Every book lands with a *thump*. I'm careful, but too much pent-up frustration is pumping through me to be gentle.

"Nothing. I just want to freshen up the table with some new books. Romance readers are voracious. They will find their favorite books no matter where we put them. It's the more general reader we want to capture as soon as they walk in the door. We got some new recipe books in that I think will look great and appeal to a wider audience."

Ruby takes the book in my hands before I can slam it down on top of the others. We both hold on until I look up into her emerald eyes.

"You're spinning. Take a breath," she says.

All the fight leaves me.

My sister smiles sweetly as I let go of the book and she puts it back on the table instead of the cart.

"The table is great. They're always great. You have a fantastic eye for pairing books and creating beautiful displays. You need to lighten up. Who cares if some committee of people voted Plot Twist as the best bookstore in Lake City? We have a very loyal clientele, and since you took over last year, revenue is up. You completely overhauled the entire store. Gigi was thinking about closing and now look at this place. It's thriving."

"They were going to close?" I ask, feeling panic at just the thought.

"That's all you heard from my big speech?"

I let out a breath. "Thank you."

I've worked hard on this place, and it means so much that she sees it. I just can't help but want everyone else to see it too.

"You're welcome." She eyes the remaining books on the table. "You're still going to swap out the table, aren't you?"

"Organizing keeps me sane," I say with a more relaxed smile.

Together we put the books on the cart, and she walks with me as I place them on their shelves in various spots of the store.

"Were they really going to close the bookstore?" I ask her.

She nods. "I'm not sure if they would have gone through with it, but they talked about it. Gigi wanted to travel, and Grandpa thought it was too much for her to maintain on her own after she had that bad fall. But then you stepped in."

Ruby gives me a smile that's all admiration and pride. I know she loves this place as much as I do, but she never wanted to work here. Even as a kid, she did more writing than reading. I'd go through three or four books in a week and when I had nothing else to read, she'd some-times let me read her stories.

The thought of the store closing, of not being able to walk in here every day, makes my chest ache. From the time I was little I knew I wanted to work here. Sure, I thought I'd go off to college first, maybe work at a library or for a publishing house for a few years, but eventually ending up here was always in the plans.

When I got pregnant with Greer the summer after high school, I decided to stay and take classes locally instead of going away to college as planned. Gigi gave me a job and I worked at the store full time until I had Greer. Then I transitioned to part time until she started pre-school.

This store really has been a lifeline for me in so many ways. At every phase of my life, it's been here for me, the same way my grandparents always have been. It's such a reflection of them and their unwavering support and love. What they've created is so much more than a bookstore. To imagine it closing breaks my heart.

The bell on the front door jingles as we finish putting away the last of the books. Ruby's eyes widen.

"Oh no, what will they think of the empty front table?" she asks with mock horror.

"Shut up." I backhand her lightly and then take off to greet our customer.

"Welcome in," I say as I come around the corner. But when I see who it is, my steps come up short.

"You." My hands go to my hips.

One side of his mouth hitches up and he gives me that easy, sexy smile. "And you."

"How did you find me?" My arms fall to my sides. It seems there's no avoiding this guy.

"I asked around." His gaze lifts and he smiles as he takes in the store. "This is cool. Exactly as you described."

"Liv, I'm going to—" My sister's voice cuts off as she takes in the scene in front of her. She looks from me to Flynn and back. "Sorry. I didn't mean to interrupt."

An awkward silence stretches out until Flynn takes a step toward her with his hand outstretched. "I'm Flynn."

"Ruby."

"The sister, right?"

"That's right." She gives me another side-eye as she shakes his hand. "How do you two know each other?"

"He's the baseball player that was signing at Plot Twist this morning."

"Oh." Ruby smiles tentatively. "You're Flynn Holland. The new pitcher. Our grandfather—"

"Loves baseball," I finish for her, sending my sister a traitorous look. "Is it okay for you to be in here cavorting with the enemy?"

His lips twitch with a smile. "I didn't know bookstores had rivalries."

"Oh, yeah." Ruby nods along. "We throw down once a year. Who can stack the most books or make the best window display."

Flynn's chest shakes with a silent laugh.

"You are not helping," I tell her.

"Sorry. I thought we were being nice to our customer."

"He isn't a customer."

"I might be." He takes off, heading farther into the store like he's browsing.

Ruby fights a laugh, and I go after him. "You can't just come in here and… and… look at books."

"Why not?" Flynn asks, continuing on.

"What's the last book you read?"

"Are you book shaming me?"

"What? No, of course not. Just making a point."

"Books are cool. I'm thinking about taking reading up as a new hobby. Where are your sister's books?"

"I knew I liked you," Ruby shouts from wherever she's eavesdropping.

"Really, really not helping," I mutter, but I take off toward our Ruby Madison display. I pick up her newest book.

He takes it with a grin. "Vampires. I dig it."

I pick up two more and he takes those as well.

"Anything else?"

"Your number."

Turning on my heel, I head to the front counter. Flynn follows me, standing on the other side. I feel a little better with a few feet of distance between us.

"You already gave me yours," I say as I ring him up and put his books in a tote. I can feel him watching my every movement and it's unnerving.

"Yeah, but you haven't texted."

"You only gave it to me three hours ago."

"So, you were planning to text?"

When I don't reply, he says, "That's what I thought."

He rests one elbow on the counter. "You know I thought you'd be more excited to see me. I meant it when I said I thought about that night in New York hundreds of times. I was kicking myself for not getting your name or number."

"A thousand."

"What?"

"At Sabrina's engagement party, you said you thought about that night a thousand times."

He grins. "A million, probably."

"Wait. You're the guy from New York?" Ruby appears out of nowhere and gawks between us.

I want to die inside.

Flynn, on the other hand, lights up. "You talked about me?"

"Only to say terrible things." I usher him toward the door before my sister can say anything else.

"Nice to meet you," Ruby calls after him. "Enjoy the books!"

He throws a hand over his shoulder. "Yeah. You too."

I walk him all the way outside. Flynn laughs, still smirking at me. "What terrible things could you possibly have said about that night?"

"Oh, I don't know, maybe the part where I woke up and you'd snuck out." I wish I could take the words back because I fear they give too much away. I was so embarrassed that morning. I still am.

"I did not sneak out." He must read the thoughts swirling in my head that are screaming they don't believe him because he adds, "I swear."

"Well, you weren't there when I woke up, so either you left me there or were hiding and hoping I'd see myself out."

"My agent showed up at my door early that morning and said the general manager of the Renegades was in the lobby waiting to talk to me. I went downstairs to meet with him. I wasn't gone long. Thirty minutes tops. You were asleep. I thought I would be back before you woke up. When you were gone, I felt awful. I knocked on the room next door and looked for you around the hotel. I even asked the doorman if he'd seen you, but he didn't have much to go on since all I could say about you was that you were a gorgeous blonde with the prettiest blue eyes I'd ever seen and a smart mouth."

I open said mouth and close it when I can't think of a single thing to say in response. He hadn't been running away from me? Maybe it says something about my luck with men that my mind automatically went there, but honestly, I never considered any other scenario.

"Let me take you out. We can catch up over dinner or drinks. I want to hear what you've been doing since then."

The answer to that is not much. Work and Greer take up all my time. And the reminder of my daughter gives me another reason to shut this down. Flynn is interested in the single, carefree woman he met in New York. Not the busy, single mom who swore off dating after one too many disappointing dates. He likes the person he thinks I am. Not the one that I actually am.

"I can't."

Surprisingly, he doesn't push. He does linger a moment longer as if hoping I'll change my mind.

When I don't, he finally nods. "It was good to see you again. Thanks for the books."

My stomach dips with an uneasy sensation that might be disappointment. It's for the best, but I still don't like it.

"You're welcome." I force a smile. "Try not to use them as coasters."

CHAPTER SEVEN

Flynn

FRIDAY AFTER OUR FIRST WEEK OF SPRING TRAINING, JT invites me to go out with him and a few of the guys. We hit up a dive bar near the stadium, taking up two long tables in a quiet corner.

Most of the days, pitchers and catchers work out separately from the other positions for a good portion of the day. Which means I haven't had a lot of time to get to know the team. We eat together twice a day and there are team meetings and scrimmages, but there isn't time to sit and relax.

And if I'm completely honest, I think a good portion of the team is holding out judgment on me. I can't tell if they're worried I'm going to ruin their season or if they're just so used to guys coming in for one season and ditching that they don't bother getting to know newbies.

Whatever the reason, tonight seems to be breaking the ice. Gunnar Cruise, the Mustangs' first baseman, and Bo Mitchell, an outfielder, are deep in conversation about *The White Lotus*. While JT and one of our relief pitchers, Freddie, and I sit in a quiet, companionable silence.

It was a long week, filled with long days, and we're all beat.

"Anyone want another round?" Freddie asks as he stares down at his nearly empty pint glass. He's only a few years older than me but had an elbow injury two years ago that he's battled on and off, which has kept him from seeing a lot of time on the mound.

"Nah. I should probably get home to the wife and kids," JT says. "I've barely seen them this week."

Freddie looks to me.

"I can stay." My apartment, though I've barely been there except to sleep, is too quiet. No way I want to go stare at the blank walls all night.

"Yo, Gunnar," Freddie calls down the table. "Another beer?"

"Yeah, but can we go someplace where women aren't afraid to step through the door?" He nods his head toward the big, burly men at the bar. Their Harleys are parked out front and they're all wearing leather and sporting beards. They look tough, even though I'd wager most of them are as friendly as they come, unless you touch their bike. I know from experience with my brother Knox. The fastest way to piss him off is to touch his bike… or his woman. Both and you're a dead man.

Again, Freddie looks to me.

"Let's do it," I say.

JT drove us all over from the stadium so as he heads home, the rest of us pile into an Uber. I don't bother asking where we're going since anyplace but home is fine by me.

We pull up in front of Lilac Lounge, a popular night club. Sabrina used to work here as a dancer. It's a cool place. Inside there's a bar and tables spread out for groups who want to sit and chill. But outside there's a patio surrounding a giant pool. They have a DJ on the weekends, and he's set up at the back with cage dancers on either side of the stage.

"Now this is more like it." Gunnar rubs his palms together as we enter the club. It's packed tonight, making it hard to walk.

"This place has the hottest bartenders," Freddie says to me.

I nod, but my brain swirls with something Archer said: Olivia bartends here. Or she did. That's how she and Sabrina met and became friends. Olivia wasn't here the night I came with my brothers and Sabrina though so maybe she quit? Except now that I think about it, she mentioned she bartended that night in New York.

I detour away from the rest of the group, speaking over my shoulder, "I'll meet you guys out there."

Freddie nods and I head toward the inside bar. There's

a chaotic crowd, trying to get close enough to order. Being tall gives me an advantage to see over the madness. Hanging back, I let my gaze scan the full length of the bar looking for a familiar blonde bombshell. Brunette, Brunette, Dude… but no Olivia.

Disappointment trickles in. With spring training, I haven't had a lot of time to sit and think about anything else. But I have thought about her. She's a tough one to crack. I know she's attracted to me because she said as much in New York. Maybe it's weird for her because I'm her best friend's fiancé's brother but that seems like a stretch. There's something else holding her back and I intend to find out.

I pull out my phone to text Sabrina. I feel like there's a good chance I can convince her to give me Olivia's number or at least help me bump into her again. My future sister-in-law loves me. The feeling is mutual. She's funny and protective of my brother. And anyone who makes Archer as happy as she does is okay in my book.

While I'm tapping out a message, someone bumps into me from behind.

"Sorry, man," the guy says.

I glance up and turn to tell him it's no problem, but that's when I see her. She's carrying a tray over her head as she squeezes through the crowd. The way her arms are lifted pulls her purple tank top up, exposing a whole lot of smooth, alabaster skin. Her tits are pushed up and her hair is pulled back into a ponytail. She's dressed sexier than any other time I've seen her. Even though I know it's a uniform meant to make people stare at her, I feel a jolt of possessiveness.

It takes some effort and time for her to push through and make her way behind the bar. She sets the tray down and moves to the far side of the bar to help the other bartenders.

I move in that direction, but still hang back while I watch her. A smile curves my lips. She's quick, pouring drinks and taking the next order with an ease and skill that's impressive. Other people notice too and move toward her side. Mostly men. Even without hearing her exchanges with some of the guys, I can tell they're hitting on her. It's in the way they lean toward her or linger a little longer than necessary.

She offers a few flirty smiles and even a wink to one older guy, but she's moving so fast no one can pin her down long enough for more than a quick back and forth.

A group of guys celebrating someone's birthday come away from the bar with drinks and shots, but a disappointed air surrounds them as they all pat the birthday boy on the shoulder. He must have been rejected.

I feel your pain, bro.

Every so often the female bartenders switch sides, so that each of them moves to work the opposite section they've been on. I don't know the reasoning, but I can't help but note that each time Olivia switches to work a new area, the guys up next in line that she leaves behind, groan with frustration.

I don't know how long I watch this whole thing go

on. I don't even have a drink in my hand yet, but this is too good to miss. I inch closer without deciding. It isn't like I planned to gawk at her from afar all night, but from a distance at least she can't crush my hopes and dreams of taking her home.

Eventually a barstool frees up and I snag it. The new bartender on this side, a pretty brunette with a septum piercing, smiles at me.

"What can I get you?" she asks.

"Jack and Coke."

She nods and gets busy pouring my drink. I lean back, staring across the bar at Olivia. The crowd is gradually starting to move outside, and the bartenders slow down a bit, taking a little more time getting orders, smiling and talking more. All except Olivia. She moves with that same hurried pace. It seems like she's in a whole zone, not really seeing anything or anyone around her.

My drink is nearly gone when the bartenders switch again. Olivia moves toward me, only looking up at the last second.

"Can I get you another—" Her sentence comes to abrupt halt as her blue eyes lock on mine.

"Hey there." I wave with the fingers around my glass.

She looks behind me like she expects to see Archer and Sabrina or anyone that explains my presence. When she doesn't find anyone, she asks, "Are you stalking me?"

A small chuckle leaves my lips. "I came with some teammates. They're outside."

"Oh." She tugs on the hem of her tank top.

"Purple is a good color on you. My new favorite in fact."

"Are you expecting that line to work on me?" She raises her voice slightly to be heard over a group of noisy women nearby.

I get that familiar zing of excitement at her words. I love that she's such a ball buster.

"That depends. Is it?"

"No." She shakes her head, but a hint of a smile pulls at the corner of her mouth. Her gaze drops to my drink. "Want another?"

"Yeah. Thanks. Jack and Coke."

While she pours it, I say, "You should have prepared me better for chapter twenty-eight."

I guess I should have expected some spicy sex scenes, but as a new reader of the genre (or any genre, really), I did not.

She freezes, brows raised. "You read the book?"

"Yeah. In nearly one sitting. I'm working on the second one now."

"I'll let Ruby know. She'll be thrilled to know she has a foothold in the male demographic." Olivia places the new drink in front of me.

"I only have one critique."

Her body language stiffens immediately. I lean forward, closing some of the distance between us. "Nine inches is not the perfect length."

Her cheeks flush as she understands my meaning, but she keeps that haughty body language. "No?"

"Too big." I lean back. "Chicks think they want that sort of size, but they're never prepared for it."

"And you know this because…"

I grin back at her, waiting… waiting… waiting…

Her mouth falls open. *There it is.*

"I don't believe you." She won't quite meet my eyes though.

"I could prove it to you, but I think that might get me kicked out of here." I glance down quick at my crotch and back to her.

"Possibly arrested." Her smile widens. That excitement and sparkle I remember from the night we spent together makes an appearance for the first time since then. There's something intoxicating about being the one responsible for making her smile like that. Her carefree smiles are hard-earned, and it makes me that much more determined to get them out of her.

"Guess you'll just have to come back to my place tonight then. What time are you off work?"

As quickly as her excitement appeared, it fades away. "Sorry. I'm busy."

"What about tomorrow night?"

"I'm busy then too."

"Sunday?"

"Busy," we say at the same time. The busier she claims to be, the less I believe it.

"My ego is taking a real hit here, Liv."

"Only my friends get to call me that."

"Ouch."

She grins, clearly loving baiting me as much as I love being baited by her.

"It's okay. I like your name too much to shorten it anyway. O-liv-ia," I say it slowly, enjoying every syllable.

"Don't do that. Don't say my name all sexy."

"So you think the way I talk is sexy?"

She groans and turns away from me. Yep, she's definitely into me.

She gives me a smirk as she moves to the side to take another drink order. For the next half hour or so I sit and drink and watch her work. Between customers she lingers near me, so I take that as a cue to keep talking her up.

"How's the bookstore rivalry?"

She lifts both brows and gives me another exasperated look.

"Okay, fine, we won't talk work. What was your first car?"

Clearly amused by the random question, she huffs a short laugh before she answers, "I had an old red Toyota truck."

"A truck? Really?"

"It was my grandfather's. He sold it to me cheap."

"And now?"

"Surprised you don't already know, stalker."

"I'm in the intel gathering phase."

After another short laugh, she says, "Honda SUV."

"Color?"

"Black."

"Nice vehicle."

"It was one of the top safety picks last year."

Now it's my turn to be amused. Do people actually look at that stuff before they buy a car? I mean, they should but I've never heard someone say it before. Olivia is full of surprises.

"Let me guess, you drive a shiny new truck. A Ram maybe, something lifted with big tires."

I shake my head.

"I've got a new Chevy outside, sweetheart," some guy two seats down says. He has a bushy beard with twinges of gray in it. He strokes said beard as he continues, "Just drove it off the lot yesterday. Want to take a drive?"

"No thanks," she says politely but firm.

He shrugs and takes another sip of his beer.

"You don't seem like a sports car guy." Her gaze narrows.

"I'm not sure if that's an insult or not, but you're correct. I do not drive a sports car. I wouldn't mind having a McLaren someday though. Any more guesses?"

"Creepy white van?"

I chuckle. "Closer than your other guesses."

She arches a brow.

"I have an old '67 Ford F100 Ranger."

"Damn." The guy two seats down is clearly eavesdropping but the appreciative whistle he gives me is welcomed. "That was a good year."

"You remember it?"

"I meant the truck." He scowls at me. "How old do you think I am?"

"Uhh…"

Olivia fights a laugh, and I send the guy an apologetic tip of my head.

"Get him a round on me," I say to her.

He minds his business after that, and Olivia and I continue trading random facts. I want to dig deeper, beyond the surface, but I'm afraid she'll close up on me if I do.

"Did you really come with teammates or was that a line?" she asks as she pours another customer a drink.

"Oh shit," I say, glancing toward the outdoor area.

Her lips curl together as she holds in a giggle.

Fuck, they completely slipped my mind.

I give her a sheepish smile. "I guess I should get back, so they don't think I ditched them."

A flicker of what could be disappointment crosses her face, but it's gone so quickly I can't be sure.

"Have fun!" She flits off to the other side of the bar before I can respond.

I leave cash on the bar in front of me and take my drink with me as I head outside. The music is louder out here. Lots of girls in bikinis and guys in trunks are in the water or sitting on the edge. The whole vibe is just… more. People are drunk and having fun. It's the kind of environment I'd usually be all about, but tonight I'd rather be back inside sitting and talking to Olivia.

Still, I walk around until I find the guys. They're at a table on the right side of the patio. Three women are sitting on the edge of the pool, their feet dangling in the water as they talk to them.

The girls look first as I approach, and the guys' attention follows.

"We thought you bailed," Gunnar says, then quieter adds, "Everyone always bails."

That feels like a loaded statement that I don't want to address tonight.

"I ran into someone I know inside," I say then tip my head to the women with a polite smile.

"I know you." One of the women narrows her gaze at me like she's trying to place me. She has short black hair and light brown skin. I'm proud of myself for noticing anything other than her giant boobs because, damn, they're basically falling out of her top.

"Flynn." I lift a hand in a wave and take a seat beside Freddie.

"You're on that billboard." She points then nods excitedly as if she's more sure of it now that she's said it. "You're one of the Holland brothers, right?"

"That's right."

"Ooooh. Can you introduce me to your brother? The motocross racer." Another girl, sitting across from me, grins wide as she waits for my answer, then lets out a dreamy sigh. "He is so hot."

"Sorry, he's married."

"Too bad. I guess you'll do then. I'm Sadie." She smiles and bats her lashes innocently. She's fucking with me… I think. Her demeanor reminds me of Olivia a little.

A surprised laugh escapes my lips. "Lucky me."

As the seven of us talk, Gunnar and one of the girls pair off, clearly into each other. Bo and her friend with the very large boobs are in deep discussion about *The White Lotus*, I'm starting to sense it's a hot topic for him, and that leaves me and Freddie with Sadie.

Sadie's pretty cool actually. I'm not into her, mostly because I can't stop thinking about Olivia, but I'm enjoying talking to her. Freddie, on the other hand, is silent. When Sadie goes with her friends to get a new drink, I look to the guy next to me.

"Is everything okay with you?" I ask him.

"Yeah. Fine." He drags both palms over his thighs.

He's not fine, and after I stare at him a few seconds longer, he finally adds, "I just can't talk to women. I get all flustered and nervous."

"Seriously?"

He looks embarrassed as my brows lift in surprise, and I let out a low chuckle.

"Sorry, I don't mean to laugh. I'm surprised. You're a cool dude and not terrible to look at." I'm fucking with him. He's got this good ole country boy vibe about him. Blond hair, blue eyes, golden skin. If he pulled his shirt off in here, he'd look like he was modeling for some popular clothing line.

"At best, I'm an eight out of ten. Then knock off three or four points when I open my mouth, and nothing comes out."

"You haven't said a single thing to them all night?" I

ask, thinking back if I can remember him uttering a word since I've been here.

He shakes his head.

Well, fuck.

The girls are walking toward us, so I don't have time to ask him more. Sadie drags a chair over next to me. She's pulled on a pair of jean shorts with her white bikini top. She's sexy as fuck, but I'd be leading her on by pretending to be interested in her while I can't stop thinking about Olivia. And Freddie needs a win.

I clear my throat. "Hey, I've got a question for you."

"Sure," Sadie says.

"Say a guy wanted to impress a girl but he keeps messing it up. He says the wrong thing or does the wrong thing, or maybe he doesn't say or do anything at all."

Freddie next to me is taking a drink from his beer and coughs. His cheeks turn pink.

"Are you okay?" I ask him.

"Fine." His tone has a little grit to it as he blushes and sneaks an embarrassed glance at Sadie.

"A bad first impression isn't a deal breaker," she says with no hint of recognition that I meant Freddie. In fact… I'm not just talking about him.

"Good to know. How does he recover?" I ask.

She takes a second to consider it. "At our core, women just want to be acknowledged and recognized for who we are individually. Everything is so surface level nowadays. Ask her questions, show an interest in getting to know her. Most men, and even other women for that matter, barge in with their own agenda and unless it magically matches my energy we never connect."

Well shit. I'd expected a noncommittal reply about complimenting her hair or some shit. Sadie doesn't strike me as vapid, but I wasn't ready for her to drop reality bombs either.

"That's a real fucking good answer," I say as I think back to my last few encounters with Olivia. I've been so certain that we had this great connection that I jumped right in like we were going to pick up where we left off. Clearly, that hasn't worked.

"Thank you." She beams. "Who's the girl?"

"Am I that obvious?"

"Let's just say if you were hitting on me the past hour, you're doing a terrible job."

I bark out a laugh. Freddie snickers too.

"I can help more if I know the full details." She crosses one long leg over the other and leans forward.

So, I tell her everything. Or a lot of it anyway. About New York, and then running into Olivia now.

"Maybe she's seeing someone else. It's been months." Freddie finally finds his voice.

The idea of Olivia dating someone else makes me scowl. "I don't think so."

"Are you sure?" Sadie asks. "That's actually a good point."

"Thank you." Freddie is loosening up and blushing less. I'm glad my misery could bring them together.

"I don't think that's it." Olivia doesn't seem like the

type to keep that to herself. If the reason were that simple, she'd just say so.

"Have you asked her?" Sadie's brows lift as she questions me.

"Of course. She says she isn't dating at all right now."

"That's bullshit," Freddie says, then looks at Sadie. "Right?"

She preens at him. "Yes, *but* there's a story there. Figure that out and you'll be closer to figuring out what the real problem is."

The conversation shifts after that. Freddie seems to have gotten comfortable, but while they switch topics, I'm stuck on Olivia. Seems to be a common problem lately.

"I think I'm going to head out." I elbow Freddie. "You good?"

"Yeah. Are you?" He briefly studies me, then glances toward the inside of the club as if to remind me of Olivia.

"Fantastic." I grin. "See you tomorrow."

We bump fists and I stand.

Sadie smiles softly. "Good luck."

"Thank you."

I set my drink glass on a small empty table just before I step inside the club. A new crowd has gathered in the time I've been outside, and I fight through people again to get to the bar.

One giant group of guys, fraternity brothers judging by the college name and Greek letters on their shirts and hats, is gathered in a big huddle in the center of the room. They're loud, drunk, laughing and having a good time.

For the briefest moment, a flicker of longing for that kind of carefree fun hits me. Not that long ago, I was out with my college buddies at a place a lot like this. I was so ready to be playing professionally, to get to that next level, that I probably didn't enjoy it as much as I should have. I feel older than I am, but that's always been true.

Maybe it stems from being the youngest in a family of successful athletes or maybe I just have an old soul, but I've spent my life working so hard for the next step that I often wonder if I missed out on enjoying the moments as they happened.

I don't want to go back to the minor leagues or to college, but it's difficult to stop myself from wondering how things might be different if I hadn't always been so eager to be where I am now.

As I'm edging around the frat guys, I spot Olivia. She's out from behind the bar again. One hand holds up a tray of shots as she navigates through the crowd with a grace and steadiness that is sexy and impressive.

My body tingles as I watch her. She's a knockout, but it's more than that. I just dig her, and I refuse to accept that night in New York wasn't indicative of how good we could be together.

As I'm walking toward her, one of the guys in the group of fraternity brothers approaches her. I can't hear him, but her reaction is all I need to know he's hitting on her. She shakes her head with that same firm but polite look she's given a lot of other men tonight. I hate to admit that I enjoy watching her turn down some other guy, especially since she's done the same to me a few times now.

I don't have long to enjoy that feeling though because as she tries to walk off, he wraps an arm around her waist from behind and I have an "oh shit" reaction. My brows rise in surprise and my blood boils. It's fucking slimy to put your hands on a woman without her permission, and even I can tell from here that she wasn't interested in whatever he had to offer.

I move toward them quickly, but by the time I get there she's already extracted herself from his hold.

"Aww, come on," he says. His eyes are heavy-lidded, and he reeks of beer. He extends a hand like he might touch her again, but I grab him by the forearm.

"You good?" I ask her as I hold on to the guy.

"Fine." Relief flashes in her eyes for a second.

"Dude." The drunk guy pulls free and looks at me with disdain. I really didn't have *bar fight* on my agenda tonight. *Fuck.*

I don't even bother giving him my attention. My gaze stays on Olivia. She regains her composure quickly and puts another step of distance between her and the idiot.

"What the fuck? We were having a conversation," he says to me.

"You touched her." I finally flick my stare in his direction.

"I was just playing around."

"Really. I'm fine." Olivia's tone is hard, and her

stunning blue eyes bore into me with a clear signal not to get involved.

But there's little to no chance I'm going to stand by while some creep violates her personal space.

"See?" He grins at me like he's proved his point.

I don't like it, but the situation seems to be under control.

"As I was saying." He steps in front of me and sways.

Motherfucker. This time when he reaches out for her, I don't catch him in time. His fingers spread across her stomach and while I'm grabbing him by the back of the shirt and putting myself between Olivia and this asshole, she does one better. She tosses a beer from her tray into his face. Or mine since I'm now blocking him.

"Everything okay here?" The question comes from a deep voice to my right.

When I blink away the beer stinging my eyes, I find one of the bouncers has positioned himself in front of Olivia.

"Great," I mutter as the cold liquid drips down my face and seeps into my shirt.

As the bouncer takes in the scene, he must decide it is in fact not great, because the next thing I know he's guiding me and the drunk dude toward the front door.

A couple of his fraternity friends follow us out, and when their brother starts protesting, they offer me sympathetic smiles.

"Get him out of here," I say to them. "And when he

sobers up, tell him the next time he puts his hands on a woman, he better be damn sure she's consented."

"She was into me," he tries to argue with me more, but they're pulling him away from me. Smart choice.

I pull off my T-shirt as I walk around the side of the building. I wring out as much of the beer as I can and then sigh. What a fucking night.

My adrenaline is still pumping as I pull up the ride-share app. I'm about to request a Lyft when Olivia appears out of an employee door. Her steps falter when she spots me.

"I'm so sorry," I say as I look her over. She has her keys in hand and her purse over one shoulder. I don't move in case she's still feeling spooked.

"I was about to say the same thing. I wasn't aiming for you, in case that wasn't clear." Her gaze dips to my bare chest and then lower. A ripple of lust shoots through me as she stares a little longer than necessary.

A smirk plays over my lips when she meets my stare again. "No apology needed. I should have known you had it handled."

"I did try to warn you."

"They didn't send you home because of that guy, did they?"

"No. I was supposed to be off about thirty minutes ago. That was my last walk-through before clocking out."

I nod, still not moving toward her. She doesn't budge either.

"Well, I guess I should go." She glances around the dark parking lot.

"Let me walk you," I say.

She opens her mouth like she might argue, but I motion with my head and take a step.

"Come on. It'll make me feel better to know you're safe. And keep me from getting into a bar brawl," I mutter the last part.

She laughs lightly and we fall into step together. I let her take the lead and she walks up to a small black SUV. She hits the key fob, and the vehicle unlocks, lights flashing.

"I made it. Safe and sound."

I open the door for her, and she cocks one brow. "You just can't help yourself, can you?"

"Being a gentleman, you mean?"

"It is a lost art," she says.

"One more reason you should go out with me."

"Good night, Flynn."

I think about what Sadie said about how maybe I wasn't really listening to her now, but then I think about the drunk idiot and how he couldn't take no for an answer.

While I'm deciding whether or not I should shoot my shot again, she gets into her vehicle. So, I shut the door and step back, then lift a hand in a wave.

CHAPTER EIGHT

Olivia

MY NERVES ARE SHOT. I'M SURE FLYNN ASSUMES it's from the creep who put his hands on me, but I'm more spun up about him. Talking to him, seeing him, seeing him with his freaking shirt off. I was not prepared. He's tall and broad so I assumed underneath he would be muscular but seeing it is a whole other thing.

I fumble with my seat belt twice before it clicks into place, then start the engine. My heart is still racing so it isn't until I go to put the SUV in gear that I realize all the dashboard lights are on.

I glance to my left. Flynn stands a foot away,

watching me through the closed window. I give him a wobbly smile and try to start it again.

The engine turns over slowly but doesn't start. I groan. "Come on. Don't do this to me now."

Another two tries give me the same result.

He steps closer and speaks through the glass. "Won't start?"

I roll down the window. "Guess not."

"Pop the hood. I'll take a look."

"It's fine. You've done enough. I can get a—"

"Pop the damn hood, Olivia." His bossy tone does something to me that I'd rather not examine in this moment, so I do as he says and then get out and walk around the front of the SUV.

Flynn's got the hood propped up and is using his phone's flashlight to peer underneath.

"Do you know what you're doing or is this another play from your gentlemanly playbook?"

He cracks a smile and tosses a wink back at me. "Why can't it be both?"

He goes back to looking at my car's engine and I stand there awkwardly.

"Can I do anything?"

"Here." He holds his phone out to me.

Stepping up beside him, I aim the light approximately where he had it. His attention is on the car, so I take the moment to study him.

Impressive back muscles ripple as he leans forward. When he reaches out to mess with some knobs or wires or…whatever they are, his bicep flexes. He has this pensive look on his face, and he pushes the tip of his tongue between his teeth.

His reddish-brown hair is covered by a blue Mustangs hat. He has one of those straight Nordic noses and a jawline that looks like he's perpetually clenching.

That tattoo on the inside of his right forearm is the only ink in sight. Five black circles in a horizontal line. The last circle is filled in, but the others are empty. I saw a picture of when they got the tattoos on Brogan's social media page while I did my deep dive of all things Flynn Holland (Flynn's page was far less active). Five circles for five brothers and the solid dot represents where they fall in birth order.

As he pulls back, his arm brushes against mine. His skin is warm and a waft of his cologne or deodorant hits me.

"Do you have jumper cables in the car?"

"Umm…"

He flashes me another grin. "Your battery looks pretty new, but we could try to jump it if someone has cables."

"I replaced the battery a couple months ago."

"Probably your alternator then," he says. He takes the phone from me and moves it closer to the problem. "This wire is a little worn."

I glance to where the light shines. "I'll be honest, I'm not sure what I'm looking at."

I know it's such a cliché girl response, but I've always had my grandfather around to ask about car stuff. And he'd smile and take my keys, and then voila, my vehicle would be good to go. Everything I know about cars, I know from him. Which is probably less than he'd like.

"This is the alternator." He touches it with his free hand. "It charges the battery and powers the electronics in the vehicle."

I nod along.

As if he can tell I'm not really getting it, he adds, "Easy fix. If I had tools and parts, I could do it for you."

"Of course, you could." Oops. I did not mean to say that out loud. I so don't feel like dealing with the hassle of calling a tow truck tonight. "Thank you. I'll get a ride home and call someone in the morning."

Grinning, he shuts the hood and then asks, "Can you leave it here overnight?"

"Yes."

He nods and holds up his phone. "Want to share a ride?"

"I can change a tire, you know? And change the oil. Although I only did that once because it was so messy."

He's wearing a knowing smirk as he pulls on his wet T-shirt. Even soaked in beer, he makes it look good. It probably says something that I don't want him to think I'm a complete idiot, but it's not just for me. It's for women everywhere. We can know stuff about cars or sports. I hate the stereotypes. Even if I happen to fall into a few of them. I could be good at car stuff. I just don't want to be.

"Is that a no to sharing a ride? Xavier will be here in thirty seconds," Flynn says.

I open the door to my car, intending to sit and wait by myself while I call a ride. I'm used to doing things on my own, not needing or depending on anyone else. Sure, I have my family and they're great, but outside of that I don't let a lot of people in. Certainly not men who are only offering up their services with one goal in mind. Maybe that isn't fair. Flynn seems like a good guy, and he probably doesn't have some conniving ulterior motive by offering to share a ride with me or take a look at my car, but I know too well how easy it is to get lost in those small acts of service. Pretty soon you're expecting it or relying on it. And when they're gone, it hurts all that much more.

I already rely on other people more than I like. My family helps with Greer, my grandparents dote on me any way they can, my sister is babysitting for me tonight. And my schedule is so chaotic I rarely get to repay the favor for any of them.

I wave at Flynn from the safety of my car. He waits a few feet away until his ride arrives. The car sits there, unmoving until my driver shows up minutes later.

Only once I'm in the Uber does Flynn's driver finally take off.

"Freaking gentleman through and through," I mutter, but I can't help but smile.

I breathe a sigh of relief when I get inside my apartment. The lights are out but the TV in the living room is on and the colors from the screen shine bright enough I can make out my sister on the couch.

She wakes when I sit on the far edge.

"Hey." Her voice is gruff. "How was work?"

"The usual," I say, even though Flynn's face and words are on a constant loop. "How was Greer?"

"Perfect. As always."

I snort a laugh. My daughter has her aunt wrapped around her cute little finger.

"Thank you for watching her tonight." A little of that guilt for needing someone to help me with my daughter slinks in. If the bookstore wins best in the city and gets the attention and recognition to bring in more customers, then maybe I can finally quit the club.

"Are you kidding me?" Ruby yawns. "I love hanging out with her. She helped me replot a scene in my book."

"You let Greer read it and not me?"

"No." She laughs softly and yawns again. "She made me watch *Tangled* again and it gave me an idea."

"In that case, I've seen it about a billion times so maybe if you let me read it, I can help even more."

"Nice try." She smiles, eyes barely open.

"Are you staying over?" I ask as I stand. Exhaustion

is creeping in, and I can't wait to wash my face, brush my teeth, and fall into bed.

"I should go back to my place," she says, and then curls onto her side before her eyes fall shut again. Ruby lives in the same building, two floors up.

"Night." I toss the throw blanket from the back of the couch to her and then turn off the TV.

The door to Greer's bedroom is cracked open. I push it another inch and peer in on her. The bedside lamp casts a warm glow over the space. We aren't able to paint the walls here since it's a rental, but we compensated by hanging pictures and posters, plus stringing pink twinkle lights.

She's on her back, snuggled up in the light pink comforter and sheets, clutching her stuffed pink rabbit under one arm. She loves that thing. I have a backup in my closet just in case something happens to it. Though at this point she's loved it so hard that it doesn't really look like the original. My heart squeezes, and my body relaxes for the first time in hours.

It's a reminder that everything I'm doing is worth it. The long hours at the bookstore, followed by late nights at Lilac Lounge. I want to give her everything. Opportunities and love, security. I had a great childhood filled with happy memories, two parents who loved each other and me and Ruby. Plus, grandparents who were active and involved in our lives. Basically, I have the family most people could only dream about. It's hard not to compare what I had to her situation. She has a great family and life, but her parents aren't raising her together and she doesn't see her dad that often. Some days I let it get to me more than others. I hope my loving her more than anything else in the world is enough.

I cross the room to her and pull up the comforter tighter around her shoulders. Her lashes flutter open and then right back closed.

Leaning down, I brush her blonde curls out of her face and place a kiss on her forehead. She smells like toothpaste and lavender. God, I had no idea it was possible to love someone so damn much. I'd do anything for her.

"Momma," she whispers, still half asleep. She lets go of her bunny and her arms go around my neck.

"Hi, baby girl." I lie in the small space next to her and wrap my arms around her.

She cuddles right into my chest and falls back asleep. And so do I.

I wake up with a groan.

"I'm hungry." The volume in which Greer speaks does not account for our close proximity or the early time.

I crack open one eye. Her face is inches from mine, making her green eyes look like one big eye.

"Me too. You should make me an omelet," I say, voice

thick with sleep. "Oh, and some yogurt with strawberries too, please."

I roll over and pretend to go back to sleep.

Greer isn't fooled for a second. "You said I can't use the stove, remember?"

"Right."

She giggles and climbs onto my side. Her blonde curls fall into my face as she peers down at me. "I want pancakes!"

"How about cereal for both of us, then?" I suggest, sitting up and rolling my neck. I slept in my clothes, including my shoes, and there's a painful kink when I move my head to the right.

"Okay!" She bounds from the bed and out of the room. She has endless energy, but she's such a happy, easy-to-please kid.

With a groan, I rub at my sore muscles and get up a lot slower than my daughter had. I follow her into the kitchen and help her get her cereal.

Ruby is already gone. The blanket is folded neatly and laid over the arm of the couch, and she made a pot of coffee before she left. Bless her.

I pour myself a cup to take with me as I get ready for the day. By the time I've showered and changed and finished my coffee, I almost feel human again.

When I come out of my bedroom, Greer is sitting on the floor in front of the TV. She's changed out of her pajamas into one of her many princess costumes. Today she's Belle in the big, yellow dress and gloves, complete with a tiara on top of her head.

"Are we going to the nursery?" she asks when she spots me in my pink overalls.

"Yep. Do you want to wear that?" I ask.

She nods quickly as she gets up and twirls. "Can we get roses like in Beauty and the Beast?"

"We'll see." I laugh quietly. "Find your shoes."

I take my empty coffee cup to the sink, rinse it out, and then put it in the dishwasher.

The doorbell rings as Greer is coming back out of her room with her sparkly tennis shoes in hand.

Greer looks to me like I can see through the door better than her.

"Maybe your Aunt Ruby?" I move to the door and open it, smiling when I see who it is.

I glance back at Greer and then slowly inch it wider to reveal Sabrina.

"Aunt Brina!" Greer has perched herself onto the couch and she jumps up and down.

Before I can tell her not to stand on the furniture, she's already launched herself off and is coming toward us.

"What are you doing here?" I ask my best friend as my daughter wraps her arms around Sabrina's waist.

"I missed my favorite girls." Then she looks at me. "And I heard you had an interesting night."

My skin flushes at the indirect mention of Flynn. "How did you find out so fast?"

"Archer," we say at the same time.

"We're going to the nursery," Greer tells Sabrina.

"Well, you are dressed perfectly." She takes Greer's hand and spins her. The two of them giggle.

"We can go later if you want to hang out," I say.

"Can I tag along?" Sabrina asks.

"Yes," Greer and I say in unison.

The nursery is within walking distance—one of the perks of our apartment location. Greer holds on to Sabrina's hand and talks a mile a minute on the way, leaving me to my own thoughts.

I find myself wondering what Flynn said about last night and about me. As much as I want to pretend he hasn't gotten under my skin, he has. I like him. Okay, I've always liked him. Basically, from the moment I laid eyes on him I felt something. But I've spent a lot of years second-guessing myself when it comes to feelings and navigating dating relationships. I don't trust myself more than I don't trust him.

At the nursery, Greer runs ahead to the cut flower display. Every morning, they put flowers that have fallen from their plant or needed to be pruned in a cute display for the kids made of pallets with attached mason jars filled with water for vases.

"You're quiet this morning," Sabrina notes as we watch Greer pluck a pink rose from one of the vases.

"I fell asleep in Greer's bed last night," I say as I absently rub at the sore spot on my neck again.

"Are you sure it doesn't have anything to do with running into a certain baseball player?"

I cut her a look that must not be intimidating because she laughs.

"Fine. Not ready to talk about it," she says.

Greer runs back with her flower clutched in one hand.

"An enchanted rose!" Sabrina picks her up and bops her on the nose. "I hope you don't turn into a horrible beast!"

I grab a cart, and we wander down the aisles of the nursery. I'm easily distracted by the plants and flowers, and Sabrina and Greer chat happily about roses and beasts.

I got into gardening at a young age with my mom. She'd bring me and Ruby with her to pick out flowers or plants and then we'd get home and she'd plant them while we played in the yard.

As soon as I moved out on my own, I filled the apartment with greenery. Something about it just makes every space feel more like home.

I stop by a section of succulents. I need something small and low maintenance that doesn't need a lot of sun for a shelf in my bathroom.

Sabrina steps up beside me while Greer wanders just ahead of us where I can still see her.

"I have news on the bachelorette party."

"Ooooh." I look from an aloe plant to Sabrina. For weeks now she's been going back and forth on where and how she wanted to celebrate her upcoming wedding. She and Archer are getting married this summer. They want to keep the wedding simple, but they are going big on all the fun activities leading up to it.

"How do you feel about a mountain getaway?"

"What happened to Vegas?" That was her most recent plan. One night on the strip, gambling, drinking too much, and dancing the night away. Followed by a spa day.

"I realized I don't really want to deal with other people. I just want to hang out with my friends."

"Mountains are fine by me."

"Perfect. There are these cute cabins just out of the city. We'd all go up on a Friday, have a chill night in and then Saturday do all the usual fun bachelorette things."

"That sounds great."

"I'm trying to finalize everything this week. Does the first weekend next month still work for you?"

I nod. "I already asked my grandparents if they could watch Greer."

I don't love leaving her for that long, but I know how important it is to keep my friendships too. Sabrina has been a real friend to me. I lost most of my closest girlfriends when I got pregnant. A few tried to keep in contact, but we were just at two different points in life. I couldn't go out with them, and I was worrying about breastfeeding while they were figuring out college or dealing with boyfriend drama. It wasn't all their fault. I'm sure I wasn't as interested in their lives as I should have been either.

But with Sabrina it's different. Maybe it's our age or maybe we just get each other. We met at Lilac Lounge when she first moved to Lake City. She worked as a dancer, and I was bartending. I thought she would be one of those work friends who as soon as I mentioned my daughter would never ask to hang outside of the club. But she surprised me. She not only wanted to hang out, but she also wanted to meet Greer and made a point to suggest kid-friendly activities. We went to all the parks and museums in the city, and she didn't blink an eye when Greer would have a meltdown, or plans had to change because suddenly Greer wasn't feeling well or needed a nap.

Being a parent is a constant game of agility, and people who haven't experienced it, don't always understand. I didn't.

"I can't believe you're getting married," I say, smiling when she gets that soft, happy expression that makes her pale skin flush from head to toe. "What is Archer doing for his bachelor party?"

"He hasn't decided. Brogan came up with more than a dozen ideas and has been pitching them to him one-by-one each night. Last night he suggested bungalows over the ocean in the Maldives. He had a slideshow and wore a Hawaiian shirt."

"I feel like I got invited to the wrong party."

She elbows me playfully. "I told Archer he couldn't go anywhere I haven't been. We still need to pick a honeymoon spot."

We fall quiet for a beat as I continue to look at the succulents. I have two aloe plants, one in each hand.

"Maybe I should get a plant for the apartment."

Sabrina picks up a beautiful Easter cactus. I have one at home on our entertainment stand, where it gets just the right amount of indirect sunlight.

"Oh no, that one is finicky." I decide to get both aloe plants and put them in the cart. I pick up a potted moon cactus and hold it out to her. "This one is basically impossible to kill."

Laughing, she takes it. "Thanks. I think."

I take the Easter cactus from her and put that in my cart too.

After I've bought too many plants, we pay and start back toward the apartment.

Greer wore herself out twirling around the nursery and Sabrina carries her while I lug the plants in a paper bag.

"Okay, I told myself I wasn't going to bring it up, but I have to know about Flynn."

That uncomfortable, skin too tight for my body sensation spreads through me. "There really isn't much to tell. He came into the club with some of his teammates."

"And almost got into a fight defending you from what I heard."

"I nearly forgot about that," I admit. "It wasn't that big of a deal. Some guy got handsy. I had it under control."

"Still, had to feel good to have someone there in the moment." She shudders in a way that says she might be remembering her own interactions with drunk people at the club. It doesn't happen that often, thankfully, but the exchanges always leave me feeling gross.

"Yeah, until I accidentally tossed the beer at him."

"What?" she asks, clearly having not heard that part.

"I was aiming for the other guy and Flynn stepped in the way," I defend myself, then finally laugh. The look on his face was priceless. So damn adorable, even with beer dripping down his forehead and soaking his shirt.

"That reminds me, I need to call someone about my car." I don't have to work tonight, and I can walk to the bookstore for my usual Sunday afternoon week prep, but I'm going to need my vehicle eventually. I start to take out my phone and Sabrina places a hand on my arm.

"You can borrow mine until then. Archer has been driving me to the studio every morning anyway."

"Adorable." I grin at her and pocket my phone again. How many guys would wake up early to chauffer their partner to work just because they want to spend time with them? "Ruby rarely drives her car, so I'm sure I can borrow hers, but thank you. I appreciate it."

"Any time," she says, and I know she means it.

As the apartment complex comes into view, Greer lifts her head from Sabrina's shoulder.

"Can we go to the studio and have a dance party?" she asks with those big, pleading eyes.

"Sorry, sweetie," Sabrina says and sets her on the sidewalk in front of her. "Miss Zoey is teaching an adult tap workshop this afternoon."

Greer sticks her bottom lip out and stares at her feet.

"Who is going to help me pot our new plants?" I ask as I reach out and take one of her hands.

She thinks for a moment and then asks, "Can I paint the pots?"

"Absolutely."

Greer is mostly appeased by that, though I have no doubt she'd leave me with my gardening in favor of twirling around Sabrina's studio if she had her way.

A truck pulls up to the curb in front of us. I glance up at the driver absently and then squint.

"Is that Archer?" I ask Sabrina.

"Yeah." She moves toward him as he opens the driver's door.

"Momma. That looks just like our car," Greer says as another vehicle pulls up behind Archer's truck.

"That's because it is," I say, feeling dumbfounded. It's an odd thing to see big, hulking Brogan sitting behind the driver's seat of my little SUV.

"What are you doing here?" Sabrina asks, draping her arms around Archer's shoulders and hugging him.

When they break apart, he looks to me.

"We're just dropping off Olivia's car." Archer smiles, tipping his head to me slightly, then he stares down at Greer.

How? And why? And what the ever-loving-hell? Those and many more questions float through my brain, but I don't ask any of them because I already know.

Flynn.

"*Uncle Arch!*" Greer signs his name as she says it, then goes right into showing him all the new sign language words and phrases she's learned since the last time she saw him.

He squats down and signs back, praising her and giving her attention and adoration that has my heart squeezing. I want that for her. Don't get me wrong, I'm so happy she has it with Archer and Brogan and Grandpa Earl. But what would it be like if she had a father that was around more to give her these moments daily?

Brogan is out of my SUV and standing in front of me with a big grin before I've snapped myself out of the weird thoughts swirling around.

"Drives like a dream." With a wink, he holds out the key to me. It's attached to a little purple tag that has Sabrina's name written on it. I gave it to her months ago when she needed to borrow my car and never bothered to get it back from her.

I glance to Sabrina, who is wearing an appropriately guilty expression.

"You gave him my keys, didn't you?"

"I still had the spare and it was for a good cause." She smiles hesitantly.

"So much for offering up your car. You knew this whole time?" I ask her.

She laughs before saying, "The offer was legit. I didn't know if he'd be able to fix it, only that he was going to try."

Brogan scoffs. "You wait until I tell him that. Flynn can fix anything. He's just like Knox."

Archer nods. "It's true. He's great with engines and

even if he weren't, he's stubborn enough that he would have done whatever it took. Especially for a girl."

"Lucky me," I quip, then sigh because I am lucky, and this is nice. Too much, but really nice. "Thank you, guys. I don't know how to repay you. I'll cover the parts and labor, of course, just let me know what I owe you."

That all too familiar feeling of gratitude mixed with discomfort makes it hard to look any of them in the eye.

"Not necessary. Happy to help," Archer says.

"We barely did anything," Brogan says. "It was all Flynn."

"He would have loved to drop it off himself, but he had to be at the field early," Archer adds.

Which begs the question, when did he find time to fix my car?

While I'm spiraling, Brogan picks up Greer and spins her around until she squeals with delight. It sometimes takes her a beat to be comfortable with men, but Archer and Brogan won her over with their fun, goofy personalities and being so consistently interested in her. It's a rare thing, honestly, that adults, especially my peers, treat Greer and other kids like they're worth getting to know.

Sabrina steps closer and her arm brushes against mine, pulling me from my thoughts. She has this knowing smirk that tells me she is acutely aware that I'm spinning out and why.

"Baby Holland has a crush," she says in a singsong voice.

"Don't tell me you're in favor of this." I wave a hand

toward my vehicle, but what I really mean is, there's no way she can want me and Flynn together or dating or whatever it is that he wants.

"I'm in favor of people doing nice things for you," she says in a very matter-of-fact tone. "No matter who they are."

CHAPTER NINE

Flynn

"**N**ICE PITCHING TODAY," JT SAYS AS HE SLUMPS DOWN on the bench next to me.

"Thanks." I rub at my upper arm. "It felt good."

Freddie drops to the other side of me. "That makes one of us. I feel like hell."

"Late night?" JT asks as he starts pulling off his gear. "I swear I don't know how you guys do it. I was out by ten o'clock and it was still painful to get out of bed this morning."

"I'm too amped up this week to sleep even if I'd gone home early." Freddie's right leg bounces as if to emphasize that even now after a full day of workouts he's got this underlying energy coursing through him.

"Wait until you have a couple of kids. You'll be stealing a few minutes of sleep any chance you get too."

"That why you were sleeping in your car this morning?" I ask him. When I pulled up to the stadium, JT was sitting in his parked truck. The engine was off, driver's side window down, and one arm resting on the sill. At first, I thought he was on the phone or pumping himself up for the day, but upon closer investigation, his eyes were closed and his mouth gaping wide. The fucker was asleep.

"Bella woke me up at four to have a tea party." He grimaces as he says it but then a soft smile lifts the corners of his mouth. "I couldn't say no to that adorable little face. Then her brother woke up screaming an hour later. He's teething."

The mention of his kids makes me think of Olivia. She hasn't said much about her daughter, but when I was fixing her car this morning, the evidence of her was everywhere. Car seat in the back, an abandoned stuffed animal on the floorboard, and a sparkly beaded necklace looped around the gear shifter.

I bet Olivia was pissed when she realized I fixed her vehicle. I wish I could have been there. She would have insisted it wasn't necessary and that I didn't need to do it, maybe even told me all about how she can take care of things on her own. But honestly, it wasn't that much work. The alternator was good. It just needed a new cable. Easy fix. I liked doing it for her. And fine, I still want to impress her.

Once JT is gone, Freddie steps closer to me with a shy smile. "I'm going out with Sadie again this weekend."

"Yeah?" A smile stretches across my face. "That's awesome. Congrats, man."

"Thanks, and, uh, thanks for last night. That was really decent of you."

"It was nothing."

The excitement radiating off him is thanks enough.

After Freddie leaves, I sit for another twenty minutes, icing my arm and watching the locker room clear out. Some of the guys are making plans to hang out at Gunnar's place but no one has invited me. It's fine. I should really rest tonight. We have our first spring training game tomorrow against Chicago, and it'll be my first chance to show everyone that I deserve to be here, playing with the best of the best.

Despite my misgivings about the team, I've had a decent week here. And JT's wife's coffee cake muffins were as good as he promised. My stomach growls, finally pushing me to action. I shower and put on fresh clothes.

As I'm leaving, I run into Earl. He holds up a rectangular name placard like the other guys have above their lockers. This one has my name on it.

"Finally came in," he says with a smile. "I'll have it up for you this evening. It's official. You're a Mustang."

"Thanks."

We pass each other, but he calls after me.

"Nice pitching today. Your delivery has improved, and you did a great job controlling the inside fastball.

You're finding your place out there, and the whole team looks better for it."

I pause, looking back at him. "How long have you been with the Mustangs?"

"Longer than you've been alive probably." He grins.

"It's the baby face. I'm not that young."

"Uh-huh."

Who am I kidding? He probably knows exactly what day and year I was born.

"Did you ever play or coach?" I ask him.

He nods. "I played as a kid. Nothing serious. I spent a couple of years on the pitching staff here a long, long time ago. Another lifetime."

"I knew it."

His brows lift as an amused expression plays over his face.

"It's the way you talk about it. Most people don't really understand pitching mechanics, not that they need to."

"When you've been around as long as I have, you're bound to pick up a few things," he says.

Nah, it's more than that. I've had actual coaches that seem less insightful than him. Or maybe it's just that sweet grandpa look about him that makes me want to listen.

"What happened?" I shift my bag and wait for his reply.

"Had a daughter. The apple of my eye."

Okay. Not what I expected.

"And?"

His smile widens. "That's it. I didn't want to spend as much time away from home anymore. The travel life can be hard. Gone two or three nights a week for nine months out of the year. It wasn't for me."

He's not wrong, but I can't believe he'd give it up just like that. People would kill for a coaching job with a major league team, even this one.

"Of course, things were different then," Earl says. "We didn't have cell phones and video calls. It's easier to stay connected now."

"She must be grown up. Why not get back to it?"

He shakes his head as he wipes down the spot where the placard will go above my locker. "Too much time away from it. Things have changed. I don't know the latest trends and advice. Plus, who'd keep this place up?"

I chuckle softly and watch him as he removes the back of the placard to stick it in place. I like Earl and he's right, this old stadium would probably look a hell of a lot worse without his meticulous care. Still, it feels like a shame that he gave up that sort of position and now cleans up after everyone.

"Thanks for the placard," I say to him.

He glances quickly at me, smiling still. "See you tomorrow, kid."

I push out the back door into the parking lot. The sun is at that perfect level where it's impossible to look up without squinting. I pull my cap down farther to cover my eyes and head in the general direction of my truck, staring at the pavement as my feet eat up the distance.

I glance up as I get closer, gaze landing on my truck and then the vehicle parked next to it. Pausing, I squint harder.

Either I'm seeing a mirage in the desert or Olivia is here to see me. If it's the former, I hope I die of dehydration before she disappears.

She's standing close to her SUV dressed in a soft pink dress. Her blonde hair is down and blowing around her shoulders. She has a potted plant in one hand, and she shifts from foot to foot as if she's uncomfortable as I approach.

"Hi," I say, trying and failing to keep the surprise out of my tone.

"Hey." Her voice is low with a hint of uncertainty that makes me feel the same way. I don't know if anyone has made me feel more... well, anything than Olivia does.

Excitement, nerves, a dash of fear. But more than anything, it's curiosity. I want to know her: what she thinks, likes, wants, her hopes and dreams. I don't think there's any little detail about her that I would find boring.

"How's it running?" I ask, stopping in front of her.

"Good." She glances back at her SUV. When she meets my gaze again, that familiar sass is back in her eyes. "You just couldn't help yourself, could you?"

"You're welcome." I unlock my truck and toss my bag inside.

As I turn back to her, she takes a step closer to me and holds out the plant. "Thank you."

"What's this?" I take it from her. I stare down at the prickly-looking cactus. "Is this another way of saying you think I'm a prick?"

She lets out a soft laugh that makes her mouth curve into a sexy, amused smile. "It's a angel's wings cactus. Indirect sunlight is best, and you should only need to water it once a week or so."

I feel my brows rise as I stare down at the green paddle-like leaves with sharp needles. It's in an orange pot with pink and purple splotches of paint.

"If you don't want it," she starts and moves another step closer.

"Nah." I pull it toward me instinctively. "This is cool. No one has ever given me a plant before."

Probably because they assumed I'd kill it, which is likely.

"I also want to pay you for the parts and your time. Archer told me you had to replace some cables for the alternator. I looked it up online and this was what it said. If it was more, let me know and I'll get the rest to you."

A little dumbfounded I take the envelope she's holding out to me and look inside. I see at least four one-hundred-dollar bills before I close it and hand it back to her.

"This is way too much, and I don't want your money anyway."

"Don't be ridiculous. It must have cost you to get the

part, plus the time you spent fixing it." She tries to give it back and I sidestep her, putting distance between us.

"It didn't take long at all, I had the tools, and the part was cheap."

She gives me one of those no-nonsense scowls that makes me want to kiss it off her face. For some reason it doesn't seem like she wants people doing nice things for her. Maybe she thinks I have a hidden agenda. I don't. Well, not much of one. Sure, I want her to go out with me, but I'd have fixed her car either way.

"The cactus is payment enough. I love this planter. Did you make this?"

"My daughter painted it," she says, then adds, "The cactus and pot were less than ten dollars."

Knowing her kid had a part in it makes me smile more. "It's a one of a kind, which makes it priceless."

She lets out an exasperated but amused sigh. "You're not going to take my money, are you?"

"Nope," I say proudly.

We stare at each other for a beat, neither giving in. Adrenaline rushes through me and my gut swirls with a pleasant but uneasy feeling.

"Thank you," she says finally.

"You're welcome."

Her gaze flicks to the quiet stadium. "How are things going with the new team?"

"Pretty good. We have our first game tomorrow if you want to come cheer me on."

"My family has season tickets."

An unexpected but exciting development. And here I thought I'd have to pull off a miracle to get her to a game.

"So, you'll be in the crowd cheering for me?"

Without answering, she steps back toward her SUV. "Bye, Flynn. Good luck."

"What section are you in?" I call after her.

She wiggles her fingers in a wave and ducks into her vehicle.

I smile as she starts the engine and pulls away.

A new resolve washes over me. I don't need luck. I have a steely determination for tomorrow to: a) prove my worth to the entire league, and b) win over Olivia.

CHAPTER TEN

Olivia

"**W**HY ARE THERE SO MANY PEOPLE HERE?" RUBY asks as we walk to our seats in Fletcher Stadium where the Mustangs play.

"I have no idea," I say, stepping past people in the narrow aisle and offering apologetic smiles as they shift and move to let us pass by. "Maybe they're here for the other team."

It's the first spring training game for the Mustangs, and in my grandfather's mind, a local holiday. But in reality, these games aren't usually this well attended. It's die-hard locals, mostly. Or snowbirds who are here for the winter, looking for something to do.

The weather is still too cool for people to be out

simply enjoying the weather, and there isn't the same pomp and excitement of a regular season game with all the flashy things that can make coming fun all on its own. Although Mischief, the Mustangs mascot, was at the gate when we walked in and made Greer's whole day.

As we get to our seats, I scan the field. Players are warming up. Some have bats in their hands, others are playing catch. But my attention goes to the side where a couple of pitchers are warming up. It doesn't take long for me to pick out Flynn. My body does most of the work if I'm honest. Goosebumps rise on my arms and my stomach flutters the instant I locate his broad shoulders and bulging biceps.

Ruby and I sit. Greer stands in front of the empty seat between us, leaning against the metal fence rails that box us in. We've had the same seats, looking out at first base, for as long as I can remember. We have a great view of the field, something I'm infinitely more grateful for in this moment.

Flynn looks good in a baseball uniform. I mean, yes, he always looks good, but damn. I've not let myself really admire him since I found out who he was, but with a little distance between us and his playful smile not aimed at me, it's impossible to deny how attracted I am to him.

"Did you hear me?" Ruby leans over from her seat.

"Sorry. What?" I blink several times and look over at my sister.

"I said, she's a whole vibe." She tips her head toward Greer.

"I know," I say with a small laugh as I admire my daughter's fashion sense. She's dressed in a Mustangs T-shirt with a pink tutu and tiara, beaded bracelets are looped around both wrists all the way up to her elbows. Since she was able to dress herself, she's been adamant about wearing what she wants. It caused a few fights early on when I thought I needed to make her look a certain way or wanted her to wear a cute outfit I bought for her, but parenting is nothing if not humbling. And now, I love that she has her own style.

We fall into on and off conversation as we stare out at the field during warmups. It isn't long before the players jog to their respective dugouts.

My stomach bottoms out and I pull down the bill of my baseball cap, shielding more of my face.

"Hey." Ruby pinches me.

"Ow." I pull my arm back instinctively. "What was that for?"

"I'm over here talking to myself. What is up with you? And why are you so jittery?"

"I'm not." I absolutely am. I don't even know why. It isn't like I came for him. We do this every year. The entire family comes to the first spring training game.

Only this year there are two empty seats.

"It's weird without them here," I say to Ruby, looking past my sister to the vacant chairs on the other side of her.

Our phones ping at the same time and Ruby smiles at me knowingly. I check my phone as she does the same, and yep, it's exactly who I expected. Mom checking in from somewhere in the Caribbean with a "Go Mustangs!" and a selfie of her and dad in matching Mustangs shirts. I've lost track of where they are or will be next because their schedule changes so often.

Last summer they randomly decided to apply for chef positions on a cruise ship. They're both chefs and owned a small catering business that did weddings, business luncheons, and private parties. Now they're cooking for thousands each day as they sail around the ocean. It's the most adventurous thing they've done during my whole life. I still have a hard time believing they did it.

"They'll be back next season," Ruby says after sliding her phone back into her front shorts pocket.

"You think? They seem happy."

"It's killing Mom not to be around for Greer's school stuff. I can't tell you how many times she texted me to be sure I recorded her music performance last week." My sister changes her voice to a high-pitch, slightly nasal impression of our mother, "I want to see every second my grandbaby is on that stage."

"You sound just like her."

Ruby tosses a piece of popcorn at me.

"You do." I sit back as Gigi comes down the aisle with lemonade for all of us. It's better here than anywhere else in the world. I have the best memories of eating a hot dog and drinking lemonade while watching the Mustangs play. I was never a big fan of baseball but being here with my family is an experience that transcends the game.

"Is Grandpa coming?" I ask, taking my drink and settling back into my seat.

In front of us, the teams take the field.

"He's around somewhere. Probably a last-minute maintenance issue."

The announcer calls out the starters for the Mustangs as they run out to applause and cheers.

"Your catcher, JT Ryan." The stadium gets loud. He's one of the most beloved players on the team. I couldn't tell you exactly why. He seems to be good at catching, but I think more than that it's because he's been with the team so long. A lot of players come and go. The Mustangs aren't exactly known for winning so it makes sense that they move on. I imagine playing for a team that routinely loses takes a toll on you.

"And your starting pitcher, Flynn Holland!"

The applause around the stadium is even louder than it had been for JT. The people I assumed were here for the other team… now I'm thinking they're here for Flynn.

"Ooooh. There's your pitcher." Ruby cups her hands around her mouth and yells for him, along with everyone else.

"He isn't my pitcher."

She flashes a teasing smile that makes my stomach swoop.

"What do you think the odds are that a guy you met in New York lives here? *And* that he's related to your best friend's fiancé? That's too much coincidence to not be the tiniest bit romantic."

I have had the same thought a thousand times. I'm not sure if I believe in fate, but I do think the universe has a sense of humor. The question is, what does it mean?

"Did you forget that he is working with Plot Twist?" I ask, deflecting. I have gotten really good at that. Not that Ruby isn't aware of exactly what I'm doing. Sisters are the worst at calling out your bullshit.

"It must have slipped my mind after he bought my books." Her grin lifts higher. "I love my readers."

I can't help but laugh and then blush when I think of him reading chapter twenty-eight.

Greer takes her seat, blocking my sister from any more annoying quips, and I go back to watching Flynn.

The announcer is talking about the batter, and his walkout music plays, but my gaze doesn't leave the pitcher's mound.

Flynn looks focused and a little intense. On the mound, he seems bigger somehow. He drags his right foot along the ground then digs his toe in. He stares down, but his mouth moves almost as if he's talking to himself. When he finally looks up, I can practically feel the calm that's washed over him. He pushes his shoulders back and turns to the side.

I hold my breath as he winds up and throws the first pitch. I watch him even after the ball leaves his hand. For a moment, it feels like everything stops and the only sound is the ball sailing through the air.

"Striiiike," the umpire calls out, and the crowd claps.

Flynn's expression doesn't change as JT throws the

ball back to him. My body is tense, like I'm the one out there as I watch him do it again and again. I lose track of the number of pitches, and I barely see the batters. It isn't until he's jogging off the mound that I realize they've managed to get three outs.

"Impressive." Ruby turns and stares at me over Greer's head. She raises her voice so I can hear her over the applause around us.

"What?"

"He didn't let a single batter on base," she says like duh, weren't you watching?

"Really?" I glance back to the field as Flynn is getting to the dugout. A few players tip their head to him as he makes his way to the bench.

My sister's only response is to laugh at my surprise, and possibly my inability to look away from Flynn.

The innings pass with more of the same. While the Mustangs are up to bat, I'm willing them to hurry up so Flynn will run back out onto the field. And when he's out there, I can't look away.

Gigi and Ruby are talking about some book tour Ruby's publisher wants to send her on; meanwhile, Greer is playing happily with her stuffed pink rabbit. She chatters quietly. I only hear enough to know she's explaining to Bunny about the game and using words she must have picked up from Grandpa or the announcers. "Wooowee, that was a beautiful slider," she says as Flynn throws another pitch.

I bite back a smile and turn my attention to the man

on the mound. JT tosses the ball back to him. Flynn catches it in his glove and then grabs it with his right hand. His fingers move over it as he gets back into position.

He takes his time, adjusting his hat and wiping his brow, even looking out at the crowd for a beat before he gets into the familiar pitcher stance.

Anticipation thrums under my skin as I watch him.

Flynn stares down the batter. His hair curls up around the back of his blue hat, broad shoulders and muscular arms fill out the jersey. He's tall and imposing in his uniform and his usually playful, boyish smile is gone.

He shakes off two signals before nodding at JT. He does that thing pitchers do, checking the bases. There's a runner on first and he takes two sidesteps toward second. Flynn looks away from him and then quickly back, firing the ball to the first baseman. The runner barely gets back in time.

"Safe." The umpire makes the signal, and the ball is thrown back to Flynn.

I lean forward in my seat as he gets set again. A shiver rolls through me as he goes through his whole routine. The more I watch, the more turned on I get. Who knew baseball was so sexy?

I can't tell a good pitch from a bad one, but I know he's throwing fast and hard based on the way the crowd reacts. When Flynn fires another pitch to JT, an older gentleman in front of me takes off his hat and fans himself with it.

Chuckling, he says, "That kid's got some arm on him."

The man next to him agrees with a nod.

"I need to go to the bathroom," Greer says to me, drawing my attention away from Flynn and the game.

"Can you wait until the inning is over?" I ask her. I've started tracking and I know the count is full and there are two outs.

"I'll take you. I want to get a hot dog or maybe nachos," Ruby says, standing and holding out her hand to Greer.

She flashes me a smug knowing grin. "Need anything? An ice water maybe?"

"No, thank you," I say pointedly, but I can't help let a small smile slip. Sisters are somehow the best and worst at the same time.

Gigi moves down to sit beside me after they're gone. She studies me for a moment. "Are you okay? You look a little flushed, honey."

"Must be the heat." I train my gaze back to the pitcher's mound.

"The heat?" She scoffs. Rightfully so since I haven't taken my sweatshirt off. "Are you sure it isn't that cutie pitcher you've been staring at for four innings?"

My jaw drops and I give her my full attention, as if that could prove her wrong. "I was not."

She laughs, probably at the high-pitched squeak of my voice—a dead giveaway I'm lying.

"He's cute. Nothing to be embarrassed about."

The tension leaves me, and I laugh with her.

"Want me to ask your grandpa to introduce you?"

"Definitely not." I shake my head as a new kind of panic washes over me. The last thing I need is my grandfather talking to Flynn about me. What would Flynn think about me if he knew my grandparents are trying to set me up? He'd think it was hilarious probably.

"Fine. Fine. We'll just keep staring at him then. Maybe he'll look over here and notice you in this big crowd of people."

The way she says it I know she thinks that's impossible, but that's only because she doesn't know Flynn. I wouldn't put anything past him. I slump down in my seat an inch instinctively and she laughs again.

When Ruby and Greer return, Gigi moves back down to her seat.

I lean over Greer to my sister. "Did you tell Gigi about Flynn?"

"What? No, of course not."

"She said he was cute and accused me of staring at him."

"He is cute, *and* you have been staring at him." She stares at me, daring me to argue either point as she takes a bite of her hot dog.

I use my middle finger to scratch the side of my nose.

"So mature." Ruby laughs and then I can't help but join in.

Grandpa finally joins us at the bottom of the sixth inning.

"Hi." I stand and hug him. He's beaming underneath

his familiar Mustangs hat. "I wasn't sure you were going to make it."

"Ran into some snags with the plumbing in one of the locker rooms," he says.

"Eww." Ruby makes a face but then smiles as she steps up to hug him next.

Greer bounces impatiently waiting her turn. He scoops her up and drops a kiss on the tip of her nose.

"How are they looking?" he asks Greer.

"Great!" she exclaims, pushing both hands into the air and making us all laugh.

Grandpa sits in Greer's seat next to me with her on his lap.

"Have you been able to see any of the game?" I ask him. There are a lot of TVs up around the stadium, so it's possible he was able to watch while he was working.

"No, but I heard our new pitcher is having a good day."

"He is," I say, feeling a hint of pride for him.

"So good that Olivia can barely look away. You might make a baseball fan out of one of us yet," Ruby says from the other side of him.

I shoot her a murderous look and then smile at Grandpa. "Flynn is Sabrina's fiancé's brother, remember?"

"That's right." He nods. "Are Sabrina and his brothers here?"

Greer moves to stand again, and Grandpa crosses his arms over his chest and leans back in his chair.

"I don't think so. Sabrina didn't mention it."

Grandpa nods. "Seems like a good kid. A lot of pressure on him this season."

"Why's that?"

He takes his time answering like he's mulling over his thoughts. "A lot of people think he was brought up too soon, that he isn't ready for this level of baseball, and his performance against Kansas City proved that."

My brows knit together in confusion. That seems harsh.

"What do you think?" I ask.

One side of his mouth lifts in that familiar smile of his. "I think our team needs someone who has as much to prove as he does."

I glance back out to the field. Flynn stands in the dugout with his profile to me. He takes off his hat and runs his fingers through his hair, then looks in my direction. I freeze, but his stare moves quickly, and then I feel silly for thinking he could pick me out of a crowd at this distance.

Grandpa leaves us as soon as the game is over. The Mustangs won, five to two, and there seems to be a hopeful feeling in the air for fans.

I lose sight of Flynn as people stand around us and start to leave. I have the strangest urge to tell him that he pitched a good game. I'm sure he has lots of people already patting his back and telling him how great he is. And who knows, maybe I'll see him around again soon.

"Can we get another lemonade?" Greer asks. She

looks tired. She rarely naps anymore, but I have a hunch she's going to fall asleep as soon as we get in the car.

"No, but we can make some cookies later after dinner," I say.

She gives me an only half-appeased shrug. Gigi is going to sit and wait for Grandpa to be done, so I hug her.

"I'll see you Monday morning," I say as she wraps her arms around me, and I breathe in her familiar floral scent.

She hugs Greer next, then Ruby.

I have my back to the field and the seats around us are mostly emptied when a familiar, cocky voice sounds behind me.

"Enjoy the game?"

I jump and let out a squeak as I whip around to see Flynn standing on the other side of the metal fence. A few people are walking around him, giving him curious looks. One girl snaps a photo of him. It's hard to blame her. He's even better looking in that uniform up close.

I swallow thickly and ignore the way my pulse has sped up in his presence. "I did."

His responding smile is all charm and ego.

I glance around. "How did you find me?"

"I put a tracker on you," he deadpans to which I glare playfully.

Chuckling, he says, "I looked up from the pitcher's mound and there you were."

My brows lift. "Just like that?"

He shrugs.

I feel Greer press into my side and Flynn's gaze slides

over to her, then to me, and back. His expression softens as he says, "You must be Greer."

I drop a reassuring hand to her shoulder and open my mouth to encourage her to say hello, but to my surprise she beats me to it.

"You're Uncle Archer's brother," she says confidently.

Flynn nods. "That's right. I'm Flynn. Nice to meet you. I've heard a lot about you."

And then he signs to her, something I don't follow but Greer does.

Her grin widens and she signs back. It's such a small thing, but my heart squeezes in my chest as I watch my daughter interact with Flynn so easily. Even with Archer and Brogan it took a little time before she warmed up to them.

"Well, if that isn't the cutest freaking thing," Ruby mutters quietly. I didn't even see her step up beside me.

I elbow her, hoping to silence her. It doesn't work.

"All I'm saying is, if I were writing this, my heroine would be swooning about now."

"I don't swoon," I say.

"Liar."

When Flynn and Greer are done signing with each other, he glances up and smiles at Ruby.

"Good to see you again. I enjoyed your books. Your characters are hilarious and that twist at the end of *Love Bites*? Never saw it coming."

"Thank you." My sister beams.

She leans over to whisper to me, "Swoooon."

Before I can reply, she stands tall again and says louder to Flynn, "Come back to the store and I'll let Olivia sell you some more."

"I'll do that." His stare finally moves over to Gigi, and he tips his head, expression going a tad more serious.

"I didn't realize my granddaughters knew the new pitcher," Gigi says to him, then looks to me for an explanation.

"Flynn, this is my grandmother, Gloria."

"Nice to meet you," he says to her.

"You too," Gigi replies.

"He came into the store last week," I tell her before Ruby or Flynn gets any ideas to share more. I know Gigi and Ruby would have us mentally engaged with a dozen babies if she knew the whole story.

"A book lover?" she asks and then smirks at me. Who was I kidding? She's going to picture us living happily ever after no matter what I say or do.

"He's working with Plot Twist," I say.

"Ah." Her expression goes serious, and she nods with understanding.

Flynn offers a sheepish smile. "That's true. And honestly, I've never been a huge reader, but I liked your store. It was…charming."

"It's all Olivia's doing," Gigi praises me. "Since she took over running the store, we've been runner-up for best bookstore twice."

It's so obvious what she's doing and my cheeks flush.

"Is that right?" Flynn beams at me. "In that case, you should let me take you out to celebrate."

"You want to celebrate the store being runner-up?" I quirk a brow.

"Sure. It sounds like a big deal."

A laugh bubbles up and slips out. "If you had lost today, would you want to celebrate it?"

"With you? Probably." His eyes still twinkle, but his smile falls a fraction.

Before he can ask me again, because I have a feeling he will, I say, "Greer and I need to get home."

"All right." He looks at my daughter and signs something to her.

She signs right back and my heart squeezes.

"You look like Uncle Archer," she says as she slips her hand into mine.

"Really?" Flynn asks. "Are you sure I'm not more handsome?"

He winks at her and Greer giggles sweetly.

Flynn pushes back from the fence and waves to Gigi and Ruby, who wave right back very enthusiastically.

He then walks backward away from us.

"What are you doing? You should absolutely go out with him," Ruby hisses.

"I'm not dating right now."

Gigi makes a noise that I'm pretty sure is a disbelieving huff.

We start to walk down the aisle to leave, but something makes me turn back.

I lean over the railing to call at him, "Flynn!"

He stops and glances back over his shoulder.

"You pitched a great game today."

His lips curve up as he flashes me that charming smile that I feel everywhere. "What was that?"

"I said, you—"

I stop when he starts chuckling. He totally heard me and just wanted me to yell it again. I shake my head at him, and he winks at me just like he had Greer before he turns away.

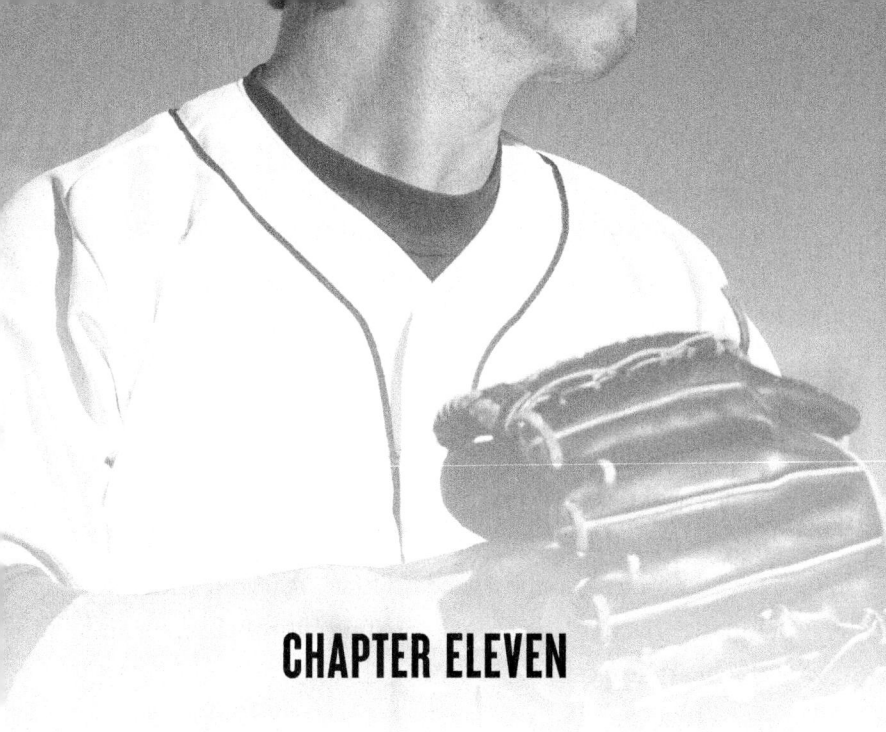

CHAPTER ELEVEN

Flynn

A WEEK INTO OUR SPRING TRAINING GAMES AND
they're all starting to blur together.

While I warm up, my gaze drifts to the seats
beyond first base. The ones where Olivia and her family
sat last weekend. She hasn't been back, but every game I
keep checking just in case.

I fire another pitch. It's feeling good today. I'm locked
in and ready to have a better showing than Tuesday, where
I had a setback with inconsistent throws. Some days I
can't seem to find that rhythm no matter how hard I try,
and other days it comes so easily. Our pitching coach,
Wayne, says to give it time, but time feels like the one
thing I don't have. I only get into a game twice a week

and the rest of the time I'm sitting on the bench impatiently waiting for my next turn. I know how important it is to get it right when opportunities show up and today feels like one of those moments.

JT stands with the ball in one hand. He lifts his face mask. "Be right back. I think I got something in my left eye. I can't see for shit."

I nod and he takes off toward the dugout. I'm in my head, trying to lock in this feeling right now. Turning it over in my mind, memorizing it. What did I eat for breakfast? Which shoe did I lace up first? Without thinking, I glance back to the crowd trickling into their seats and my heart stops.

Olivia.

Her blonde hair is pulled back into a ponytail, and she wears the same Arizona Mavericks' hat she had on last time. Is she trying to torture me by wearing my brothers' team swag?

My pulse races as I watch her take her seat. She's looking at Greer next to her, but I stare long enough she finally looks up at me. My mouth curves into a smile and I lift a hand in a wave. She turns around like she thinks I'm waving to someone else.

I laugh to myself. This girl.

"How's the arm feeling today?"

The question startles me, and I turn my attention to Earl, the facilities' guy, as he approaches me.

I look at him, then back to Olivia, who no longer is staring my way.

"Really good," I say, giving him my attention.

I like the guy. Every time I see him, he has a kind word and a smile for me.

"That's what I like to hear. My wife's coming today, and I promised her a good game."

"That makes two of us hoping to impress a woman."

"Girlfriend?"

"Not yet, but I'm working on it."

"Ah, I see." His smile grows. "In that case, I like our odds. Men tend to do their best work when they're motivated by a woman."

JT jogs up to us. He flashes a smile and nods at Earl. "Good to go. Sorry about that."

"Have a good game today, boys," Earl says, tipping the brim of his hat to us as he walks off.

As JT and I continue warming up, Earl's words keep coming back to me. Coach Wayne comes over and watches me throw a few, nodding and giving me a few pointers.

"All set?" JT asks when we're done and walking toward the bench. It's almost game time, and I like to have a few minutes before I take the mound to visualize and get my head right.

"Yeah."

I must look as in my head as I feel because JT gives me a strange look.

"I need to do something really quick, then I'm ready."

He keeps staring then nods as if he's pieced it together. "Nervous pooper?"

"What?" I ask, laughing.

"It's fine. I've seen it all. Freddie used to run off the field before the start of every game to vomit. By the end of his rookie season, it finally went away. Eat light and drink lots of coffee early in the day to clean out your system."

"My stomach is fine, but thanks for the tips." I clap him on the shoulder and then take off past the dugout to where the tunnel leads to the locker rooms. There's a stairwell off to the left that goes to the stadium seats. I nod at a guard and pass by him, then quickly make my way up to the first level.

Greer spots me before her mom does. She aims a shy smile at me and says, "Archer's brother!"

Olivia's head snaps up and those stunning blue eyes lock on me. Her surprise morphs to amusement quickly.

"Flynn Holland. Watching the game from the stands today?" she asks with a taunt in her voice that makes my body come alive.

"You came!" I try to hold back my excitement, but the smile on my face doesn't want to relax.

"Was I not supposed to?"

No, I've just been looking for you at every game.

"I'm glad you're here. I've been meaning to stop by the bookstore, but practices and games have been long."

"Need more Ruby Madison recommendations?"

"That depends. Does she have a book on how to convince you to go out with me?"

She lets out a nervous-sounding laugh. "I can't go out with you."

"I know you said you weren't dating, but that's just

because you've been out with some real ass—" I stop myself when I remember Greer is listening in. "Jerks. Let me prove to you that good guys still exist."

"Are you one of the good guys in this scenario?" she asks all sass but smiling.

"You know that I am."

"Do I? Because I seem to remember you leaving me all alone in a hotel room."

"A mistake I won't ever make again," I say playfully, but I'm dead serious.

"It isn't a good idea."

"Because your best friend is engaged to my brother? Because you know I think I could break them up if needed."

She lets out a loud laugh and her shoulders relax. "It isn't because of that."

"Good because I was lying. Archer is more likely to disown me than break up with her."

Her smile pulls higher.

"Go out with me, Olivia," I say. I don't have much time before Coach realizes I'm missing and mingling with the fans.

She stares at me, a million emotions crossing her face. I can tell she's conflicted, which means there's a part of her that wants to say yes.

"You have a game to win." She looks past me to the field, which probably means people have noticed I'm gone.

"If we win, then will you go out with me?"

She stares at me with an incredulous look, but still doesn't give in.

Some older gentleman with a bald head and deep lines around his eyes and mouth calls out to her, "Make him throw a no-hitter, honey. I've never seen one and this might be my last chance."

I give him a *stay-the-hell-out-of-it-, old-man* look and glance back at Olivia.

"You heard the guy," she says with a twinkle of amusement in her eyes.

"Done. If I throw a no-hitter, then you'll go out with me."

"You're serious?" Her brows lift.

I nod my agreement.

"Do you know how rare those are?" she asks.

Now it's my turn to laugh. "As rare as meeting a woman like you probably."

Her jaw drops like she can't believe I just said that. My brothers would give me so much shit for a line like that, but I mean it.

"Only three in the last three years. None in history for the Mustangs," the old guy pipes in.

Olivia looks nervous for me. Too late now.

"Do we have a deal?" I ask.

"Sure, Hotshot. You throw a no-hitter, and I'll go out with you." The way she smirks I know she thinks there's no chance in hell I'll pull it off.

But this is one bet I know I won't lose.

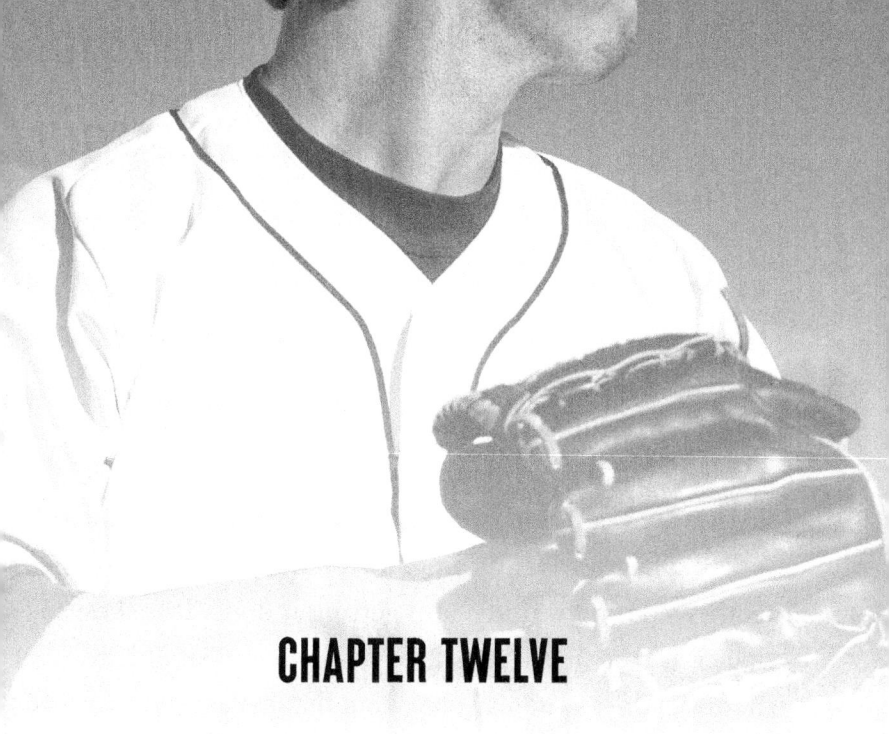

CHAPTER TWELVE

Flynn

AFTER THE GAME, THE LOCKER ROOM ISN'T AS celebratory as I would have imagined for a team pulling off a no-hitter. The guys all celebrated in the moments after the final out, but as the high has worn off, most of them are back to ignoring me.

"I never thought I'd be a part of something like that. Even in a spring training game," JT says to me. "Thank you."

"I couldn't have done it without you," I tell him truthfully. My arm aches and my under-shirt sticks to my body. I have ice wrapped around my right shoulder. Coach wanted to pull me after the seventh inning to rest my arm, but I was too close to winning my bet with Olivia to let a little pain hold me back.

A no-hitter. Something only a handful of pitchers have ever done. Sure, we were playing a team that's only marginally better than us and their best hitter is out with an injury, but no matter the situation, pitching a no-hitter is still damn hard to do.

I was on fire for the first five innings, but after that it was my team that pulled it off. We looked like we knew what we were doing. Error-free, working together, communicating, and getting it done. It makes me even more inspired to keep at it and get out of here next year. I want to play on a team that makes this kind of magic every night.

I check my phone while I let the ice work on my muscles. I have a bunch of texts from people congratulating me: friends, college teammates, my agent, and of course, my brothers. Brogan's been busy changing the group name again by the looks of it.

FLYNN HOLLAND SUPAFANS

BROGAN

Daaaaamn! A no-hitter??!!!

ARCHER

I'm kicking myself so hard for not being there.

HENDRICK

Congrats, little bro. We had the game on at the bar. Place went nuts. Jane is working on a special drink menu for game days—all named after you.

BROGAN

Oh, please tell me one is called The Flame Thrower?

KNOX

Damn good game. Hope you have another one in you next week. Avery and I are driving up for the weekend.

BROGAN

Dirty Slider?

I close out without reading the next ten drink name suggestions from Brogan. I'm too tired to tap out a reply right now. One person is missing though. My dad is doing a cross-country drive with some friends and the woman he started dating recently. I haven't seen or heard from him in a month. I thought by the time the season started he'd be back, but still nothing.

Once I'm showered and ready, most of the team has

cleared out of the locker room. It hadn't occurred to me earlier how I was going to meet up with Olivia, but I pull up my texts again now with plans to bug my future sister-in-law for her best friend's number.

I glance up as I push out of the locker room and, to my surprise, spot Olivia and Greer. Only family are generally allowed in this area, but however she got here, I'm not about to complain.

"You waited," I say as a smile spreads across my face. I half-expected her to bolt when she realized I'd won our bet. Then again, I don't take Olivia as someone who backs down from a challenge.

"Congrats, Hotshot. I underestimated you."

Greer holds her mom's hand, beaming up at me. She signs with her free hand to me, *Hotshot*.

I wonder if Archer taught her that one. Either way, it makes me laugh. I freaking love this kid. She's the coolest.

"Thank you," I say and sign.

"We wanted to say congrats, and I thought I should tell you in person that I can't go out with you tonight."

"Why not?"

"I don't have a sitter and it's a school night anyway. We have a whole bedtime routine."

"We read books together and sing songs," Greer tells me proudly.

Right. I hadn't considered that she'd be busy or not have a sitter. I'm disappointed but at least she's not bailing for some bullshit excuse.

"Sounds fun." I tamp back my disappointment and give Greer a small smile.

"Here's my number. Text me and we can figure something out for next week." Olivia hands me a piece of paper with her number written in blue ink.

My excitement over finally having her number is short-lived. Next week? No way I want to wait that long.

"Why don't we just grab ice cream or something quick?"

"Ice cream!" Greer's eyes light up.

Oops. I flash Olivia an apologetic smile. I don't know a ton about kids, but I think sweets are one of those things that parents try to limit.

"You want to use your one date to go for ice cream?" she asks, one brow stays quirked when she's around me, like she's prepared to challenge every word out of my mouth.

"Sure. I know a place not too far from here."

"Please, Mom?" Greer asks in a pleading tone that mirrors the one inside my head and gives her mom big, puppy dog eyes.

Olivia's gaze narrows slightly on me. Not in a defensive way, more curious.

"Please?" I repeat Greer's plea.

"Okay." Olivia nods. The relief I feel is palpable. "If you're sure that's what you want, then let's do it."

Olivia and Greer follow me in their vehicle to the ice cream shop. It's a bright-colored place with boppy music playing. There's a claw machine in the back of the store and Greer is pumping quarters into it trying to win a pink bouncy ball while Olivia and I sit at a table a few feet away.

"She's cute," I say as we watch her.

Olivia smiles, the first uninhibited smile she's given me since we got here. I get the sense she's nervous. Or seriously second-guessing agreeing to this date.

"I love that she signs for Archer."

That uninhibited smile stretches wider. "She adores him."

"The feeling is mutual," I say, then ask, "What's up with her dad? Is he still bailing on stuff?"

"I forgot I told you about that," she says and then stares down at her scoop of Neapolitan.

"We shared a lot of things that night. I haven't forgotten any of them."

She looks up and holds my gaze for a moment then nods. "He lives in California, so the distance makes it hard for him to see her regularly, but he calls every Sunday, and they video chat."

I don't know if that's normal for parents sharing custody or not, so I just nod. It wasn't normal for my dad, but even he would agree that he wasn't a good example back then. "Is he why you don't date?"

"Only partly. I don't have a lot of free nights, and I already rely on sitters and my family a lot when I'm working. I guess I don't want to be away from her more than I already am. And definitely not for the dates I've been on recently."

"You're a good mom." The words come out with little thought, but instantly I know they're true.

"I don't know about that, but I'm trying my best."

"I know. She's a great kid and you're doing it mostly on your own. I admire that." My mom did it mostly on her own too. I don't remember much about the situation or her. She died when I was young, but I've heard enough from my brothers to know she was a badass single mom. Just like Olivia.

"Thanks." Her cheeks take on a light blush. "So…the game today was wild. Have you ever thrown a no-hitter before?"

"Change of topic, huh?" I grin at her. She really hates compliments. We'll work on that, but for now I don't press. "Definitely not. Maybe never will again."

I scoop a hunk of mint chocolate into my mouth and hold the spoon there as I let that sink in. Nah, I'm going to throw more. A lot more. I can't stomach the idea that my best is behind me. Not with the Twins and not today. There is so much more I want to accomplish.

She leans into me, pressing her shoulder and arm to mine. "All just to get me to go out with you?"

"I would have thrown a perfect game if I had to." A smirk tugs at my lips. "You may not have noticed, but I like you."

"I'm starting to see that." Her dry tone carries a hint of sarcasm.

"Starting to, huh? I need to rethink my entire strategy of picking up women."

Light laughter slips out of her. She looks happier, lighter than I've seen her since New York.

"I think you're doing just fine in that department."

I shrug. It's true I haven't had a lot of problems finding dates. "I'm only interested in you."

"Why?"

"You want a list?" I ask with a chuckle.

"You could date a million other women who are way less…"

"Awesome?"

"Complicated. Greer is amazing and I'm not ashamed or anything, but my life is different."

"I like different."

"You're twenty-one. You should date someone who doesn't have to check her schedule a month in advance to make plans or spends her nights packing lunches and sometimes can't remember the last time she washed her hair."

My lips quirk as she spirals in front of me. I feel the anxiety rolling off her and while that's not funny, the fact she thinks she can scare me off with unwashed hair is hilarious.

She still has on the Mavericks hat and her hair is in a ponytail that hangs over one shoulder. I reach out and wrap my index finger around a silky, blonde lock. "You know, I spent a lot of my life being told what I should or shouldn't do. I have four older brothers who all thought they knew what was best for me. But I'm not them. And I'm not any of the guys you've been out with who obviously didn't realize what they were missing out on."

"You have a good answer for everything."

"Is that a yes?"

She fights a smile. "It isn't a no."

God, I love that she makes me work for it at every turn.

"How about double or nothing?"

"What?" she asks with a laugh.

I let my hand fall away from her hair. "I'm going to win your daughter that pink ball and when I do, you're going to go out with me again."

I push my chair back to stand and walk over to join Greer. She stomps her foot as the mechanical claw closes over the top of the ball, not gripping it well enough to grab a hold of it.

"Can I give it a try?" I ask her.

She takes a step to the side. We got five dollars' worth of quarters when we came in and she's worked her way down to the last three coins.

I put in a quarter and the machine hums to life.

Greer presses up onto her toes next to me and peers

through the glass as I move the claw into position over the pink ball.

"Is this the one you want?" I ask.

She nods her head, blonde curls bouncing with the movement.

I move the claw another inch to the right, then carefully examine the position from every angle. "Okay. Want to hit the button?"

Greer's smile is the sweetest, purest thing I've seen as she brings her little palm down on the red button. I squat down to her level as we watch the crane slowly lower and the claw open.

A shadow falls over us and I glance over my shoulder quickly to see Olivia has stepped up behind us.

I turn back in time to see the claw close over the top of the pink ball and then ever so slowly grab and lift it.

Greer bounces with glee as the claw drops her prize into the shoot where she can retrieve it. She snatches it up with a huge grin and then she must have misunderstood my intention of winning it for her because her smile falls, and she holds it out for me.

"Here's your ball," she says.

"It's all yours," I say and instantly that adorable grin is back.

She clutches it to her chest protectively. "Thank you, Hotshot."

"Welcome, munchkin." She really is the cutest dang kid.

I open my stance to meet Olivia's gaze.

Her arms are crossed over her chest, but she's smiling. "That isn't how double or nothing works. You already got your date."

"Then go out with me because you want to."

She glances over at her daughter holding her pink bouncy ball and then back to me. "Okay, Hotshot."

"Really? That worked?" I clear my throat. "I mean, of course it did."

She laughs, shaking her head. "Text me this week?"

"I'll text you tonight."

CHAPTER THIRTEEN

Olivia

"**Y**OU ARE STARTING TO MAKE ME NERVOUS," RUBY says as I pace in front of the counter. Gigi had an early dinner date with a friend, so my sister is watching the bookstore while I finally go out on my date with Flynn. It's taken two weeks and a lot of planning between his schedule and mine.

"I should cancel. This is a terrible idea."

She looks up from her laptop. "Want me to go instead? He's pretty cute. Plus, he likes my books."

I glare at her, and she laughs.

As I pace away from my laughing sister, I unlock my phone and call someone who will be more reassuring.

"Hello?" Sabrina answers with a smile in her voice.

"HELP!"

"Is this an actual cry for help or are you panicking about your date?" she asks with a chuckle.

My nervous system is a wreck and there's a pit in my stomach that's growing as the time inches closer to Flynn walking through the door. "Why can't it be both?"

"It's going to be great. Flynn's a good guy."

"I know but…" My words trail off and a heavy silence hangs between us. I know it's just a date and that he's a good guy and that there are a thousand other reasons that to anyone else this feels like no big deal, but it's huge for me.

The way I feel around him is beyond a typical first date. I don't know if I can handle another heartbreak and I know, deep down, that if I open myself up to him, I'm only going to like him more. That night in New York was…magical.

The music in her dance studio breaks through my spiral.

"How's Greer?" She's watching her tonight while I'm on my date. I dropped her off at dance class an hour ago and she's going to hang there with Sabrina until she's done teaching for the day.

"She's an angel, as always. She's helping Miss Beth teach tap to the three-year-old class."

I smile as I picture that.

"I think you might have a little dance teacher or choreographer on your hands," Sabrina says.

"Thank you for watching her tonight."

"Any time. You know I love hanging with her."

I do know that, but it still feels like an imposition when I constantly need to rely on my friends or family.

The bells on the front door jingle and my heart lurches until I see a young woman step inside.

"Hello," Ruby greets her.

"I'm guessing that's not your hot date," Sabrina says.

"No. Not yet, but I better go. I need to reapply some deodorant. I think I've already sweat through mine."

Sabrina laughs again. "Are you going to sleep with him?"

"What?" I screech. "Of course not."

"It's not the craziest idea."

"It's bananas. We haven't even kissed."

"Well, start there and see what happens."

My body flushes hot. "I might need to brush my teeth again too."

I run my tongue along the front of my teeth.

"Have fun and I'll see you tonight."

I nod.

"Olivia?"

"Sorry. I was nodding. Yes. I will see you later. Text me if you need anything or if Greer does."

"We'll be fine."

"Okay, then text me if I need anything."

"I don't think you're going to need it, but I will text you in a couple hours to give you an out just in case."

"Thank you. You're a true friend."

"Love you."

"Ditto."

I hang up and then let out a long breath. Ruby is talking with the customer as I walk back to the office. I check my teeth in the mirror and swipe on another layer of deodorant before I check the time.

Three minutes. My stomach is performing Olympic-level somersaults and twists. Sabrina wants me to think about sleeping with him. Is she for real? It's taking all my effort to keep breathing at the thought.

Inside the office, I close the door and let out a long breath. I wander over to the back wall where the lunch notes my grandfather has written Gigi are pinned up. I'm always struck by the sheer volume. One every day doesn't sound like that many until you see how that adds up over a decade or two. The entire wall is covered in them.

Newer notes cover old ones, but I occasionally like to peel them back to read something that might have been written five or fifteen years ago. I do that now, lifting the bottom of a yellow Post-it that says, *I love you*, and revealing a faded receipt with the words, *Don't forget the milk*, scribbled onto it.

Not romantic but very real. And isn't that sometimes the most romantic thing?

I get lost in them, rereading my favorites and find-ing new ones.

"Wow." Flynn's deep voice filled with awe startles me and freezes me in place. Goosebumps spread over my arms and legs as I slowly turn to face him.

My breath hitches as I take him in. He's dressed in

jeans and a plain white T-shirt. No hat tonight and his reddish-brown hair is wavy and curls around his ears.

"You look…" He trails off as he keeps staring at me, then his throat works with a swallow.

"Thank you." I shift my weight from foot to foot. I wore my favorite dress, a simple black one that fits me well, and heels that are already pinching my toes. Flynn is so tall I felt like I needed an extra few inches. "How'd you find me back here?"

"Ruby said you were finishing up. Are you done?"

I'm grateful she covered for me and didn't tell him I was hiding back here fighting off a panic attack. "Yeah. I'm ready."

He nods, then his gaze finally slides past me to the wall of notes.

"What is this?" he asks as he steps toward it.

I turn with him to face it again. "Notes my grandpa has written Gigi over the years."

Flynn's brows rise. "That's a lot of notes."

"One every day. He puts them in her lunch."

"I love that," he says, smile lifting on the left side. His gaze roams over the wall as he takes it all in.

I step away from him, steady my breathing with a couple deep inhales and slow exhales, and grab my purse.

"Ready?" I ask him, finally letting myself feel the one thing I've fought all day. Excitement.

He moves his attention from the wall to me and he gets a cocky, flirty look on his face. "For months now."

Something about his playfulness makes the rest of

my nerves retreat. They're not gone completely, but I feel more like myself.

"All right, Hotshot, let's go."

"Where are we going?" I ask once we're in Flynn's truck.

It's nicer and more comfortable than I expected it to be, and while I was taken aback at first at the idea of him driving something like this instead of a new, flashy vehicle, I have to say it suits him.

"When's the last time you went roller skating?"

"Roller skating?"

"Yeah." He takes his eyes off the road long enough to smile at me. "I figured you've been on a million dates that included dinner or drinks. I want to take you somewhere different."

That's exactly the kind of thing I was expecting, if I'm honest.

He pulls into the parking lot of a huge nondescript building with no windows. If it weren't for the neon lights above the front doors, it could pass for a warehouse.

"I feel like I might be overdressed," I say as I step out of the truck. The nerves I was feeling earlier have turned into butterflies. I'm on a date with Flynn and we're going skating of all things.

Flynn comes around the front to my side. The grin on his face is all boyish charm. "You look perfect."

Inside, Flynn pays for our skates and socks for me. We walk over to a bench on the side of the rink to change our shoes. Only a few people are skating right now, but the music is loud and the lights are flashing.

Flynn gets a locker and shoves our stuff inside while I stand on wobbly legs.

"You got it?" he asks with a hint of a smile. He looms even taller on skates.

"I think so."

He holds out his hand to me. "We'll take it slow."

My heart speeds up as I place my palm in his. His fingers close over mine and we move carefully together. He gives my hand a reassuring squeeze before we step off the carpet to the smooth floor of the rink.

It takes a few seconds to get my bearings and not feel like I'm going to fall on my face. If Flynn has any of those same feelings of unsteadiness, it isn't obvious. He looks as graceful and athletic as always.

"When's the last time you skated?" I ask him.

"I don't know," he says, keeping his stride short and in sync with mine. "High school, maybe?"

"So not long, then?" I grin at him.

"Ha ha," he replies dryly. "I'm not that much younger than you."

"Three years."

"I'm mature for my age."

"Says the man who brought me roller skating," I tease.

He speeds up, tugging me after him. I squeal as he pulls me faster. His grip on my hand tightens almost like he's determined to keep me upright by my fingertips if necessary. When I get my bearings again, he says, "I just wanted an excuse to hold your hand."

Laughing, I pull free of him and skate ahead then turn to face him. His jaw drops slightly and he lets his head fall back with a chuckle. I'm grateful that I don't fall showing off for him.

"Greer gets invited to a lot of skate parties," I say when I turn back and fall into stride with him again.

"Impressive. I bet you're the hottest mom of the group. So much for original, huh?"

That pulls a surprised laugh out of me.

"How is Greer? I heard Archer and Sabrina are watching her tonight."

"She's good. Probably forcing Archer to play dress-up and teach her new words in sign language."

"She won't need to force him into anything."

That's probably true. He's really good with her. So is Flynn for that matter. I have replayed that moment in the ice cream shop where he handed her the bouncy ball over and over. I love seeing her so happy and open. It's a gift that I doubt Flynn or even Archer realizes they've given us.

"Is it hard being away from her?" he asks as a teenage couple rolls past us. They're holding hands, looking carefree and happy and so in love.

Flynn finds my hand again.

"Yeah," I admit with a nod. "It's weird because I look forward to bedtime when I finally get some time to myself or a night doing adult things—"

"Like skating." He waggles his brows playfully.

"Exactly."

We laugh together.

"But fifteen minutes after she falls asleep or an hour into a date, I usually find myself wondering what she's doing and missing her." I probably shouldn't admit that to a guy mid-date, but it's the truth.

"Do you want to call her?"

"No." I shake my head. "I know she's having fun with Sabrina and Archer."

We've gone around the rink a few times now and have found a steady rhythm. The music changes from the upbeat pop song to a slower one.

I finally get brave enough to ask the question that's been on my mind lately. "Have you ever dated someone with kids before?"

"No. How am I doing?"

"You get points for asking about her. Most guys pretend like she doesn't exist."

"Really?"

His surprise makes me feel slightly better about the male species.

"Aside from maybe not liking kids or the idea of me having one, I think they don't love switching the mental image of me out on a date in a sexy dress to picturing me reading bedtime stories and folding laundry in front of the TV while watching cartoons."

"Everything I've seen you do is sexy. Hell, you even make rented skates and tube socks look hot. I'd venture a guess that folding clothes and reading bedtime stories looks just as good on you." His gaze drops over my bare legs and flicks up. He's so vulnerable and honest in his attraction for me that it constantly catches me off guard. I don't know if he truly understands my life as a single mom or not, but he isn't pretending that I'm something different than I am, and I appreciate that.

After skating for three more songs, we take a break to get food.

I stand at the concession counter, perusing the menu. Flynn is behind me. He leans forward and rests both hands on the glass, caging me in.

"Hot dog, pizza, or nachos?" he asks.

"So many options," I tease.

"Nothing but the finest cuisine." He winks at me, then orders one of each, plus two cherry ICEEs from the teenage boy working the concessions.

We take all our food to a little booth that overlooks the rink. His skates bump against mine under the table.

"Next time we should bring Greer. Is she a good skater like her mom?"

My heart flutters at the casual way he mentions a second date, including my daughter.

"She's pretty good. She falls more, but she makes it look cute."

"I'll bet."

I take a bite of the cheesy, greasy pizza. It's terrible. I follow it with a sip of the frosty, cherry drink. The sugar goes straight to my head.

I feel thirteen again. God, maybe that was the last time I was this hopeful while out with a guy.

Flynn makes a face as he chews a tortilla chip covered in nacho cheese.

"Good?" I ask with a laugh.

"Awful." He grabs another chip smeared in the orange sauce and holds it out to me.

I lean forward and take a bite. I'm not sure awful was a strong enough word for how bad it is. The chip is stale, and the cheese is cold. My expression must tell him exactly what I'm thinking because Flynn laughs.

He pops the rest of the chip in his mouth and smiles at me. "Next time, we'll go to a real restaurant first."

My stomach flips as he casually drops the promise of another date again. I'm not even sure he realizes he's doing it. Or maybe he's just that confident.

"Or I could cook for you," I suggest.

"You cook?"

"Yeah."

He groans. "Marry me?"

"Because I can cook?" Laughter flows out of me easily around him.

"I'm living on takeout. My teammate brought in these coffee cake muffins his wife made, and I swear to God

I had dirty dreams about her for a week." His grin is all boyish mischief. "Don't tell JT."

"Your secret is safe with me, Hotshot."

We pick at the food, leaving most of it uneaten. It really is bad, and I feel like my standards are low. Chicken nuggets and Goldfish crackers make up a large part of my daily diet.

"Want to take another spin?" Flynn asks after we throw away our trash. More people have trickled into the skating rink. Teenagers, families, and other couples.

"Sure."

Flynn holds one hand out to me, but with his other, he reaches into the front pocket of his jeans. I left my phone in my purse since my dress doesn't have pockets and it's been a nice reprieve from all adult responsibilities.

"Sorry. No one ever calls me," he says as he laces his fingers through mine absently and stares at his screen. "It's Sabrina."

My pulse races with alarm. Ever since Greer was born, I've known a new kind of panic when someone calls me while they're watching her. My mind immediately goes to all the worst-case scenarios before I can stop it.

"Answer it," I say at the same time he puts the phone to his ear and says, "Hey, Sabrina."

My throat is thick, and my stomach ties itself into knots as I watch Flynn's usual playful expression twist into something like concern.

"Got it. We'll head out now." His brown eyes meet mine and his thumb glides over my knuckles reassuringly.

"I'm going to hand you to Olivia so you can tell her, okay?"

I grab his phone the instant he drops it from his ear.

"Sabrina," I say in a rush. "What's wrong?"

"Greer is okay," she says immediately. "She started coughing at the studio, but I didn't think anything of it. Then when we got to your apartment, she complained her throat hurt. I just checked her temperature, and she has a fever. I'm so sorry. I should have checked sooner."

"A few of her classmates have been out sick recently," I admit. I thought we'd been lucky to avoid it. Guess not.

"Do you want me to give her meds or wait until you get here?" she asks.

In the background I hear Greer cough and my heart aches.

"No, I'll be there as soon as I can."

"Okay," Sabrina says. "I'll just give her cuddles then."

"I hope you don't get it too," I say, feeling guilt wash over me. It's one thing if Greer gets me sick, but I feel terrible that she might have infected my best friend and everyone else she was around at the studio today.

"I'm fine. Don't worry about me."

"Okay. See you in a few." I hand the phone back to Flynn.

"Poor kid," he says as we skate to the lockers. "And poor, Mom. Are you okay?"

"Yeah. I just feel terrible for not being there when she needed me."

Silently, he nods, and we change our shoes quickly

then head out of the skating rink. It isn't far from my apartment, but every mile feels like it takes an eternity.

Flynn waits until we're close to speak again. "It's good for kids to have a lot of people they can depend on in tough times."

"Yeah," I say, hearing him but the words not really sinking in.

"Greer trusts Sabrina and Archer. And more than that, she knows you trust them. While I'm sure she wishes you were there right now, she isn't blaming you. So don't blame yourself either, okay?"

I glance over at him. One hand on the steering wheel, dark eyes darting my way and back to the road. I don't know how he knew I was sitting over here feeling terrible for being out on a date having fun while my daughter is home sick, but his words help more than he could know. They don't completely wash away the guilt, but it at least makes me aware that it isn't rooted in reality.

"Thank you."

CHAPTER FOURTEEN

Olivia

T HE RELIEF I FEEL AT SEEING GREER IS PALPABLE. She's snuggled up in her bed, eyes closed. Her ever-present Bunny is next to her. So is the pink bouncy ball Flynn won for her.

Flynn. I think I thanked him for tonight and getting me here so quickly, but it's a little bit of a blur. The second he pulled up, I was out of the truck and rushing to get to Greer. Flynn followed me up to the apartment and is talking with Sabrina and Archer in the kitchen as I look in on my daughter. The floor creaks as I step closer and her eyes open.

"Momma," she says, voice scratchy, then she coughs.

"Oh, baby." I move to her, sitting on the edge of the

bed and placing the back of my hand on her forehead. She's warm and sticky.

"My throat hurts."

"I know. I'm so sorry."

She coughs again. Big, body-wracking sounds that make my heart hurt.

"I'm going to get you some medicine, okay? I'll be right back."

I'm in autopilot as I leave her room. I head to my bathroom in search of medicine. I find a nearly empty bottle of children's Tylenol and some cough drops. I take them with me to the kitchen, then search in the cabinets.

"How can I help?" Sabrina asks. "What do you need?"

I stop my rummaging only long enough to give her an appreciative smile. "Nothing. I've got it. Thank you for looking after her."

"Of course. I'm so sad she's not feeling well. Do you think it's strep?"

"I hope not, but I'll probably make an appointment with the doctor tomorrow just in case." I close another cabinet.

"What are you looking for?" Flynn asks.

I feel a flicker of disappointment about the way our date ended. We were having such a nice time and now he's getting a good, hard look at what it's really like to date a single mom. I doubt he's going to ask me out again.

"I thought I had cough syrup, but I guess not," I say.

"We can go get some," Sabrina offers, and Archer nods his agreement.

"No. Really. You've done enough. I have Tylenol and I can Instacart anything else I need."

No one looks like they're going to budge.

"Go home before you're all contaminated." I step forward and hug Sabrina, then Archer.

"Hope she feels better," Archer says.

"Text me if you need anything," Sabrina adds.

I start to move toward Flynn to say goodbye to him too, but Greer calls out for me.

"Thank you, guys," I say to them and lift a hand in a wave. I let my gaze linger on Flynn a little longer than the others before I turn to head back to Greer's room.

Once I give her some Tylenol and crawl into bed beside her, Greer falls right asleep. I lie there, listening to her breathe and letting her sticky forehead rest against my arm.

I should get up and order some more medicine, maybe some food with it. My stomach growls. Slowly, I inch away from my daughter, careful not to wake her, then tiptoe out of her room. I leave the door open, only a crack, and let out a breath.

It feels like it's been hours since I got home but a glance at the clock on the coffee pot says it's only eight o'clock.

I pull my hair back into a ponytail and pad to the refrigerator to look for something to eat. I'm starving. The food at the skating rink seems like days ago.

I get lost in a flashback of Flynn grinning at me over a plate of nachos and then him holding out his hand to keep me upright on the skating rink. Not that I needed it, but it was still sweet.

A light knock at the front door pulls me from my thoughts, and I walk to it without giving much consideration to who might be on the other side. The last person I expect is Flynn.

"What are you doing here?" I ask him as he stands on the "hello" doormat with grocery bags in both hands.

"I thought you might need a few things," he says as he walks into my apartment. He goes to the kitchen and sets the bags on the counter.

I stare after him dumbfounded.

"Who knew there were so many kinds of cough syrup?" Flynn must pull out a dozen different bottles of children's cough syrup. Every brand, all the flavors and types.

"Did you buy out the store?" I ask.

"Too much?"

I laugh softly. "You didn't need to do this. I could have ordered it."

"I know. I wanted to, though. And I wasn't ready for our date to end." The sincerity in his words makes my heart flutter.

"There's more," he says, grinning. He reaches into another bag.

"More?" I ask, incredulously.

"Since the skating rink food was a bust, I stopped and got a few things." The same way he filled the counter with medicine, he now adds a variety of take-out options.

Tacos, noodles, salad, burgers, and pizza. "In case you're hungry."

"This is…"

"Yeah." He rubs at the back of his neck and wears a sheepish grin. "Now that I'm seeing it all laid out, it looks borderline creepy."

"It's really nice," I say as I step closer. "And thoughtful. Thank you."

That cocky smirk returns.

"Dare I ask what's in the last two bags?"

He pulls out two cartons of ice cream—Neapolitan and chocolate. And from the last bag, a stuffed horse wearing a Mustangs team jersey.

"A kid can never have too many toys, right?" He holds up the stuffed animal with a boyish smirk.

"You thought of everything." I am in shock. And touched.

"How is she?"

"Sleeping for now."

"How are you?" he asks as he comes around the kitchen counter.

My cheeks puff with a breath I let out slowly. "I hate it when she's sick. I feel so helpless."

He reaches out with both hands then rubs up and down my arms. "Anything I can do?"

"You mean aside from all that." I tip my head toward the haul of medicine and food with a smile. "No, but thank you for asking."

His hands drop away and instantly I wish he were still

touching me. Not in a *please take off all my clothes* kind of way, just a reassuring, *I'm here for you* caress or hug. I'm too worried about Greer to think about sex.

"You should take half that food with you," I say.

He gives me a strange look.

"There's no scenario in which I'm going to be able to eat all that in the next day or two."

"I'm staying," he says and goes back into my kitchen, looking somehow at home and completely out of place in the small space.

"You are?" I ask, then add, "She might be contagious."

"If she is, then you are, and I'm already screwed."

"I'm not going to be much fun to hang out with."

My basic plan for the night was to hover nearby, checking on Greer every few minutes to make sure she's breathing, until I passed out on the couch.

"I know. Pretend I'm not here."

"You want me to pretend you're not here?" I repeat his words in the form of a question.

"Mhmm."

"Unlikely."

"Because I'm so handsome?" His playful side is back, and it relaxes some of the tension I'm holding.

Every scrape, bump, sickness leaves me emotionally wrung out. From the moment it happens until she's back to feeling better, it consumes me. I don't know if that's healthy or not, but she's depending on me, and that is a responsibility I don't take lightly.

Instead of answering him, I smile and take a seat at one of the barstools in front of him.

He slides the take-out containers into a line in front of me. "What sounds good?"

I reach for the pizza box.

"Really?" he asks, grinning wide. "I had you pegged for a noodles or salad kind of woman."

I flip open the box and the smell of cheese and bread wafts around me. My stomach growls.

"Plates?" he asks, looking around.

I direct him, and Flynn moves around my kitchen, getting plates and napkins. He even fills glasses with water. I can't remember the last time someone not related to me did something simple for me, like serve me food.

He sits next to me, and we fall quiet while we eat pizza.

"When you said you were into gardening, I was imagining a yard filled with flowers and a little vegetable garden," he notes as he reaches for a second slice. "This is cool though. You brought them indoors. It has a whole greenhouse vibe in here."

I glance around, trying to see the apartment and greenery with fresh eyes. "I'd love to have a real garden someday, but for now this is more practical."

"How'd you get into it?"

"My mom."

"You're close then?"

I nod.

"Does she live nearby?"

"Sort of." I explain to him about the chef positions my parents took on a cruise ship and not being certain when or if they'll come back.

"That's awesome," he says. "I'm sorry you don't get to see them more though."

"Yeah, I miss them, but they're having a blast. How is it living near your brothers again?"

"Good, most of the time." He gives me a half grin. "Don't get me wrong, I love the shit out of them, but they can't help but treat me like a kid no matter how old I get."

I realize the more he talks that I hadn't really opened myself up to getting to know him before and now I want to know it all.

"How so?" I ask.

"I'm not sure how much Archer or Sabrina has told you, but my mom passed away when I was eight. After that, my brothers raised me. Knox, mostly. Hendrick was off at college and Archer and Brogan were only a few years older than me."

"I'm sorry. That had to have been hard."

"Thanks." He bobs his head.

"What about your dad?" I ask him.

"We're pretty close, yeah."

"Really?" I asked the question, but I thought I knew the answer.

"Yeah. Why? What'd you hear?"

"Sabrina mentioned in passing once that Archer's relationship with him was strained."

"It is," Flynn admits. "I'm the only one that has much

to do with him. Archer's been making a little effort, but Knox and Hendrick have basically written him off."

"Why?" I ask, then think better of it. "Sorry. None of my business."

"It's okay." He takes a bite of pizza and then sets the slice down.

I wait in suspense while he chews and then takes a drink of water.

"He wasn't around much when we were kids. He drove a truck all around the country, sort of popped in and out when he could. Then when our mom died, he stepped in to take care of us. Or he tried. Dad didn't know how to handle us. He hadn't really ever done any of the parenting, and we were all a wreck after losing mom. I'm sure we didn't make it easy on him. Anyway, he stuck it out for a while, but eventually he took off again. After that, we managed on our own."

"And you forgave him?" I don't mean for it to come out full of accusation and skepticism, but as a parent it's hard for me to imagine leaving my kids to fend for themselves.

"You sound just like my brothers." Flynn smiles at me. I try to see past it for any hint that he's covering up pain underneath it, but he seems genuine.

"I'm not saying I agree with it or that I don't wish he'd been around, but I guess I've made peace with it. He screwed up and made a lot of bad choices over the years, but he's still my dad. I'd rather have him in my life now and in the future than hold on to resentment for the past."

"Wow."

"You think I'm naïve or stupid for forgiving him and expecting him not to disappoint me again?" he asks, then adds, "Trust me, I've heard it all. And I get it, but the thing is I know what it was like not having a relationship with him. If it's a risk, then it's one I'm willing to make. People change."

"I don't think you're naïve or stupid."

"No?" he asks, brows lifting and a smirk pulling at his lips.

"It's incredibly pragmatic and far more understanding than most people would be to someone who hurt them like that. I don't know what that was like, but I'm not sure I could be as forgiving." The more I think about it the less I think I could do the same. I stare down at my plate as I wonder about Greer. Will she resent her father one day for not being around more?

Flynn's knee bumps against mine gently. "You okay?"

"I was thinking about Greer's dad and what her relationship will be like as she gets older. Right now, she adores him, but she's starting to realize that she sees him less than other kids see their dad. I don't want her to feel like she's missing out, you know?"

"She's not missing out. She has the best mom possible."

I laugh softly. "Thanks."

"I mean it. She's a dope kid and you're amazing with her. It's sexy."

"It's sexy?" A far heartier laugh bubbles up in my chest.

"Hell yes."

I have no response to that. Zero. But I must be feeling better because my libido has entered the chat.

He leaves his leg resting against mine and we finish our food in silence. Is it weird that this is possibly the best date I've ever been on?

"I should go check on Greer," I say as I push my plate away.

"Of course." He stands and takes his plate and mine. "I've got cleanup."

I stare at him a beat, watching him move around so comfortably in my space. When he realizes I'm sitting and staring at him, he tosses a wink over his shoulder. "Go check on your girl. I'll have ice cream ready when you're back."

Who could say no to that?

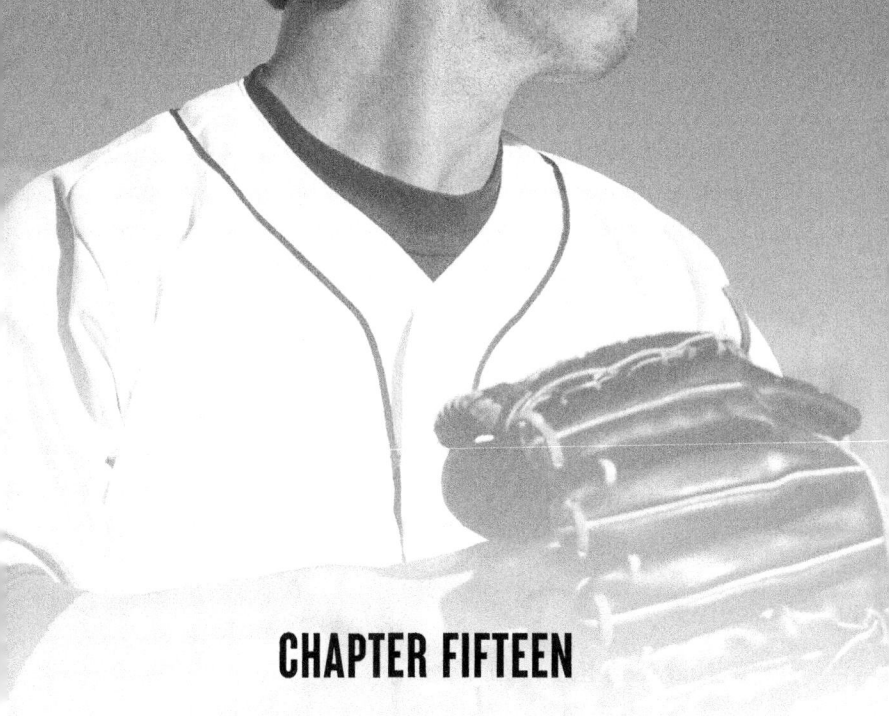

CHAPTER FIFTEEN

Flynn

"**W**AKE UP, HOTSHOT." OLIVIA'S VOICE CUTS through my hazy dreams. My lids flutter open and she's standing over me looking as sexy as ever. She holds out a mug of coffee to me.

"Thanks." I sit up and take it from her as I get my bearings. "What time is it?"

"Five. You fell asleep while I was checking on Greer. I wasn't sure what time you needed to be up for baseball."

"How is she?" I take a sip of coffee and grimace.

"Good. Her fever finally broke."

"That's great." I roll my neck side to side. "Do you have any cream or sugar? This is the strongest fucking coffee I've ever tasted."

She laughs, plopping onto the couch next to me. "There's sugar in the cabinet next to the microwave."

I get up, stretching and groaning. I dump two big spoonfuls of sugar into the drink before I attempt another sip. On the way back to the living room, I snag a slice of cold pizza.

Olivia looks tired. Her hair is pulled up in a ponytail, but a few strands hang loose around her face and the nape of her neck. Sexy as hell, but tired.

"Did you sleep at all?" I ask her, taking a seat next to her.

"A bit."

That feels like a no.

"I can come back after practice today."

She lets her head fall to the side to look at me. "I'll be fine. Besides, my grandfather will disown me if his star pitcher isn't ready for this weekend's game."

"He's really a diehard, huh?"

Some sort of emotion flickers across her face, but it's gone too quickly for me to make it out. "He loves baseball and the Mustangs more than just about anything."

"Well, he's safe. I'm not pitching again until Saturday."

"Right."

"Will you come?"

"To the game?" she asks.

"Yeah. I like seeing you in the stands while I'm pitching. You have this anxious, hopeful expression on your face."

"You cannot see my expression from that far away."

"I can," I insist.

"You are so full of it." Her eyes narrow in disbelief, but her lips curve into a smile.

I should go. She needs sleep and I need to run by my apartment before practice. But I don't want this night to end. The only thing that gets me up is the hope that this won't be the last time.

"All right. I better go. Tell Greer I said to feel better, and if you need more medicine or food, I know all the best spots."

She laughs.

"Text you later?" I ask, still not wanting to leave. My gaze drops to her mouth. All night I've thought about kissing her, but it hasn't felt like the right moment with everything else going on.

Her stare is locked on me, and I think maybe she's thinking the same thing. "Sounds good."

I force myself to my feet, then take one more sip of coffee before I hold it out to her. "Here, I think you need it more than me."

She takes a drink and then coughs. "That is straight sugar."

"Sweet, just like me." I wink at her.

She shakes her head at me as I head toward the door. Damn, I really, *really* don't want to leave.

"Take care of yourself."

She nods. "Later, Hotshot."

Practice is killer. I'm dragging from lack of sleep, and my mind wanders to Olivia and Greer every second the ball isn't in my hands.

"Better. Sink in a little more on that back hip as you drive forward. You're opening up a little fast," Coach Wayne says.

I nod, taking in his words as I kick at the dirt with the toe of my shoe. Despite my no-hitter a couple of weeks ago, I've struggled ever since. I'm back to throwing like shit. Every fifth pitch or so is right on the mark, but I can't find it with any consistency. It's the most frustrating thing to know I'm capable of so much more but can't do it every time I step onto the mound.

When we finish up, I head to the locker room with JT. The atmosphere all around me is optimistic and happy. I feel like the only black cloud.

JT smiles as I drop to the bench with a groan, sweat pouring off me.

"Chin up, Holland. You'll get it."

"Will I?" I ask, not really expecting an answer.

He chuckles. "I remember feeling the same way you do right now."

That gets my attention. "You do?"

"My first year, I stepped onto the field every day with the weight of my future bearing down on me."

"This is different. I already blew it once. I don't know how many more chances I'm going to get."

"You just threw a no-hitter." He shakes my shoulder and laughs. "No one is looking at you right now thinking you're blowing anything."

I crack a smile, but it doesn't last long.

"Don't be so hard on yourself. One day at a time."

"Patience is not my strong suit. I was pitching in the biggest games of baseball last season and now I'm…" I trail off.

"Playing for the worst team in the league?" he asks, one brow cocked.

"I didn't say that."

"It's fine. Nothing everyone else isn't saying about us." He's quiet as he stands and grabs his phone and wallet from his locker. I didn't mean to insinuate that I think the team sucks, but I do wonder how he's able to show up every day and not dwell on that fact.

"We've had a rough few years with injuries and trades, but this is a great group of guys. We have the talent and the heart to do big things. Our time is coming. I believe that."

"Is that why you've stayed all these years?" I ask, keeping my voice low. There's no way he hasn't had opportunities to play for other teams over the years. I'll never understand why he's stayed as long as he has.

"This place is home. Winning somewhere else wouldn't feel as sweet."

"At least you'd be winning though."

His upper body shakes with a silent chuckle. "Winning isn't the only thing worth playing for."

"We're going to have to agree to disagree on that point."

He flashes me a smile. "See you tomorrow, Holland. Don't forget tomorrow is your day to bring food."

Looks like I'll be making a trip to the grocery store.

When JT is gone, I pull out my phone and send Olivia a text to see how Greer is doing. While I wait for her reply, I take a quick shower and get dressed. I don't feel like going home so I go to the media room to watch film of Milwaukee's last game. I'm starting Saturday and I need to see what I'm up against.

The video equipment is clunky, and it takes a bit of effort to get it to work. I'm cussing out the screen, which keeps flickering on me, when Earl finds me.

Smiling, he walks in and takes over, jiggling some wires and blows the dust off the projector.

"That should do it," he says as the screen comes into focus.

"Thanks."

With a nod, he steps back. "Preparing for Saturday?"

"Yeah. I haven't faced them before. Any words of wisdom?"

"They have some talent over there for sure." He glances to the video as the first Milwaukee batter walks out to the plate. "That's Foukes. He likes a fastball, but he has a hard time being patient. Mix it up. Keep him guessing."

Intrigued, I watch as Foukes swings at the first pitch, a two-seamer that moves a little too far inside.

"Did you already watch this game?" I ask him.

"Nah." He crosses his arms over his chest as we watch the next two pitches. A beautiful fastball that he lets go by him, then a changeup that he can't resist but swings too early.

"Damn. You were right," I say to Earl as Foukes strikes out.

"What else are you holding back on me?" I ask playfully, but as the question lingers, I really want to know.

"Seriously," I say. "You have any tips for me?"

"You've got coaches for that. I've already said too much."

"I know what they think, but what about you? Don't tell me you haven't been paying attention because I don't buy it." He sees everything around here.

I pause the video and wait for him to answer.

"Your front foot."

"What about it?"

"You step a little too far inside as you release the ball."

I nod, thinking. "Wayne thinks I'm not sinking in enough on my back hip."

"You should listen to him. He's a good coach."

"Something tells me you are too."

Before I can ask him more questions, and I absolutely want to, Earl heads for the door. "You're a smart pitcher with a great arm. Trust your instincts out there Saturday and I like our chances against any batter."

"Thanks, Earl."

By the time I get to my apartment later that evening, I still haven't heard from Olivia. Archer texted to invite me over, but I'm not sure if I'm feeling up to it.

I pull a beer from the fridge and look around the empty space. The cactus that Olivia gave me sits on the kitchen counter.

I check my phone again in case I missed her text, but still nothing. Hopefully she got some rest today and Greer is feeling better.

Taking my drink and the cactus with me to the living room, I set the plant on the coffee table in front of me and then down another long swig of the beer. I haven't spent a lot of time in my apartment so there still isn't a lot of furniture or décor. I wonder if Olivia knew how much my place needed some life in it when she gave me this cactus. Maybe she really was just trying to call me a prick.

My phone vibrates and I swipe to unlock it so fast.

OLIVIA

We're good. Thanks for checking on us. No strep, thank goodness. Hope you weren't too tired today.

Instead of texting her, I record an audio message. "Hey. I'm glad to hear from you. I'm home now. I survived the day, although I did spend a lot of it wondering how you were. Need anything? I can bring food or medicine or anything you need."

I drink my beer and tap my thumb against the side of the phone while I wait for a reply. My lips pull into a smile when a new audio message comes through.

I click play and her teasing, sweet voice hits me in the gut. "I am good on food and medicine but thank you. We're taking it easy tonight. Greer's fever came back for a bit today, so she is staying home from school again tomorrow and is currently working her way through all her favorite movies while I'm organizing the pantry. Sexy, right?" She laughs. "Greer says thank you for the stuffed animal by the way. She hasn't put it down since I gave it to her."

I quickly reply, "Everything you do is sexy. Want some help?"

Another laugh starts her message. "You want to come over and organize my pantry?"

"I want to see you again. The activity doesn't matter."

"I'd like to see you too, but if you come over, Greer's going to get excited, and she really needs to rest."

Her being such a thoughtful mom is so fucking hot. But damn, I really want to see her.

CHAPTER SIXTEEN

Olivia

G REER STAYS HOME FROM SCHOOL ON THURSDAY AND Friday, which means so do I. I manage to find people to cover me at the Lilac Lounge, and Ruby helps Gigi at the bookstore. By Saturday, my house has never been cleaner. It's fueled from boredom and sexual tension. Once Greer started feeling better, my brain switched from obsessing over taking care of her to thinking about Flynn.

We've been sending voice messages back and forth for two days. I don't want to admit how many times I've played each one. His voice, deep, playful, teasing has been the soundtrack to my manic deep-cleaning. And I can't stop smiling.

"Morning." His voice is raspy with sleep. "How are my girls this morning?"

He sent that fifteen minutes ago and I'm on replay number four. Okay, fine, fourteen.

"Morning," I chirp in reply. "Good. We're finally leaving the apartment today. Good luck at the game. Sorry we won't make it."

The Mustangs play this afternoon. Flynn is pitching, and Sabrina and all his brothers are attending. I hoped to take Greer, but I don't think she's quite up for that yet.

Greer comes out of her room as I'm sliding my phone back into my pocket. She looks a thousand times better. The cough is still there, but she's been fever-free since yesterday morning. By Monday I think we'll be back to our normal routine.

"Ready?" I ask her.

She nods happily, holding her new horse in one hand.

We go to the bookstore first. Oh, how I've missed it. Gigi hugs Greer before my daughter runs off to the kids' section to see what new books she might have missed.

"She looks better," Gigi notes.

"She is," I say. "How is it going here?"

"It's been quiet."

My stomach drops. "Really?"

She picks up on my disappointment and gives me a reassuring smile. "The weather is nice. People are out enjoying it. They'll be back."

I hope she's right. Keeping the store afloat is a constant challenge. Some months things look great and then it seems as soon as I get comfortable, we have a month or two where it feels like we'll never get back into the black. It's one of the many reasons I'm so determined to win the best bookstore in the city award. It comes with extra media coverage, newspaper articles, social media posts, and a very fancy-looking trophy to display in the store.

"Thanks for looking out for everything. Did the new shelving arrive?"

"It's in the back."

"Great," I say, heading in that direction. We have a new stack of advanced book copies from publishers, and it looks like a new shipment of restocks came in too. I pick through each box, then examine the long, heavy boxes that must be shelving. I might need Grandpa to come in and help me get those together. We are expanding the teen section with a private nook outside of the kid area. I've noticed more and more young readers popping in, and I want our store to be inclusive.

After I've looked through everything, I go to the note wall. I can easily pick out the newest notes from Grandpa. A white sticky note with the Mustangs logo up top says, *Extra sweets for my sweetie*. And a torn piece of newspaper with *Have a good day* in red Sharpie.

I pull out my phone and snap a picture of it, then send it to Flynn.

His reply is almost immediate. Instead of typing out the words, "you too," he's written it on the palm of his hand and taken a picture.

After we leave the bookstore, I take Greer to get sandwiches at our favorite little café before heading back to the apartment. Ruby is waiting at my door.

"Aunt Ruby!" Greer runs and launches herself at my sister.

"Oh, I missed your germy face," Ruby says as she picks up Greer and hugs her.

"I'm not germy anymore." She coughs immediately after and the three of us laugh.

I unlock my apartment, and we all go inside.

"Can I steal my niece for a bit?" Ruby asks.

"Are you sure? She doesn't have strep, but she still might get you sick."

"I'm willing to risk it."

"Avoiding writing?"

She gasps dramatically. "How dare you. I want to spend time with my favorite girl. But also, yes. I'm pretty sure I've forgotten how to write a book."

As I'm laughing at my sister, Greer bounces up and down.

"Can I, Mom? Please?" Greer whines but in the most adorable way.

"Yes, but take it easy. Your body needs rest." I kiss the top of her head. I give my sister my best no-nonsense glare. "No junk food."

They start for the door.

"Does ice cream count?" Ruby asks with a wink.

I can't remember the last time I watched a baseball game on TV, but that's exactly what I do while Greer is with my sister.

Flynn looks just as good, no, better, with the camera zooming in on him before each pitch. The time in the sun has turned his skin a golden tan that makes his hair look redder, especially in the sunlight.

The Mustangs are up by one run in the top of the eighth inning. Flynn's shoulders lift and fall as he lets out a long breath. He's tired. The announcers have been tracking his pitches and noting that he's thrown a lot today. They've also noted that he's been very inconsistent since coming up to the Major, and I feel instantly defensive of him.

He just threw a no-hitter two weeks ago. How quickly people turn from praise to criticism.

I cheer for him alone in my living room. He strikes out the next two batters and the top of the inning ends. I feel such pride I'm giddy with it.

Lake City gets two more runs in the bottom of the eighth, and then Flynn strikes out the first three batters in the ninth inning, ending the game.

"They won," I say to myself, wishing so badly I was there. The announcers are back to singing Flynn's praises. Jerks.

I send Flynn a voice message. "Congrats, Hotshot."

Greer returns around dinnertime, cranky and sassy. She fights me over every bite, pushing her green beans around the plate and looking sullen.

"Finish up. It's bedtime."

"I'm not hungry."

"Okay," I say and take her plate. "Time to take a bath."

"Can we watch a movie after I'm done?"

"Not tonight. You need sleep."

She stomps her foot, and I have to fight a smile. She's in that irrational mode where she doesn't realize that her bad mood is because she's tired.

Her footsteps echo down the hall to the bathroom, but by the time she gets in, I can already hear her singing happily.

I clean the kitchen, checking my phone every few minutes for a new text from Flynn. I've gotten so used to hearing from him that I'm disappointed when two hours have passed since the end of the game with still no word from him.

I'm about to go check on Greer and give her a

five-minute warning that it's time to get out of the bath when there's a knock on the front door.

My brows pull together as I cross the apartment. Maybe Ruby wants to talk out her story.

I pull open the door, faltering when it's the man I've been thinking about for three days straight on the other side.

"What are you doing here?" I ask, then step forward and hug him.

I think my action takes us both by surprise because he chuckles as he wraps his arms around my waist.

"I needed to see you."

Those words make my pulse race.

I step back and stare at him in amazement.

"Is it okay I'm here?"

"Yes." I blink a few times and wave for him to come in. "Greer is taking a bath."

I forgot how good he looks in my apartment.

"Something smells good." He lifts his chin and sniffs.

"We had spaghetti. Want some?"

"Absolutely."

"Really?" I offered, but I did not expect him to say yes.

He nods. "I came straight here from the stadium."

I check in on Greer and let her know we have company, then pull out the leftovers and reheat them while Flynn wanders around the apartment like he's seeing it for the first time.

"Is this your favorite flower?" he asks, pointing to a framed print of a night-blooming epiphytic cactus.

"I don't have a favorite," I say before realizing that might sound weird. Everyone has a favorite. Well, except me. It would be like picking a favorite book. Impossible.

I set his plate on the counter, and he moves my way.

"It's a queen of the night," I tell him. "They only bloom once a year."

"That's a real thing?" he asks.

"Yeah." I laugh lightly.

"That's awesome. Have you ever seen one bloom?"

"Not in person." I shake my head as I take a seat next to him. I can't believe he's really here.

Flynn rubs his hands together then picks up a fork and shovels in a big bite. He groans as he chews. "It's official: We're getting married."

My face heats. "Because of my spaghetti?"

"Food is the third most important thing in my life, and I can't cook for shit."

I'm about to ask him what the first two things are when Greer comes running out. Her pajamas stick to her like she didn't bother toweling off before she got dressed.

"Hotshot," she says as she comes to a stop next to him. Her wild curls are dripping with water.

He drops his fork and turns to face her. "How are you feeling?"

"Aunt Ruby says I'm a germ fest."

Flynn lets out a hearty laugh.

"Do you want to watch *Tangled* with me?" she asks him.

"No movie tonight," I remind her.

Her face twists into a pout.

"Another time," Flynn says.

Her smile returns. "Do you want to see Sweetie?"

"Uhh…" He looks to me for help.

"Come on." She takes his hand, and he lets her lead him to her room. I follow behind, giving them some space.

She goes to her bookshelf and picks up Sweetie, the stuffed horse he gave her. I place a hand over my mouth to keep from laughing. The horse has been upgraded with a tiara, pink beaded bracelets as necklaces, and a tutu.

Flynn's expression is filled with amusement as she hands it to him.

"Isn't he cute?"

"The cutest," he confirms. "It looks like you've given him a great home."

His gaze roams around the rest of the room, finally landing back on the bookshelf.

"You like books like your mom, huh?"

Greer nods. "Want to see my favorite?"

She doesn't wait for his answer before pulling out a stack of books and sitting on the floor with her legs crossed.

To my surprise, Flynn sits down with her. He looks adorably tall and big in the small space between her bed and the bookcase. She opens the book and holds it out to him. My chest squeezes as I watch them interact so easily. He's a good sport and she's completely enamored with him. I stay in the doorway, letting them have a moment. Flynn looks up and meets my gaze, then winks at me.

After Greer has flipped through three books, making him read each one to her, I finally intervene.

"Okay, let's give Flynn a break. You need to get to bed," I say.

Greer opens her mouth and looks like she's going to object, but Flynn holds up Sweetie and says, "I think he needs his beauty sleep."

Greer giggles. "Will you come back tomorrow?"

"Sure," he says, then glances at me. "If it's okay with your mom."

She gives me those big, pleading eyes. I nod and she lunges forward to hug Flynn. I think it takes him by surprise, much like my hug at the door had, but a second later, he wraps one arm around her back.

When she pulls away, Flynn gets to his feet and helps her put away her books.

"Brush your teeth," I tell her.

She rushes out of the room, leaving me with Flynn.

"She only has one speed, huh?" he asks.

"It's running or asleep," I confirm.

His smile stretches wider. "She's a trip. I can see why Archer is wrapped around her finger."

"She's pretty great."

He crosses over to me, stopping a foot away. With one hand, he reaches out and takes my hand, interlacing our fingers. "So is her mom."

My heart races faster when his gaze drops to my mouth. We've spent two nights together now and still haven't kissed. I feel like if it doesn't happen soon, I might die.

"How long does it take her to brush her teeth?"

An odd question, but I answer it without thought. "A couple of minutes. Why?"

He tugs me to him with our linked hands and his other hand moves to the side of my neck as his mouth crashes down on mine. His fingers glide around to the back of my neck. My lips part in surprise and invitation, and Flynn doesn't waste any time sweeping his tongue in to play with mine.

My heart leaps in my chest. It isn't a typical first kiss. It's filled with months of anticipation and longing. He isn't soft or gentle, and he doesn't hold back. Neither do I.

I step closer, pressing my body against his. My pulse races as he groans softly. He nips at my bottom lip and his fingers at the nape of my neck tangle in my hair. He pulls gently, tugging my head back to give him better access. Our height difference means he's leaning down, so I lift onto my toes and bring my free arm up to rest against his shoulder to help him out. He's hard and warm and smells faintly of some sort of crisp citrusy soap.

He drops my hand and then uses both of his to pick me up. I giggle as he backs me up against the wall and then continues to kiss me, this time without needing to bend down to reach me.

I cup his face in my palms and revel in being face-to-face with him. His cheeks are scratchy with light stubble, but his lips are soft.

Blood pounds in my ears as we keep kissing. I loop my arms around his neck, and he squeezes me to him until there's no space between us. He's every bit as good of a kisser as I imagined. I never want to stop, but too soon he's setting me down and standing tall. I'm dizzy with sensation when Greer comes running back into her room.

"Can we read another story?" she asks as she climbs into bed.

I manage to compose myself, or at least I attempt to, as I walk over to her bed. "Not tonight."

"Can you at least sing me a song?"

Nodding, I pull up the covers over her feet. She wiggles down until only her head is visible. Quietly I sing the first verse and chorus of "Dream a Little Dream". I'm not a great singer, but I don't have time to be self-conscious because Greer joins in, and her voice overpowers mine.

As soon as we're done, she yawns.

"Get some sleep." I give her a hug and a kiss.

When I get up, she signs what I assume is good night to Flynn.

He grins. "Night, germ."

She giggles.

I turn off the light as Flynn and I step out of the room and close the door behind us.

I stop with my back against the door and laugh quietly.

"We almost got caught."

"I don't want to throw the kid under the bus, but I don't think she brushed her teeth for two minutes." His mouth quirks up on one side.

His head dips, and he brushes his lips over mine again.

"Mom, can you leave the door open?" Greer yells from inside her room.

Flynn steps back with a quiet chuckle and I push her door open.

"Night," I say to her again.

Flynn and I go to the living room. He sits down on the couch, and I take a seat next to him. He drops one open palm to my thigh.

I am buzzing with adrenaline, giddy and light. God, how long has it been since I had a kiss that made me feel this way? Maybe never.

Flynn groans and then makes a tsk noise. "I know what you're thinking and I'm not a piece of meat."

A surprised laugh bubbles up in my chest and slips out. "I don't know what you're talking about. I was only thinking about laundry."

It's the first thing that came to mind and a complete lie. And judging by the cocky look on his face, he knows it too.

"I watched the game," I say, changing the topic before I admit that I want to climb into his lap and tear off all his clothes.

"Yeah?" he asks as the corners of his mouth lift.

I nod. "You pitched a good game."

He runs a hand through his hair. "I did okay. Still struggling to dial it in, but we got the job done today."

"I don't know what dialing it in means, but I'm confident you'll figure it out."

"I hope so. Otherwise, I might be a Mustang forever."

"That's a bad thing?" I feel defensive of my hometown

team, if for no other reason than I know it means so much to my grandfather.

"I didn't mean it like that. I am grateful that they took a chance on me and I'm really enjoying the team and coaches and the community that has stayed so loyal, but I want to play with the best of the best. It sucks but money matters in professional baseball teams. Everything from equipment to salaries."

"I guess I never thought of that."

"But if I can prove myself this season, then I'll have more options."

My stomach feels like someone dropped a cinder block in it. Obviously, I know that baseball players come and go from teams all the time, but Flynn just got here.

"You're only going to be here for one season," I say it more as a statement to myself than a question, but Flynn answers anyway.

"If things go well, maybe. There are a lot of talented pitchers out there." His brows knit together. "Is something wrong?"

"Sorry. I guess I just assumed you'd be here for a few years at least." I'm withdrawing into myself, which maybe isn't fair to him, but I can't help it.

"The season is long, and it just started," he says, smiling in a way that I can't seem to reciprocate.

"Still. It doesn't make a lot of sense to get involved if you're planning to leave."

"Hey. Don't do that." He wraps his arms around me. "Nothing has been decided for sure."

I rest my head against his chest and do my best to calm the anxiety coursing through me. But the truth is, I don't know if I can pretend like I don't know this has an expiration date.

He pulls back and aims one of his playful, charming smiles at me. "What do you say to a redo date? No roller skates or bad food."

"I liked skating with you," I tell him honestly.

"Same. How's Wednesday night? I know Greer has dance class with Sabrina and she could watch her after like last time."

"Can I think about it?" I ask.

His brown eyes flicker with some unnamed emotion. Disappointment maybe.

I decide to be honest. There's no reason to hide my feelings from him. It's obvious I like him, but I can't pretend I don't know he's planning on leaving. "I like you, but I'm not sure it's a good idea for me. It's not just me. I have to think about Greer. She already worships you. If we keep dating, she's going to get more attached."

He nods and a muscle in his cheek flexes. "I understand."

We fall quiet, staring at each other but neither knowing what to say.

"I guess I should go." He stands slowly and I follow him to the front door.

The mood has shifted. The thought that this could be over before it really started is gut-wrenching, but I need time to process.

"Text me later?" he asks, holding my hand and swinging it lightly.

"Sure."

"This sucks. I want to kiss you again, but…"

I step to him and lift onto my toes. If this is the last time we're going to hang out like this, then I want to have kissed him with every emotion buzzing in my body.

Flynn is quick to wrap his arms around me and pick me up. My hands go to his hair, and I pour every ounce of myself into the kiss. He's given me a gift, to feel this way again. Before him, I was happy not dating, or at least I thought I was.

He hums quietly as he explores my mouth and crushes me against him. I don't know how long it goes on, but when we finally break apart, my lips are swollen, and his hair is a mess.

He continues to hold me up. I scrape my nails over his scalp.

"Fuck, Olivia." His eyes flutter closed. "I don't want to be a gentleman right now."

I don't want him to be either.

He buries his head in the crook of my neck and places a soft kiss to my collarbone before whispering, "To be continued, I hope."

Once he sets me down, he opens the door and steps out. He looks back once, aiming that playful smirk at me. And then he's gone.

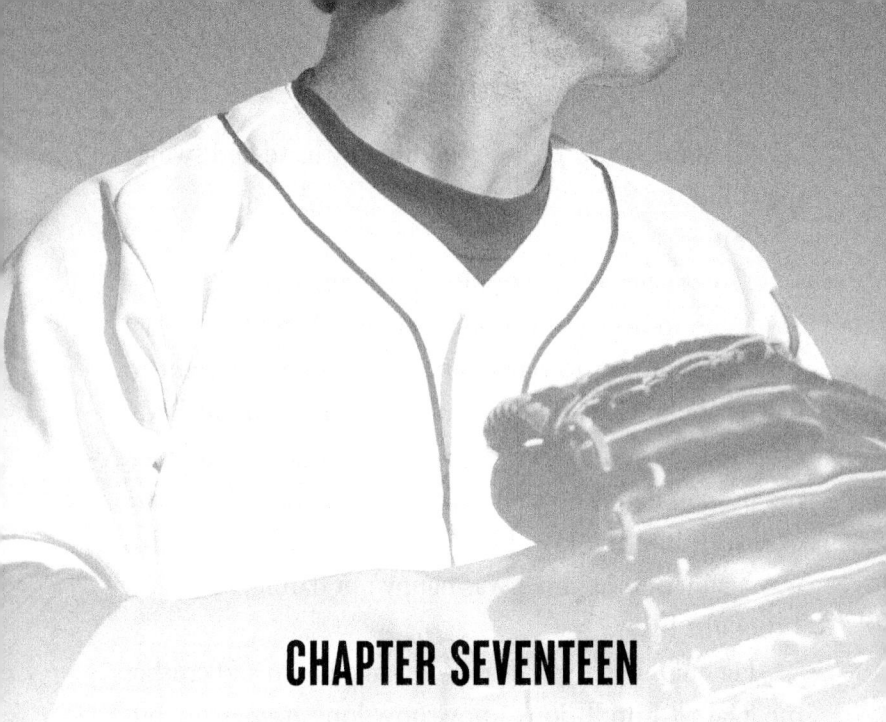

CHAPTER SEVENTEEN

Flynn

"To Baby Holland!" Brogan lifts his beer into the air.

"I'm going to be thirty and still be called *Baby* Holland," I say with a shake of my head, but a smile slips free anyway.

My brothers came to my game again this afternoon and the five of us are having a rare night out. I've missed them, but it's inevitable when we're together that we fall back into our old roles. Which means, I'm the little kid they all want to tease and poke at playfully.

Maybe I'm just sensitive to it after everything with baseball. My age and my experience always seem to come back to bite me. To be fair, we all do it to each other, so I can't really complain.

"Better than being the old man of the group," Hendrick says to me.

"That's true. Tell me, have you started drinking Ensure yet? Taking a multivitamin? How about anti-aging moisturizer?" If I'm going to take it, you better believe I'm going to dish it right back.

"And don't forget the sunscreen," Archer pipes up.

"Fuck all of you." Hendrick hides his grin behind his glass as he takes a long drink of his soda.

"Anybody want to throw some darts?" Archer asks as he stands.

"I'm in." Hendrick gets to his feet.

So does Brogan. "Me too."

The three of them head across the bar to the dart boards and billiards. Knox waits until they're gone to turn to me.

"Nice game today," he says.

"Thanks." We didn't win, but I threw better than I have in practice all week, so I'm not totally dissatisfied with my performance.

I check my phone, more out of habit than anything. And maybe a little hopefulness. I haven't heard from Olivia since last week. I'm doing my best to give her space, but it is not easy.

"I didn't see Dad today," Knox says as he takes another drink.

"He's still out of town."

"Still?" There's a challenge in Knox's voice any time the conversation revolves around our dad.

"It hasn't been that long." I let out a short laugh and shake my head. "I don't get you. You're pissed if he's hanging around and you're pissed if he's not."

"How I feel doesn't matter. How are you? I know you've gotten close to him, and I remember what it's like when he flakes out."

"I'm fine." I take a drink, not loving the line of questions and not understanding exactly why. "He took a trip with Terri and some friends. It's not a big deal."

"Okay," Knox says in a way that means he's dropping it…for now.

The back of my neck flushes with heat. I know our dad wasn't perfect, but he's different now. He's trying and that's good enough for me.

"I hear you're dating Sabrina's friend. What's her name? Olivia?"

My brows lift, but it doesn't take a lot of guesses to figure out where he heard that.

"Archer has a big mouth," I say under my breath.

"It was Brogan, actually." Knox smirks at me.

"We went on a date."

"And?"

"I'm not sure there's going to be another. She's worried about getting involved when I'm not going to be around that long."

"Because she has a kid and doesn't really date casually?"

"Jesus, Brogan," I grumble and shoot daggers at his

back across the bar. There's no privacy to be had with these guys.

"Partly, yeah. I also think she's just been burned in the past. Getting her to go out with me in the first place was not easy. I had to throw a no-hitter."

Knox erupts into deep laughter. "Wait, wait, wait. That was because of her?"

"She said she'd go out with me if I did."

He barks out another amused laugh. "I should have fucking known."

He reaches over and musses my hair. I shove at his shoulder in response.

Despite him treating me like I'm still a kid, I'm glad to see the more easygoing version of my brother has returned. He's had a chip on his shoulder about our dad for years. And I get it. Knox took the brunt of the parenting when Dad left. He quit high school, got a job so he could pay the bills, and put his life on hold. I'll always be grateful for that. Who the fuck knows where I would have ended up without him.

But since I graduated high school and he's been able to regain some of his independence, our relationship has shifted. He doesn't have to be my parent and can just be my brother.

"A kid is a big responsibility," Knox says, voice returning to that serious, paternal tone.

"Definitely. You should see this kid though. So fucking cute and sass for days. Reminds me a little of Avery."

"Oh yeah?" That peaks Knox's interest. He loves few

things more than his wife, Avery. Scratch that, I'm not sure he loves anything more. I might have a slight edge but only because I'd never make him choose. Avery is cool as hell. She's an Olympic gymnast and gives Knox so much sass it's a fucking blast to watch them together.

"Yeah." I nod. "And Olivia's a good mom. It has me remembering back to little things Mom would do. Remember how she would put music on in the kitchen while she was cooking and any time someone would gripe or complain about whatever she was listening to, she'd turn the volume up another notch?"

Knox smiles. "Yeah. On an old radio that had to have been from the eighties. It was all staticky, and the songs would go in and out."

"I don't remember that," I say. "I thought she had that iPod that sat in the dock with speakers."

"No, she had this white cassette player with a big antenna." He gets a faraway look on his face as if he's picturing it. "Hendrick bought her that for Christmas one year after the radio finally died."

I nod like I remember, but I don't. It guts me to admit that I don't remember a lot about her, and the things I do, I often think are just stories my brothers have told me so often my brain has convinced me that it's my memory.

"Anyway, back to Olivia. I'm sure she's awesome but dating a single mom is a complication you don't want. Not now when you're just getting started. Be young and stupid and selfish."

I hear him, but Olivia isn't just a single mom. She's

this absolutely fire chick who is stunning and smart and keeps me on my toes. I like who I am with her. And I like that she's such a good mom, too. Greer is lucky and so am I for getting to hang with them.

"You did it and you were still young and stupid. And look where you are now. Beautiful wife, badass career…" I trail off. "What am I missing?"

"You forgot about my good looks," he chirps.

"Obviously your good looks." I wave a hand toward his face. "And humility."

He chuckles softly. "It was different for me. You were my brother. It wasn't a choice."

"It was a choice," I insist. "If it weren't a choice to leave family, then dad wouldn't have left us in the first place."

"All I'm saying is I don't want to see you make things harder for yourself. Right now, you have no one to answer to but yourself and that's a beautiful thing."

I fall quiet, mulling over his words. After a moment, I shake my head.

"I hear what you're saying, but I don't see it. Maybe because I was that kid who had other people filling the role of parent, but I can't picture Greer as an obligation. She's a freaking blast. I'd be lucky to spend more time with her and Olivia."

Knox studies me carefully, then his lips part with a smile. "You have it bad, little bro."

I huff a laugh. He's not wrong there.

He tips his glass to me. "I'm happy if you're happy."

Within the next hour, my brothers start losing interest

in brotherly bonding time. Archer says he needs to help Sabrina with something at the studio and takes off; Brogan goes with him while practically foaming at the mouth to see London; Hendrick starts talking about heading back to Jane and the bar, and Knox thinks he's being sly, but I see him texting Avery nonstop.

"Thank you, guys, for coming today," I say when Hendrick pulls up in front of my apartment to drop me off.

"We'll be back," Knox promises as he gets out of the vehicle and hugs me. "First regular season game. I expect a no-hitter now that I know you're holding them back for bets."

"What now?" Hendrick asks as he comes around to hug me next.

"I'll tell you about it later," Knox says to him.

"Love you guys." As Hendrick pulls back, I put my hand on the top of my head and move it out to show him I'm taller now. He hates it, and it makes me laugh every single time.

When they're gone, I head into my apartment. I pick up Dick and carry the potted plant around with me as I heat up some leftover pizza and then sit in front of the TV.

I have some texts from friends that are going out tonight, and Freddie is having a few people over later, but the only thing I really want to do is see Olivia.

I lie back, sinking into the couch, and place Dick on my chest. "What do we do now?"

CHAPTER EIGHTEEN

Olivia

ABRINA SITS ON THE BALCONY ACROSS FROM ME AS I repot a Monstera plant. I can see Greer through the sliding glass door in the living room. She has the tablet propped up in front of the TV as she video chats with her dad. She's currently showing him all the new sign language she's learned, which makes me smile.

"Have you heard from him at all?" Sabrina asks, pulling my attention away from my daughter.

I spent the past hour telling my best friend everything that happened with Flynn. *Everything.* From Flynn showing up with bags of food and medicine the night Greer got sick, to that amazing first kiss, followed by an even better second kiss, how I've spent the past week dreaming of said kisses, and finally him planning to leave at the end of the season.

"No, and I hate that I'm so disappointed."

"Then reach out to him."

"I can't." I shake my head as I add a little soil to the pot and then smush it down with my fingers.

"Sure you can. Here, let me help." She clears her throat and then does a high-pitched voice that I'm pretty sure is supposed to be me. "Hey, Flynn. How are you? I've been, like, thinking about you for days. I can't focus. Food has lost all flavor, and I find myself staring out the window daydreaming of your body. Can you please come over and kiss the crap out of me? Naked."

My face flushes. I reach into the soil bag and pinch some between my thumb and pointer finger, then fling it at Sabrina.

Her jaw drops. "How dare you."

"Serves you right. That was a terrible impression of me. And I'm eating just fine. I finished off two cartons of ice cream in the past few days."

"You're sort of proving my point for me."

"Which is?"

"You want to date him or at least kiss him some more."

"I mean, can you blame me? It was the best kiss of my life. Better than sex."

Her brows rise. "Better than sex?"

I suddenly realize how pathetic that sounds. "Maybe it's just been so long I don't remember."

"You should look into that." She grins. "With Flynn."

I give her my best Mom-stare and she laughs.

"I'm serious. You two obviously have chemistry and you could use some no-strings fun."

"What, like friends with benefits?" I scrunch up my face. "I tried that once. It wasn't for me. I was always second-guessing when to text or call. It was the most stressful relationship of my life."

"Yeah, I'm not great at it either." She thinks for a moment. "And dating him knowing it might have an expiration is definitely out?"

"What would be the point?"

"Uh…kissing. Kissing is the point."

"It was a really, really good kiss," I admit again. It's just my luck that the one guy that's made me want to date again is leaving. My life is here in Lake City. My family and friends, the bookstore, Greer's school and activities. It isn't like I never thought about living somewhere else when I was younger, but those were dreams of a carefree girl who didn't really know what she wanted and liked the idea of it more than the reality.

I would miss seeing my family every day, and what would come of the bookstore? For that matter, where would I work? I can't imagine working anywhere else.

Later when Greer's in bed, I shower and get into my pajamas. Usually, I stay up watching TV or scrolling on my phone, but all I want to do is climb into bed and fall asleep. My determination to forget about Flynn has resulted in a lot of very tiring days.

I turn off the light and then stare up at the ceiling. My mind spins. Sabrina's words keep replaying in my mind. Could I keep seeing Flynn knowing he's going to leave? Would we be dating? Hooking up? Friends with benefits? Cringe.

I glance over at my phone on the charger. I know if I pick it up, I'm going to be awake for another two hours.

"You know what?" I ask myself out loud. "I've got this."

I open the drawer on my nightstand and pull out my vibrator. You wouldn't believe how difficult it is to find time even for self-love when there's a six-year-old living in the room next door. I flip it on and it sputters and dies. I try again with the same result.

Of course, the battery would be dead. Okay, universe, I hear you. I toss it back into the drawer and grab my phone instead.

Fuck it.

ME

Free tomorrow night?

His reply is immediate.

FLYNN

Yes.

ME

Pick us up at seven.

At exactly seven o'clock, Flynn knocks at my apartment door.

"Hi. Come in." Nervous energy courses through me as I open the door and step back to let him in. My heart flutters at the sight of him. He's in jeans and a navy T-shirt that makes his brown hair look a tinge redder than normal.

"You look great," he says. I'm dressed more casually, in leggings and a T-shirt, than any other time we've hung out.

"Thank you."

Greer comes running to the door and hugs Flynn around the legs.

"We're going cactus jumping!" she shouts.

"Cactus jumping?" Flynn asks her, then glances at me.

I chuckle. "It's a trampoline park, The Jumping Cactus."

One side of his mouth pulls into a smile. "A trampoline park, huh? That sounds awesome."

"It's Ben's birthday."

"Who's Ben?" he asks her.

"A kid in my class. He has two dads."

Flynn's smile lifts higher. "Is that right?"

She nods excitedly.

"Grab your grip socks and Ben's present," I tell Greer, and she runs back to her room.

"Her kindergarten class is doing family trees," I explain her fascination with Ben's parents. She's just now figuring out what's "normal" among her classmates and comparing her situation. "I think she's jealous he has two when she barely sees her dad."

"I remember feeling like that," he says.

"Really?"

"Oh yeah. I dreaded all those school events, Donuts with Dad and Muffins with Mom." He visibly shudders. "Even sporting events were awkward sometimes. People who didn't know my situation assumed my mom and dad were both alive and in attendance. I hated correcting them, but the strained apologies when I finally had to set them straight were worse."

"I'm sorry." I was probably one of those kids who assumed everyone was like me, and before I had Greer, I never thought about how other kids who didn't have a parent to come along must have felt. "If it makes you feel better, they've rebranded. It's Donuts with Grown-Ups now."

A real smile spreads across his face. "Nice."

"It doesn't stop her from realizing other people see their dad more than she does, but it's something."

"She'll be okay." He tips his head toward Greer's room.

"Thanks for that." It's an ever-present fear of mine.

That she'll feel less-than or not get the love and attention she needs.

But that's not something I want to dwell on tonight. Greer comes out with her socks in one hand and Ben's present in the other.

"You ready for this?" I ask them as I grab my purse and phone.

"Are you kidding? I've been dying to go cactus jumping." His eyes twinkle with amusement.

We take my SUV to the trampoline park. Greer chatters happily the entire ride and Flynn is a good sport, talking with her and answering her every question.

Once we arrive, she spots Ben and other classmates already jumping and takes off to join them in the trampoline area. I lead Flynn toward the party room to drop off Ben's present and say hi to his dads, who are setting up the room with balloons and cute dump truck themed plates and party favors.

Flynn is gracious, shaking their hands and introducing himself. Especially when one of them, Blake, gives Flynn that side-eye, you-look-familiar look.

"Were you at Donuts with Grown-Ups?" he asks Flynn.

If they knew he was a professional baseball player, they'd be losing their minds right now. It makes me feel like I'm in on an inside joke with Flynn.

I fight a smile as Flynn shakes his head. "No, sadly I missed that."

"Well, good to meet you," Blake says.

There are a few other parents arriving with their kids. Flynn greets them all like it's the most natural thing. He has that easy, likeable way about him that makes me feel less anxious. I'm one of the youngest parents, if not the actual youngest, and sometimes I feel out of place among them. Especially the moms. They all seem so accomplished and put together.

As we mingle with the adults, Flynn reaches over and takes my hand. It's funny that he's doing most of the talking when I'm the one that's been interacting with them since the start of the school year, but I love that I can just be present without feeling like I need to be on.

When the conversations start to die off, we head back out to check on Greer. We flash our wristbands to the teenager at the gate and he lets us into the jumping area.

"This is awesome," Flynn says.

"You brought me roller skating, so this seemed right up your alley."

"If I'd known this was here, I might have brought you here instead."

"Next time," I say.

"Why not now?" He bends down to take off his shoes and then walks over to a small trampoline that's currently kid-free.

I watch him as his face lights up more with each bounce. He is such a big kid. I like that about him.

"Come on." He waves me over with both hands.

I glance over where the other parents are sitting with

no intention of participating. Some have their cell phones out, one even brought their laptop.

While I'm deciding, Greer and three of her classmates have spotted Flynn and run over to join him. My daughter's face is full of the same carefree excitement as my date's. She bounces in front of him, holding on to his hands. He makes her go higher by jumping opposite of her and she is living for it.

I kick off my shoes and join them. We go from one area of the park to the next. There are small trampolines and bigger ones, a zipline, dodgeball, and basketball hoops. The kids adore Flynn. I think it's a combination of his height and how playful he is with them. He challenges each one in the jousting area over a foam pit. By the time Ben's dads call the kids over for cake and ice cream, I'm sweaty and my face hurts from smiling so much.

Flynn and I follow slowly, stopping at a bench inside the park to put our shoes back on.

"I think you're the hit of the party," I tell him and mean it.

"This was a blast. I'm so glad you invited me."

We haven't talked about the elephant in the room, him eventually leaving town and my hesitancy to get involved, but tonight feels like we've taken a step past it.

"I missed you."

"Same." He bumps his shoulder against mine and his gaze drops to my mouth.

Butterflies swoop low in my stomach as he leans down and kisses me. It's not the all-consuming, toe-curling, make-out session style of our first two kisses, but it leaves me lightheaded all the same.

"I'm not sure how good I'm going to be at this," I confess.

"This?"

"Dating and not thinking about the future."

"Planning ahead is always a gamble. Nothing goes the way we think it will or want it to."

"That's true, I guess."

"It's not even a given that I'll leave for another team. I might be with the Mustangs for the rest of my career."

I know he doesn't believe that or if he does, then it's because he's feeling like he's far away from his goals.

"Yes, it is." I nod. "You are going to do amazing things and every team in the league is going to want you. But for now…"

Instead of finishing that sentence, I lean over and press my lips to his.

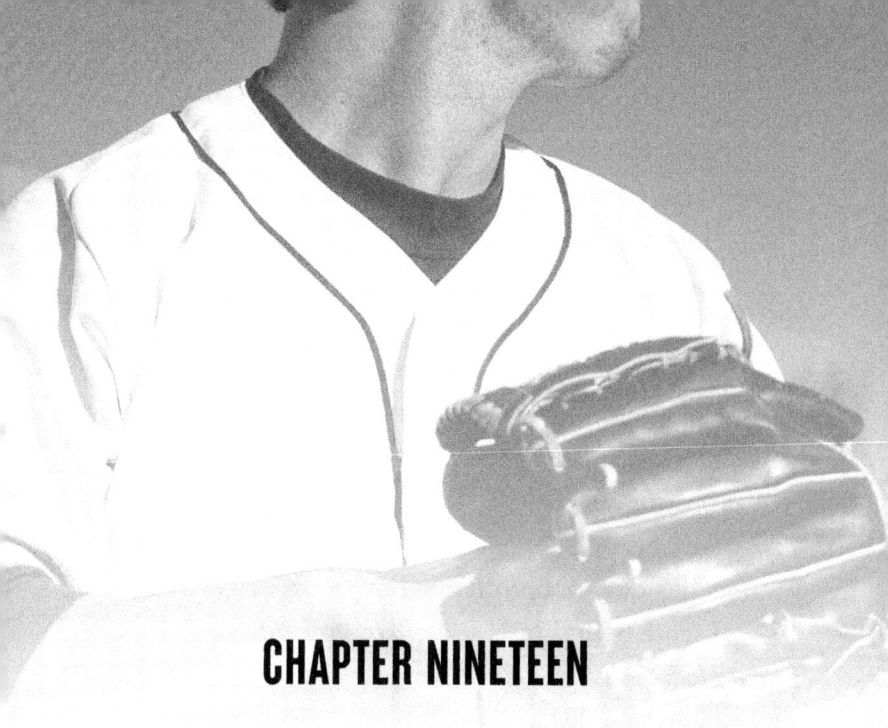

CHAPTER NINETEEN

Flynn

"**T**HOSE MOMS WERE ABSOLUTELY CHECKING YOU out," Olivia says, giving me that haughty, one-brow cocked smirk that dares me to disagree with her.

"Did you claw their eyes out?" Sabrina asks her.

We're out with Archer and his fiancée for coffee while Greer is across the street at the dance studio taking a tap class.

My arm rests along the back of Olivia's chair and my fingers trail up and down her shoulder. It's been hard to find time to go out between my schedule and hers, so when she said she had an hour while Greer was at tap class, I jumped at the opportunity to hang out.

"No." She shakes her head and then glances over at me. "He's pretty. I don't blame them."

"Pretty?" Archer asks. "Did she say Flynn was pretty?"

"Sorry." Olivia flushes as she angles herself so Archer can better read her lips.

"He heard you. He's just being a dick." I squeeze her for reassurance. It can be tricky in group conversations with Archer if everyone isn't signing, but in this case, he's just busting my balls.

Archer smiles at her. "Gotta give my little bro a hard time. Besides, we both know I'm prettier, right?"

I scoff, then sign as I say, *"I'm obviously the best-looking Holland. No contest."*

Sabrina rolls her eyes at us and Olivia relaxes.

I lean over to her and whisper, "I'm definitely prettier, right?"

She laughs softly and lets her stare roam over my face. "Let's just say those school moms would not have gotten off so easily if they'd done more than look."

"Ooooh." Pleasure zips through me. Is it fucked up that I'd love to see her throw down for me? Probably, but damn it's a good image. "I love a woman that fights for me."

She shakes her head at me. "You're hopeless."

"Hopelessly into you."

"Hopelessly cheesy."

"Hopelessly turned on. What do you say we ditch these two and go make out in my truck?"

She laughs louder, then smacks me playfully.

"I wasn't really kidding."

"This is the only time I have to see you and Sabrina."

"Fine. Fine." I sit back in my chair but drop the hand that was around her shoulders to her thigh.

I'm so fucking into this girl. I've never been so all in so quickly. I'm a walking hard-on, but it isn't only about wanting to sleep with her. I'm turned on, but I want to tease and flirt and be cheesy almost as badly as I want to get her naked.

Maybe it's because I have no idea when that might happen. We're already sneaking small moments to be together, most of which include Greer, so sex hasn't really been an option. Well, unless she decides to take me up on my offer to have a quickie in my truck.

At five 'til the top of the hour, Sabrina stands. "I need to get back to the studio to get ready for my next class. I'm teaching an adult ballet class."

"Sounds fun," Olivia says.

"You should come next time. Greer can hang in the lobby."

"What I meant by sounds fun is that sounds fun for someone who knows ballet. I would be so bad at it. And that would not be fun."

"Give me three classes and I'll change your mind," Sabrina says as she walks off.

Archer pushes back and stands to go with her. "Nice to see you, Olivia."

Then he flips me off.

I bark out a laugh and sign to him, *Love you too, asshole.*

He grins as he follows Sabrina out of the coffee shop. I turn to Olivia, ecstatic to finally have her to myself, even if it's only for five minutes.

"Thanks for coming," she says, wrapping both hands around her coffee cup.

"Are you kidding? I was thrilled to come hang. When are you free again?"

"I'm not sure. I work at the club tonight and tomorrow. Maybe Monday night. I'll have Greer."

"I love hanging with Greer. Maybe we can take her skating."

She smiles. "I should get back before her class is done. What time is your barbecue with the team?"

"I think some of the guys are already there."

"Sounds fun."

"Eh..."

"No?"

"They're not my biggest fans."

"How come?" The surprised look on her face, like how dare anyone dislike me, is cute.

"They've had a lot of guys come and go. Every team deals with it, but I think they've felt it more than most."

"Yeah. That makes sense. Loyalty is big here, even for the fans."

"I just want to play great baseball."

She laughs softly.

We get up and toss our trash then head outside. We've

had a stint of warm days this week, but the sun has set, giving the night air a chill.

"Thanks for the coffee." She starts to leave me, but I reach out and take her hand.

She grins as she turns to face me. I grab her other hand and swing them between us.

"If Greer sees you, she's going to be mad at me for hanging out with you without her."

That makes my grin inch higher.

"Fine," I say with a sigh. I step to her and drop a kiss to her lips then step back with the intent to let her go.

But I can't. I drop one hand and pull out my phone.

"I'm going to be late," she says, smiling and inching backward.

I hold my phone up in front of my face.

"Are you taking a picture of me?" she asks.

"No, but that's a good idea." When I'm done with my original task, I snap a photo of her too.

Her phone pings, and she reaches for it with a questioning glance.

"What is this?" she asks, then reads my text out loud, "Coffee should have cream and sugar."

"It should," I say. She ordered black coffee today and I still can't believe anyone willingly drinks it without any cream or sugar.

"And you texted me that because?"

"I was going to write you a note, but my handwriting sucks."

Her gaze narrows.

"Like your grandfather does. Every day at…" I look at the time, "6:59 I'm going to text you my love letter."

"You can't steal my grandpa's sweet gesture!"

"It's so good though." I tug her back to me by our joined hands.

I capture her laughter as I slant my mouth over hers. An hour wasn't enough. I wish I could go back to her place, but JT is having the team over to watch hockey, and I feel like I should take every opportunity I get to know the guys, even if most of them are still not acting that warm toward me.

She groans and pulls away. "I have to go."

"All right. All right." I wrap my arms around her and give her one last hug. "P.S. Your butt looks really good in leggings."

She's wearing them again tonight and goddamn.

"I do love a postscript."

"Good to know." I bury my head in the crook of her neck. It feels physically impossible to let her go. I breathe her in and then scrape my teeth over her collarbone.

"P.S.S. It didn't matter if the school moms were checking me out or not. Everyone there knew I only had eyes for you."

Her cheekbones take on a pinkish tint as she smiles shyly. "I gotta go, Hotshot."

"Okay." This time I finally let her go.

She takes two steps backward smiling at me and then turns and crosses the street to the studio.

The following day, I'm leaving the stadium after a long practice when my dad calls to say he's in town. I head straight to the bar to meet him.

He stands and smiles as I approach him.

"You look good," he says, embracing me. "Did you grow another inch?"

"I don't think so," I say, taking a seat on a barstool next to his. "I think your memory is failing you, Pops."

Grinning, he waves over the bartender for another beer, and I order a Coke.

"When did you get back?" I ask him once we both have drinks in front of us.

He gives his head a shake as he gets a pensive expression on his face. "I'm not sure. Two or three weeks ago."

"Weeks?" That catches me by surprise.

"Yeah. The last leg of our trip didn't pan out. The weather was crap, and my back can't handle riding for those long stretches anymore."

"Really? You haven't called or stopped by. What have you been up to?" I ask. I assumed he was still gone since I hadn't heard from him.

"Oh, you know, working on the bike, doing a couple odds and ends jobs when I get them, and Terri keeps me busy with her honey-do list. She's decided to paint the entire house in daffodil."

My brows rise.

"It's a fancy paint color way of saying yellow. I'm living inside a banana." He chuckles softly.

I try to mimic the sound, but I'm still caught on the fact that he's been back in town, and I haven't heard from him until now.

"I wish you'd have called. I thought you were still on the road or I would have checked in sooner."

"Eh. I knew you were busy with the team. I saw the highlights from your no-hitter. That was some game."

"Thanks." I do my best to shake off any weird lingering emotions. "How was the trip? Did you make it to Yellowstone?"

For the next half hour or so he tells me about the places they rode through, the ones they stopped in, and his favorites and least favorites. By the time I've finished my soda, and we decided to get dinner, I've successfully managed to put any hurt feelings aside.

I tell him about the Mustangs and how I'm still trying to find consistency from game to game and inning to inning.

"You'll get there," he reassures me. "Consistency is just putting in reps. You have the talent and work ethic. It's just a matter of time."

"Patience is not my strong suit."

His mouth quirks up on one side in a smile that reminds me of Knox. They're the most alike, from their love of motorcycles and really anything with an engine to their facial expressions. Knox would hate me saying it, but it's true. But all of Dad's faults as a parent, Knox has gone the other way. He's loyal, dependable, and up-front about everything. There is no guessing how Knox feels at any given moment whereas, Dad is an enigma sometimes and his dependability is questionable.

These are things I already knew and accepted, or thought I had.

"I can get you tickets any time. Just say the word."

"I appreciate that," he says, but it isn't lost on me that he doesn't automatically jump at the opportunity to take me up on it. Of course we're still in spring training. A lot of fans don't really get invested until we're playing regular season games.

We spend the rest of dinner talking about random shit. He asks about my brothers, and I give him the rundown. It's a tight rope to walk in safeguarding their privacy and not feeling like I'm giving Dad information that they might not want him to know. I imagine it's different in other families, but my brothers have chosen not to have a relationship with our dad, and I try my best to respect that.

"Have you talked to Archer?" I ask him. He's recently been communicating with him more, but I'm guessing if I haven't heard from Dad neither has Archer.

"No." Dad shakes his head and drops his gaze to his food. "I figured he's enjoying the off-season."

My brows pinch together. "He'd still want to hear from you."

It's a guess but since that's how I felt it seems like a safe bet.

"Yeah. Maybe." He nods his head and pushes his plate away from him.

We only stay a few minutes longer. Outside of the bar, we stop along the sidewalk, and I step forward to hug him.

"It sounds like you're going to be sticking around for a bit. Do you want to do something for your 60th birthday?"

He groans. "Fuck no. I don't need a reminder that I'm getting old."

I laugh lightly as he grimaces. "Okay, a birthday celebration where we won't mention the number. It might be a good way to get everyone together."

And by everyone, I mean my brothers. It's happened a few times by accident over the last couple years, my brothers sharing the same space as my dad. They're all good at showing up for me, which is another thing they have in common, even if they're too stubborn to realize it.

Dad mulls that over, clicks his tongue, and then nods. "Okay, sure. If you think you can get them to come."

It's still a few months away, which is good because I might need that long to convince them.

He doesn't quite meet my gaze. I know from previous conversations that he carries a lot of guilt and regrets from the past. His attempts at reconnecting with Knox and Hendrick have been met with a lot of resistance. So much that dad hasn't made any new attempts in a while.

As I've built a relationship with him, it's ignited a

dream in me to have all of us together again. I love my brothers, and I love my dad. I know it'll never be perfect, but it seems like we'd all be happier if we could figure out how to let go of the past and start fresh.

"Leave it to me," I say.

"All right, Son." He places a hand on my shoulder and squeezes. "If you make it happen, I'll be there."

CHAPTER TWENTY

Olivia

THE FIRST REGULAR SEASON GAME IS ON A SATURDAY afternoon at Fletcher stadium. Late March in Arizona is gorgeous. The sun is out, there isn't a cloud in the sky, but it isn't unbearable to be outside like it will be by June.

"You're so jittery," Ruby comments as the pregame festivities are taking place.

Flynn is standing in the dugout, staring out at the field and looking focused and so damn sexy.

"I had too much coffee this morning."

"Is that the problem?" she asks with a smirk.

"Go, Hotshot!" Greer yells as Flynn walks out onto the field behind the rest of the team.

Ruby chuckles and then joins in clapping and cheering with my daughter.

The truth is I am a nervous mess. I don't even know why because when I talked to Flynn this morning, he was calm and collected. I guess it's knowing how much it means to him. I might not want him to leave Lake City, but I still want him to succeed.

We've only been hanging out a short time, but I can see how hard he works. Long days of practice, extra pitching coaching, workouts, therapy, and no doubt there are even more things that I'm not aware of him doing.

And somehow, he still makes time to text me or swing by for a few minutes on his way home or take me and Greer out to dinner or ice cream. We haven't been out on another date, just the two of us, but I look forward to the little moments. Holding hands, flirty texts, Greer making us laugh, and stealing kisses when she isn't looking.

"Are his brothers here today?" Ruby asks as the cheers and applause die off and the first batter for the opposing team steps up to the plate.

"Yeah. They're sitting behind home plate."

"Why doesn't your boyfriend get us fancy seats?"

A small laugh slips from my lips. "He isn't my boyfriend."

"Oh, I see we're still in denial. Got it." She tosses a handful of popcorn in her mouth and turns her gaze to the field.

"We've only been on one date."

"So?"

"We haven't spent enough time together yet to be that serious. We're still hanging out and getting to know each other."

"No."

"What do you mean, no?" Another laugh bubbles up in my chest.

"You are not the kind of person who dates casually. You're one and done or all in."

I shift uncomfortably in my seat. She isn't wrong. Before Flynn and before I decided dating was awful and I didn't want to do it anymore, I went on a lot of first dates. It didn't take me long to tell if we had chemistry or had things in common. So many of the guys I went out with I could tell within minutes that they either weren't for me, or they had a life that would never match mine. I don't hold any judgment for my friends or peers who spend every night going out and want to pick up at a moment's notice and travel the world, but it makes their lives the opposite of my very structured, stable one.

I work hard to give Greer a life that makes her feel safe and loved, and right now that means less spontaneous adventures and more routine.

One of the things I like about Flynn is he makes everyday activities feel fun and original. He's steadfast in working toward his goals and maintaining relationships with his family and making time for me, but he reminds me that everything else is just not that serious. It's why Greer likes him so much too. He plays with her and listens to what she has to say. Nothing is silly or childish.

He'll watch cartoons or play arcade games or play trampoline dodge ball. He's a good sport in all the ways he's bent his life to be a part of mine.

Grandpa joins us as Flynn is striking out the second batter. Gigi is working the store today and, honestly, I think she's grateful to have an excuse to sit this one out. She has sat through a lot of baseball games during their forty plus years together, so I think that's fair.

"No facility emergencies today?" I ask, smiling at him and then glancing back at Flynn. He's going through his whole routine, kicking the dirt, rolling the ball in his hand, staring down the batter and shaking off signs from JT.

"If there are, they'll have to wait until after the game." Grandpa leans back in his seat and adjusts the old Mustangs hat on his head. He's been wearing the same one for as long as I can remember. The team made it to the division playoffs that year. I remember Ruby bought him a new hat one year because his was looking old and worn. He thanked her, then hung it up on a hook in his and Gigi's mudroom, where it still hangs today.

No one has bought him a new one since, and eventually I realized that the hat was a symbol for him. The Mustangs didn't win that year, but it was one of those years that gave my grandpa, and so many other hardcore fans, hope that we might get back there again.

"Yeah, right," Ruby says from the other side of me. We both know he wouldn't be able to enjoy the game if he thought something needed his attention. He takes such pride in the stadium. It isn't as big or fancy as others, but it's clean and well-maintained.

We watch the first inning without talking much. It's easy to get wrapped up in watching Flynn, or at least it is for me.

When the Mustangs get the third out and Flynn starts for the dugout, I let out a breath. I'm clapping and staring hard at him for any sign of how he's feeling when Grandpa nudges me.

"Your grandmother said Flynn stopped by the bookstore this week."

I'd been waiting for someone to spill my secret.

My face flushes. "Yeah, he did. He's reading through Ruby's entire backlist."

Grandpa grins. "Oh yeah? I didn't picture him as a romance reader."

"I have a small, but loyal male fanbase," Ruby says.

His smile smooths out into a more solemn expression. "Is it serious? Should I give him the talk?"

"Oh my gosh. No." Just the thought makes my face flame hotter. "We've only hung out a few times."

My traitorous sister speaks up again. "He texts her every day, little notes like what you do for Gigi."

"He saw the wall in the office," I add.

"The kid is stealing my moves." Grandpa shakes his head, but his smile brightens. "You like him?"

"Yeah. He's great." I'm sweating in my seat. I swear I feel like a teenager whose parents found out she had a crush. "And as you can see, he's already won over Greer."

She's wearing a shirt that he gave her with his name and number on the back.

"Hotshot took us to get pizza last night. He ate half the pizza *by himself.*" Greer says the last part with complete awe in her voice.

"Hotshot, huh?"

Greer nods rapidly. "I made him a bracelet."

She holds up a pink beaded bracelet. I helped her spell out his name and she used an I and B for his number, eighteen.

"That's real nice," he tells her, then turns his attention back to me. "You know, about a month ago before he threw that no-hitter, he told me he needed to impress a girl that was in the crowd watching."

I blush. "He did?"

He nods. "If I had known that girl was you, I would have messed with him a bit."

"Does he know?" I ask him.

"That you're my granddaughter?" He shakes his head. "Not unless you've told him."

"No. I wanted to tell you first."

It isn't that I was worried Grandpa wouldn't like me dating a baseball player, but I did think there was a possibility he might have an opinion on Flynn. And I guess I didn't want anyone else's opinion to change mine.

"You don't owe me any explanations. Your dating life is your own. And Flynn seems like a good kid."

My stomach dips. "He is."

"Then I'm glad, sweetheart. You deserve to be happy."

"I was already happy. I have the best family and friends ever."

"Then you deserve to have someone to share that with."

I lean my head over onto his shoulder and breathe in his familiar spicy aftershave and minty gum. "I'm so lucky to have you as my grandpa."

After the game, Grandpa takes me and Greer down to the field. Flynn spots us and a surprised smile stretches out on his face as he moves our way.

"Congrats on the game," I say, stepping forward and hugging him. He's warm and a little sweaty, but I feel a rush of pride when he wraps his arms around me.

"What are you doing down here?" he asks. "Never mind. However you got here, I'm not asking questions."

Greer squeezes in between us, and Flynn reaches down and scoops her up. My stomach flutters as he grins at her.

"What'd you think?" he asks her.

She thinks for a moment, bringing her pointer finger to her chin. "Nice game. Slow start but you really pulled it together by the fourth inning."

Flynn lets his head fall back and barks out a laugh.

"I made you a bracelet." She holds it out to him.

"No way. For me?"

She nods with a proud smile on her face.

Flynn takes the bracelet and slides it onto his left wrist, then holds it out for inspection. "I love it. Thank you."

He sets Greer down, still smiling at us, then his gaze moves to my grandpa.

"Did you meet Earl?" he asks me, then says in a loud whisper, "He's my favorite staff member at the Mustangs."

"I did."

Grandpa and I share a knowing look.

"He's my favorite staff member as well," I say. "And my grandfather."

Flynn's mouth hangs open as he looks from me to Grandpa and back. "Seriously?"

"Yeah. I've been meaning to tell you."

His easy smile returns. "I guess it makes sense why he's my favorite now."

"I'm not quite as pretty as my granddaughter, but I'll take credit for all the rest." He winks at me.

"Don't be so hard on yourself, Earl," Flynn says. "You've still got it."

Grandpa chuckles. "I better get to work."

I step forward and hug him. "Thank you."

"See you later, sweetheart." He hesitates and then glances at Greer. "Do you want to help me this afternoon?"

"Really?" Her eyes get big. She loves going on "adventures" around the stadium.

He nods and clicks his tongue. "Maybe we should make a whole night of it."

"Like a sleepover?" she asks and immediately looks to me.

I know what he's doing, trying to give me time alone with Flynn. I'm torn between being excited at the prospect and then feeling guilty about it.

"Please, Mom?" Greer's voice is all excitement.

"Are you sure?" I ask her. "I can wait while you help Grandpa."

"I want to have a sleepover with Grandpa and Gigi!"

I meet Grandpa's expression to double-check it's okay. He gives me a reassuring smile and nod.

"Okay," I relent.

"Yes!" She bounces toward Grandpa and takes his hand.

"Give me a hug first though." I squat down and she comes back to let me hug her. "Be good. Have fun. If you change your mind, tell Grandpa and I'll come get you."

I give her a kiss and then she runs back to him.

"You kids have fun," Grandpa says to us.

"Bye, Hotshot!" Greer waves at Flynn.

Once they're gone, I turn back to Flynn. "Free tonight?"

CHAPTER TWENTY-ONE

Flynn

"**T**HIS IS IT," I SAY AS I STEP INTO MY APARTMENT. Olivia follows behind me. I flip on a light in the kitchen and drop my keys onto the island.

"It's nice. When did you move in?" She bypasses the kitchen and walks into the living room, turning slowly to take in the main space. The kitchen, dining room, and living area are all one big open space. Although, I don't have a table or chairs, so the dining area is empty. In the living room there's a fireplace that I use quite often. Plus, I have a TV, couch, and coffee table, only the essentials. I also bought a couple barstools for the kitchen island.

"January." I grin sheepishly. "I hate picking out stuff and I'm not here that often."

She laughs softly and picks up the cactus she gave me off the coffee table. "You still have it."

"That's Dick." I cross over to her and take the plant from her. "I'm trying not to kill him and he's attempting not to take it personally when I forget to water him."

"You named him?" Her blue eyes spark with amusement.

"Yeah, I talk to him sometimes." I set Dick down on the coffee table and then wrap my arms around her. "It's not as homey as your place, but for now it's fine."

"You just need a few more plants and then it's basically my place only bigger and fancier." She rests both palms against my chest as she grins up at me. "And a few dozen princess costumes strewn about."

The image of Greer today in my shirt with a tiara on top of her head flashes through my mind. That kid is a riot.

"You haven't seen my closet yet."

She giggles and I dip my head and cover her mouth with mine. I'm having to hold myself back from mauling her. Weeks of hanging out but rarely being alone has me wanting to immediately capitalize on the moment. But I sense Olivia needs to take this slower. Confirmed when she pulls back, cheeks flushed, and a shy smile is splashed across her face. "It's been a long time since I was at a guy's apartment. I feel a little out of my depth."

"I just introduced you to my plant, Dick. I think you can safely relax." I step back, running my hands down her shoulders to her hands. "Are you hungry?"

"I could eat."

Olivia sits on one of the stools, watching me as I move around the kitchen. She hasn't stopped smiling since I told her I was going to cook instead of order takeout.

"I haven't had pancakes for dinner in so long," she says, propping her elbows on the countertop and leaning forward.

"It's one of five things I can make and the only thing I have all the ingredients for," I admit. I stop what I'm doing and lean over the counter to kiss her again.

"We could have gone out," she says when I pull back.

"No way. I finally got you all to myself."

Her smile grows wider. "What are the other four?"

"Scrambled eggs, omelets—"

"Are those different?" she asks with a laugh.

"For the sake of my pride, let's say yes."

She laughs again. The sound makes my chest tighten and then release. I can't remember having this much fun hanging out with anyone. It's easy but somehow still thrilling. Every smile, every laugh, every haughty brow quirk. Every little thing she does is interesting.

"What else?"

"Uhh…" As I beat the batter for the pancakes, I think. "Grilled cheese and spaghetti. Does it count if I buy the marinara sauce?"

"I'd say that still counts."

"Oh." I point excitedly. "Mac and cheese. Six things!"

Her lips smush together like she's fighting off a retort at my cooking abilities. "Greer loves macaroni and cheese."

"And you?"

"I'm not big on pasta."

"There goes two of my meals." I toss a wink at her.

I make way too many pancakes, piling them up on a plate in front of her.

"They smell so good." She leans forward and inhales.

From the fridge, I pull out butter and syrup, then grab forks and knives. Instead of divvying up the food, we eat off one plate. She giggles as I fit a huge bite into my mouth, then take a much smaller forkful.

"It's good." She holds a hand in front of her mouth as she talks.

"Were you afraid it wouldn't be?"

"It did cross my mind after your whole 'I can cook five things' speech."

"Six," I remind her.

"What's your favorite food?" she asks as she cuts another bite of pancakes.

"Pizza probably."

"Greer and I make pizza almost every week."

"Now you're just showing off," I say to her, then lean in for another syrup-y kiss. "I usually order mine."

"I'll make it for you sometime. Homemade is so much better."

I have a mental image of the three of us cooking together that makes me smile. "I'd like that."

After we eat, Olivia insists on helping me clean up. I play music on my phone and we hand-wash the dishes instead of putting them in the dishwasher, and wipe down the counters. It takes a lot longer than it should because I can't stop kissing her. I can't help it. It's the most domestic thing I've ever done with a woman but somehow still the sexiest too.

She's rinsing off a plate when I come up behind her. I wrap my arms around her waist and nuzzle into the crook of her neck.

"You smell like syrup." She turns her head, and I kiss her.

Laughing, she hums as she pulls back. "Taste like it too."

She sets the plate down and shuts off the water, then turns around to face me. Her wet hands come up to rest on the front of my shirt.

"Oops." She giggles as she realizes what she's done.

"Guess I'll have to take that off."

Her laughter grows, warm and airy. Reaching down, I pick her up and carry her to the island where I set her down in front of me.

Those stunning blue eyes spark with desire as I stand between her legs.

"I like having you in my apartment," I admit.

"I like being here."

"Next time we'll have to bring Greer."

She nods then reaches out and slides her hands under the hem of my T-shirt on either side. "Then we better enjoy having the place to ourselves tonight."

They are the exact words I want to hear, but I still hesitate.

"We don't have to rush things. Hanging out with you, talking and laughing, kissing… it's already the best night I can remember." To prove my point, I offer up the first ideas that don't involve getting her naked that come to mind. "We could watch a movie or play cards. I think I have an old Monopoly game around here somewhere too."

"I despise Monopoly."

"Cards it is." I take a step back and she grabs a hold of the front of my shirt, keeping me from getting any farther away.

"I don't want to play cards."

"Movie?"

She slowly shakes her head, and a saucy grin pulls at the corners of her mouth. Her fingers roam up my sides and over my stomach and chest. My dick twitches.

My next suggestions come out in a low, gruff tone. "Karaoke? Dancing? I think I have some marshmallows around; we could roast them by candlelight."

"Stop talking and kiss me, Hotshot."

"Yes, ma'am." I crash my mouth down onto hers.

Her fingers continue to explore my bare skin under

my shirt as I savor every taste of her. Sweet and heady and so fucking perfect.

Eventually, she grabs hold of my shirt on either side and tugs upward. I break the kiss and lift my arms until she can get it all the way off. Her stare moves to take in every inch of me. When her fingers return to my chest, goosebumps dot my skin.

"Your body is incredible," she says, holding my shirt in her hands. "I think I changed my mind about letting you see me naked."

"Gorgeous, there is literally nothing you could be hiding under there that's going to change how badly I want you."

"Always the charmer."

"It's true though."

Her gaze bores into me as if she's deciding whether or not she believes me. Then she sets my shirt down and removes hers.

Her pale skin is smooth and only covered by the lacy, black bra that dips low and pushes her tits up.

Whatever expression she sees on my face must reassure her because a playful smirk dances across her lips, and she hooks one finger under the waistband of my jeans to pull me back to her.

I wrap my arms around her back and crush her to me. Our tongues tangle and taste, only stopping for the occasional nip of a bottom lip or to catch our breaths.

When we're both panting, I drop my forehead against hers.

"I like you."

Her body shakes with a quiet laugh. "Oh yeah?"

"So fucking much."

"I like you too in case that wasn't obvious by the way I can't stop touching you." Her nails rake down my bare chest. "I can't get over the muscles in your stomach. I didn't even know we had that many."

I want to touch her too, but I'm not sure I trust myself to keep taking this as slowly as she needs. Instead, my mouth finds hers again. Time seems to stand still, like nothing else matters right now but the two of us.

Her phone rings out from the end of the counter. We both freeze and turn to stare at it.

"I'm so sorry," she says as she leans to grab it. "I have to check in case it's Greer."

"Yeah, of course." I let out a slow breath and step away from her as she answers the phone.

"Hello?" She sounds a hell of a lot calmer than I feel.

I back up all the way to the other counter and lean against it as I try to pull myself together. I'm strung tight, muscles clenched, heart racing, brain foggy. This girl has me spinning.

"Sorry about that," she says as she sets the phone back on the counter.

I blink away some of the haze. "Is everything okay?"

"Yeah." A tight, quiet chuckle leaves her lips. "Gigi wanted to know if it was okay for Greer to go on a hike with Grandpa tomorrow morning."

The corner of my mouth hitches up. I still can't believe Earl is her grandfather. I can see the resemblance though.

"It sounds like they're good with her."

"Yeah. The best. I don't know what I would have done without them. They help a lot. My sister too." She places both hands on the counter, bracing herself, shoulders lifted. "Anyway."

"I get the sense you don't let people help you."

"That obvious?"

I nod. "They love you. And Greer. You both deserve to have people like that. Who will jump in and lighten the load. It doesn't say anything about your ability as a mom. Actually, no—it does, but not in the way you think."

"What does it say?" she asks.

"That they think you're doing an amazing job and think you could use a break occasionally. People don't generally offer to help out someone they deem unworthy."

"I guess that's true." She smiles then wrinkles her nose. "I still don't like it."

"Of course not."

She wouldn't be Olivia if she weren't trying to tackle everything herself. It's one of the many things I like about her. Doesn't stop me from wanting to swoop in and do a lot for her though.

We fall quiet. Her smile falls and we stare across the

kitchen at each other. Tension crackles in the air and I'm still just as keyed up as I was before the phone rang.

Her tongue darts out to wet her lips. She glances down as if only now realizing she isn't wearing a shirt. Fuck, she's stunning.

"Do you still want…" The question trails off and she looks anywhere but at me. "Of course you don't. Answering a call mid-make-out sesh is about the least sexy thing. Can you hand me that?" She points to her shirt lying on the floor between us.

I feel one brow lift. Is she for real now? Can't she see how badly I want her?

I push off the counter slowly and bend to pick up her shirt, then close the rest of the distance between us.

"Thank yo—" Her words cut off as I scoop her up and toss her over my shoulder.

She squeals as I head toward my bedroom. "What are you doing?"

"Showing you how unsexy I think you are." I swat her ass, and she squeals again.

I cross the apartment and walk into my room, not bothering with the light. The window in my room faces a courtyard with just enough light that filters in and help me see where I'm going.

Carefully, I shift and place her on top of the navy comforter. She stares up at me, smiling but looking shy.

I toss her shirt to the floor.

"Better," I say.

She laughs again, then pushes up to a sitting

position. Her hands lift and rest on the waistband of my jeans. All the blood rushes to the bulge straining against the zipper of my pants.

"Can I?" she asks as her thumb swipes across the button.

"If you don't, I might die."

Her lips pull higher, smiling in that sassy, assured smile that I fell for all those months ago. She's more layered than I expected, insecure and struggling with certain things in the same ways we all battle shit. But in this scenario, I never want her to feel anything but confident.

She undoes my jeans and pushes them down with my boxers. My dick springs free, happy to be uncontained and happier that she's here.

There's a long stretch of silence. Her eyes widen and her breaths come quicker as she stares slack-jawed at my cock. "Holy shit. You were serious."

"I would never lie about something so important." My tone is teasing and light, but she continues to look at me with shock. "We can still play Monopoly instead if you want."

"No, I…" She swallows and then takes a breath. "You can't dangle that giant thing in front of me and then suggest a board game. Give a girl a second."

A silent chuckle shakes my body, and she smiles up at me.

"You're stunning. All six foot five and nine inches of you." Her smile pulls higher on one side. She reaches around and undoes her bra, then lets it fall around her shoulders.

My breath hitches as she tosses it to the floor with her shirt. I already knew she was going to be perfect, but she's so far beyond.

"Come here." I beckon her with one finger. She stands and I kiss her while removing her jeans and panties.

When we're both naked, she drapes her arms over my shoulders. The movement presses those full, gorgeous tits against my chest.

We've kissed plenty of times, but with nothing between us and the rest of the night to ourselves, my patience wavers. Part of me wants to take my time, and the other part wants her so badly that it's nearly impossible to hold back when she's offering herself up to me.

"What am I going to do with you?" I ask, walking us slowly back to the bed.

"I don't know," she replies breathlessly. "I have a few ideas though."

"Oh yeah?"

She sits on the edge of the bed, and I inch closer, forcing her onto her back.

"Do any of them include me being inside you?"

"All of them."

My heart is beating so hard it feels like it might pound right out of my chest.

"I'm not going to lie. I'm a little intimidated." She bites her bottom lip.

The corner of my mouth twitches with a smile. "Don't worry. He's gentle like me."

"I don't want gentle."

Fuck me.

"I need to make sure you're ready for me." I kiss a trail down her body.

She sucks in a breath as my lips graze over one hip bone, then the other. I hook one arm around her leg and slide down farther.

Her body trembles underneath me and she grabs hold of the sheets on either side of her. Keeping my eyes locked on hers, I swipe my tongue over her pussy.

She inhales sharply and lets her head fall back against the pillow.

"Was this one of your ideas?" I ask, then taste her again.

She answers in moans and unintelligible whimpers until I pause to readjust and push her legs farther apart.

"No, but it should have been. That feels…oh god, so good. I should have known you'd be good at this."

I chuckle softly, then push one finger inside her before I reply. Her pussy tightens around my knuckle.

"And I should have known you'd taste like heaven."

My finger pushes in and out of her as I flick my tongue over her clit. She writhes underneath me and keeps giving me those sexy little moans.

"Flynn," she says my name on another breathy moan.

"Hmm?" I ask, not moving my mouth from her pussy. I add another finger and step up the pace.

"I'm so…" She leans up on her elbows and stares at me with those big, blue eyes. Her lips part and make a perfect "o."

"Are you going to come for me?"

She nods rapidly and those stunning eyes widen seconds before her body tenses, and she cries out, "Flynn. Oh, god. Flynn."

Her mouth hangs open and her face is flushed as she orgasms. It's the most beautiful thing I've ever seen, and I decide on the spot I want to claim a thousand more. Whatever ideas she had, I'm going to see that we do them. Again and again.

As Olivia recovers, she starts laughing.

"Something funny?"

"That was the best orgasm of my life." She laughs harder.

I reach into the nightstand and get a condom. While I'm covering myself with it, she doesn't take her eyes off me.

"And you're surprised by that?" I ask as I climb back up her body.

She lifts her arms and loops them around my neck. "No, Hotshot. I don't think I am."

She tugs me down to her and kisses me. She kisses me hard and wraps her legs around my back. My dick nudges her center, and a jolt of pleasure moves through me.

I wait until she's lifting her hips up to create friction against me and giving me those sexy little moans before I guide the head of my dick to her pussy.

I meet her gaze. "I'll go slow. Let me know if you want to stop."

I push in a few inches and watch her lashes flutter closed. A lazy smile lifts the corners of her mouth.

"Don't stop."

"We have all night," I say, but what I mean is I don't want to hurt her. I'm not being cocky when I say I'm a lot to take.

Her eyes open and she drags her nails down my sides. "If you don't start fucking me, I am going to die of anticipation."

"So bossy." I nip at her full bottom lip and then give her more.

Her brows pinch together, and her mouth stays in that perfect "o" shape as I work my way in and out, each time sinking farther into her pussy.

I'm strung so tight that I'm already in danger of coming. I do my best to memorize every detail of this moment because I know I'll want to replay it later. She's so damn sexy and everything about this feels perfect.

"I'm going to come again," she warns as she bucks up into me, forcing me a little deeper.

"Me too," I tell her, swiping my lips over hers and pressing our foreheads together.

Our ragged breaths mingle together as her second

orgasm seizes her body. Her pussy locks onto me and sends me over the edge.

I'm panting her name and wishing on every possible entity for it to never end or for a million repeats as we both come down from that post-sex high.

"Fuck, gorgeous. Your pussy was made for me." I pull out of her with a groan and fall onto the mattress beside her.

Olivia's sweet laughter starts up again and I glance over at her with a mixture of amusement and concern.

"Everything okay?"

"Better than okay," she says and flings an arm over my chest as she nuzzles into my side.

"I can't think straight yet to come up with anything witty, but I'll take better than okay."

She lets out another short laugh. "Way, way better than okay."

CHAPTER TWENTY-TWO

Olivia

"**M**ORNING," I SAY AS FLYNN PULLS ME AGAINST him, so my back is flush against his chest. One beefy arm wraps around my waist and he throws a leg over my hip.

"I could get used to this." His words come out gruff and muffled.

Same. I wriggle my butt against his crotch. My body lights up in a way that shouldn't be possible after last night. I'm sore but in the best way.

"Ooh. Feeling feisty?" His arm around my waist lowers. I fell asleep in one of his T-shirts. I tried a pair of sweatpants, but they were comically big on me, so I skipped pants all together. As his fingers slip under the hem of the shirt and glide across my lower stomach, I'm grateful there's one less thing in the way.

"Yes."

He groans.

"I have bad news." The pad of his thumb drags over my inner thigh.

"What's that?" I ask breathlessly. I can feel him growing harder against me.

"Brogan and Archer texted to see if I wanted to go to brunch with them this morning. London loves brunch and I figured you'd like an excuse to hang with Sabrina."

"That's sweet," I say. "And incredibly inconvenient."

I turn in his hold. I'm all revved up. Who needs food?

"What time?" I ask.

"Fifteen minutes." He gives me a sheepish grin.

"That is not nearly enough time."

"It never is with you." Flynn leans in and drops a kiss to my lips and then sits up, pulling me with him.

After brunch, I take Flynn to the nursery to look at plants. I figured he could use a few.

"Here?" Flynn asks as he moves a Ficus over a foot.

"Umm…" I bite on the corner of my lip as I take in his living room. I picked out a variety of things for his apartment. Mostly succulents because they're easy to care for, a couple potted trees, and accent plants for surfaces and small spaces like the bathroom.

Flynn stands tall, a crease forming between his brows. "What's wrong?"

God, I love how well he can read me and how quick he is to jump in and help. And the more he does it, the easier it is to let him.

"I think I might have gone overboard," I admit.

He whirls around, looking at all the plants we brought into his apartment. It looks more like a greenhouse than an apartment. He laughs first, then I join in.

He walks over to me, eyes glinting with amusement.

"I'm so sorry," I say as his palms glide around my sides to rest on my lower back. "I got excited about adding some green to your apartment and now it looks like you're living inside a terrarium."

"It isn't your fault. The place was so bare before. Now all you can see are the plants." He chuckles as he scans the space again.

"I can take a few to my apartment."

"Nah, I love them. Although, there is a good chance I'm going to need to hire someone to water everything while I'm traveling."

"I'll do it." It feels like the least I can do after convincing him to get so many. I went a teensy, tiny (read: a lot) overboard.

"Yeah?" His lips pull into a smirk. "You want to be my plant lady?"

"Yeah, I think I do." My heart rate speeds up as I hold

his gaze. I'm pretty sure we're talking about more than plants right now.

His mouth captures mine and, like every other time he's kissed me, I get lost in him. There's something about him, or us together, that puts me at ease while also making every nerve come alive. I trust him and I've trusted very few men. The knowledge should freak me out, considering his plans to leave, but it doesn't, at least not in this moment.

"How much time do I have?" he asks as he trails kisses down my neck.

"I have to pick up Greer in an hour."

"I can work with that." He takes my hand and tugs me with him toward the couch. He sits and pulls me down on his lap.

My knees bracket his hips and as I settle onto him, his hard length presses into my core. His hands tangle in my hair, and he continues kissing my neck down to my collarbone.

One arm circles around my waist and he shifts quickly so I'm on my back and he hovers over me. He sits back and helps me out of my clothes. Slow and unhurried, taking time to kiss me between removing each piece.

The result leaves me squirming and anxious for more.

Flynn chuckles as I wrap my legs around him to hold him in place.

"Don't worry, gorgeous. I'm not going anywhere." With a wink, he removes his shirt and unbuttons his jeans.

I watch while he undresses, savoring every inch of his body. My throat goes dry, and a delicious throb starts between my legs. His right hand drops to his dick, and he strokes himself as he stares down at me, eyes roaming over my nakedness and that same desire I'm feeling is reflected at me.

Sitting up, my gaze lingers on his thick cock. He's huge and I probably shouldn't be considering it, but I want to taste him. To see if he'll fit.

I place my hand under his and follow his stroke over his length. He groans, deep and low in this throat.

His dark brown eyes are locked on me as I lean forward and wrap my lips around the head of his dick. Surprise flickers in his expression, followed by undeniable heat.

"Fuck, Olivia." His hand moves to my face, and he cups my cheek. His thumb brushes gently over the corner of my mouth. "You don't have to do that."

"I want to at least try. You're kind of a lot."

He smirks.

Electricity ripples over my skin as I take him farther into my mouth. I stop when my eyes start to water and pull back. It's embarrassing how little of him I can fit. Determined, I try again. This time I push past my initial instinct and slide down another inch.

The hum of approval I get in response lights me up and encourages me to take more. One tear leaks out from the corner of my eye and Flynn's thumb is there to brush it away.

"I should have known you'd take me so good. You're incredible. Do you know that? So fucking sexy with my cock filling that perfect mouth of yours."

More tears pool in my eyes, then slowly fall. He catches each one with the pad of his fingers. He's too big for me to go fast, but I bob over his length slowly, letting him hit the back of my throat every time.

It's intoxicating. The way he looks at me so adoringly and the high I feel from his praise and the pleasure etched into his features.

My nipples are tight buds that ache and my pussy clenches. I've never wanted someone this much before. My body is already humming with pleasure and he hasn't touched more than my face.

"That's it. Oh, fuck. Just like that. Your mouth is heaven." His head falls back, and he stares up at the ceiling. His Adam's apple bobs and the muscles in his neck strain.

My jaw is tight, and I have to force myself to relax to keep going. I want to make him feel as good as he makes me feel. While his gaze is lifted, I miss having his eyes on me. There's something about having him watch me and seeing the adoration in his expression. As soon as I think it, they're locked back on me, and then he's guiding me off him and crushing his mouth down onto mine. We tumble back onto the couch, me underneath him. He nips at my bottom lip and his knee nudges my legs apart.

"We're going to need to move this into the bedroom soon," he says as the head of his cock slides over my clit.

We let in a collective inhale and a shiver rolls through me.

"I don't have any condoms out here," he adds.

I wrap my arms around his neck and my legs around his back. "Let's go, Hotshot. We have a clock, remember?"

"Don't rush me, woman." He chuckles and navigates to a stand with me strapped to his front like a koala.

He kisses me as he walks us to his room. His steps are slow and controlled, but his long legs eat up the space quickly all the same.

As gingerly as he had last night, he sets me on his bed, then grabs a condom from the nightstand.

"Do you have to buy the Magnum XL?" I ask with a grin. He really is huge. Long and thick. Intimidating but still aesthetically pleasing.

"I think you already know the answer to that." He covers himself and then leans down and catches one nipple between his teeth.

My back arches as pleasure rolls through me. I'm expecting his dick, but it's his hand that reaches between my legs.

"Thank fuck you're already soaked for me because I'm dying to be inside you," he says as he pushes in one finger, and then a second.

He continues lavishing my breasts with attention, biting and licking and fingering me until I'm writhing and moaning. Only when stars are flashing in front of my eyes does he remove his hand and line up his dick.

As he pushes the tip inside, my pussy clenches around him.

"Goddamn, baby." He groans and gives me a little more. "Are you sore?"

"If you pull out now, I will kill you."

"I love it when you talk sexy to me." He bites the side of my neck and then kisses the same spot. "If it's too much, let me know."

Staring down at me, Flynn waits until I nod in understanding before moving. He keeps a slow, steady pace, inching farther each time until it feels impossible that I can take more. I feel so full of him and it's a heady thing that I'm pretty sure I could get addicted to.

"I won't break," I tell him when I can see he's holding back. It's in the crease between his brows and the strain in his arms, as if he's physically restraining himself.

His expression smooths out and is replaced with a look of hesitation.

I bring both hands up to his face. His unshaven jaw is bristly as I smooth my palms over it. "I promise I'll tell you if it's too much."

"So fucking perfect," he mutters almost more to himself than to me. His lips press to mine. "This pussy was made for me."

Our kisses are hard and messy, like neither of us can get enough. I don't know if it's the ticking clock on our time together or if it's just him, but every moment with Flynn feels big and important, and I don't want to waste a second.

CHAPTER TWENTY-THREE

Olivia

"WHERE HAVE YOU BEEN?" MY SISTER ASKS AS I walk into the back office of the store.

"I had lunch with Flynn before the team leaves for Chicago this afternoon." He was antsy and keyed up. And I was happy to distract him for forty-five minutes.

"Lunch or making out at his place?"

My face heats. "He ordered takeout."

"I'll bet he did." Ruby quirks a brow, pen poised at her chin as her lips pull into a knowing smirk. "You're glowing."

"What?" My hand rises to my face, and then I brush my hair back and tuck it behind my ear. "No, I'm not."

"You are. I'm totally jealous." She sighs. "I love those

first few months of dating. Lingering kisses, sweet text messages, feeling like you'll die if you go more than a day or two without seeing each other, sex is still fun and exciting."

Yep, that pretty much sums it up. It's only been a few weeks since Flynn and I slept together but to say I'm falling fast would be the understatement of the century. He's amazing. And yes, the sex is out of this world. Our schedules make it difficult to see each other every day, let alone have sex, but let's just say we make it count when we do.

"You have it so bad. It's written all over your face, little sister." She makes a loop in the air with her pencil as if circling my face.

"Shut up." I take a seat across from her and pick up a stray rubber band before shooting it at her.

She laughs as it flies by her to the right. "I'm happy for you."

I'm happy for me too. I feel so full of life right now. Maybe it's a post-high orgasmic bliss or too many pheromones, but I'm not questioning it.

"Is he still planning to leave at the end of the season?" Ruby asks, effectively dousing all the good feelings I was just basking in.

"Nothing is set in stone," I say, ignoring her gaze. I don't want to think about that. It's months away and it might not even happen. Though I don't really believe that. Flynn is a great pitcher. I know nothing about baseball and even I know that.

I flip through a stack of mail, and eventually Ruby

goes back to staring at her laptop screen and I can't stand the silence.

"How's the book coming?" I ask her.

"I think I finally have something. Can I run it by you?"

"Really?" I sit straighter, happy for something else to focus on.

Her expression is a mixture of excitement and nerves as she nods.

"Absolutely." I've been dying for her to tell me about what she's writing. It's such a sacred process for her that I never want to push.

"Okay." She flashes a tentative smile before starting in.

"I got the idea when we were at the Mustangs game."

I hang on her every word. Ruby is a fabulous story-teller, but when she's in this mode, she talks fast and in circles, sometimes inserting something she forgot to say at the beginning that was important for the characters or plot. It's like a puzzle to follow along and try to piece it all together.

It's only when she's finished that I offer any feedback. Which really isn't feedback at all, but more like me fangirling over my genius sister. A sports romance from Ruby Madison? It's so unexpected that people will lose their minds.

"Have you told Grandpa?" I ask when we finally fall quiet.

"No." She shakes her head so quickly she looks like a bobblehead. Ruby is buzzing with nervous energy. She always gets like this right before she holes up for a few weeks and pounds out words. "I thought I'd surprise him once I know I can pull it off."

"You can," I assure her. "And if we have any baseball questions, I have an inside source."

"I know baseball. Unlike you, I paid a little attention over the years."

"I'm sorry, you *know* baseball?" Ruby is a lot of amazing, talented things, but sporty isn't one of them.

She waves one hand around. "There's a ball and bases."

I fight a laugh.

"The pitcher throws the ball and the guy with the bat tries to whack it out of the park." She points like she's making her closing statement. "There are quarters or—wait, no, innings and whichever team has the most points at the end wins!"

"Points?" My body folds over with laughter. Excitement and that giddy high of books mixed with my sister and her idiosyncrasies is too much to hold back. When I glance up at her, she wears a sheepish grin.

"Okay. I might need help with the baseball stuff, but the story isn't about baseball. It's a romance between a beloved hometown bad boy shortstop who gets in trouble and is forced to do a charity auction to save his reputation."

"Where the heroine's twin sister bids and wins for her sister because she knows how big of a fan she is," I add. "I love stories where a regular woman is confronted with a celebrity only to find out he's a big ole jerk in real life."

She pauses. "Would it be better if he turned out to be a werewolf? Or an alien?"

She looks so serious that I don't want to laugh, but one slips out anyway. Ruby grins and joins in.

"I think I might have broken my brain. It's all this sports talk. I'm going to take a walk and get some fresh air." She stands and packs up her laptop and many notepads and pens. She smiles as she zips up her backpack. "Thank you."

"For what?"

"Not harassing me over the past few months and letting me figure out the book in my own time. I know it was killing you."

"So painful. I was on death's doorstep. Truly."

With a chuckle, she heads out of the office, leaving me alone with the mail. The store is quiet in the afternoon. We got hit with a cold front that brought in wind and light rain. I can't blame people for wanting to stay home. Curling up on the couch with a blanket and a good book sounds like the perfect way to spend the day.

In the late afternoon, I brave the cold for a coffee break. Inside the café, I order my usual black coffee, then decide to add a dash of cream and sugar. Flynn would be so proud. I move over to the end of the counter to wait.

"I was in your store this morning." The voice comes from my left side and makes me jump.

When I turn, I come face to face with Walter, the owner of Plot Twist. That I didn't even notice him speaks to how much I'm in my head lately. It's possible falling in love makes people dumber. I wonder if Ruby can use that for plot material.

"You were?" I ask, unable to hide the surprise in my voice. He must have stopped by while I was at Flynn's house. I wonder why Gigi didn't mention it. She had to have recognized him.

"I received some of your mail by accident," he says.

"Oh." Well, that makes more sense. I can't picture him browsing our store unless it was to scope out the competition, and that's more something I would do than him, from what I've gathered in our few interactions.

"There's quite a big romance section."

"The largest in the city," I say proudly. "If you ever want recommendations for your store, I'm happy to help."

As soon as I offer, I want to kick myself. What am I doing? I can't help the enemy.

It doesn't matter though. Walter's lips smash together, and he makes a disapproving hum. I'm fairly certain that's a no.

The barista calls out his name and Walter gives me a polite nod instead of responding to my offer. He picks up his drink and leaves the café. I really don't get that guy or how he's managed to create such a cozy, friendly bookstore when he's…not.

I'm hot when I get back to the store. I tell Gigi about the run-in, and she confirms he dropped by earlier with a stack of mail.

"He seems lonely," Gigi says. "Go easy on him."

"He dissed the store and made a face like romance is an unworthy genre."

"I don't think that's what he did." She smiles. "He said we have a big romance section, which is true."

"The biggest in the city," I add, just like I had done with Walter. "And he completely dismissed my offer to help him, like I couldn't possibly have any knowledge worth sharing."

"By your own account you didn't really want to help."

"But I would have," I say defensively.

Gigi gives me a patronizing look but doesn't say any more.

I'm still stewing over it when Grandpa stops by at the end of the day with Greer. The latter trudges in with a frown that would be comical if it weren't also heartbreaking.

"What's wrong?" I ask, smoothing her curls away from her face.

"Nothing," she says in a voice that basically says the opposite.

I look to Grandpa who shrugs.

Gigi steps out from behind the counter and motions for Greer. "Why don't you help me in the back? We got in some new princess books today."

A flicker of excitement crosses her face, but she slams the door on it quickly, returning to her sullen mood. When they're gone, I step closer to Grandpa.

"What's that about?" I ask him. Greer is usually a bundle of joy when she greets me after school. She gets this look of pure happiness when she sees me and then runs to hug me like she just can't wait another second. I live for those moments.

"She wouldn't say, but she had this with her." Grandpa hands me a piece of paper and then squeezes my shoulder. Confusion and concern mar my brow as he heads the same direction Gigi and Greer went.

I focus on the paper. Greer's familiar stick people art makes me smile. I recognize myself by my big blue eyes, she always exaggerates them in pictures, and Greer by her wild, curly hair. She's holding my hand and on the other side of her is a man I immediately identify as Flynn. He's in a blue cap with a baseball glove.

She's gotten attached to him, which doesn't concern me as much as maybe it should. Maybe he won't always be in her life, but isn't it better to have this relationship with him now so she knows what's possible?

I'm mulling that over while simultaneously trying to figure out why this could have prompted her to be so upset when she stomps back out. Gigi and Grandpa follow her, looking as perplexed as I feel. Rarely do her bad moods last this long and almost always a new book pulls her out of a funk.

"I want to go home," Greer says as she crosses her arms over her chest.

My brain spins on what to say in response. It's so out of character for her that I'm at a loss.

"I can close up here," Gigi offers.

I nod. Part of me doesn't want to give in to her tantrum, but the other part knows something is going on and I want to figure it out so I can fix it. ASAP.

CHAPTER TWENTY-FOUR

Flynn

HOLLAND BROTHERS

ME

How's June 10th?

BROGAN

Not my favorite day of the year, usually, but not bad.

ARCHER

I don't think he was asking about your personal feelings on the date.

ME

Let me try again, are you guys free on June 10th?

BROGAN

For you, always, baby Holland.

HENDRICK

I should be able to get away for a day or two. Big game?

KNOX

I have a race the day before but it's local so I'm in.

ARCHER

Is this for Dad's thing?

KNOX

Wait. Dad's going to be there? Pass.

ME

It's his sixtieth birthday and I'm throwing him a party.

HENDRICK

Did Dad put you up to this?

ME

No, it was all my idea. If you don't come, I get it, but it would mean a lot to me.

ARCHER

I'll be there, but I'm bringing Sabrina as my security blanket.

HENDRICK

Count me and Jane in.

BROGAN

I'm coming for you, not him.

ME

Knox?

KNOX

I'll think about it.

We get back to Lake City Wednesday afternoon after our games in Chicago. I go straight to the stadium for a pitchers' meeting and then treatment. By the time I'm free, I'm so amped up to see Olivia and Greer that I'm waiting on their doorstep when they get home.

"Hi!" Olivia's face lights up when she spots me, and she comes forward to hug me. "What are you doing here?"

"I couldn't wait to see you." I tear my gaze from her to Greer. "How's my favorite munchkin?"

She stares down at her feet, which shuffle almost nervously.

Olivia nudges her. Something is up, but I can't guess what.

Greer finally glances at me but doesn't meet my eyes. "Hi, Hotshot."

Olivia unlocks the door, and her daughter slips by her into the apartment without another word.

"Is she alright?" I ask of the usually bubbly six-year-old.

"She's been like this for two days." Olivia's mouth pulls into an unconvincing half smile. "Come in. I'm so glad you're here."

I follow her into the apartment.

Greer is in her bedroom. The light streams out into the hallway from her open door, but unlike the other times I've been here, she's quiet. I follow Olivia to the kitchen, where she drops her purse on the counter and sighs.

"How was Chicago?" she asks. "I caught part of the game, but I fell asleep once I was certain you were going to win."

I love that she watches the games. "Terrible."

She smirks and lets out a small laugh.

"It was cold and windy, and you weren't there."

"I missed you too," she says as I step into her space.

I drop my mouth to hers, savoring her soft, slow kisses.

"What's for dinner?" At the question from Greer, I pull back and Olivia turns to face her daughter.

"I don't know yet. What do you want?"

"Pizza."

"We don't have time for pizza. I need to be at work in an hour."

"Fine! Whatever." The words come out in a haughty tone I didn't think Greer was capable of.

Before Olivia can respond, her daughter stomps back to her room and closes the door.

The shock pulsing through me must be written all over my face because Olivia nods and says, "I know. It's awful."

"And you don't know why?"

"She won't tell me. I've tried a dozen times. I asked if something happened with a friend at school or if someone hurt her and she says no, but she won't say much else. I called her teacher, but she didn't know either. She said Greer had been playing by herself more the last couple days, but she hadn't witnessed anyone treating her poorly."

I'm surprised at the rage I feel, thinking someone might have hurt Greer, and the immediate need to figure out who, what, and when.

Olivia's phone pings, and she digs it out of her purse. A crease forms between her brows.

"What?" I ask, thinking it's something to do with Greer. My mind is stuck there. Somewhere along the line while I was falling for Olivia, I fell just as hard for Greer.

"Sabrina is sick. She was going to watch Greer for me tonight while I work."

"Yeah, everyone at their apartment has it," I confirm. I texted with Archer and Brogan this morning and they were talking about painting a red X on their front door.

"I'll have to call my grandparents and see if they can watch her," she says, not sounding happy about the prospect.

"What about Ruby?"

"She's deep in the writing cave."

I don't know what that means exactly, but that only leaves one option. "I can watch her."

Olivia's brows lift.

"Don't look so appalled by the idea. I'm great with kids. Or at least with Greer."

"Of course you are." She shakes her head and smiles. "But hanging out with her for a couple hours while we go to the trampoline park or somewhere fun is different than getting her to bed. Especially in her current mood."

"I grew up with four brothers. Someone was always in a bad mood. I know how to handle it."

"The peacekeeper," she says, stepping closer and wrapping her arms around my middle. She places her head on my chest. "I'm worried about her."

"Me too." I cup the back of her head and then let my fingers flow down her hair. "But we'll figure it out."

I pull back and stare down into her eyes. "Now tell me all the rules, Momma."

"You really want to watch her only hours after getting back into town? Have you even been to your apartment yet? I don't get off until two."

"Yes and no. I like your place better anyway. It has my two favorite people. And I'll crash on the couch once she's in bed. That's allowed, right? Wait, do you sleep or do you stay up and watch her breathe all night?"

She smacks at my chest playfully.

"I got this."

She bites on the corner of her lip, then nods slowly. "Okay. But only if you're absolutely sure. It's fine to say no. My grandparents won't mind if I drop her off there."

"If Greer's cool with it, then I'd love to hang with her tonight. I missed her too."

She chuckles, grinning in a way that tells me she doesn't quite believe me. That's okay. I'm still a little taken back by it too.

"Let me talk to her." Olivia leaves me in the kitchen, disappears into Greer's room, and comes back only a couple minutes later.

I don't know why, but I feel a little nervous. It's possible Greer would rather go to her grandparents' house than have me watch her. And I guess I want her to like and trust me.

"She wants to stay with you," Olivia says, a small grin lifting one side of her mouth. "She nearly cracked a smile when I asked her."

"See? I've totally got this."

"Keep her alive, make sure she brushes her teeth, and is in bed by eight."

"That's it?" I ask with a huff. "Easy."

She laughs again.

While Olivia gets ready for work, I order takeout for the three of us. Olivia barely gets to eat before she rushes off to work.

"I love you." She kisses Greer's head. "Be good for Flynn."

Then she walks to me.

"I promise I'll be good too." I wink.

"Thank you. Text me if you need anything. I'll check my phone when I can."

"We'll be fine," I assure her and myself. Greer still isn't her usual self, so my confidence is already wavering a little.

When she's gone, I look to Greer.

"What do you want to do?"

I get a shrug in response. Okay, not killing it right out of the gate.

"Wanna know a secret?"

"What?"

"I've never babysat before. It's my first time. I don't know what to do."

A tentative smile tugs at the corner of her mouth, but she shuts it down quickly. Whatever has her upset isn't going to be pushed aside so easily.

"Anything you want to do?" I ask her.

Another shrug.

"We could watch a movie," I suggest. "Have any favorites?"

"A new *Bunny Ballet* movie came out yesterday."

"There's a new one?" I ask, wide-eyed. "I had no idea. We must watch it!"

Her expression softens the tiniest bit, and we move to the couch. Once I find the movie and hit play, Greer inches closer to me. We watch the first twenty minutes or so in silence.

I love a good cartoon as much as the next person, but I find myself too worried about Greer and what's bugging her to get invested in the movie.

Reaching over, I tug on a curl.

"Hey, munchkin. Want some ice cream?"

Her head nods quickly and I get the first real smile out of her all night. After I pause the movie, I head into the kitchen and pull out the ice cream cartons. "Chocolate or Neapolitan?"

"Chocolate!" She sits on a stool at the counter.

"Great choice." I find two small bowls and give us each two big scoops. I slide her bowl in front of her and then walk around to sit next to her with mine.

I wait until she's had a couple of bites before I ask, "How's school?"

Her demeanor changes immediately. Her shoulders slump forward, and the corners of her mouth turn into a frown. Is there anything sadder than a kid eating ice cream with a frown? If there is, I haven't seen it.

"It's fine."

I guess it was naïve to think she'd tell me so easily, but I'm disappointed all the same.

"That's good," I say, focusing on my bowl. "Baseball is *fine* too."

She peeks over at me. "Grandpa said you're the best pitcher he's ever seen."

"He did?" Genuine surprise lifts my brows. The old man and I chat whenever we see each other and occasionally he gives me his opinion on what's working or what isn't. As soon as I mentioned to Wayne that I thought my front foot might be landing a little inside, he watched and agreed. It was a small tweak, an inch or less, but it's made a big difference.

I told Earl as much, but he's slow to give guidance. I imagine he doesn't want to step on the toes of my coaches, but I'm not opposed to feedback, no matter where it comes from. And I think he's got plenty of it that could help me.

She nods and we fall quiet while we finish our ice cream. When we're both done, I rinse the bowls and spoons and put them in the dishwasher and then we head back to the living room to continue the movie.

I get lost in the story, and so does she—evidenced by the way she unconsciously inches closer to me while watching. I rest my right arm along the back of the couch, and she nuzzles against my side. Apparently, I was stressed because by the time the movie is over, I'm more relaxed than I've felt in days.

"Can we play a game?" Greer asks as the credits

roll. "My dad sent me the Disney Princess edition of Monopoly, but my mom doesn't like to play it."

I hold back a laugh as I remember Olivia telling me how much she didn't like the game and then what happened after. "Sorry, munchkin. Time for bed."

"Fine. I'll just wait until I see my dad again to play it."

Man, the kid really knows how to lay on the guilt.

"Are you going to see him soon?"

The nonchalant shrug she gives me makes my heart squeeze. I remember that feeling of not knowing when you'd see your dad again and not wanting to answer questions about it for fear of people judging you.

"You miss him, huh?"

She nods.

"Can I tell you another secret?"

"Sure," she says, looking the tiniest bit excited but like she doesn't want it to show.

"I didn't live with my dad when I was growing up either."

"You didn't?" Her eyes widen a fraction.

"Nope. My brothers raised me."

"Really?"

"Mhmm." I want her to know that she's not alone, but I don't want to dismiss her feelings either, so I add, "It was tough. I used to sit around and wish that he'd call or stop by, that I could tell him about my day or show him something I did in school."

Shit, I still feel that way sometimes.

"I video chat with my dad every Sunday," Greer offers.

"That's cool."

She nods, finally smiling. "Where's your dad now? Does he come see you play baseball?"

It feels like a punch to the gut. "Sometimes he does, yeah."

I'm lost in my own emotions until Greer yawns so big her eyes water.

"Time for bed, munchkin. You don't want to be tired for school in the morning." I stand and so does she.

"I hate school. I don't want to go anymore."

My pulse kicks up and I consider my words carefully as I follow her to her room.

"Why not? Don't you basically just play with your friends all day?" I ask, keeping my tone playful in hopes she'll keep answering my questions.

She turns and gives me a very serious stare that reminds me of her mother. "We *only* get three recesses."

"My mistake." I fight a smile.

She picks out pajamas and then heads to the bathroom to change and brush her teeth. I wait for her in her room, sitting on the edge of her bed. It's pink and covered in stuffed animals, including the stuffed Mischief Mustang I gave her. She comes back and moves her stuffed animals, one by one, to the floor in a line next to her bed.

"So, what's up with school? Why don't you want to go?"

She keeps focused on her task as she answers, "Sara

Stites is telling everyone I'm a liar because I said I knew you."

My brows pinch together. "Me?"

She moves the last few stuffed animals off her bed and then goes over to her bookshelf and picks up a piece of paper. She brings it to me.

"No way. You drew this?" I ask as I stare down at the picture of Olivia, Greer, and me. The three of us together, adorable little stick people. I'm towering over them, a baseball glove on my left hand. She stands between me and her mom, holding both our hands. My stomach swirls with some unnamed emotion.

"The teacher told us to draw a picture of our family doing something fun. It's me and mom at your game, when we walked down to the field."

"Yeah, I remember." I smile at her, then frown. "What does this have to do with Sara whatever her name is?"

"She called me a liar in front of the entire class and said I was making it up. Even after Ben stood up for me and said he knew you too. Although I'm not sure if that was a lie or not since he only saw you at the birthday party. Does that count as knowing you?"

"Yeah, I think that counts."

She nods like that makes it final.

"Is that all? Anything else?"

She shrugs one little shoulder.

"It's okay. You can tell me."

"That's pretty much it. Sara keeps calling me a liar

and now no one will play with me. Even Ben is avoiding me."

"I'm sorry." My heart cracks right down the middle.

"It isn't fair." Her temper flares in the most adorable way. "I *do* know you."

"Of course you do. You're my favorite kid in the whole world."

The corners of her mouth pull into a smile, and she wraps her arms around my neck.

Fuck. My entire body hurts at the idea of this sweet little girl being picked on. I don't have a lot of experience with kids, but there have been plenty of times I've had to ignore the naysayers, haters and trolls. Plus, I had four big brothers ready to fuck shit up if I needed it.

"You can't worry about what people say. The important thing is knowing that you're being honest. I know that doesn't make it easier, but it's true."

She nods, but I can tell she doesn't love that answer. No one does. It's life. Fighting the bullies never gets easier, but sometimes you're better off just not playing their game.

"But if they bring it up or pick on you again, then you tell your teacher."

"That's what my mom would say."

"Oh, thank goodness. I thought I was screwing up this whole babysitting thing."

She giggles and plops her entire body into my lap, then yawns.

I try to hand her the picture back, but she shakes her head. "You can keep it."

"Have you told your mom about Sara?"

"No," she says, sounding guilty.

"I bet she'd have some good advice. Your mom is super smart."

"She'll be mad and make a big deal about it," Greer whines.

A small laugh breaks free. "It *is* a big deal. She loves you and when someone hurts the people we care about, we can't help but get mad and want to fix it."

She's quiet, considering. "Can we watch *Bunny Ballet* again?"

All right. Guess that conversation is over.

I glance at the time on my watch. "Sorry, munchkin. It's already past your bedtime. If your mom comes home and you're bouncing off the walls, she'll never trust me again."

"Yes, she will. She likes you."

"Yeah? How can you tell?" I'm fishing for information and have zero shame about it.

"She smiles a lot when you're around and she wears her favorite perfume any time you come over."

My chest squeezes. "I like her a lot too."

"I can tell that too."

"Because I smile a lot?"

"And smell nice. Except after games." She wrinkles up her nose.

A laugh rumbles from my chest. God, I love this kid.

"I do like her, and I like you too."

"I'm your favorite kid in the whole world," she says proudly.

"That's right." I hug her to my chest and breathe in the top of her head.

She climbs into bed, and I read her a book until her eyes look heavy, and she can't stop yawning.

"Night, munchkin. Thanks for letting me hang with you tonight."

Sitting up, she holds her arms up and drapes them as high as she can get on my shoulders to hug me. "Night, Hotshot."

CHAPTER TWENTY-FIVE

Olivia

THE APARTMENT IS QUIET WHEN I WALK THROUGH the front door. The TV is on, but muted.

I place my purse on the counter and then round the couch to find Flynn asleep on it. His long body doesn't fit, and his feet hang off the end. One arm is thrown over his face and the other rests at his side.

He stirs as I get closer.

"Hey." The arm over his face moves and he aims a sleepy smile at me. "How was work?"

"Long and boring." I climb on top of him, resting my cheek on his chest.

His arms wrap around me, and he hums a deep, gravelly sound.

"How's Greer? Did she give you any trouble going to bed?"

"She was great. We had fun."

"You did?" Nothing about my daughter's attitude when I left here indicated they would be having *fun*.

"Yeah. She's a good kid. We watched a movie, had some ice cream, and then it was bedtime."

"For both of you apparently." He's warm and still faintly smells of his cologne.

"Yeah, I gotta say. This couch is fighting me a bit."

Laughing quietly, I stand and take his hand. "Come on, Hotshot."

I tug and he slowly gets to his feet. I stop to peek in on Greer and then lead him to my room.

I take off my shoes. "I'm going to shower. I smell like beer and fried food."

"You smell incredible." He pulls me to him, then drops his face to the crook of my neck and breaths me in. My body lights up as his hands find the hem of my shirt and slip underneath. I'm so tired, but I missed him.

We kiss as we fumble around to the bathroom. I start the shower and then we get undressed, stealing more kisses as we go. By the time we make it under the hot water, I don't feel the least bit tired.

He studies the shampoo and conditioner bottles carefully before selecting the body wash next to it. As soon as he flicks the top on it, he grins.

"Now I know why you always smell like coconut." He pours a generous amount into one palm, sets the bottle back on the shelf, and then rubs his hands together.

He sets to work, lathering me up, in slow, sensual strokes. His hands are big and strong. I love the way his rough palms glide over my skin.

When I'm practically vibrating, core aching and breathing quick, his hand finally slips between my legs.

"Spread them farther for me."

I do as he says, stepping my feet apart. He cups my pussy and then slowly strokes my sensitive flesh with his big, rough fingers.

My hands go to the shower wall on either side of me. The sensations rocking through me already have my legs feeling wobbly.

"Already so close," he mutters softly. "Were you thinking about me at work?"

"Always," I admit. Though there was something extra exciting about knowing he'd be waiting for me at my place when I got home.

"Same." He pushes two fingers inside me.

I let out a gasp as he pumps in and out, finding a slow, steady rhythm.

"I think about you, about us, about making you come, and waking up beside you…" He trails off as I let out a low moan.

"That's it, baby. Give it to me." He swipes his thumb over my clit as he pushes his fingers into me, and I fall apart.

I drop my head to his chest as the orgasm rolls over

me in waves. It's never been like this with anyone before. The chemistry is like nothing I thought was possible. I like him—his playful personality, how considerate and thoughtful he is, the way he is with Greer, the lengths he's gone to show me he cares about me. But I also think he's the hottest man I've ever seen and want him to tear me to pieces. I've never had that combination in a guy before. Good for me and good at making me come.

Only after my body stills, does Flynn slowly pull his fingers away from me. His hand reaches up and lifts my chin so he can place a soft kiss on my lips.

Some of my earlier exhaustion is creeping in post-orgasm. He must read it on my face because he smiles at me, then says, "Bedtime. I get to tuck two ladies into bed tonight. Lucky me."

"Wait, that's it?" I ask as he steps into the stream of water.

His mouth pulls into a smirk. "I didn't bring any condoms."

"Oh." Well, that's an oversight. Once upon a time I kept one in my purse but that's been so long that even if I did have one, it'd probably have expired.

"It's fine. You should sleep. It's been a long day." He motions with his head for us to get out of the shower.

Longer for him probably. By the look of him though, he's not going to sleep very easily. His dick is so hard it looks painful.

"What if I'm not ready for bed yet." I reach out and wrap my hand around the base of his shaft.

His body stiffens and then relaxes. His lashes lower until his brown eyes are barely visible.

The high I get from his reaction to me touching him never gets old. I'm addicted to it.

"You better make it quick then or no bedtime story." His jaw tightens and the words come out clipped.

"Like this?" I ask as I move slowly up and down the length of him.

"Little tighter."

My grip closes around him, and he lets out a guttural laugh mixed with a moan in response.

"Was that a happy sound?"

"Ecstatic," he grits out. "Don't stop. I'm already so close from feeling you fall apart around my fingers."

Another thing I'm addicted to—how he revels in my reaction to him as well.

His hands move to the shower wall behind me, caging me in. His forehead drops to mine and he kisses me hard.

The sounds that leave his throat are raw and primal. Followed by little streams of consciousness like, "So good" and "I'm so fucking gone for you." Each one lights me up and makes me more eager.

"That's it. Don't stop. I'm coming." He bites down on my bottom lip as he finds his release. His cum coats my hand and my stomach, but the water rinses it away quickly.

"Goddamn," he mutters as his breathing slows.

Our mouths linger together without really moving.

"Do I still get a story?" I ask, batting my lashes.

He laughs then bites the side of my neck.

We soap up a second time, this time more quickly and with less kissing. The full extent of this long day is finally starting to sink in.

He steals one last kiss as I turn off the water.

"Thank you for watching Greer for me tonight," I say as we get out of the shower and dry off. "Did she say what was bugging her?"

"She did." He nods slowly. "A girl in class called her a liar for saying she knew me."

"What?" My tired brain comes to life as I try to process his words.

He looks sheepish and adorable as he runs the towel over his wet hair. The usually brownish-red locks are darker and fall onto his forehead.

"She drew a picture of the three of us and, I don't know, the girl accused her of lying in front of the class and then teased her later."

"I saw the picture," I say and smile before I process the second part of his sentence. "Who?"

Flynn chuckles. "Easy, Momma Bear."

I hold the towel a little tighter in my hands. "Which girl?"

"Sara something or other."

I nod, fighting back the anger bubbling underneath the surface. Listen, I know Greer isn't perfect and that she might even be the villain in some other little kids' stories on occasion, but none of that makes me any more reasonable. Actually, I take it back. Greer would never call someone a name and then tease them like it sounds like Sara did to her. My daughter is a lot of things, but she isn't a bully.

"I'm not sure what the rules are for telling you this stuff…" He trails off.

"I won't tell her that you told me."

"Thanks," he says, smiling and looking relieved. He steps closer and runs his hands up my arms. "If it's any consolation, the only reason she didn't tell you is she knew how much it would upset you."

"She said that?"

"Yeah." He wipes a water drop off my cheek and then brushes his lips over mine. "You're a good mom, Olivia."

I soak in his words and hope he's right.

The next morning, I wake to my alarm. Flynn's arm is draped over my middle.

"No," he mutters when I move to silence the incessant noise.

I laugh and turn in his arms. Greer's bedroom door creaks, interrupting our happy bubble, and Flynn and I both go wide-eyed. We hadn't discussed him sleeping over or what Greer would think, but it seems like it's too late to worry about that now.

She comes bounding in, all smiles, and bounces onto the end of the bed. Seeing her so happy for the first time in days lessens my panic a smidge.

"Good morning," I say to her as I sit up.

"Morning, munchkin." Flynn waves and then we both wait to see what Greer will do or say.

"Can we have pancakes this morning?" she asks.

"Uh…sure. I think we have time for that."

"Okay." Then she squeezes her body between us, right into the nook of Flynn's outstretched arm.

My heart feels like it might burst.

"You have to get ready for school," I tell her.

"I know." Her voice is despondent.

"Five more minutes?" Flynn asks with pleading eyes that match my daughters.

"Yeah," I agree and lie back down with them. "That sounds perfect."

The extra minutes make our morning a little more cha-otic. I get ready and start on making breakfast and Greer's lunch.

Flynn comes in shortly.

"Perfect timing." I add another pancake to his plate. "Food is ready."

"It smells great." He finds Greer in the living room packing her backpack. He picks her up and raises her onto his shoulders.

She squeals with delight as he walks her over to the kitchen and deposits her onto a stool, then takes the one next to her.

Everything about this morning has been so surreal but watching them eat together, drenching their pancakes in syrup the same way, and then taking equally big bites is the final punch to the gut.

I'm in love with Flynn. Not only am I in love with him, but I want this every day. Me, Greer, him, waking up and having pancakes and getting ready for the day.

I keep that realization to myself as we eat breakfast. As soon as we're done, it's time to go.

"Do you walk her into her class?" Flynn asks as I grab my purse, and Greer puts on her backpack.

"Yeah," I say. "Sometimes I drop her off, but I like seeing her classroom."

"We have a reading loft!" Greer proudly exclaims.

"Cool. Can I tag along?" Flynn asks.

Greer looks thrilled at the prospect.

"Sure," I say.

Flynn rides with us after I agree to drop him off at the stadium afterward. He says he'll get a ride to his truck later and I selfishly hope that means I'll get to see him again tonight.

At the school, we get out of the car and Flynn puts on a jacket that I didn't even realize he had with him. Plus, his Mustangs game hat. He looks like he just stepped off the field, which is admittedly a very good look on him.

As I round the back of the vehicle, he and Greer are already waiting for me. It's good to have my happy child back.

Flynn smiles and the three of us fall into step.

"Why are you wearing your team jacket?" I ask, leaning in so I can whisper the question. I've only ever seen him wear it during games between innings. It's a bright blue with *Mustangs* written across the front and his number embroidered into the right arm.

"Because I don't have my jersey."

"That is not…" My words trail off as he takes Greer's hand. She bounces with every step, glancing up at him and grinning as wide as her little mouth will allow.

She leads him into the school and down the hall to her kindergarten room. The door is decorated with construction paper flowers. Each one has a different kid's name on it. Greer's is hot pink with a bright yellow center and her name written large in all capital letters.

Greer's teacher, Mrs. Kadia, smiles and looks from Greer to Flynn.

"Good morning," she says in a slightly chirpier voice than normal.

"Morning," I reply, stepping in behind them. Flynn gives her a polite nod.

Greer is still holding on to Flynn's hand.

"Have a good day, munchkin," he says to her.

"You too, Hotshot."

I lean down and hug her, dropping a kiss to the top of her head. "Love you. Grandpa will pick you up."

"Love you too." She heads off to the coat and backpack rack.

Flynn steps closer to me. "Which one is Sara?"

"Pink shirt sitting at her desk," I say without a lot of thought and then it hits me.

"Got it." He takes a step toward the desks.

I grab a hold of his arm. "Oh my god, Flynn, you cannot yell at her."

His deep chuckle skates over my skin and he carefully removes my fingers. "I'm not going to yell at her. I'm going to introduce myself."

I watch in terror as he starts toward Sara. She's a cute girl. Shiny brown hair, dimples, and always dressed in very trendy outfits that were clearly picked out by an adult.

But before Flynn reaches her, Greer's friend Ben steps in front of him.

"You're Flynn Holland," he says loud enough that the entire class can hear.

Little heads turn to him.

"Oh my goodness." Mrs. Kadia beams. "I thought I recognized you. You pitch for the Mustangs."

"That's right," Flynn says with all the abashed

charm of a man who wouldn't normally want to draw this much attention to himself.

"Greer was telling the truth," another kid says.

I look right at poor Sara whose face turns red. Everyone else flocks to Flynn. The kids ask him questions like, "How tall are you?" and "Can you stay and play kickball with us at recess?"

He stands behind Greer and places both hands protectively on her shoulders as he answers every single one. It's only when the first bell rings that Mrs. Kadia instructs everyone to say goodbye to Mr. Holland. He offers the kids high fives, and they go to their desks with big, awe-filled smiles.

Greer is the last one with him. He squats down in front of her. I can't hear what either of them says, but it ends with her hugging him and me feeling like I might cry.

Emotion clogs my throat as I wave one last time to Greer. Flynn and I leave, and Mrs. Kadia calls the room to attention.

In the hallway, I wait until we're out of sight of the kids and then hug him. He's taken by surprise, but his arms circle my waist, and he hugs me back. I squeeze him hard, still fighting back tears.

"That was really nice of you." The words are muffled into his chest.

His grip on me loosens and I peer up at him.

"It was mostly selfish."

My brows pinch together.

"I couldn't stand the thought of anyone thinking Greer is a liar. Nobody picks on my favorite little girl."

Now I'm the one laughing while he looks like he wants to march back into the classroom. I get it though. Nothing makes me angrier than when someone hurts Greer. It's nice to have a partner that loves my daughter as much as I do. She's lucky. We both are.

Stepping back from him, I lace my fingers with his. "Come on, Hotshot. We're both going to be late for work."

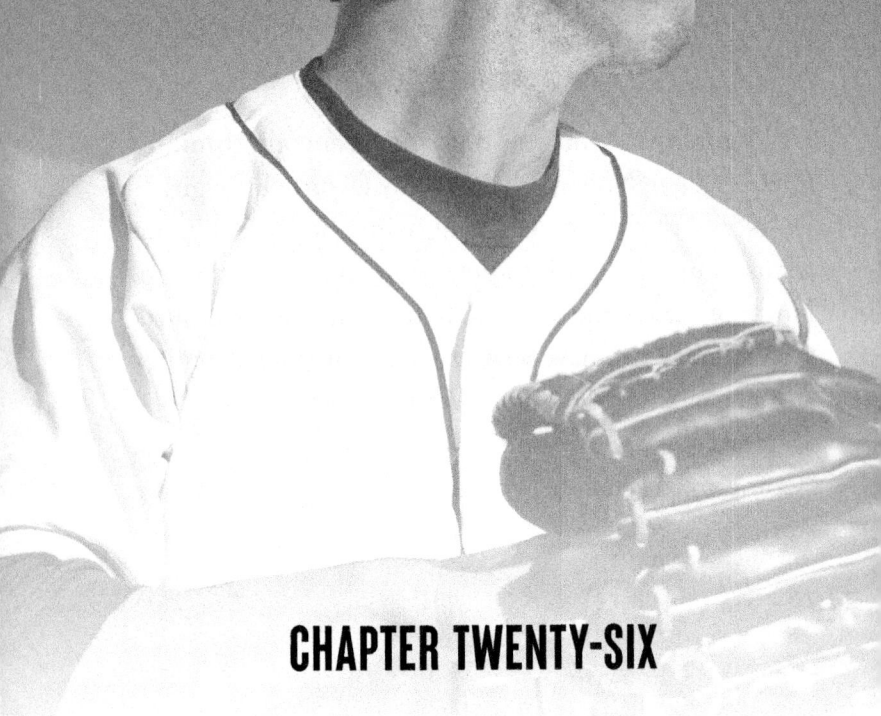

CHAPTER TWENTY-SIX

Flynn

THE FIRST MONTH OF REGULAR SEASON GAMES GOES by in a blur. When I'm not pitching, I'm sitting on the bench antsy to get back out there. Working with the coaches here has been good. Between them and little tidbits I pull out of Earl, it's made a difference. I'm finding my way and starting to be the pitcher I knew I was capable of being.

Unfortunately, my performance hasn't kept us from losing. We're coming off back-to-back losses on the road and I desperately want to get us another win at tonight's game. It's a big game for a lot of reasons, but for me it's the first time I'll be facing the Twins since they let me go.

I get to the stadium hours before the game starts. I

take my phone with me to the training room. The trainers are here, but I'm the first player to arrive.

I tip my head to them and move to a corner of the room. The game is late tonight, so Olivia and Greer aren't making it. Archer and Brogan will be in the stands though. They come to every game they can. Knox and Hendrick too. Knox even made it to see me in Texas. He had a race the next day nearby. I appreciate them and the way they always show up for me. I don't know what I would do without them.

The more time I've spent with Greer, the more I've thought about that. I know my brothers have a hard time with my relationship with Dad, but the truth is I didn't feel his loss the same way they did because I had them. I didn't need a dad because I had them, but I still *want* one.

I click on his contact to call him and then put the phone to my ear. He answers on the third ring.

"Hel-lo." He always says it that way, emphasizing each syllable. The background is noisy with lots of people talking.

"Hey. Where are you?" I ask him.

"Took a little drive up to Sedona."

I guess that answers my question if he's coming tonight. He still hasn't been to a game this season and it's starting to get to me. I know it's early in the season, but it seems like he could have made it to at least one. Last season he was at nearly every game. I don't get it. What's changed?

"Oh."

"You still there?" he asks, and the background is quieter now, like he moved away from people.

"Yeah, I'm here."

"Did you need something or just calling to check in?"

"Both. I haven't heard from you in a couple weeks. Everything good?"

"Yeah. All good here. How about you? Couple of tough losses last week. Your team isn't giving you a lot of help. Someone needs to figure out how to swing a bat over there."

I feel defensive of the guys, especially because JT was feeling down yesterday about his batting average this season. Baseball is a tough game, and everyone is fighting either to get on top or stay there.

"Hoping to turn things around tonight," I say, suddenly feeling like I'm giving a publicity quip instead of talking to my dad.

Things are weird between us lately and I don't know why.

"What did you need?" he asks, pulling me back to the conversation.

"Your birthday party. It's all set up for June 10th. It's a Saturday. Hendrick agreed to host it at The Tipsy Rose. Feel free to invite Terri and whoever else you want."

He's quiet for a beat and I really hope he isn't going to bail. My brothers will never let me forget it.

"Okay."

I breathe a sigh of relief. "You'll be there?"

He makes a grunt of agreement. "I'll be there, but no mention of the number sixty."

"Done." A small smile tips up the corners of my mouth. This is going to be so great. I know it'll be awkward for him and my brothers, but hopefully it's the first of many family get-togethers.

"All right," Dad says. "I better get back out there before someone drinks my beer. Have a good game tonight."

"Thanks."

We hang up and I go through my normal warm-up routine. The rest of the team starts to trickle in too.

Gunnar and Bo arrive together. I give them my usual nod of greeting and go back to warming up, so I'm surprised when they head toward me.

My first reaction is nerves. We've reached a mutual understanding, and they've stopped excluding me outright, but they don't usually seek me out to chit-chat.

"We've got your back tonight," Bo says.

Confusion tugs my brows together.

"You strike them out and we'll make sure we get on base." Gunnar holds out a beefy hand like we're going to arm wrestle.

Hesitantly, I put my palm in his. He grips my hand tight and then pulls me in to his broad chest.

"Pitching arm," I remind him.

"Right." He eases up and I step back, still not sure what to make of the change in them.

As they wander off, I rub my right arm protectively.

319

Earl walked in at some point, and he smiles as he watches Gunnar and Bo retreat.

"Big game tonight," Earl says.

"Yeah," I agree.

"How are you feeling about facing your old teammates?"

He remembered. To be honest, half the reason I'd called my dad was because I wanted someone to talk to about the extra pressure of tonight. My first time going up against my old team. I don't hold any grudges against them for letting me go, but that doesn't mean I don't want to be at my absolute best tonight.

"Barely feels like they were my team anymore," I say. I never thought I'd say this, but I'm enjoying being a Mustang. The things I didn't like about it in the beginning have become quirks that make this place unique. From the weird smell in the showers to the vending machine that routinely steals money, I don't know, this place feels more like home than other teams did.

"Still, I'm sure you want to show them what they're missing out on."

"Yeah." I don't deny that.

It feels like good timing honestly. My pitching is the most consistent it's ever been and now that I'm getting that under control, I should be able to start throwing harder.

I nudge Earl with my forearm as I prepare to change the subject. "You were right. I had JT start watching my front foot. It's made a big difference."

Earl grins proud but then smooths it out, almost like he's embarrassed to have noticed it all. "Someone else would have noticed eventually."

"Maybe." I shrug. "But they didn't. You did. You ever think about coaching again?"

"I'm too old for that. I had my time. And who would keep this place up?" He waves a hand around the room before giving me a face that tells me he thinks it's a ludicrous idea.

"You're good at it. A lot of guys could benefit from your eye. You see things other people don't."

"I appreciate it, kid, but I'm happy where I'm at and the team has plenty of coaches with a lot more experience than me."

I can't tell if he's telling the truth or not about being happy, but I decide not to push. At least for now.

JT walks into the room and moves to his usual warm-up spot. When I catch his eye, he grins wide and gives me a thumbs-up.

"Looks like your teammates are ready to help you show the Twins what they're missing out on," Earl says with a small chuckle.

"Yeah." I return the thumbs-up at JT and then look off in the direction Gunnar and Bo disappeared. Is that what earlier was about? No matter the reason, I'm glad they're ready to play tonight.

"I need to do my rounds, but give 'em hell out there." He pats me on the shoulder.

"I will."

I go over to JT and fall back into stretches next to him.

"You ready to do the damn thing tonight, Holland?" he asks me, his head bobs to the music playing over the speakers.

"Yeah. I am."

He glances at my right arm. "Any soreness or pain?"

"Nah, man, I'm good to go."

"Need an early pep talk?"

I laugh. JT is by far the best catcher I've played with. Not only is he great at correcting me during the game, he's also just a good guy. He knows my quirks and patterns. He reminds me to take my time when I rush or notes differences in my mechanics that cause bad outcomes. I'm at my best when I'm feeling somewhere between playful and competitive. If I try too hard, I get in my head. If I'm too mellow, then I can pull back. JT has strung together the best pregame playlists and warm-up pep talks to keep my mind right.

"I'm good," I say. "You need anything?"

He lunges to the right side, stretching his quads and hips. "That depends. You know any good pep talks?"

"No. Just a warning. I'm going to throw hard tonight."

"That's the best pep talk I've ever heard." His expression softens and his eyes crinkle at the corners with a smile. He holds out a fist to me and I bump mine against it.

CHAPTER TWENTY-SEVEN

Olivia

"I'M NERVOUS." MY LEGS BOUNCE RAPIDLY, AND I TAKE a deep breath.

"You're making *me* nervous," Sabrina notes beside me as she takes another handful of popcorn.

"He's got this," Brogan says on the other side of me.

I nod, letting his words soothe me. The whole crew is here. All Flynn's brothers and their partners. Hendrick and Jane, who I immediately recognized as a former actress from one of my favorite childhood TV shows, Knox and Avery, who look like complete opposites, her in pink and all smiles and him in black with a scowl (except when he looks at her), London came with Brogan, and of course Sabrina with Archer. And me. Flynn doesn't know I'm here. It was a last-minute thing, and I wanted to surprise him.

Flynn nods at JT and then stands tall, winds up, and throws another pitch. I hold my breath in those short seconds before the umpire yells, "Striiiike!"

"Yes," I say quietly, clenching one hand into a fist. The entire row of brothers stands to give Flynn a standing ovation as he jogs off the field.

It's been a tense game. Every inning feels long. Flynn is pitching well. He's only let three batters on base through eight innings. Despite that, the Twins are up 1-0.

"All right. They need to make something happen here," Knox says. He's the last one standing, watching Flynn all the way into the dugout.

I can see the pride in his face. All the brothers wear their support for him proudly, but none more than Knox.

After he accepts high fives and butt pats from his teammates and coaches, Flynn takes a seat to wait through the bottom of the inning.

JT steps up to the plate first. He's been hot on the bat tonight. He was robbed of a home run in the fourth inning when an outfielder made a phenomenal catch, jumping higher than anyone should be able and snatching it before it went out of the park.

He takes a big swing on the first pitch and sends a line drive down the third base line. He takes off for first as the crowd cheers loudly. Everyone is amped up. It's surreal to see this stadium so alive. True, I haven't been to a lot of games over the years, but enough that I can say this season the fans are showing up. I'd bet anything that Flynn is the catalyst for that.

JT is safe at first. The next batter walks out to heavy rock music.

"Let's go, G-Cruise." Two guys in front of us stand and yell down to the field. One of them is wearing a Holland jersey and it makes my lips pull into a smile.

Gunnar Cruise is broad and muscular. His biceps fill out the sleeves of his jersey in a way that looks like he might Hulk out at any moment. He digs in his back foot as he moves into position at the plate.

Again, the first pitch is magic. Gunnar sends the ball soaring out to center field.

Everyone stands to see if it's going to go. My pulse races. The second the ball clears the fence, the stadium roars. The Mustangs have taken the first lead of the night.

I glance back at Flynn amidst the chaos. His body language is relaxed. He leans back against the bench and his head falls back slightly, but he's grinning. I bet he's tired. Eight innings, throwing harder than he has all season, according to the announcement on the jumbotron. The coach could pull him and let someone else finish out the game, but I know Flynn wouldn't want that. Not with the game this close. It's going to be up to him to hold off the Twins and win the game.

The next batter hits a grounder and is thrown out, then Bo hits a pop-up that is caught by the short stop. The inning ends with a strikeout.

Again, I look to Flynn. He stands quickly. His

expression is all business as he grabs his glove. The coach moves to him, and they have a short exchange. Flynn nods and then steps out of the dugout.

I sit back in my seat and immediately feel like I want to throw up. Sabrina pats my leg and holds back an amused smirk.

"You look more nervous than he does," she says.

"That's his superpower, but sadly not mine." It's true. He's so effortlessly chill and I like the illusion of control.

She gives me her hand and I take it and squeeze out some of my anxiety.

"Okay. Ouch. Ouch."

"Sorry." I loosen my grip and a nervous laugh escapes. "I want this for him so badly."

"He's got this," Brogan says again, putting an arm around me and shaking my shoulders lightly.

I nod. "You're right. He's unstoppable."

"Exactly." Brogan gives me one last shake before releasing me.

"The best Holland brother," I say and glance sideways to see his reaction.

"All right. Let's not get carried away," Brogan mutters with a mock frown.

"If he pulls this off, then I think he can claim that title at least for tonight," Knox says.

The first batter for the Twins steps up to the plate. Flynn goes through his usual routine, taking his time and looking confident but at ease on the mound. I try to channel that same energy.

He can do this. He's had an incredible night. Three more outs.

He splits the first two pitches. One ball, one strike. On the third pitch, the batter foul over the third base line. The next pitch is high and inside. The crowd lets out a collective "oooo" as the batter jumps back to avoid being hit. And the next is high.

"Come on, Baby Holland. Show 'em what've you got," Brogan mutters so quietly I barely catch the words.

Flynn takes a little longer setting up for the next pitch, shaking off signals from JT until he finally nods. The pitch looks better, but the umpire rules it as a ball and the batter walks to first base.

I know that inconsistency has been an issue for Flynn, and probably most pitchers. It's why the Twins let him go. No matter how calm he might be out there, he has to feel the pressure to show them they were wrong and not let the last couple pitches determine the rest of the game.

JT runs out to the mound. Flynn keeps his head down as his catcher places the ball in his glove and says something. It's a short exchange, but when Flynn lifts his chin, I can see the change in his expression. The nerves finally fall away. Brogan's right. Flynn has this under control.

The next batter steps up to the plate looking cocky and smug. My heart races as Flynn gets set. I suck in a breath as he fires the first pitch.

The umpire raises his hand in dramatic fashion as he makes the sign and says, "Striiiiike!"

Air leaves my lungs in a whoosh.

By the time Flynn strikes him out, the batter looks a whole lot less cocky. I'm so happy, I want to run out onto the field, jump into his arms, and kiss the crap out of him.

The momentum has shifted, and the next two batters find the same fate.

The stadium goes wild as the last strike is called. The guys in front of us are jumping around and hugging.

"Ahh!" I bounce on my toes and throw my hands over my head, which makes Sabrina laugh.

We're among the last of the fans to trickle out of the stadium. Instead of waiting for Flynn in the family area, we decide to wait for him in the parking lot. Brogan puts the tailgate down, and he and London, Archer, and Sabrina all take a seat. Hendrick got a call from the bar, so he and Jane are standing a few feet away. Which leaves me standing with Avery and Knox.

"Did you text him to tell him you were here?" Avery asks.

"No." I shake my head, then have a moment of panic. "Should I have?"

Her smile is instant, and she reaches out and squeezes my arm lightly. "He's going to be so excited. I've heard nothing but amazing things."

"Really?" It takes me by surprise. I mean, sure I know Archer and Brogan pretty well, but I hadn't really considered that Flynn talked about me.

"Really. He—" She starts to say more, but we're interrupted by Brogan's loud, booming voice as he yells Flynn's name across the parking lot.

I whip around in time to see him walking toward us. Suddenly I don't know what to do or where to stand. I feel exposed and somehow nervous and excited all at once. Maybe he wanted to spend the evening with his family and now I'm interrupting. Admittedly, it doesn't make sense even as I think it, but I still stress all the way until he's right in front of me. He cuts through straight to me.

His brothers call out to him, wishing him a good game and pumping him up. He doesn't look away from me, like he's afraid I'll disappear if he does.

"How are you here?" He grins, scanning me from head to toe.

"Ruby needed a writing break, so she and Greer are having a slumber party, and I didn't want to miss your game."

I wait for him to say something else in reply. Instead, he continues to stare at me. Then the next thing I know he has one arm wrapped around my waist and he's dipping me and bringing his mouth to mine while everyone around us hoots and yells in delight.

I kiss him right back, smiling as I do. His brothers catcall us, and I feel Flynn's mouth curve into a smile. He turns his hat around so he can deepen the kiss. I'm so proud of him and I feel so lucky that he's mine. I don't care who watches us make out in the parking lot.

When he finally pulls me back to standing. He's beaming and I'm pretty sure I'm blushing.

"I have you the rest of the night?" His excitement is

almost more visible than after they won. And he looks damn good in a backward hat.

"I'm all yours, Hotshot."

We pile into vehicles and head to the guys' favorite bar. Once we're there, we pull together a couple of tables and order drinks. I check my phone and open a text from Ruby. She and Greer are cheesing at the camera, both wearing big tiaras and bright blue eyeshadow.

Flynn leans over to look at the image as I heart it.

"I miss her," he says, tone sincere with a hint of surprise like maybe it just occurred to him.

"She misses you too."

That makes him smile.

"Why don't you stay over tonight, and you can see her in the morning?"

Despite Greer's blasé reaction to our first sleepover, he still stays at his place more often than mine. A lot of nights his games go way past Greer's bedtime, or he needs to be at the stadium early in the morning, so it's easier for him to stay at his place since it's closer.

"Yeah. I'd love that. I hate staying at my place now. It's just me and Dick."

I laugh softly. "What about all your other plant babies?"

"Dick is still my favorite and even he doesn't compare to you and Greer."

"That's sweet, I think." Another laugh leaves my lips.

He grins, brown eyes twinkling with amusement.

"You were really great tonight," I say.

After we came up for air, his brothers crowded around to congratulate and hug him. It was great to see them interact, but he and I haven't had a chance to talk about the game yet.

"Thanks. It was a good game. JT and Gunnar really came through." He grins a little wider.

"So did you."

"I should have known you were there. I always play better when you're around."

"I don't think I should take credit for that, but I will anyway. I love watching you pitch. You have this incredible confidence and ease about you up there. It's sexy."

"Yeah?" His grin hitches higher on one side. "You think I'm sexy?"

"Was that not clear?" I arch a brow at him.

He chuckles softly. "Nah, totally knew it, just wanted to hear you say it again."

I can't help but join in laughing with him.

"Was it weird playing against your old team?"

"No," he says immediately. "I thought it would be, but no."

I take that in. I can't imagine moving from team to team like he's done. It must be hard.

"I'm still really happy to pull out a win against them though." He gets a mischievous grin.

"You made them rue the day, for sure."

He chuckles, nodding his head.

"Speaking of victories, I have one more to pull off tonight," Flynn says. "I'll be right back."

He kisses me and then winks as he hurries after his brothers.

I watch him go. He stands between Knox and Brogan, putting his arms around their shoulders playfully. Seeing him with his brothers, so happy and carefree, makes me want to be a part of his life. Not just right now, but all the time. When Flynn is around, he makes everything feel simpler and better. He does that not only for me, but for his brothers too. They all smile more when he's around. He has this way of acknowledging the bad but not lingering in it.

"All right. Time to spill." London's voice pulls my attention to the girls at the table.

They're all staring at me.

I smile hesitantly. "Me?"

"Yeah, you." Avery's sweet-looking smile is aimed right at me. "We're all dying to hear about you and Flynn."

I open my mouth and look around to each of the girls, unsure what to say. I finally settle on, "What do you want to know?"

"What's he like as a boyfriend?" London asks.

"Have you said 'I love you?' Because the way he looks

at you… he's one hundred percent in love." Avery places both elbows on the table and leans in.

"You should see him with Greer," Sabrina adds. "So cute."

"Is he good in bed?" Jane asks.

All of us look at her.

"What?" she asks innocently. "We're all thinking it."

She glances at the others for confirmation, but they just laugh.

"He's great. We're taking it slow. And he is both good with Greer and good in bed." I laugh. "Those are weird thoughts to put together."

"I knew it. Must run in the family," Jane says.

"I heard about what he did for your daughter—showing up in his baseball garb to prove that bully wrong," Avery says. "Classic Flynn. He's always had such a good heart."

"I wish I could have seen that little girl's face." Sabrina looks vicious. She's great with Greer and her kids at the studio, but she does not tolerate bullying.

"It was pretty adorable," I admit.

"Are you in love with him?" London asks.

Again, all eyes are on me, and I feel my face flush.

"It is none of our business." Avery nudges London.

"She absolutely is," Sabrina says. She knows me too well.

"It is none of our business," Avery says again, but she still looks at me expectantly.

I do a quick glance around the table, meeting each

of their eyes. I know how much Flynn means to them. They want to know that he's with someone who cares about him. I get that. So I nod. I am a thousand percent in love with him.

They squeal in unison.

CHAPTER TWENTY-EIGHT

Olivia

ON THE WAY HOME FROM THE BAR, I CHECK IN WITH Ruby who lets me know Greer is fine and that they had a blast. She sends me several pictures of their hang, including one of my sweet daughter asleep in Ruby's bed.

Flynn and I get dropped off at my place, then decide we're hungry so we walk to an all-night diner a block from the apartment.

"I really like your family," I tell him as we walk, swinging our hands between us.

"They're pretty great, huh?" His smile is infectious. I don't think I've ever smiled more around another person.

"Just like you," I cheese, reaching over and squishing his very square and hard jaw together to try to make him look young and cute. It doesn't really work. His brothers might refer to him as Baby Holland, but he is all man.

Flynn laughs as my hand drops away. He opens the diner door for me, and I step inside. It smells like coffee and greasy food. My stomach growls. It's nearly empty. A group of women, maybe a little younger than me, sit in the back talking and laughing loudly, and a couple of customers are at the counter.

I nuzzle into Flynn's side as the hostess greets us.

"Have a seat anywhere you'd like," she says.

As I'm taking another scan of the place, I spot a familiar face at the counter.

"Is that Walter?" I ask Flynn.

"Yeah, it is." He sounds as surprised to see the bookstore owner as I am but then takes a step toward the front counter.

"Wait." I latch on to Flynn's arm to stop him.

"Come on. You can put your rivalry aside for one night."

I don't have the heart to tell Flynn it's a one-sided rivalry. Walter is kicking my ass with little to no effort, at least that's how it looks.

I hide behind Flynn as we approach him. Walter has a mug in front of him as well as a book. Half a sandwich and some fries are abandoned on his plate.

"Walter," Flynn says in a cheery tone.

The older man looks up from his book and swivels to face us. His smile is slow to inch up but does eventually.

"Flynn." He removes his glasses and holds them in one hand. "It's good to see you."

"You too." Flynn opens his stance. "And you know my girlfriend, Olivia. Her family owns The Book Nook down the street from your store."

I think it's the first time I've heard Flynn call me his girlfriend. If he's trying to distract me or butter me up so I'm nice to Walter, it's working on both accounts. I can't fight the smile that tugs at the corners of my mouth.

"Hi." I lift a hand in a small wave.

"Of course. Nice to see you as well."

"I've been meaning to stop by and sign your new stock of jerseys and merch," Flynn says.

Walter makes a face that shows his indifference on the matter.

"Whenever you get a chance. No rush. Congrats on the game tonight. They had it on earlier." He points his glasses toward a small box TV on the wall. It looks like it's been there for several decades.

Flynn's phone vibrates in his jeans pocket. We're standing so close I can feel it. His brows pinch together as he pulls it out.

"Ah. It's my agent," he says to me.

"This late?"

"She's traveling on the West Coast with her husband's hockey team. I better get this. Grab us a table and I'll be right back." He kisses me quick on the cheek. "I'll stop by this week, Walt."

Flynn hurries off with his phone to his ear and leaves me with Walter… or Walt. Leave it to Flynn to have befriended the grumpy bookstore owner and have a nickname for him.

"I should…" I trail off, hitching a thumb over one shoulder to indicate I should find a table. I pause when I see the book in his hands.

"That's one of my top five books of all time. Is that the original cover? I've never seen it in person before." I nod toward the book. It's an old historical romance published more than forty years ago. It's about a farmer and a schoolteacher set in North Dakota in the early nineteen hundreds. I stumbled upon it in my high school library. It's the book that made me fall in love with reading romance, or one of them anyway, and ever since, I've fallen in love over and over again. That's one of the many great things about books.

"It was my wife's favorite. I read it every year around this time. It reminds me of her." He smiles in a way that transforms his whole face. "She passed away three years ago."

"I'm so sorry."

I find myself taking a seat at the counter beside him. "She loved books too?"

"Oh yes. Reading was her sport, that's what she used to say. She read two or three novels a week, always had one with her anywhere she went." Another smile tips the corners of his mouth as if he's picturing it in his head. "It was her idea to start a bookstore once we both retired. Of course, it took longer than planned. I was a history professor with tenure and a cozy office. We thought we'd have plenty of time."

It's the saddest thing anyone has ever told me, but beautiful too.

"You opened the store for her?"

"And for me. I like being surrounded by books. They remind me of her."

That makes sense, but it's so sad.

"And the window art?"

"A hobby of mine." He gives me a conspiratorial glance. "You?"

"Don't tell anyone."

"Why not? They're beautiful. People walk by just to see it."

"I draw for me," he says simply.

The diner door jingles as Flynn walks back inside. I stand from the seat next to Walter.

"Do you want to join us?" I ask him. Maybe Gigi was right and he's just lonely.

He glances back at Flynn, then shakes his head. "Thanks for the offer. You two enjoy your night out."

"Okay," I say, then give him one last smile.

After dinner, Flynn and I head back out to make the walk to my place. It's late, but neither of us is tired.

"What are the odds that his late wife and I share the same favorite book?" I ask, a little dumbfounded still.

Flynn chuckles. I've probably said the same thing a dozen times.

"I'm not sure, but that would make a great trivia question in your bookstore competition."

I swat at him playfully and his grin widens. I shake off the weird encounter, at least for now.

"Tell me again what your agent said."

Now it's his turn to wear that happy, slightly dumbfounded grin.

"She said, and I quote, 'If you keep it up, you're going to have so many offers at the end of the season you'll have to wade through them.'" He chuckles softly. "Everly has a flair for the dramatic."

"She's not wrong though. You played such a great game tonight. Everyone is finally seeing what I knew from the second I met you."

"What's that?" he asks.

"You're a superstar."

He takes a second like he's soaking that in. Good. He should.

"Is everything ready for your big bookstore event?" he asks as we keep walking toward my apartment. It's a novelty for me, being out this late, having him sleep over, and not worrying about Greer—or at least not as much. I want to soak it up. If Flynn does get traded at the end of the season, then I don't want to miss out on a single second like this.

"Yes." Excitement zips through me. I cannot wait. I read an early copy of a debut mystery book and when I reached out to the publisher to let them know how much I enjoyed it, they asked if I'd be interested in hosting a release party for the author. It's turned into a whole event, and I am so excited for it all!

"I'm proud of you." He kisses my knuckles. "Raising the coolest kid, managing a bookstore, bartending at night… it's inspiring."

"Thanks." I laugh lightly. He's the one getting national media attention and still somehow, he's proud of me.

"Hey." He stops.

I take another step but don't get far when he pulls me back with our joined hands. Laughing, I rest a hand on his chest to keep from colliding into him. I look up into his eyes, expecting them to be playful but finding them serious instead.

"What?" I ask, searching his face.

"I love you."

My chest expands and my pulse speeds up. "You do?"

He nods, throat working with a swallow as he keeps looking at me with that same expression.

I drape my arms over his shoulders and then lift onto my toes to lace my fingers behind his neck and pull his head down to mine. "I love you too, superstar."

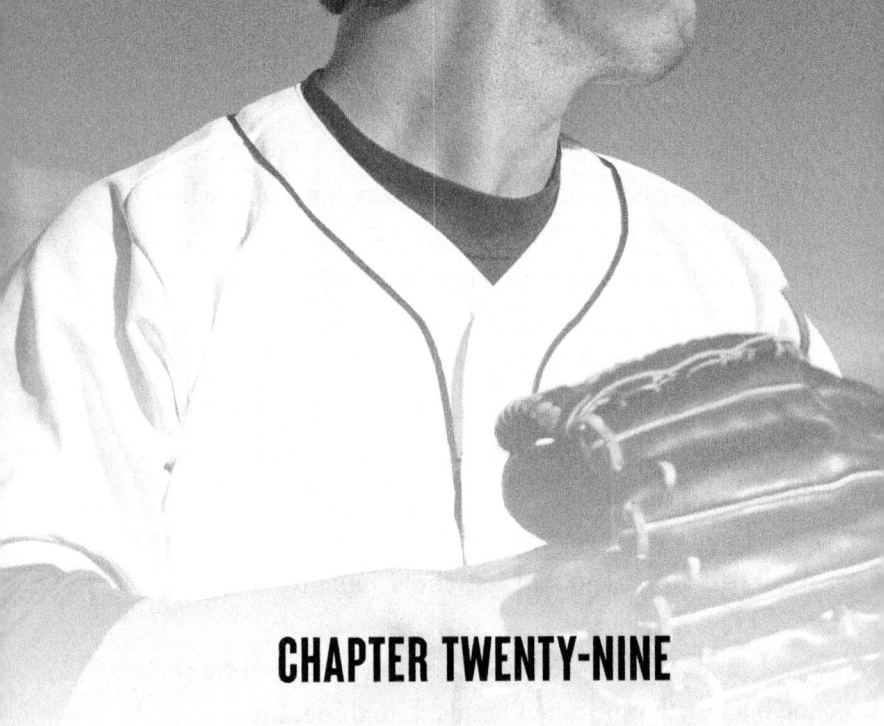

CHAPTER TWENTY-NINE

Flynn

WE HAD A ROAD GAME ON SATURDAY AFTERNOON in Vegas. It's our fourth win in a row and the flight home feels like a party. The guys are all in a good mood, playing cards and listening to music. JT tells stories from previous seasons—the wildest, funniest things that have happened in his years with the Mustangs, and I take it all in.

I want to celebrate with the guys and feel that same sense of excitement for how great the season is going— we're proving to everyone that we're better than they gave us credit for. And just maybe we have what it takes to go all the way this year. But my mind keeps drifting to my dad.

I didn't really expect him to show since we're on the road, but there's always that hope. I can't help but feel like I did something wrong. Last year he went to every game, traveling all over to watch me, and now that I'm finally making something of myself, he's all but disappeared. If I didn't call to check in, would I ever hear from him?

I think of Greer and her dad. Olivia said they talk every Sunday and at the time I thought that was sort of sad, but I'd give just about anything to know my dad was going to call every week at the same time. The not knowing, the second-guessing and mulling it all over and over, is the worst part.

"Hey." JT drops into the seat next to me. "What are you doing back here? You should be celebrating. You are the man of the moment. All those teams that passed you over are kicking themselves."

I flash him a weak smile. "Tired, I guess."

"Tired?" He huffs a laugh. "What, like you threw for seven innings or something?"

He breaks out into a wide smile. "Thank you for this season."

I look at him with confusion.

"I know you didn't want to be here, but you've given these guys something they haven't had in a long time."

"A better winning average?"

"Hope," he says.

"Holland!" Gunnar yells my name in his big, booming voice. Then he and Bo appear in the aisle next to JT.

"What's up?" I ask them.

"I'm having a party at my place tonight. JT can give you the address."

"Actually, I have—"

JT elbows me before I can finish the statement. "We'll be there."

Once they're gone, I say, "I can't stay long. I have something I need to do."

"Yeah, me too, but you have an hour. After that, they'll be drunk and partying and no one will notice when we cut out."

I nod. He's right and I know it's a big deal to be included, but all I want to do is see Olivia and Greer. It's been three days and that's three days too long.

As JT predicted, about an hour after arriving at Gunnar's, the party is so big and wild that no one cares when we head out.

"Thanks for inviting me," I say to Gunnar.

"We have a tradition." He places one hand on my shoulder.

"What kind of tradition?"

JT takes my phone from my hand. I give him a strange look but then Gunnar picks me up.

"What are you doing?" I ask, gripping his big biceps to steady myself.

He marches toward the pool and his intent becomes clear.

"Woah, woah, woah."

"Sorry, Holland," he says seconds before he tosses me into the pool. When I surface, the party is cheering and laughing.

Gunnar is waiting by the side. His hand stretched out to me.

"Like I'm going to trust you," I say and move to the pool wall next to him to pull myself out. My wet clothes are heavy and it's a struggle.

He grabs a hold of my arm and helps, then pulls me into a bear hug, crushing me against his huge chest, water splashing around us. "You're one of us now, Holland."

It's getting dark when I pull up in front of Dad's house. After the party, I went home to change and then planned to go straight to Olivia's house, but when I got in my truck, it seemed to have a mind of its own.

Dad's Harley is in the driveway, and I spot Terri in the front yard trimming her rose bushes.

She smiles at me as I get out of the truck. "What a pleasant surprise."

"Hi, Terri. Is he here?"

"In the garage." She tips her head in that direction.

"Thanks."

The one-car garage is on the right side of the house. As I walk around, the door is open, and rock music plays from an old radio on a workbench. For a moment, I'm struck with the familiarity of it. A memory floats just out of grasp. Dad tinkering on his bike in the garage, music playing. There's something simple about it that feels like home.

The hood is up on his truck and Dad bends over the engine.

"Timing belt acting up again?" I ask him.

He glances up, then stands tall as a smile pulls at his lips. "Flynn. What are you doing here?"

He wipes his hands on a rag and then comes toward me, holding his arms out for a hug.

"It seemed like the only way I was going to see you," I say as we pull back.

He looks me over like he hasn't seen me in a long time, which to be honest is accurate. "You want a beer?"

"No." I shake my head. "I can't stay long."

He grabs a bucket and flips it over for me and we take a seat across from each other.

"To what do I owe the pleasure?" he asks.

"I hadn't heard from you or seen you. I wanted to see how you were."

"Good." He bobs his head up and down. "I saw the highlights from your game in Vegas. Another win. You're having a hell of a season."

I wish I could feel the pride in his voice, but I'm too

stuck in my head. Is he really that proud if he can't even make it to a game?

"What's new with you?" I ask.

"Not much. Getting ready to head out on the road again next week, so I'm getting the truck fixed up."

"Where are you headed?"

"A friend is building a house about an hour north of here and needs some guys for the job. He has a camper I can hook up to the truck, so I won't have to drive back and forth."

An uneasy sensation builds in my gut. "How long will you be gone?"

"A month, maybe two. Depends on how fast things go."

I nod and then something hits me. "You're going to miss your birthday party."

He gives me an apologetic smile. "I don't care about my birthday, and I doubt anyone will miss me."

"I will."

He smiles softly, but I can't mimic the expression. I'm pissed. This is such bullshit and so typical that I can't believe I didn't see it coming.

"I don't get you." My voice comes out louder than intended. "I thought you wanted to repair things with us."

"I do. You and I are good."

"Are we? I haven't seen you in months, you don't call or text, you haven't come to any of my games this season."

He looks like he has a retort ready, but I don't give him time to speak.

"And what about Archer? Things were finally getting better between you two. Have you reached out at all?"

I know the answer by the guilty look on his face.

"I can't keep making excuses for you. I keep saying you've changed, but you haven't. Not really. You're the same selfish guy that comes and goes as he wants without thinking about anyone else." God. I feel so stupid.

"It's just a party."

"No, it isn't. It's another time that you've dipped out on us. How many more chances do you think you'll get with Knox and Hendrick?"

"None, I expect. They wrote me off a long time ago," Dad says as if that's all the rationale he needs for not going.

"Which is exactly why you should come. They're giving you an opening, and you're shitting all over it. Nothing is going to change unless you make the first move. Maybe that isn't fair, but that's parenting. You walked out on us, and now you have a chance to fix it."

"If I'm such a disappointment, then why are you here? Sounds like you're better off without me too." His jaw flexes in a way that reminds me of Knox. And then the memory comes into full view. It isn't Dad working in the garage listening to music, it's Knox. Dad wasn't around because he was never around. But my brothers were. They raised me. I am who I am because of them. I owe them everything. Maybe that isn't how I want the story to go, but it is. How it happens from here on out is on him.

"Do you know what it's like for your own father not

to give a shit about you?" A sardonic laugh leaves my lips. "Let me just tell you, it fucking sucks. I spent my whole life looking for you in the stands, wondering where you were and why you couldn't make it. I'd never wish that on anyone."

He says nothing, though, what is there to say?

"The past is the past, Dad. I don't hold that against you. I never have. But what you do from here on out will determine the relationship that we have." I stand from the stool, ready to leave, but there's one more thing I need to say. For me, for Greer, for every kid like us.

"Someday I'm going to have kids, and I'm going to be there for them in all the ways you weren't. Every game, every birthday, every milestone. I won't be like you, and they won't grow up questioning whether or not their dad gives a shit about them. I let you have a lot of chances to be in my life, but you'll get a lot less to be in theirs. I will protect them from you the same way Knox tried to protect me from you. So, it's on you. Come to the party, or don't. But decide if you're in or out once and for all."

I get it now. I know why Knox has carried a chip on his shoulder all these years and why he was so reluctant for me to have a relationship with Dad. He was trying to keep me from feeling the very thing I feel right now.

I take one last look at my dad. I don't know what the future holds for us, but I feel okay about that for the first time.

CHAPTER THIRTY

Olivia

T HE DAY OF GREER'S KINDERGARTEN GRADUATION, Flynn takes off practice early to come with me. Gigi, Grandpa, and Ruby are also in attendance. I'm under strict instructions to send Sabrina and Archer videos and pictures, as well as her dad. Ruby is standing in the back of the gym where the graduation is being held so she can video chat with my parents so they can see it in real time.

The kids still have two more days of school, but it's almost summer and they are buzzing with excitement for break. None of them can sit still, and I have no idea how the teachers are managing it all.

"Are you okay?" I ask Flynn quietly. His leg is bouncing a mile a minute.

"Yeah," he says quickly. "Great. Look how cute she is up there."

He's been a little off-kilter since his confrontation with his dad over the weekend. I don't know all the details, but he said that they finally had it out over him continually walking in and out of his life. I'm proud of him for standing up to him.

I lace my fingers through his, resting on his leg, and the bouncing stops.

"You did the right thing," I tell him, not for the first time.

"I know." He nods. I think he believes that, but I also know it doesn't make it any easier. Not facing things is easier because you can still believe what you want. Once you force people to commit, you have an answer that you can't ignore. I'm familiar with that, but I can't imagine dealing with it from my own parents. My heart breaks for him.

I squeeze his hand a little tighter and then the principal walks to the microphone to start the program.

It's the most chaotic and adorable hour. Each of the kindergartners walks across the stage in a red cap and gown. There is a slideshow with their picture and a prompt for what they want to be when they grow up.

When it's Greer's turn, our entire row stands and cheers. Greer grins big as she hurries across the stage. Her blonde curls bounce under her cap. I'm vaguely aware that all eyes are on Flynn as he yells loudly. His bond with Greer is more than I ever could have imagined.

"Look."

Gigi points to the slideshow as the principal reads, "When she grows up, Greer wants to be a professional baseball player or a princess."

The audience laughs and I hear more than a few "awws." Tears well in my eyes as I smile and clap. Greer accepts her certificate and then skips off to rejoin her class, sitting on the floor in front of the stage.

"Did you hear that?" Flynn asks as he sits down. He could not look prouder. "Baseball player came before princess."

I lean over and press my lips to his.

As soon as the ceremony is over, we say goodbye to Ruby and my grandparents then Flynn and I take Greer for ice cream to celebrate.

Flynn has Greer on his shoulders as we walk down the sidewalk. I snap a few pictures of them as I follow behind.

He sets her down as we step inside the ice cream shop, then reaches into his pocket and pulls out some money for the claw machine. She takes it eagerly and bounds to the back of the store.

Flynn and I order and then take our ice cream to the same table we sat at a couple of months ago.

"Greer is visiting her dad for ten days in June," I say. It's something I've been meaning to bring up in hopes we could spend some of that time together.

"That long?" His eyes widen.

I love him for that reaction. Here I thought he would be excited for a kid-free week to do whatever we wanted. I should have known better. That's not Flynn's style.

"Yeah. She's excited. They're going to Sea World and the beach and…anyway, I was thinking we could have our own adult vacation, so we don't spend the entire time feeling sad and lonely."

His brows lift and a smirk plays across his face. "Good thinking. What did you have in mind?"

"A weeklong sleepover where we only leave the apartment for food and mandatory activities."

"Mmm. Thinking, thinking," he says playfully as he pulls his phone from his pocket. "Let me ask Everly if I can call in sick to my games that week."

He holds up a finger as if to signal one second, and then puts the phone to his ear. "Hey, Ev. Good timing."

His laughter trails off and slowly his expression changes. I scoop another spoonful of ice cream into my mouth and glance at Greer. She has a look of deep concentration on her face as she moves the crane over to a stuffed blue bunny.

"Are you serious?" Flynn's voice pulls my attention away from Greer.

The happy, playful expression is gone and in its place is one I can't make out.

"That's…" He doesn't finish the sentence. Instead, his throat works with a swallow.

Goosebumps travel up my arms. There's something in his voice that has me on high alert even though he sounds…happy.

"Okay. Yeah, that sounds good," he says, nodding. His leg starts bouncing under the table. "Thanks, Ev."

Flynn moves the phone away from his ear with a dazed expression. He stares straight ahead like he's completely forgotten where he is in this moment.

"Is everything okay?" I ask.

He blinks and then turns to face me. "A trade offer came in today. The Renegades want to buy out my contract."

"Next season?"

His head shakes side-to-side. "No. Like…now."

"What?!"

At my panic, he seems to snap out of it. "Their pitcher is out the rest of the season with an injury. Everly made sure we had a no-trade clause as part of my contract with the Mustangs so I wouldn't end up in another situation like last season. That means it's my decision if I want to go or not."

He stares at me, seeking some sort of reaction.

"That's…amazing." I force a smile because it *is* amazing. This is exactly what he wanted, and he worked hard for it. I wrap one arm around his neck and hug him. I spot Greer and a lump forms in my throat. She's going to be devastated. Tears prick the back of my eyelids. No. Not now. Later I can be sad, but right now I just want to be the support he needs.

"Congratulations." The word is barely a whisper. "I knew you could do it."

CHAPTER THIRTY-ONE

Olivia

"**O**KAY, THIS IS SERIOUSLY COOL," RUBY SAYS AS SHE walks around the bookstore.

It's the night of the book signing for the debut mystery author I read and loved. I put so much work into planning the event. I really want it to be a success, but I hadn't predicted that the rest of my life to be in chaos. It's a good distraction, at least for a few seconds at a time.

"Jealous?" I ask, arching a brow at my sister.

"A little bit."

"We'll throw an even better one for your next release." I adjust the bookmarks and stickers on the swag table. "Speaking of, did you write the ending today?"

"No." Her tone goes glum. "The last chapter continues to elude me."

"Just write a bad chapter and we'll fix it later."

She gives me a horrified look. "You know that is not how I work."

A small laugh escapes my lips. The first one in days.

The first few guests arrive, followed by Sabrina and London.

"You guys came." I hug each of them.

"Of course. We wouldn't miss it," Sabrina says.

"Look at this place. I love it." London turns in a circle, looking around the store. "I'm not a huge reader, but I have the sudden urge to buy a whole shelf full of books."

"Well, in that case, let me show you around," Ruby says with a laugh.

As Ruby and London walk off, I glance around. It looks pretty good, if I do say so myself. We have games and activities; there are chairs set up for a Q&A with the author later, and a reading area for people who want to sit and quietly partake in the night. It's like an open book club with themed food and fun.

Sabrina moves closer and lowers her voice. "How are you doing?"

Flynn left yesterday for New York to meet with the coaches and GM. He said he didn't want to decide right away without talking to them, but he's excited. How could he not be? It's his dream.

"I'm…good." I settle on the word because terrible and heartbroken feel too depressing for such a fun night.

She smirks in a way that says she isn't buying it. She shouldn't. I'm a terrible liar.

"I can be sad after tonight. For now, I need to focus. I want this event to be perfect." I think this could be our niche. Maybe we host monthly book clubs or more regular author signings and events. I love the bookstore, but it's connecting people through stories that makes me happiest. Funny how I'd forgotten that until talking with Walter about his wife's favorite book. Every year he reads it just to feel closer to her. How incredible is that? Stories are powerful and healing and the closest thing to magic that I know. Tonight, I need to harness that magic for myself.

Sabrina nods and a look of determination etches its way into her features. "Okay, let's do this. How can I help?"

For several hours, I manage to push all thoughts of Flynn and New York out of my brain. The bookstore is packed and it takes all of us to keep things going. The author is charming and engaging, and he stays after to sign books. They love him and we sell out of our stock.

I'm putting the last box of swag out on the table when an unexpected face walks through the door.

JT Ryan smiles when he spots me. He's holding the

hand of a stunning woman with dark brown skin. Her lips are painted cherry red and she tilts her head toward him in this cute, adoring way as she stands by his side. I walk to them, stunned. I've only met JT once, but he has that air about him that makes him stand out in a crowd. He has on a blue Mustangs hat, the same one Flynn so often wears, and his hazel eyes twinkle with a friendliness that puts me at ease as I approach him.

"Hi." The greeting comes out like it's a question. What is he doing here?

"Hey. Nice to see you." His deep voice is filled with warmth.

"You too." I turn my gaze to the woman. "I'm Olivia."

"I know. I've heard a lot about you. I'm Whitney," she says with a knowing grin.

"You have?"

"Flynn doesn't shut up about you," JT says.

"And we've run out of new and interesting topics that don't revolve around diapers, teething, and sleep deprivation." Whitney shoots JT this adoring look as she lets out a small laugh.

"Teething. Yikes. I remember that." I suck in air through my teeth.

The three of us share a laugh.

"What are you doing here?" I angle my body so I can glance at the author still signing books on the right side of the store. "Are you a fan?"

"Uhh…" JT follows my line of sight and then looks

back to me. "No. Flynn mentioned your bookstore was having a big event tonight."

"He did?"

"Oh yeah. He made sure the entire team knew. He's so proud of you."

My stomach flips and the ache in my chest deepens. "The feeling is mutual."

"We just wanted to stop by and say congrats. I used to be a big reader. I'm hoping when our little guy starts sleeping through the night again, I might be able to pick it up again." Whitney's smile widens. "Now I know where to come."

"Thank you. I love that and yes, come back any time. I have loads of recommendations for you."

She nods eagerly. "I will take you up on that."

JT lifts their joined hands and places a kiss on her knuckles. The gesture is small but sweet and makes me miss Flynn even more. How many little moments like that do we have left?

Ruby calls for me from behind the counter. I catch her eye and hold up my finger to indicate I'll be there in a minute.

"I better go," I say. "Thank you for coming. And thank you for the way you've welcomed Flynn to the team. He speaks highly of you."

"He's a hell of a guy, but I think you already know that."

I nod, throat tight.

JT's happy expression dims for only a second and

then his smile hitches higher. "Congrats on this. Flynn said it would be packed."

He steps back toward the front door. Whitney offers me one last smile as she says, "It was nice to meet you. I'll be back."

I lift a hand in a wave as they exit.

I have only a moment to sit with the knowledge that Flynn told his teammates about the event and that he expected it to be a success before I jump back into the action.

Our author stays to sign and chat with every single person in line. But even after he's gone, people linger. Small groups form all around the store. The introverts reading in the corner, the extroverts laughing as they play games, and the hardcore fans are gathered around in a huddle, discussing books in detail.

I almost don't want to make them leave, but the store needs to close and I'm running out of energy to keep my emotions at bay.

Ruby stifles a yawn.

"Go home," I tell her. "I've got it from here."

"No. It's fine." She yawns again.

"Go," I say more adamantly. "You need sleep so you can write the last chapter tomorrow."

She gives me a look but doesn't argue this time. While she grabs her backpack from the office, Sabrina, London, and I continue to clean up.

Ruby reemerges and hugs me. "This was incredible.

I'm so proud of you. Best bookstore in the city, at least according to me."

"We'll see," I say.

With a wave to the other girls, Ruby heads out.

"Well…" London places both hands on her hips. "Is it time to kick them out?"

"Yeah. Unfortunately." I really hope they'll come back. I love seeing the store this full.

"Hi, everyone," Sabrina says, raising her voice in the same way I've heard her do in her dance classes. "Thank you for coming tonight. We hope you had a great time. The store is now closed, so please gather your things and head out in an orderly fashion."

"An orderly fashion?" London asks.

"I forgot they aren't five." Sabrina's cheeks pink a little.

I stand at the door and thank everyone as they go. When the last person is gone, I let out a long breath. We did it. The rush of adrenaline washes over me and even with the sadness creeping in, I take a second to feel happy and grateful.

"I feel like I ran a marathon," London says as I shut the door and lock it.

"Same." Sabrina walks behind the front counter and fishes a bottle of champagne from her purse.

"You just carry around booze now?" I ask with a smile.

"I had a hunch tonight would be a smashing success, and we'd want to celebrate." She pops the top and London grabs paper cups for us.

"To Olivia," Sabrina says after we each have our drink.

"To Olivia." London taps her cup against mine. Sabrina does the same.

We walk over to a table with chairs that was used for one of the games tonight and have a seat.

"Thank you, guys, for helping tonight." Gigi is watching Greer, and I thought it was going to be no big deal without her, but I underestimated the work. I don't know what I would have done without them.

"You're welcome," London says.

Sabrina smiles. "You can repay me by telling me how you're really feeling. No bullshit."

"Well, now this feels like bribery booze," I say but take another sip anyway.

London laughs quietly, then says, "If it's any consolation, Brogan is really bummed out, too. He's been moping around ever since he found out."

Sabrina nods in agreement. "Archer too. He's happy for him, of course, but I think they've really enjoyed having him close again."

"I feel sad for me but proud of him. This is his dream, and he's worked so hard for it." I think of the late nights he's spent at the stadium, the aches and pains he rarely complains about, and the way he has done all that and still made time for me and Greer. I mean, amidst all this he somehow found time to tell his teammates about tonight.

"You could still visit on weekends and during the off-season," London says. "During the busiest part of football season, I barely see Brogan and we live together."

"Does Greer know?" Sabrina asks.

"No." I shake my head. "I don't want to tell her until everything is settled, but I won't be able to keep it from her for long. New York wants him there next week."

She'll be sad, just like me, but we'll get through it. I knew inviting him into our lives was risky, but I still believe the good he brought in was worth it. I hope I was right.

"He asked me if I'd consider going with him." I glance down at the cup in my hands.

"He did?" Sabrina squeaks her surprise. I can tell she wasn't expecting that.

"Are you going to go?" London asks.

"We've been dating for such a short time. I can't uproot Greer's life. Her family, friends, school… everything is here. And the bookstore." I glance around at this place that has been home as much as anywhere I've ever lived. "I can't imagine leaving this behind."

A solemn quiet falls around us.

London is the first to break it. "New York isn't that great anyway."

Sabrina and I laugh and the ache in my chest loosens.

"It's late. I think I'm going to leave the rest of the cleanup for the morning." I stand and then they follow me.

I hug each of them and walk them to the door. Once they're gone, I head to the back office to grab my stuff and turn off the lights.

The note wall draws me to it tonight. I pick a random spot and read a few of them.

Enjoy the peaches.

Be home late tonight.

Twenty years and counting x

Twenty years. Gosh, what that must be like to spend so much time with someone. I wonder what Flynn will be like in twenty years. Where will he be? Most baseball players have retired from the sport by their late thirties or early forties. What will Flynn do after that?

I have this image of him with a whole brood of kids, taking them to the park and teaching them baseball. Ugh. I have to stop torturing myself.

Since Greer is staying with my grandparents tonight, I head to the apartment by myself. As I approach my front door, a man stands from the top step.

Flynn.

My pulse kicks up as he unfolds himself and aims a smile at me.

"Hi." He stays where he is, and I'm temporarily frozen in place.

Then I rush to him.

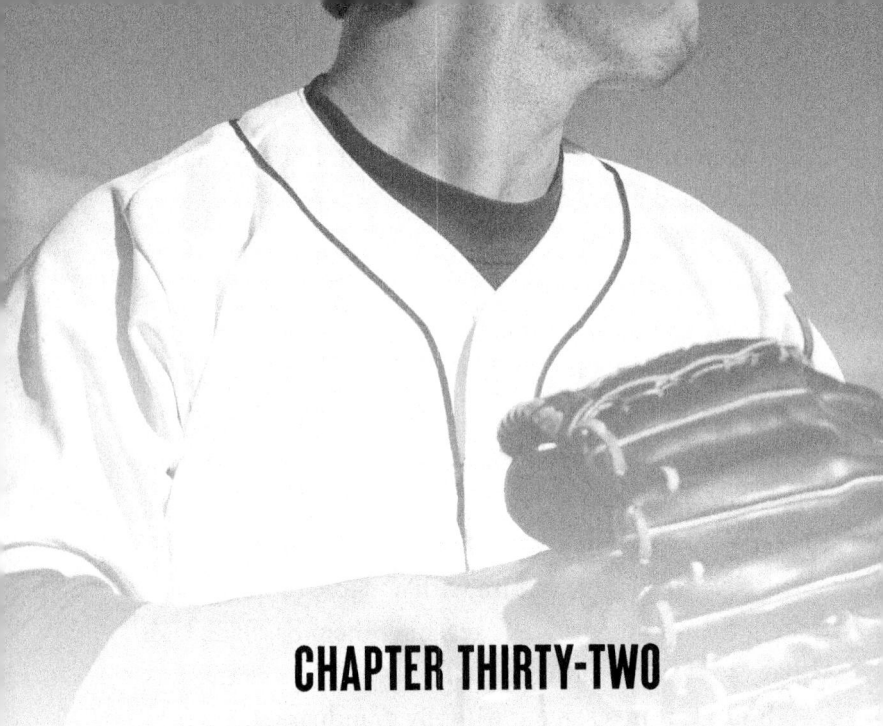

CHAPTER THIRTY-TWO

Flynn

I WAKE UP TO AN EMPTY BED. I HADN'T MEANT TO FALL asleep. The long, restless nights have caught up with me. And I think my body relaxes more when I'm with Olivia. She feels like home.

I listen for her as I get up and pull on my jeans. The apartment is quiet, but small enough that it isn't hard to find her.

Olivia sits on the couch with a book in her lap. It's closed and she stares out the dark window like she's deep in thought.

"What are you doing?" I ask.

Her attention snaps to me and she blinks several

times. She tosses the book onto the coffee table. "I couldn't sleep."

I cross the room and sit beside her, then pull her onto my lap. She wraps her arms around my neck and buries her head in my shoulder.

This whole thing sucks. New York was great. They said all the things I wanted them to say—that they were wrong, that I've come a long way, that they think I'd be an asset to their team.

I always thought this moment would be full of joy and excitement, but I can't shake the feeling that it's requiring me to sacrifice a lot. I'll have to leave Olivia, Greer, my brothers, my team.

My hands rub slow circles on her back as I breathe her in. I shift so that I can look into her eyes. I push her hair back away from her face.

"Did you give any more thought to coming with me?" I know it's a lot to ask of her, but it all feels so much more exciting with her at my side. "They'll put me up in housing for three months until I find a place. They said there are lots of great schools nearby for Greer. We can go check them out together and I can ask the other guys on the team. I want to make this work."

"So do I," she says in a sad voice. "If it were just me, I'd follow you in an instant. There is nothing I want more than to see you achieve everything you want. You're such a good man and so freaking talented."

She doesn't even have to say it. I know what's holding

her back. I know and I respect it, but it still guts me knowing she isn't coming with me.

"It's a big ask and I get it. You're a great mom. It's one of the many reasons I love you. Greer is lucky to have you always looking out for her."

I swallow the lump in my throat. It doesn't escape me that she's doing the thing I wish my dad had done for me—putting her daughter's happiness over her own.

"We could do long-distance, at least for a while. Greer and I can come up for a weekend sometime and you can show us around." She smiles, but it feels like goodbye.

"Of course. I would love that."

"I do love you," she says, like she wants to reassure me. Her hands come up and frame my face. "I love you more than I have ever loved anyone."

I blow out a breath that feels like it steals the life from me and press my forehead against hers.

"When will you leave?" she asks quietly.

"Sunday."

"As in forty-eight hours from now? *That* Sunday?" There's a slight look of panic in her eyes as the realization washes over her.

"Yeah. We play New York at home on Saturday. It'll be my last game with the Mustangs."

"You have to play your new team with your old team?"

"Yeah." It doesn't feel weird yet, but maybe it's because it hasn't really sunk in that I'm leaving.

Olivia nods and she gets that stubborn look on her

face that I fell in love with. "Then we better make the most of the time we have left."

"So you're going, then?" Knox asks.

"Yeah." I nod and fix my gaze to the bar.

Knox and Hendrick drove up today. They were already planning to make the trip to watch the game tomorrow, but they decided to come up early to hang out. It might be our last time for a while.

"So that's it? It's done? There's no changing your mind." Brogan tosses the next one out there. It's been nonstop, one question after another.

"I told them I'd let them know tomorrow, but there isn't a lot to think about."

Archer blows out a breath. "Hell of a decision."

"Is it?" Brogan lifts a brow. "Seems simple enough."

All of us look to him.

"Stay here," he says with a shrug like the answer is obvious. "We're here, your girl is here, what else do you need?"

"A team that's won in the last fifty years," Hendrick says with a light chuckle. "And he said Olivia and Greer might go with him eventually."

"Yeah, but I'm not." Brogan jabs a thumb toward himself.

Archer gives me a sympathetic smile and pats his best friend on the shoulder.

"I thought you'd be happy for me. Flynn the Flaaaaame," I mock in his big, booming voice. He's been my loudest, if not biggest, supporter.

"I am. I am. But fuck, I'm going to miss you, Baby Holland. I liked us all being in the same state again. It's nice."

"I'll still come back to visit," I promise.

Brogan's lips are in a tight line as he nods.

The conversation continues with them asking me more questions about the Renegades and Brogan looking sadder with each answer. Eventually, he heads off to the dartboard and Archer and Hendrick follow him.

"He'll be all right," Knox says, as if reading my concern.

I hate that our last night out is shrouded in sadness. I get it though. I'll miss them too.

"Am I doing the right thing?" I ask Knox.

"I can't answer that for you."

I glare slightly. "Gee, thanks."

He chuckles. "It doesn't matter what I would do, or anyone else. What do you want?"

"I've dreamt of New York all my life, but I don't hate playing with the Mustangs like I thought I would. They're a good group of guys."

Knox nods. "That counts for something."

"And I have enjoyed seeing you guys more."

"The group chat is less annoying when we don't have to track you down." His mouth pulls into a smirk.

"You know, I spent a lot of my life thinking I needed to get out on my own and prove I could take care of myself. I always had you four looking out for me. I was grateful, don't get me wrong, but I also just wanted to know that I could stand on my own."

"You stood on your own a long time. We may have been looking out for you, but you didn't really need it. You've always been a good kid."

"Kid," I grumble with a small laugh.

"Good man," he amends.

"I am the man I am because of all of you. Good or bad. You're with me everywhere. That won't change in New York."

"I know. And whatever decision you make, I'm behind you. So are they." A look that I can only describe as pride is etched into his features. That's one thing I've never second-guessed. I know without a doubt that Knox has my back. Always. It's why I've always been free to chase my dreams.

I take a drink of my beer. "I'm going to go to New York. This is my chance. And I promise I'll visit and check in more on the group chat. Brogan is fucking chatty though."

"You're not wrong about that." Knox tries a small smile. I can't tell if he thinks it's the right decision or not, but I know what he said is true—they'll all support me no matter what.

"I should get going. I want to spend as much time with Olivia as I can before I leave." I need to see her, need to make plans, need to figure out how to hang on to her amidst all this. And I need to figure out how to tell Greer. My stomach is in knots thinking about how hard that is going to be. "Any tips on how to tell a six-year-old that you're following your dream across the country?"

I think of Dad popping in and out and how many times Knox had to break it to me that he was gone.

"You're not Dad," he says as if reading my thoughts. "Be honest and don't promise anything you aren't prepared to follow through on."

Sounds easy enough, but it's going to break my heart to leave her. I blow out a breath and stand. "See you at the game tomorrow?"

"Yep. I wouldn't miss it."

I punch him on the shoulder and start to go, then pause and turn back.

"Hey, Knox."

"Yeah?" He turns to face me, brows lifted.

"Thank you."

"For what?"

"Keeping us all together, raising me, protecting me as best you could, putting your dreams on hold...pick your poison."

He stands, giving me a look of bewilderment. "It wasn't poison. I love you. You're my baby bro. I'd do anything for you. Even visit you in New York if I have to."

"It wasn't anything. It was everything."

He grabs me by the neck and then ruffles my hair. Neither of us says anything, but my throat is tight as he pulls me into a hug.

"Go see your girls. I'll talk to you tomorrow."

As soon as I walk in the door at Olivia's apartment, Greer races up to me. There's nothing else quite like the excitement and adoration in her face when she sees me. So pure and uninhibited.

"Guess what?!" She doesn't wait for me to answer. "I'm going to play baseball for the Mustangs this summer."

She bounces in front of me. Her curls are covered by a blue Mustangs hat. It's too big and falls down onto her forehead, nearly covering her eyes.

I glance at Olivia, standing next to her, then back to Greer. "Is that right?"

"Yeah. Isn't that great? I'm going to be just like you, Hotshot. Will you come watch me play?"

My chest feels like it's been cracked open.

Another quick peek at Olivia confirms she's feeling the same misery.

"Grandpa signed her up for the youth camp at the stadium this summer," Olivia explains with a hitch in her voice that makes it sound like she's as close to tears as I feel.

"Right," I say, then squat down so I'm eye-level with Greer. "That's awesome. You're going to kill it out there. Let me see your wind up?"

With glee, she lifts her left leg while holding both hands up at her chest like she's cradling a ball, then steps and throws. When she's done, she looks to me for my feedback.

I clear my throat in an attempt to dislodge the giant lump. "That was perfect."

"Duh. I learned from the best." She adjusts the hat so more of her big, green eyes are showing. "So will you come watch me?"

Goddamn this is going to hurt so much more than I ever imagined.

"Let's go sit down on the couch," Olivia says and takes a step in that direction.

She and Greer head that way. I'm slow to stand upright and slower to move toward them. Every step feels wooden.

Olivia sits on one side of the couch, Greer in the middle. I take a seat on the other side of my favorite little girl in the whole world. It isn't an exaggeration. Sure, she's the only one I really know, but it doesn't make it any less true. She's taught me so much about the man I want to be. The father I hope to be someday too.

"We have something to tell you," Olivia starts.

Greer is too young for that sentence to inspire any type of fearful reaction. She rests one little palm on my knee as she kicks her feet against the couch.

Olivia meets my gaze above her daughter's head. It feels like my cue.

"You know how sometimes baseball players get traded to different teams?" I ask Greer.

She nods, still unphased. "Like you last year. You played for Minnesota."

"That's right. Then I came here, and I met you." I smile at her. A real, genuine smile despite the warring in my body. I wouldn't change the past few months for anything.

She leans over and hugs me around the middle. My eyes burn and I swallow hard. When I look to Olivia for help, her eyes are watery, but she has a steely resolve in her expression like she's forbidding the tears to fall.

"Flynn's such a great pitcher that lots of teams want him to play for them, including the Renegades—the best team in the league. Isn't that cool?" Olivia asks her.

Greer pulls back and her arms fall from my waist, but her body still rests against mine. Her brows furrow and her feet stop kicking. "I guess, but I like the Mustangs better. And Grandpa says this season we're as good as any other team because of Hotshot."

That unabashed smile filled with joy and simplicity is back on her face. I've had a lot of people believe in me: my brothers, my dad, friends, teammates, coaches, Everly, Olivia. But none feel quite as inspiring as Greer's unwavering belief in me. If I told her I was going to throw a perfect game, she'd consider it as good as done. She thinks I can do anything. Full stop. And I want to for her.

I find my voice, speaking with gravel scraping up my throat. "What your mom is trying to say is that I'm not going to be playing for the Mustangs anymore. Tomorrow is my last game with them, and then I'll moving to New York to play for the Renegades."

It's the first time I've said the words, and it doesn't feel the way I always thought it would. I'm going to be a Renegade. A lifetime dream achieved.

She inches away slowly, moving closer to her mom. "Does that mean we can't go for ice cream anymore?"

I hear Knox's advice—don't make promises you can't keep.

"I won't be here, but I'll bet your mom will still take you."

Olivia nods. "And we can still watch Flynn play on TV."

"But I'm your favorite kid in the whole world." Big tears well in her eyes and she doesn't do anything to stop them from falling down her face.

I reach out and wipe them away with my thumb. "Always."

She turns away from me and buries her face in Olivia's side, hugging her mom hard. The Mustang hat falls off her head and falls to the ground. Olivia wraps an arm around Greer and gives me a sad, understanding smile.

"Hey." Olivia leans down to meet Greer's gaze. "How about we all go get ice cream right now? I know it doesn't feel good for us because we'll miss him, but this is exciting for Flynn. And we should celebrate when good things happen to other people, right?"

She nods the tiniest bit.

"Okay." Olivia manages to put on a smile and speak without sounding like she's gutted, even though I can tell she's still upset. "Get your shoes on and I'm going to make sure we have lots of quarters for the claw machine."

Greer gets up slowly and walks to her room. I let out a long breath and let my head fall back to rest against the couch. Olivia finds my hand and laces her fingers through mine.

I glance at her.

"She'll be okay," she says quietly.

Yeah, but will I?

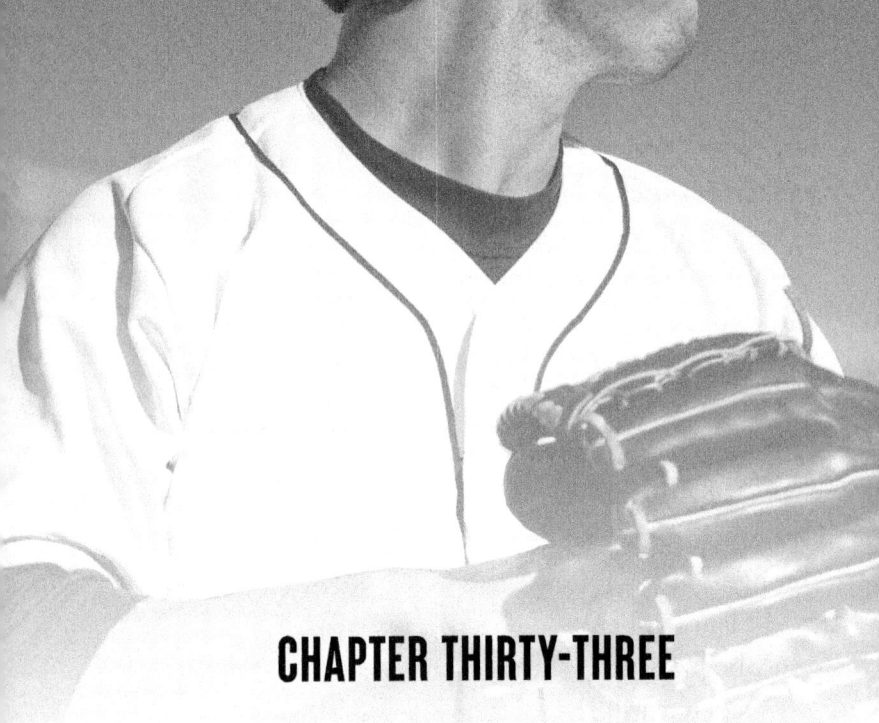

CHAPTER THIRTY-THREE

Flynn

GET TO THE STADIUM EARLY ON SATURDAY AFTERNOON. It's surreal walking into the building for the last time. The entire day has been filled with last moments. My last day as a Mustang, the last time I drive to the stadium, and on and on.

Everly is waiting for me in one of the conference rooms. Her husband, Jack, is seated next to her, and the Mustangs GM, Charles, stands against one wall.

"Hey," I say as I pause just inside the room, letting my gaze roam over each of them.

I move toward Charles first and extend a hand.

"Thank you for everything," I say as we shake.

"You're welcome. I'm sad to see you go, but I look

forward to watching your career. Best of luck." He gives me a polite nod as he steps away.

"Thanks, Charles. I appreciate it."

Once he's gone, I look to Everly and Jack.

He stands first. "Congrats. I hope you don't mind I tagged along with my wife. I've never seen her so excited."

"This is a big moment," she says, eyes lit up with excitement. "Huge."

"Not at all," I tell him. "It's good to see you. And congratulations to you as well. Surprised the Wildcats let you out of their sight."

Jack is one of the best hockey players of all time. He's crushed record after record and is a shoo-in for the Hall of Fame. His team just secured a conference championship and will play in the Cup finals next week.

"Quick trip." He smiles. "Back to business tomorrow."

I nod in understanding.

Everly stands from her chair and beams at me. "Ready to make it official?"

"Yeah." I round the table and take a seat at one end.

Everly opens her laptop and goes straight into explaining the details of the contract. I listen, not really hearing her, but nodding along anyway.

My foot bounces under the table and my heart is racing. This is it. The contract that changes everything for me. I'm going to be part of a great team. One that has the means to bring together the most talented players and coaches. Not to mention the best facilities in the league. No more potluck food or vintage video equipment.

"All that's left is for you to sign," she says finally.

My finger hovers over the track pad. I scroll to the signature box and click. Then pause. A cool sweat breaks out on my forehead. The air conditioning in the building probably stopped working. A hint of a smile tugs at one side of my mouth as I imagine the guys giving Earl a hard time and him working hard to find someone to fix it quick.

My phone vibrates in my pocket. I sit back and pull it out.

"Ah," I say, standing. "One second. I need to meet the pizza guy at the door."

"Pizza guy?" Jack asks, lifting one dark brow.

"It's my day to bring in food for the team and staff," I say, then realize by the surprised expression on their faces that somewhere along the way it stopped being weird to me.

It's kind of fun never knowing what kind of food to expect. Gunnar always brings in a big crockpot of his homemade chili, Freddie loves a salad bar, and JT's wife's muffins and other baked goods are still my favorite.

"Sure," Everly says. "We have until the end of the day."

"Great." I start for the door, then pause inside it with one hand on the frame. "Why don't you email it to me. That way you two can get out of here and get lunch or whatever… enjoy your day together."

Everly's brows pull together, but she smooths out the expression quickly. She steals a glance at Jack and then nods. "Okay. We'll get out of your way so you can prep for the game, but we'll be back tonight to watch you play. If you haven't had a chance to sign by then, we can reconvene."

"Thanks, Everly." I rap my knuckles on the doorframe and then head to meet the pizza guy.

Once I've retrieved the food, I take it to the kitchen. Gunnar and Bo are leaning against the counter, protein shakes in hand.

"Hey, guys," I say. "Bo, your pineapple and ham is on the bottom."

He grunts his acknowledgment, but neither guy says anything else. Their stoic demeanors tell me everything. Fuck. This is harder than I thought it would be. They were slow to warm up to me, but they did. And now I'm leaving them the exact way they feared.

"Thank you for welcoming me onto the team. It's been an honor to play with you guys. I know you're pissed, but how about one last hurrah?" I ask, shoving my hands in my pockets.

They both stare at me, unspeaking for so long that my back sweats and my T-shirt sticks to it. Somebody needs to find Earl and tell him there's a problem with the air conditioning.

Bo is the first to step forward. He extends a fist to me.

I bump it and then hold it up, waiting for Gunnar.

He relents without looking all that thrilled about it. "Let's do it."

After I stretch and warm up my body, I finally spot Earl. His is one of the few friendly smiles I've gotten around here today.

"Are you ready to give the fans one more show?" he asks me.

"Definitely." Another last. Standing on Fletcher field in a Mustangs uniform.

"Give 'em hell," he says with a grin.

"Will do." I take a step away, then stop. "Hey, Earl. Have you checked the air conditioning lately?"

His bushy brows pinch together.

"I've been sweating in here all day. You haven't noticed?"

His head moves in a slow nod. "Feels okay to me, but I'll look into it."

After I've changed into my uniform and gone out to the field, I take my time soaking in every little thing. I hold the ball in my right hand and look around at the familiar stadium. It isn't the fanciest in the league, not by far. Still, it's become home.

I go through my normal routine, but I take more time with each step. When the Renegades filter out to the dugout, I stare at them across the field. My gut clenches.

"Holland!" Coach Wayne hollers my name as he walks out onto the field.

I pull my gaze from the other team and start toward him. He walks with both hands on his hips and his jaw working fast on a piece of gum.

"Last-minute change to the lineup," he says when he gets close. "Freddie is starting today. New York doesn't want to go up against their new superstar pitcher."

A wave of disappointment washes over me.

"Seriously?"

He gives me a solemn nod, then calls out to Freddie who's warming up nearby. "Jones, you're up tonight."

Freddie glances to me first before he dips his chin. "Got it."

Olivia and Greer arrive early to the game and Earl brings them down to the field.

"Hi!" Olivia smiles as I approach them. Fuck, after the morning I've had, it feels so good to see them. Unfortunately, only one of them looks happy to see me.

Greer stares at her feet, holding a piece of paper in front of her in one hand. The stuffed horse I gave her is in the other.

"We wanted to wish you luck on your last game as a Mustang," Olivia says, then looks to her daughter. "Didn't we?"

Greer says nothing and won't look up either.

"*Sorry,*" Olivia mouths.

I squat down in front of Greer. Her big, green eyes are filled with tears. My heart cracks wide open.

"Hey, munchkin," I say, smiling at her.

Olivia and I told her last night. At first, she seemed pretty chill about it, until she started asking questions about when she'd be able to watch me pitch again and how often we would be able to get ice cream together or finally play Monopoly. To be fair, I didn't like the answers to those questions any more than she did.

"Hey, Hotshot." Her little voice is small and not filled with any of her usual excitement or sass.

"Excited to watch the game today?" I ask.

She nods politely. "I made you a picture."

"You did?" I ask as she holds it out to me. It's a picture of me in my baseball uniform. This time she used the Renegade red instead of Mustang blue. And written above it says, *Good Luck, Hotshot.*

"I love it. Thank you." The words nearly get stuck in my throat. I hold my arms out and she steps into them.

I lock eyes with Olivia as I hug her daughter. She wipes a tear from the corner of her eye, but she doesn't stop smiling.

"Mom said I could text you and video chat sometimes," Greer says.

"I'd love that." I want to promise her that we'll see each other, that I'll be back, or they'll come see me, but I remember what Knox said—don't make promises you can't keep.

"We better get to our seats," Olivia says, placing her hands on Greer's shoulders. "Are you still coming over later?"

"Absolutely. I wouldn't miss it." The worst of the lasts, my last time hanging with them before I leave.

I take my picture from Greer to the locker room. It's busy, everyone grabbing any last-minute things before we take the field to do our final team warm-up.

JT is sitting on the bench in front of his locker, adjusting his leg guards.

Staring down at the drawing, I take a seat next to him.

"Heard the news," he says by way of greeting. "Sorry they took your last start from you."

"Thanks. I guess I should have seen it coming." I hold up the picture Greer drew for me. "What do you see?"

"Cute," he says. "Did Greer draw that?"

"Yeah," I say. "Do you see what I see?"

"Uhh…" He glances at the picture and back to me several times. "Is this a trick question?"

I don't answer.

"It's a drawing of you, right?"

"Yes, it's me, but what do you *see*?" I stand and grab the first drawing she made for me. It's been hanging in my locker since Greer gave it to me. Now I hold them up, side by side, for JT.

He gives them both a quick glance. "She switched the color of your uniform. That's cute."

"And?"

He cocks a brow. "And what?"

"Look at the pictures. What's missing in this one?" I shake the new picture. I'm all alone. No Olivia. No Greer. Just me.

"Are you okay?" JT asks.

I let my hands fall and I slump back on the seat. "Yeah. Fine."

"All right." He looks me over but stands. "I'll see you out there."

I have never loved sitting on the bench, but it's torture tonight. The guys are all giving me a wide berth. I don't want to give myself too much credit, but it feels like my mood has infected the entire team.

We're not playing like I know we can. Errors, sloppy fielding, slow bats, and shaky pitching.

It's the bottom of the eighth inning and, somehow, we've managed to stay within one run of New York.

My leg bounces and I sit forward so my elbows rest on my knees. JT is next to me, and he keeps giving me curious glances and asking if I'm okay.

"Let's go now, Bo." Gunnar claps his hands as his friend steps up to the plate.

The pitch is fast and right down the middle. Bo gets a big cut of it and everyone in the dugout stands. It sails high out to center field and into the upper seats.

"Yes." I make a fist and turn to celebrate with my teammates, but they're already filing out to congratulate Bo as he steps across home plate.

I stay there, watching them and feeling like an outsider.

The energy shifts now that we're tied. Two more guys get on base, then Gunnar hits a double, giving us our first lead of the game.

Freddie sighs and puts his head between his knees.

"Are you okay?" I ask him.

"I don't think I can hold them off another inning," he says as he sits back.

His relief pitcher tonight is Roger, a veteran with a mean slider, but he's been struggling through some back pain lately. The trainers are out there with him, keeping an eye on things, as he warms up. His windup looks painful even from here. *Fuck.*

"Wishing you could go out there about now?" he asks with a grin.

"You have no idea."

"Us too. It'd be something to pull off a win against the Renegades for the first time in as long as any of us can remember."

"Yeah," I agree.

Some of his easygoing attitude resurfaces. "It's just one game."

Maybe, but it's my last game, and this sucks.

The inning ends and Freddie stands, blows out a long breath, and reaches for his glove.

"Wish me luck," he says before heading to the mound.

Freddie looks like he's going to be able to keep it together as he warms up before the inning. It's obvious that he's tired, but he fires the ball over the plate with a confidence and speed that has our bench feeling a sense of relief and hope.

It doesn't last long. The first batter steps up and hits a line drive down the center of the field off the first pitch. That's when Freddie unravels. I'm not sure why Coach doesn't pull him immediately, maybe he thinks there's a chance Freddie can still pull it together or maybe he's worried about Roger doing more harm to his back. Whatever the reason, it isn't until the bases are loaded that Coach walks out to the mound.

He gives Freddie a pat and the two of them walk off the field. The stadium is on their feet for him, but it's a resigned type of applause that tells me everyone has given up on this game.

Roger takes a few practice pitches with JT. He grimaces every time the ball leaves his hands. I feel like I'm going to throw up.

Standing, I pace back and forth in the dugout. I want to be out there so badly. My stomach is in knots as the next batter steps up to the plate.

The tension is palpable as Roger shakes off a signal and then nods at the next one. He winds up and lets one loose. I hold my breath as I wait for the result. The batter gets a piece of it, but it fouls off beyond the third base line.

"Shit, he's hurting," someone says down the bench.

I glance back at Roger. He's trying to walk it off, but the way he's holding himself, it's obvious he's in pain.

Coach's mouth turns down and he walks out to the mound to check on him.

Without thinking, I grab my glove and follow him.

Coach Wayne stops me. "Woah, where are you going, Holland?"

"To finish this."

"New York doesn't want—"

"I don't care. Tonight, this is still my team, and I want to finish this thing."

He nods slowly, jaw still working fast on a piece of gum. "All right, then."

While he lets everyone else know, I start to warm up beside the dugout. Someone must catch sight of me because soon I can hear a few people chanting, "Flynn the Flame, Flynn the Flame."

Brogan would be so happy to know his nickname has caught on. I let out a soft chuckle and then refocus. Three outs and this game is over. Bases are loaded and they're at the top of their lineup, which means no mistakes. Every pitch counts.

Roger starts off the field and I move to the mound. The chant gets louder. Once I'm in position, I hold the ball in my hand and look up to where I know Olivia and Greer are watching. They're both on their feet, clapping.

Next, I find my brothers. Brogan has his arms raised over his head and even from here I can see his mouth

moving along with the chant. Knox, Hendrick, Archer…
and my dad. I blink a few times to make sure I'm not
seeing things, but there he is standing next to Archer.

JT jogs up to me, pulling my attention back to the
game. "Quite a pickle you walked into."

"Yeah." I huff a small laugh and glance around the
full bases.

"I don't have a pep talk planned, but something tells
me you don't need it tonight anyway."

"I'm good," I say, confirming his thoughts.

"All right, then. What do you say? Wanna play catch
one last time?"

"Yeah." I nod, adrenaline working its way through
my body.

He turns to get back behind the plate.

"Yo, JT," I call out to him.

He stops and arches one brow as he looks to me.
"Yeah?"

"Just thought I should warn you I'm going to throw
hard and fast."

He grins. "No warning necessary. I can tell by that
look in your eye."

That's probably true. He can read me better than any
catcher I've ever played with.

We finally get set. I throw to JT until my arm is warm
and loose, then the New York batter moves to the plate.

I'm laser-focused and filled with a confidence that
I've never felt before.

I strike out the first guy in three pitches.

The next batter steps up, smirking in a cocky way that makes me want to laugh. Sorry, bro, tonight is not your night.

Three more pitches and he's walking back to the dugout with the same fate.

One more batter. One more out.

The stadium is loud now. I let the noise in for only a moment, not wanting it to distract me or pull me out of my flow. I swear I can hear Brogan's voice in the chant that still yells my name.

I used to think that all fields and all stadiums were basically the same. Interchangeable. But this one is special. It isn't the nicest, but there's an irreplaceable sense of family and community here. Fans like Earl who have loved this team through all the tough times. It would have been easy for them all to give up, but they didn't.

And I'm not going to now.

The next batter for the Renegades comes out. Nice guy. I met him when I was in New York earlier this week. I even threw him a few. He's consistent and patient. I won't be able to sneak anything by him now.

He fouls off the first pitch, hitting up and back behind the plate out of play. He's expecting my fastball, so I give him a changeup next.

"Striiiiike," the umpire calls. The crowd is electric.

I find Olivia. She thinks I'm bullshitting when I tell her I can pick her out from here, but there's no missing her. She looks as confident in me as ever. I don't know what I did to deserve her support and love, but I'm not walking away from it.

I get set and look to JT. He already knows what I'm going to throw so as soon as he gives the signal, I nod.

One last fastball. One last strike. One last win.

CHAPTER THIRTY-FOUR

Olivia

THE STADIUM GOES WILD WHEN FLYNN STRIKES OUT the last batter. His teammates crowd around him and everyone in the stands jumps up and down in celebration.

"They did it!" I say to Greer.

She grins at me, her sadness temporarily forgotten in the moment. "Hotshot was on fire!"

Ruby and Gigi are yelling and clapping along with everyone else.

"I have to get down there," I say to them.

"I've got Greer," Ruby says. "Go congratulate your man!"

"Thank you," I say to her, then hug Greer. "I'll be right back."

I rush down to the lower level, squeezing past celebrating fans. Grandpa is waiting for me, almost like he knew I'd be making my way down to see Flynn.

He lets me past. I hug him quickly and peck him on the cheek and then look for Flynn. The rest of the team has worked their way off the field, but he's over by the Renegades' dugout, talking with their coach.

He shakes hands with him and then starts across the field. He's smiling big, and I guess he should be. What a way to go out. It's hard not to think about what could have been with the team if Flynn stayed, but I'm so proud of him.

When he finally spots me, I take off toward him. There is no better feeling than being in his arms. I jump and he catches me, holding me tight while I bury my head in his neck.

"You did it! That was amazing," I say to him. "The perfect way to go out."

"I'm not going anywhere."

"What?" I ask, certain I misheard him.

He sets me down in front of him.

"I'm staying. The Mustangs are my home."

His words take me by surprise and fill me with hope. "Are you serious?"

"Yeah. I want to win here, with this team, in this city, with you and Greer and my family up there cheering me on. I thought being a part of the best team in the league was the most important thing, but now that I have the choice, I don't want to leave. This is my home. *You* are my home."

My heart beats fast in my chest. I'm speechless.

His mouth pulls into a cocky smirk. "Hope you weren't looking forward to long-distance."

"I…" Words still fail me, so I hug him again. "Are you kidding? I'm so glad. I would have missed the shit out of you. I love you so much."

"I love you too."

"Does the team know?"

"Not yet." Flynn grins. "I need to tell a few more people first."

We walk over to where his agent Everly is waiting just inside of the tunnel that leads to the locker rooms.

"If you were trying to get the attention of every team in the league, then congratulations. My phone's been ringing nonstop." She has a sly smile and a way about her that tells me she has no problem winning people over or telling them off.

"I'm not going anywhere," he says, holding my hand.

"I thought you might say that which is why I emailed you over another contract."

"I don't understand," Flynn says slowly, glancing from Everly to me and then back to his agent.

"The Mustangs want to lock you down for the next five years." She beams at him. "Think it over. I'll call you tomorrow."

Flynn's face is pure elation as his agent walks away. He dips his head and kisses me.

When he pulls back, he taps the brim of my hat. "Now that I'm staying, we're going to need to get you a new one of these."

"What? Why?" I ask. "It's my favorite."

"You can't wear my brothers' team colors. It's not even the right sport."

"It's a hat." I laugh. "Everyone knows I'm yours."

"Double or nothing?"

"What exactly are we betting on?" Another laugh slips out as his arms circle my waist.

His eyes sparkle with happiness. "Forever."

CHAPTER THIRTY-FIVE

Olivia

"**C**ONGRATULATIONS." RUBY HOLDS UP THE BEST bookstore in the city award and grins. "Do you want to take it home so you can sleep with it under your pillow?"

"Shut up." I take it from her with a laugh.

We got the news yesterday. Out of all the bookstores in the city, The Book Nook was voted Lake City's favorite for the first time. I'm so proud, but also… maybe realizing I never really needed the award. Or at least not for the reasons I thought. I love this store, this job, doing it with my family.

We've started hosting weekly events: book clubs, author signings, adult reading time, and even a collaboration with Sabrina that we called "Ballet and Books". It was a big hit with kids.

"I think we can safely leave it on the counter," I say.

Grinning, she sets it down next to the register, nearly hidden from view.

"Okay, well, maybe turn it out so people can read it." I angle the award so it's in view for the customers.

Ruby laughs again.

"Can you watch the store for a bit?" I ask. "I need to do something."

"Sure. I have nowhere to go and nothing to do. At least until my agent gets back to me with notes."

"The book is great. She's going to love it and so will everyone else."

Ruby beams. "I'm choosing to live in that bubble of hope for now."

She finally finished her book and it's the best thing she's written. Of course, I always say that but this time I think her readers are going to agree with me. Flynn does. He read it to make sure she got the sporty scenes right, or at least that was his excuse. I'm pretty sure he'd have read it either way. After all, he's read everything else she's written.

I grab a couple of things from the office and then head outside. It's summer and our little stretch of sidewalk is empty as people hide away from the afternoon heat.

Despite the sweat beading up on my forehead and the back of my neck, I stop in front of Plot Twist to admire the artwork then let out a small laugh. It says, "Congratulations to The Book Nook, Best Bookstore in Lake City." And underneath is a picture of a woman that looks a lot like me with a stack of books in her hand.

Walter is full of surprises.

Plot Twist is as quiet as our store is today, but the air conditioning washes over me, and I let out a relieved breath to be inside.

"Hello. Welcome in," Walter calls from somewhere in the store.

"It's just me. Olivia," I say in response.

He peeks around the side of a bookshelf with a stack of books in one hand. A smile pulls at one side of his mouth. "You're the first person that's come in all afternoon."

"Everyone is hiding at home today," I say as I approach him. "Thanks for the shout-out on the window."

"You're welcome." His gaze is shifty, like maybe he's uncomfortable with the affection, even though it was initiated by him.

So, instead of saying more, I take in the scene around him. There are stacks of books on the floor in front of the small romance section. I'm thrilled to see him revamping it, even if it is still the smallest section in the store.

"What's happening here?" I ask as I move to stand beside him and inspect the transformation.

"I remembered a few more of Mae's favorites, so I ordered them, and they came in yesterday."

"Wait. These are all her favorite books?" I ask.

"I don't know romance, so I let her do the talking. Seems only right."

I look over the books with new eyes. I should have guessed. There are lots of historical romance and popular authors from twenty years ago. He doesn't hate romance. He just really loved her.

"I have an idea," I say, setting the things I brought on the floor and disappearing back to the front. I grab a Sharpie, tape, and the picture of Mae he keeps at the front counter.

Walter watches with trepidation as I make a sign and then tape it over the current "Romance" sign above the shelves. Then I place her picture on the top shelf underneath it.

He nods and together we reshelve the other books.

"There," I say when we're done. I place both hands on my hips to admire our work.

"Mae's Favorites," he reads the sign and then smiles. "She'd love this. Thank you."

"And…" I lean down to pick up the book I brought him. It's Ruby's last release. I set it on the shelf with the other books.

He gives me a wry look.

"Okay, fine. It can go on the front table." I take the book back with every intent of leaving it here somewhere. It would be a real travesty for a bookstore not to carry a single Ruby Madison book.

"And this is for you." I pick up the plant I brought him and hold it out. It's become a thing. Every time I stop in, I bring him one. I can't help it. Everyone should have a little greenery in their life.

"It will look great on the front table or maybe the counter," I say.

"Thank you, Olivia," he says. "I have something for you too."

"You do?" I can't hide the surprise in my voice.

He walks to the front, and I follow him. I put Ruby's book on a front table for some lucky reader to pick up.

Walter goes around the counter, and I move to stand in front of it. He places the plant by the register and then reaches underneath and pulls out a worn paperback. He holds it in his hands for a moment, then extends it toward me.

I take it without realizing what it is, but the second my brain makes the connection I try to give it back. Even holding it feels wrong. It's too precious. Too old. Too important.

"Walter, I can't accept this."

"Yes, you can." He waves his hands to indicate he isn't going to take it from me and steps back.

I glance down at the worn cover of my very favorite book. "It was Mae's. You read it every year."

"And I still can. She'd want someone that loved it as much as her to have it."

"It's a first edition," I whisper. I'm not sure why. I think I'm in shock.

When he doesn't reply, I step forward and hug him.

I think I take him by surprise, but he eventually hooks one arm around me and pats me softly.

"Thank you so much. I will cherish it," I say as I move back. I hug the book to my chest. I've very clearly made him uncomfortable, so I discreetly wipe my eyes before I do something embarrassing like cry in front of him.

We're both saved by the front door opening. Flynn walks in with Greer on his shoulders.

"Hey," I say, smiling both at the sight of them and the surprise. "How'd you find me?"

"Ruby told us you were here." Flynn leans forward to kiss me and then pulls back and glances to Walter. He extends a hand to him. "Nice to see you. The store is looking great."

"It is, isn't it? Olivia has a good eye."

"That she does," Flynn grins proudly.

Walter tips his head to the back of the store. "I have a box full of shirts and hats for you to sign. I can't keep your stuff in stock."

In the month since Flynn turned down the Renegades' offer and decided to stay with the Mustangs, the team has continued to hold one of the best records in the league. The unshakeable hope that at one point felt illogical, has become reality, and I couldn't be prouder to watch Flynn bask in all the love and admiration. The city loves him. And so do I.

"I'll come back later this afternoon. I'm going to take my girls to get ice cream," Flynn says.

Walter nods his approval.

"I told Ruby I'd only be gone for a few minutes."

Flynn grins. "She said, 'Tell Olivia not to even think about coming back here today.' She's got you covered."

"Okay."

"Yeah?" Flynn asks.

A few months ago, I probably would have put up more of a fight or felt guilty that someone was offering to help me out, but right now I just want to spend a little more time with Flynn and Greer. Soaking up this day, this feeling, and this life.

"Will you win me something out of the claw machine?"

His smile kicks up on one side. "You got it, gorgeous."

EPILOGUE

Flynn

"**A**RE WE GOING SKATING?" OLIVIA ASKS AS I HELP her into my truck. She looks stunning in a short, light blue dress that shows off a whole lot of leg.

"It isn't our first stop, but if you're a good girl, I'll see what I can do." With a wink, I close her in and jog around to the other side.

"How was your day?" Olivia asks as I drive across town.

"Good. Tiring. Your grandfather is putting me through the wringer."

Olivia beams. When I signed my new contract with the Mustangs, I only had one request. I wasn't sure if he'd go for it, but Earl agreed to come on as a pitching coach on one condition: he'd still be able to oversee the facility needs.

He's a natural despite his insistence that his coaching years were behind him. Smart and insightful while still being able to provide feedback in a way that feels motivating instead of discouraging. I'm stoked that Freddie, Roger, and all the rest of the guys are benefiting from his wisdom now too.

"Are you excited for Sabrina's bachelorette party next weekend?" I ask her.

She smiles. "I know you guys are all crashing."

"What? How?" I lucked out on the timing. We have a game the night before so I'll have to drive up separately and maybe leave a half day early, but I can't wait. Two nights in a little cabin with Olivia.

"Archer asked me what I thought. He wasn't sure if it would be a good surprise or if he was going to walk in on a bunch of strippers and a pissed fiancée."

"And what did you say?"

"That everyone should get to enjoy said strippers and that Sabrina would be ecstatic."

I bark out a laugh. "God, I love you."

The city lights get smaller behind us and the mountains and desert land stretch out in front of us. I pull up a paved drive to a huge house built into the mountainside.

"Who lives here?" she asks. "A teammate? Coach? Some big shot in the front office?"

"You'll see." I grin and get out of the truck.

Olivia sticks close as I lead us around to the side to an

open gate. Noise from the party inside filters out. There are lights strung up everywhere and people milling about.

The summer heat still hangs in the air and the smell of flowers is so strong it's like walking into a garden.

"Oh my goodness, it's so beautiful." Olivia's voice is filled with wonder. Her mouth hangs open as she looks around at the meticulously landscaped yard. Plants of all sizes and colors. It's like something out of a magazine. In fact, I'm pretty sure this garden was featured in a magazine.

"These don't look like baseball people," she whispers.

"They aren't." I start to walk, and she pulls me back.

"Are we party crashing?"

Laughing, I lift our joined hands and kiss her knuckles and lead her through the party. I don't know a soul. It's mostly older people, a few kids that look like they were forced to attend.

We navigate to the back of the yard where a large cactus-looking plant is the star of the night. It stands about seven or eight feet tall next to a tree, stretching and climbing along the trunk and limbs. White, partially-bloomed flowers sit in the middle of spiky petals that are scattered along the stems.

Olivia gasps. She looks to me, then back to the infamous Queen of the Night.

"How?" she asks.

"I asked around, made a few calls, bribed a few sweet, old ladies with tickets to a baseball game."

"Flynn." Her hands cover her mouth and her eyes flood with tears.

"Pretty cool, right?" I'll admit, I didn't really see the appeal until now. This plant only blooms one night out of the entire year, and we get to witness it.

"I never thought I'd see one in person," she says, voice filled with awe.

"Me neither. I wasn't sure I'd be in town when it bloomed. The lady hosting the event could only give me a rough timeline of when it would happen. Ruby was my backup in case I couldn't make it."

"Ruby agreed to come in your place?"

"I had to bribe her as well."

"With what?"

"By agreeing to buy every book she ever writes."

Olivia lets out a laugh and then turns her gaze back to the cactus. "This is the nicest thing anyone has ever done for me."

"I'm evening the score. You do nice shit for me all the time."

She faces me, then steps forward and rests one arm on my shoulder as she presses her lips to mine.

Then we stand there, staring at it. Well, she stares at it. I stare at her. I don't think I'll ever get tired of that.

Eventually more people start to crowd around, and we all watch as the flowers open to a full bloom. Goosebumps rise on my arms. It's by far the coolest thing I've ever witnessed.

There are "oohs" and "ahhs," followed by a long silence as we collectively take it in. I'm not sure how long we stand there before people start to trickle away.

Unsurprising, Olivia doesn't budge. I'd stand here with her forever.

"I'm so glad I got to see it with you." Olivia rests her head on my shoulder as she hugs my arm. "This was perfect."

"Nearly."

Her brows pull together as she stands tall and then turns to face me. I use our joined hands to tug her to me. No one knows us here, but somehow it still feels like the perfect moment. Just the two of us and a once in a life-time encounter.

"Marry me?"

"What?" Her eyes widen in surprise as she smiles. Then she swats at my chest playfully. "Don't joke."

"I'm not joking." I reach into my pocket and pull out the ring box.

Olivia's blue eyes are like saucers. "Oh my god."

I flip the box open and get on one knee.

"Flynn Holland. What are you doing?" she whisper-hisses.

"Proposing, gorgeous."

She lets out a small laugh, mouth still hanging open.

"I love you, Olivia. You are it for me. I want to be your husband and a father figure to Greer. I want to have a bunch more babies, too, if you're into that. Otherwise, we can just practice a bunch. I want to do life with you, all the fun, hard, messy, chaotic things. Over the past few months, I've realized that I don't care what the future looks like as long as it includes you."

My heart pounds as I pull the ring out. "What do you say?"

"I say yes." She nods and more tears fall.

I slip the ring on her finger and then stand and frame her face with both hands. Her lips curve with a smile as I cover her mouth with mine.

HOLLAND BROTHERS

ARCHER

Congrats on the engagement! Olivia is great. Excited for you both.

BROGAN

The Holland Brothers are officially off the market. Eat your heart out, ladies.

KNOX

Oh boy. Let's not get carried away. You're sure about this, baby bro?

ME

Positive.

HENDRICK

It's a big step. Husband. Father.

ME

I'm not worried. I learned from the best. The four of you.

BONUS EPILOGUE

Flynn

"**F**UCKING FINALLY. WHERE HAVE YOU BEEN?" BROGAN asks, enveloping me in a big hug. He moves to Olivia next, careful not to squash the baby in her arms as he embraces her. He then drops a kiss to baby Sloane's head. Archer is right behind him, and we go through the hugs and baby kisses a second time.

"I wanted to show the girls around the town a bit," I say as we all step back.

"We went to the high school," Hazel pipes in, leaning up on her toes to get closer to her uncles. She's three and a half with strawberry blonde hair and her momma's big blue eyes. Tall for her age, hates peas, but loves everything else. Seriously, everything. She's the chillest kid. Happy to be doing whatever anyone else is doing. She's so full of life and wonder that it's hard not to smile around her.

Greer holds Hazel's hand. She's the best big sister. Protective, patient, and sometimes full of mischief.

"Did you know that when you're in high school you don't get recess?" Greer asks her.

Hazel gasps even though she doesn't really know what recess is yet. She's a good, captive audience for Greer. She thinks her big sister is the smartest, funniest person in the world.

"It is a real travesty." Brogan leans down and swoops Hazel into his arms while he winks at Greer and asks her, "When did you get so smart?"

"I'm eleven and a half now, Uncle Brogan," she says with all the seriousness of a girl who thinks she's mature far beyond her years.

Brogan chuckles softly, then looks to me and Olivia. "I'm stealing H-bomb here. I need a partner in the nerf war."

"Have fun," Olivia calls after them.

I smile, watching him carry her away. When I glance at Greer, she and Archer are signing back and forth. She's gotten so good at signing with him that I can barely keep up. She still wants to be a baseball player and a princess, but now she's added interpreter to the list as well.

"*Think we can take them?*" Archer asks her, tipping his head in the direction that Brogan and Hazel went.

"Definitely."

They've barely made it across the yard when Sabrina appears.

"Give me." She motions with both hands to baby Sloane. My newest girl. She's six weeks old today.

Once I decided I was staying in Lake City, everything else became crystal clear. Marriage and babies, all of it. I didn't want to wait. Neither did Olivia. My girls are my whole world.

"So bossy," Olivia carefully holds out our little girl to her best friend.

Sabrina cradles Sloane in one arm with the biggest smile on her face. "Her hair is even redder than the last time I saw her."

It's true. Where Hazel is a mixture of me and Olivia, Sloane takes more after me. Her hair is redder than mine, eyes just as dark. Hendrick says she looks a lot like our mom.

"You are just the cutest thing," Sabrina coos and talks to Sloane, ignoring us. I've noticed people do that a lot, but it's hard to blame them. My girls are dang cute.

London rushes to her side. She offers Olivia and me the briefest smile before focusing her attention on Sloane.

"It's like we aren't even here," I say to my wife, but it's impossible to sound anything other than happy. In fact, I've never been happier. Every day, every milestone gets better and better.

Looking up from the pitcher's mound and seeing my girls cheering me on, walking through the door after a long road trip, lazy Sunday mornings, and everything in between.

I lace my fingers through Olivia's as I scan the backyard. The whole family is at Knox's house to celebrate his son's birthday. Chase is this cute and fun combination of his parents. He has Avery's blonde hair and blue eyes, but everything else is Knox. His smile, his mannerisms, his love of dirt bikes. Although lately he's been showing a lot of interest in football, which has Archer and Brogan ecstatic and both me and Knox slightly offended. I'm sure I'll convince my nephew to take up baseball at some point.

Hendrick and Jane are in the pool with their daughter, Rosie. She turned four last week and is the spitting image of Jane. She's softspoken and timid, but she has the sweetest smile and loves to swim. She started swimming lessons as a baby, and ever since, it's all she wants to do. The stuff she can do in a pool is incredible. I think we have a future Olympic swimmer on our hands.

A pregnant Avery is corralling Chase and his friends to one side of the yard as they shoot each other with nerf guns. Brogan and Hazel run to join in with Archer and Greer right behind them. Brogan uses Hazel as a shield while he grabs his gun. I hear her squeal from across the yard until he hands her a nerf gun too.

It's been a wild few years with more exciting things to come. Archer and Sabrina are in the process of adopting twin three-month-old boys. One is deaf just like Archer. Greer cannot wait to teach them sign language.

Brogan and London's son, Cooper, is two. He's shy and has bright blond hair, but when he laughs, he sounds just like his dad. I look for him now, not surprised at all to see him running next to Chase. Those two have a special bond, despite their age difference.

And perhaps the biggest change…

Knox is at the grill with our dad. They're talking and smiling. It's still a strange sight to see them together, but a welcome one.

It wasn't quick or easy, but once Dad started making an effort to show up for my brothers, they slowly opened themselves up to having a relationship with him. Archer first, then Hendrick. It was when Chase was born that Knox finally came around. Don't tell Knox, but the whole parent thing has made him a big, ole softie. He's always had the biggest heart, but now he wears it more openly.

And to his credit, our dad has been a good grandpa. All the grandkids love him, and he makes them a priority—showing up for every softball game, dirt bike race, swim meet, birthday, or whatever else they have going on. They keep him busy.

I know my brothers wonder what it would have been like if he'd been around like that for us. I do sometimes too, the same way I wonder what it'd be like if our mom was still here. I like to think she'd be happy with how we all turned out.

Hendrick has followed in her footsteps, revitalizing the bar she loved so much and naming his daughter after her.

Knox has her big heart and natural caretaking side. Her fiery side too.

Archer has that same quiet but perceptive way about him that Mom had. And he's carried on her love of 80s rock music.

Brogan may not have been her son by blood, but no one made her smile like he did. He loved making her laugh, and when he cracks a joke or does something silly, I think about how she'd love that he still does that for all of us.

As for me, I don't remember her as well as I wish I did, but I see her every day in my brothers. I know she was a great mom because she's a part of all of them. So in some ways, it's like she's still here.

"Hey, Hotshot." Olivia wraps her arms around my neck.

"Yeah, gorgeous?"

Her blonde hair is shorter now (less for Sloane to grab a hold of), but she still has those big, blue eyes that cut right through me. "It's the first time we've been kid-free in six weeks."

"Well, shit, maybe we should ditch the party." I lean down and press my lips to hers. Warmth and happiness spread through me. Kissing her never gets old.

"Dad!" Hazel yells from across the yard. That never gets old either.

I look over in time to see Hazel sprinting with a nerf gun raised over head and firing bullets every which direction.

"I think your daughter needs back up," Olivia comments.

"Raincheck on…" I give her body a very thorough once-over.

She laughs. "Definitely."

I take a step back. Olivia grabs my hand and pulls me back to her. She pushes onto her toes and presses her body against mine. She kisses me like the yard isn't filled with our family.

My arms circle her waist, and I draw her closer. Someone cat calls and Chase and his friends yell, "Grooooss!"

Olivia drops from her toes and smiles up at me.

"What was that for?" I ask.

"No reason. I'm just…" She gets a dreamy look on her face like she can't quite put the feeling to words. "I feel so…"

"Yeah, me too," I say with a small laugh. I kiss her one more time before Hazel yells for me again.

As I'm running across the yard, the word finally comes to me. Lucky.

How lucky are we?

ACKNOWLEDGMENTS

Thank you so much to everyone who picked up this book. The Holland brothers consumed me over the last two years. I fell in love with the idea of this big, rowdy family and after writing their stories they are forever etched into my heart. Thank you for being a part of the journey. I hope it brought you as much joy and happiness as it brought me.

To my incredible team: Jamie, Sahara, and Tori, thank you for all your help with this release. I'm so fortunate that I get to work with each of you.

Sarah Jane, thanks again for the stunning cover illustration. This one is my fav (until the next one!). I adore you.

Lori, I know I can always count on you for the most stunning covers and this one was no exception.

Anelise, Becky, Jamie, Katie, Sahara, Sarah, and Tori—this book is so much stronger for your suggestions and notes. Thank you for always treating my words with such care while still pushing me to be a better writer.

Everyone at Valentine PR and my agent and publicist, Nina, thank you for all that you do.

To Catherine, who could not have been more excited when I told her the concept for this series. Thanks for being the best cheerleader and friend.

And lastly, to my family. Love you forever.

ALSO BY REBECCA JENSHAK

ABOUT THE AUTHOR

Rebecca Jenshak is a *USA Today* bestselling author of new adult and sports romance. She lives in Arizona with her family. When she isn't writing, you can find her attending local sporting events, hanging out with family and friends, or with her nose buried in a book.

Sign up for her newsletter for book sales and release news.

Printed in Dunstable, United Kingdom